W9-BYZ-322

Fic
Fre   Frey, Stephen W.
       The vulture
       fund

8/96

THE
VULTURE
FUND

STEPHEN W. FREY

THE VULTURE FUND

A DUTTON BOOK

DUTTON
Published by the Penguin Group
Penguin Books USA Inc., 375 Hudson Street,
New York, New York 10014, U.S.A.
Penguin Books Ltd, 27 Wrights Lane,
London W8 5TZ, England
Penguin Books Australia Ltd, Ringwood,
Victoria, Australia
Penguin Books Canada Ltd, 10 Alcorn Avenue,
Toronto, Ontario, Canada M4V 3B2
Penguin Books (N.Z.) Ltd, 182–190 Wairau Road,
Auckland 10, New Zealand

Penguin Books Ltd, Registered Offices:
Harmondsworth, Middlesex, England

First published by Dutton, an imprint of Dutton Signet,
a division of Penguin Books USA Inc.
Distributed in Canada by McClelland & Stewart Inc.

First Printing, August, 1996
10 9 8 7 6 5 4 3 2 1

 REGISTERED TRADEMARK—MARCA REGISTRADA

LIBRARY OF CONGRESS CATALOGING-IN-PUBLICATION DATA
Frey, Stephen W.
    The vulture fund / Stephen W. Frey.
      p.   cm.
    ISBN 0-525-93986-5
    1. Investment banking—Corrupt practices—New York (N.Y.)—Fiction. 2. Conspira-
cies—New York (N. Y.)—Fiction. 3. Bankers—New York (N.Y.)—Fiction.   I. Title.
PS3556.R4477V85   1996
813'.54—dc20   96-10617
                                                                              CIP

Printed in the United States of America
Set in Janson
Designed by Julian Hamer

PUBLISHER'S NOTE

This book is printed on acid-free paper. ∞

8/96   B+T   13.41

For my wife, Lil,
and our daughters, Christy and Ashley.
Everyone deserves a miracle.
I was given three.

PROLOGUE

The woman leaned back against the large granite boulder and gazed up at the thousands of black, leafless branches above her. They formed millions of intricate geometric shapes—like cobwebs—against the dark gray winter clouds beyond. She shivered. It was late afternoon, and she was freezing, tired, and hungry. What a mistake this had been.

"Hey, I think I know where we are now."

The woman glanced slowly away from the eerie shapes above and toward her husband of three weeks. He was squatting in the snow, hunched over a topographic map, gnawing on a candy bar. He didn't know where they were. He had uttered the same words at least once an hour since early this morning.

Three days ago they had somehow missed a marker on the Appalachian Trail and had been wandering through the backwoods of West Virginia since, completely lost. They might be a mile from the trail or they might be twenty miles from it. For three days they had climbed mountain after mountain, pausing only long enough at the bottom of each valley to sip water from the stream that inevitably lay at the base of each peak, before scaling the next one. She shook her head. "You don't have any idea where we are. How could I possibly have let you talk me into a hiking trip as our honeymoon? I could be lying on the beach on St. Thomas right now, being served piña coladas by a nice man in a white dinner jacket. But no, I'm lost somewhere north of Sugar Grove, West Virginia, freezing my behind off."

"And a nice little behind it is." He smiled at her.

"Yeah, well, you're not going to see any more of it as long as we're out here in the middle of nowhere. I've had enough tent sex in the last three weeks to last me a lifetime." She rubbed her aching knees.

The man watched her hands work for a moment, then re-focused on the map. "Give me just a bit longer to get my bearings; then we'll start moving again. I'm going to have us back on the trail by this evening. Promise."

The woman groaned. She didn't want to find the trail. She wanted to find a nice hot tub and lie in it for two or three hours.

"Just a few more minutes," the man said, more to himself than to her.

The woman turned and began climbing carefully up the side of a huge boulder. She was athletic, and in a few seconds she had scaled the thirty-foot outcrop. It was a remarkable view of the Appalachian Mountains from the precipice, and had they not been lost, she would have enjoyed it immensely. They had ample food supplies and were in no real danger, but suddenly she wanted to get back to civilization.

Far below and to the north the woman noticed a gaping wound in the side of a large hill. "Must be an old coal mine," she remarked to herself. Five days ago the old man behind the counter at the grocery store in Sugar Grove had told them that mining was about the only thing that kept the people in this area employed anymore. Even that revenue stream was drying up now. She wished she could turn back time to the day they had gone into that store for supplies. She would have insisted that they rent the nearest car available, drive directly to the closest airport, and fly to the Caribbean.

The woman removed a small pair of high-powered binoculars from her jacket and brought them to her eyes. Tucked beneath the hillside next to the mine were several large buildings that appeared to be abandoned and in varying states of disrepair and decay. Her breath rose before the binoculars. Just as she was about to replace the field glasses into her jacket pocket, she noticed several figures moving together alongside one of the buildings. Her spirits rose instantly. They had somehow stumbled onto civilization or at least people who would know how to get back to it. In a few hours they would be out of these damn woods and on their way to warmer latitudes.

The woman adjusted the focus of the glasses and watched intently as the figures moved past the buildings far below. Suddenly she pulled the glasses away from her face, then quickly back to her eyes one more time. Each of the figures appeared to be holding a gun. And not some run-of-the-mill hunting rifle. She had been around guns all her life—her father was an avid hunter—and those were not hunting rifles. She could not be certain from this distance, but they seemed to be assault weapons. "Jesus!"

"Did you say something, sweetheart?" the man called from below.

The woman replaced the binoculars in her coat and moved back down the rock quickly. She jumped the last several feet into the six-inch-deep snow. Her husband rose from his squatting position as she neared.

"It looks like—" But she did not finish the sentence.

The bullet entered the man's head from the back and exited just above his right eye. His skullcap exploded immediately, and fragments of brain matter, blood, and bone shot thirty feet into the air, spraying the trees and the snow with a fine red mist. As she watched in horror, what little remained of his face toppled forward with the rest of his body into the fresh white powder. The woman attempted to scream, but nothing came to her lips. It was as if her throat had suddenly become locked in the jaws of a steely vise.

Almost immediately another bullet sliced through the cold air, its high-pitched whine creating a sickening echo among the trees. The bullet barely grazed her right arm, but its tremendous force still knocked her backward into the snow. A searing pain burst through her body.

"Oh, my God." She scrambled to her feet and, holding her right hand in her left, began to run away from the spot where her husband had fallen. Whoever had pulled the trigger had not hit her husband by accident. Or her. The odds were too long that a second shot would hit her as well. They had been standing at least fifteen feet apart. This was not a case of mistaken identity, not a case of an intoxicated hunter somehow mistaking them for deer. The shots were meant to kill them. But why?

The mountainside suddenly fell away sharply beneath her boots, and she tumbled down the slope. Tears streamed down her cheeks even as she fell. God, her husband's face had been there one second, smiling at her, and then it had exploded before her eyes the next. Now they were after her. She could feel them behind her. She sensed their pursuit. And she was leaving obvious tracks in the snow for them to follow.

A tree trunk stopped her fall abruptly as she slammed into its wide base. The impact knocked the breath from her lungs, but she barely noticed the pain. Survival adrenaline pumped through her body, effectively anesthetizing her.

For several moments she lay on her side next to the tree, deathly still, clutching her useless arm to her body, listening for any sounds of pursuit. But there were no sounds save a gentle breeze moving through the upper branches of the forest.

Finally the woman rolled onto her back and gazed at the gray sky. In fifteen minutes it would be dark enough to make following her tracks much more difficult, dark enough to escape. If she could just reach a stream that was not yet frozen over, she could walk in it for a distance, leaving no tracks, and lose them. The boots were waterproof and would protect her from the icy water. Then she would make it back to civilization. She was going to make it out of here. She was.

The woman rose unsteadily, using the tree for support, and

again began to move down the hillside, maintaining her balance as best she could. Several times she slipped and fell, ten or twenty feet in a second, falling hard on the injured arm. But she managed not to scream despite the intense pain, knowing that if she yielded to the urge to cry out, she would give away her position immediately.

At last she reached the bottom of the mountain. For a few moments she lay next to a large rock, quietly catching her breath, listening intently for any sound. There was nothing but the wind in the trees. Perhaps she had somehow avoided whoever had killed her husband and wounded her. Perhaps they had lost her trail in the fading light. Perhaps she really was going to elude them. But there was no time to rest. She had to keep going.

As the woman rose to her knees, a huge hand curled about her delicate throat. She shook her head at the swarthy face beneath the black ski cap and grasped his massive wrist with both of her hands. Tears again began streaming down her crimson cheeks. "Please don't do anything to me. Help me." She gazed at the ice drops lodged in the man's full black mustache directly below his nostrils. Her eyes pleaded for mercy.

The man stared back down at her. He could snap the thin neck with one hand, but that would smack of a professional killer's work. It had to appear as if the couple had been ambushed by amateurs looking for money or other ill-gotten goods. For a moment he thought of taking her back to the men and allowing them to relieve the tension of their stressful training before killing her, but he dismissed the thought quickly. He wanted them focused. After all, they had been at the abandoned mine for only a week. If they really started complaining near the end of the training, he would accommodate them.

"It is nothing personal," he said in a thick Middle Eastern accent. "You are just a very unlucky woman. In the wrong place at the wrong time."

Then he jerked the woman to her feet, spun her around so that she was facing away from him, pulled the long hunting knife from his belt, and, with his huge left arm wrapped tightly around her neck, plunged the serrated ten-inch blade through her coat into her right lung. He withdrew the knife quickly and plunged it in again. Over and over he impaled her, careful to make certain the knife slashed across a rib each time he thrust it into her. Several times he plunged it into areas of her body where he knew there were no vital organs, all so that a coroner would not recognize the work of a professional when the woman was found. Finally he allowed the limp body to fall to the snow.

"Nice work." The assassin's second-in-command stood nearby, beneath a tall pine tree. "Almost looks as if you like doing it."

The swarthy man grunted. Killing was not to be liked or disliked. It was simply to be done. "Let's carry her back up the mountain to the other one. Then we'll get back to the base. Tomorrow we'll drive them fifty miles south of here and dump them on the Appalachian Trail. When the police find the bodies after the snow melts, we'll be long gone from the training base. If the police somehow find the bodies before we leave this place, they'll think the couple ran into an escaped convict looking for money." He paused and looked around the woods. "Probably a few of them out here."

1

Mace McLain moved smoothly into the conference room, careful to project nothing but quiet confidence to the Japanese commercial banker seated on the far side of the long table. At the last minute, as execution pages were being signed yesterday by all the other parties involved in the transaction, the man seated at the conference room table had gotten greedy and brought the billion-dollar deal to a halt just inches from the finish line. Now the rest of the money providers—the equity people, the insurance companies, and the other commercial banks—were threatening to walk away from the deal, an action that would crater Mace's seven-million-dollar investment banking fee and render irrelevant six months of hard work.

The other man rose as Mace neared him.

"Good morning, Mr. Tashiro." Mace's voice was calm, neither friendly nor unfriendly.

"Good morning, Mr. McLain." Tashiro spoke with a heavy Japanese accent.

Mace smiled quickly, towering over the other man as they came together, understanding that the thickness of the accent was being neatly manufactured. Sometimes the Japanese exaggerated their accents during difficult business negotiations so they could claim not to understand a critical point because of the language barrier. But Tashiro had been with Osaka Trust's New York branch for three

years—Mace had done his homework thoroughly—and if he tried
to pull the language barrier crap, Mace would shoot him down
quickly. As they shook hands, Mace noticed that the other man's
hand was damp with perspiration. So he was nervous. Mace laughed
to himself. He ought to be.

"Please sit down, Mr. Tashiro."

Tashiro bowed several times quickly, but did not sit right away,
instead waiting as Mace made his way back around the end of the
long table to the chair directly across from where he stood. Then
Tashiro pulled out a business card—English type on one side,
Japanese on the other—slid it across the polished mahogany toward
Mace, and sat.

Mace picked up the card from the tabletop and put it coolly
into his shirt pocket, then placed his leather-bound notebook on
the table and lowered himself slowly into the chair. It was silly to
sit across the huge table from each other, ten feet apart, in a room
big enough for an IBM board meeting. But that was how the
Japanese liked to do things, and he needed Tashiro's money. So he
would play the game.

"I assume our receptionist offered you refreshments."

"Yes, she did. But I am fine. Thank you." Tashiro attempted to
match Mace's smooth demeanor but could not. "Thank you." He
said the words again, more to calm himself than anything else.

Tashiro glanced around the ornate, impressive room, a monument to American capitalism. From every angle the dark eyes
of stern-faced men—long-dead partners of Walker Pryce &
Company, the investment banking firm for which Mace McLain
worked—bore down on him. Beautiful dark wood chairs and
tables furnished the rich setting, and a glass chandelier hung over
Tashiro from the high ceiling like a horrible guillotine. Suddenly
he longed for the drab, sterile surroundings of Osaka Trust.

"Mr. Tashiro, we've been working on this transaction for six
months." Mace leaned forward, over the table. His eyes narrowed,
and his voice became slightly stern, still calm but more forceful

than before. "Why have you picked the last minute to identify a problem? My client is not happy." Mace knew exactly why Tashiro had picked now to raise his complaint, but he wanted to see Tashiro sweat. He knew that the Japanese detested pointed questions.

Tashiro leaned back as Mace leaned forward. Americans were too direct. They said exactly what they meant, unlike his countrymen, who might circle a point for hours, discussing irrelevant issues just to test the other side for weaknesses. "I would not say it is a problem, more an issue that needs to be resolved."

Doublespeak, Mace thought. An issue that needed to be resolved *was* a problem. But his face exhibited no irritation or frustration, just stoic calm.

"Mr. McLain, I am just not certain that the tax treaties work as you say they do. And if they do not, and the interest coming to Osaka Trust is not tax-exempt, my bank will actually be losing money on this loan."

Mace stared at Tashiro. The Japanese man knew full well that the treaties were in place to stay and that the deal worked perfectly. They had an ironclad opinion on the structure's viability from the Washington, D.C., office of Jones Day, the high-profile Cleveland law firm.

Tashiro knew all this. But he also knew that Mace McLain needed Osaka Trust to get the deal done. He knew that without Osaka, the bank group did not meet a minimum Japanese content as stipulated by the treaties and the transaction would be cratered. At least he thought he knew.

Mace inhaled slowly. So Tashiro was going to hold up the deal for a better interest rate. But if he gave Tashiro the higher rate, he'd have to give all the other banks the same. Then the pension funds and the insurance companies would find out and start screaming for a better deal too. An irreversible chain reaction would begin, and everything would fall apart.

"Just how do you propose to get past this issue, Mr. Tashiro?"

Tashiro adjusted his glasses, then with his elbows resting on the arms of the chair, folded his hands in front of his mouth and stared back at Mace. So McLain was willing to negotiate. Tashiro smiled beneath his hands. His fear ebbed away like a gentle outgoing tide.

Just as Tashiro was about to speak, a large door at the far end of the room burst open. Mace and Tashiro glanced immediately in the direction of the commotion. Sherman Stevens, a partner at Walker Pryce & Company, strode quickly through the doorway.

"Jesus Christ, Mace! I've been looking all over for you." Stevens paid no attention to the Japanese banker sitting across from Mace. "The goddamned WestPenn deal is falling apart. Norfolk Southern is going to top our offer price for WestPenn shares. This can't be happening. I need this deal!" Stevens thundered.

Mace shot a glance at Tashiro, who appeared completely bewildered.

Mace's eyes flashed back to Stevens. The older man's face was beet red, and his hair rumpled. Mace shook his head slightly. Stevens was a partner, and Mace only a vice-president. Partners were supposed to be partners because they could handle themselves in pressure situations, when the deal was on the line. Yet here was Stevens standing before Mace like some green first-year associate, unable to think clearly because a huge fee seemed to be slipping away and as a result, he might not be able to buy the Grand Cayman vacation home he had his eye on.

Mace rose, then turned to Tashiro. "I apologize. Please excuse me for a moment."

Tashiro jumped up from his seat, nodding and bowing at the same time, uncertain of what was transpiring. He was suspicious that Mace was engaging in theatrics to intimidate him but did not want to insult Stevens in case the older man turned out to be *the* player.

"Sit down, please. I'll be right back," Mace said to Tashiro.

Tashiro obeyed immediately.

Mace turned to Stevens. "Come with me, Sherman." He said the words firmly, moving past Stevens as he spoke.

Mace moved out of the conference room and toward another, smaller meeting room down the hall, with Stevens in tow. So another deal was cratering. What else was going to happen this morning?

Mace and Stevens had been putting together the acquisition of WestPenn—a poorly performing short line railroad operating four hundred miles of spur tracks in western Pennsylvania and eastern Ohio—for nine months. Now suddenly the huge Norfolk & Southern Railroad was going to snap up WestPenn's shares just as Walker Pryce was about to complete its own deal.

Mace moved briskly into the small conference room. He closed the door behind Stevens as the older man followed Mace into the room. Mace did not bother to sit. "How did you learn about Norfolk's bid?" Mace asked quickly.

"I can't say." Stevens' tone was suddenly confrontational.

Mace slammed his fist against the wall.

Stevens flinched. "Jesus Christ! What's your problem?"

Mace ignored Stevens. "How did you find out?" His voice rose slightly but his expression remained calm.

Stevens hesitated. Revealing sources in the investment banking world was something one did not do lightly. But he relented as he glanced at Mace's burning eyes. "Peter Schmidt over at Morgan Stanley called me. They are going to represent Norfolk Southern."

Mace stared at Stevens, then laughed. "That little hemorrhoid. He's just trying to ruin *our* deal. Norfolk Southern doesn't really want WestPenn. It doesn't fit Norfolk's strategy. But Peter must have convinced the senior people at Norfolk to do the deal so he could get in our way. He still hasn't forgiven us for beating him to the punch on that Black and Decker financing two years ago."

"Well, it doesn't matter why or how he's done it. What matters is that he's done it!"

Mace turned, grabbed the phone sitting on a small table, and punched out a number. A secretary answered.

"Peter Schmidt, please." Mace's voice was firm.

"Peter Schmidt." The Morgan Stanley investment banker picked up the call an instant after the secretary had put Mace on hold. His tone was curt.

"It's Mace McLain."

"Hello, Mace." Schmidt's voice suddenly turned slow and sarcastic.

Mace grimaced. He could see Schmidt leaning back in his chair, smiling an obnoxious, satisfied smile. "Sherman tells me you've ginned up another bidder for WestPenn."

"That's right, my boy," Schmidt crowed.

"Norfolk doesn't want WestPenn, and you know it, Peter."

"Yeah, but I've made them think they do. And that's all that counts," Schmidt said smugly.

"How about the three-billion-dollar Chengtu Airport bond underwriting in China to be brought to market later this year?" Mace asked quickly. "There will be tremendous fees involved in that transaction, not to mention a huge amount of prestige. Does that deal count too?"

Schmidt hesitated, uncertain of Mace's tack. "What do you mean?"

"As you must know, Walker Pryce has been named lead underwriter in that transaction by the Chinese government. And we've selected Morgan Stanley as a colead. Because we have been so kind, Morgan Stanley is now guaranteed a nice fat syndication fee and lots more business in China, which we all know hasn't been an easy market for you to break into. But it's not too late to change our colead manager to, say, Goldman Sachs. You wouldn't want it to get back to your chairman that Morgan lost the Chengtu deal to Goldman Sachs because of WestPenn, because of you. Would you want that to happen, Peter?"

There was dead silence at the other end of the line. Finally

Schmidt spoke. "You need us as colead on the Chengtu transaction." But his voice was not convincing.

"No, we don't," Mace said matter-of-factly.

Again there was a protracted silence.

"Call off the dogs, Peter. Call off Norfolk Southern." Mace prompted the Morgan Stanley investment banker.

Finally Schmidt whispered into the mouthpiece, "Okay."

Mace replaced the receiver quickly, not bothering to say goodbye to Schmidt, then snapped his fingers at Stevens. "Norfolk Southern is gone. Close the WestPenn deal, Sherman. Now! Before someone else shows up at the dance and tries to make off with our date." He brushed past the partner and out of the small room.

Stevens' eyes narrowed as he watched Mace move out of the conference room. The kid was good. There was no denying that. But he could be cocky sometimes too. Mace needed to understand the necessity of showing respect to a partner, of the need to kiss the ring. Stevens made a mental note to bring up this problem at the next partners' meeting.

Tashiro rose as Mace returned to the large conference room.

"Sit down," Mace said. It was time to end this negotiation. He did not retake his seat across from Tashiro, but moved instead to a seat next to him. He stared directly into the other man's eyes. "In this instance your real issue is price, not concern over the viability of the structure. What you're trying to do is gouge me for a little extra juice at the eleventh hour because you think you can."

Tashiro swallowed hard. "You are wrong, Mr. McLain."

"No, I'm not," Mace snapped. "It's a very profitable deal as currently structured, Mr. Tashiro. There is no justification for higher pricing. I have another bank ready to go if you don't want in." Mace paused. "And if you decline this opportunity, rest assured that the New York branch of Osaka Trust will never see another deal from Walker Pryce & Company." His eyes bored into the commercial banker. He had no other banks willing to step in at this point. Osaka was the only game in town. It was a bluff, pure and simple. But he was an excellent poker player.

Suddenly Tashiro wanted no part of this game. His information told him that Mace was bluffing, but Mace's eyes said otherwise. Tashiro could feel the perspiration building beneath his pin-striped suit. It *was* a profitable deal as structured. And Osaka Trust would make a great deal of money on this loan, as it had on many other deals Walker Pryce had brought to it in the last few years. If he stood his ground for better pricing and Mace did have another Japanese bank in his hip pocket, the pipeline of deals from Walker Pryce would surely dry up. That would not make his senior managers in Japan happy.

Slowly, almost painfully, Tashiro looked again into Mace's eyes. "All right, we do the deal as structured."

Mace inhaled slowly and raised an eyebrow. "Good," he said calmly. "I suggest you return to your office and sign the necessary papers. Immediately." Mace stood as he finished speaking.

Tashiro rose also, unsteadily. The Japanese man nodded one more time, picked up his briefcase, and was gone.

Mace watched him leave, then laughed softly as he moved to the large window overlooking Wall Street far below. He glanced up quickly at the dark January clouds filled with snow, then checked his watch. Eleven o'clock. Two deals were back on track and heading toward multimillion-dollar closing fees. But there was still plenty of time left in the day for something to go wrong with his other six transactions.

He turned to go. There was so much to do. And tomorrow would be cut short because he had to leave early to teach a class at Columbia in the evening. Sometimes there really weren't enough hours in the day.

"Thank you for coming tonight. I know these meetings are logistically difficult for you, but as you must realize, complete secrecy is essential, given my position."

Lewis Webster stared at the other man, then nodded, as if it hadn't been a problem to come such a great distance in the dead of night. It galled him to be so deferential, but he had no choice. Not to cooperate, not to take the mammoth risk this man was forcing him toward, would mean a long prison sentence. That had been made abundantly clear. And the sentence would not be endured at a minimum-security white-collar-crime enclosure. He would rot with the likes of mob hit men and serial killers until the day he died. That had been made clear as well.

"Would you care for a sandwich, Mr. Webster?" The man gestured at the thin slices of roast beef and ham neatly arranged on a tray sitting on the small table next to the hotel suite door.

Webster shook his head. He was ravenous, but his desire to end the meeting far outweighed his hunger. He stared at the other man, attempting to mask the hatred he felt—and the fear. The scenario had been neatly and coldly laid out for him at the last meeting a month ago. He, Lewis Webster, senior partner of Walker Pryce & Company, one of the most prominent investment banks on Wall Street, was guilty of insider trading, securities fraud, and unlawful manipulation of client accounts. If convicted, he would face a minimum of thirty-one years in prison. Therefore, because he was sixty-two years old, the likelihood of his becoming a free man before he died would be almost zero. And he *would* be convicted. There was no doubt about it. The other man had shown him the evidence.

Webster squeezed the arm of the chair. But there was an alternative. A rather nice alternative, the man had said; Webster hated how polite the bastard was. Webster could cooperate. He could make certain resources at Walker Pryce available. If things turned out as planned, the payoff would be huge, in the billions. Walker Pryce would keep some of those billions, and since as senior partner Webster owned a large piece of Walker Pryce, he would benefit personally. Perhaps more important, he would remain a free man. He would not have to endure lock-downs, lice-infested cells, beatings, and rapes. Webster shook involuntarily at the thought.

"Are you all right? Is it too cold in here? I apologize, I'll turn up the thermostat. It's just that I like it cold." The other man smiled and began to rise from his chair.

"No, no. It's fine. Please." Webster waved his hand.

The man sat back down in his chair, still smiling. He knew why Webster did not want to eat and why the tremor shook his body every so often. He could see the fear on Webster's face. The other man laughed to himself.

"Have you had a chance to consider what we talked about at our last meeting?"

"Yes," Webster hissed immediately. He wanted this to be over.

"And?"

Webster glanced at the thermostat. It *was* cold in here. "I don't see that I have a choice. You know that; I know that. I don't understand why we waited a month to meet again."

"Two reasons. First, I have a very busy schedule. Like New York and investment banking, Washington and politics never rest. Second, I wanted you to have a chance to think very carefully about what I said to you last time we met. This is an extremely important decision you are making."

"I've thought about it enough."

The man leaned forward slowly so that he was very close to Webster. "And are you committed to what we discussed?" His voice dropped to a whisper.

Webster gazed at the man's face—strong and calm—reflecting the tremendous power he already wielded and the greater power he desired. "Yes."

"Absolutely?"

"Yes."

"You know that if this were to fall apart, you would suffer the consequences, not I." He did not await Webster's reply. "And were you to attempt to alert someone, to lay all this out for my enemies, in the best case you would endure a protracted prison sentence. In the worst case, well . . ."

As the other man made obvious his threat, Webster's feelings of hatred and fear coalesced into only fear, a deep physical fear that he had never before known. "I understand." Webster closed his eyes for several moments. "My problem is that a majority of my partners at Walker Pryce want to go public. Now. They believe the time is right. And if Walker Pryce accesses the public market, there would be no way I could convince the new shareholders to raise the pool of money you want to raise, no way I could convince them to use the proceeds of that fund the way you want to use them."

"You need to convince your partners that going public at this juncture is not in their best interest. It's that simple."

"It isn't that easy," Webster whispered.

"The decision of whether or not to go public will be made by the executive committee of Walker Pryce, isn't that what you told me at our last meeting?"

"Yes." Webster glanced at the floor.

The other man bent down slowly and picked up two thick brown envelopes leaning against a leg of his chair. He handed them to Webster. "These should help." He smiled as he released his grip on the packages.

2

R*eady? Ready, go! Go, go, go!"* The captain screamed at the twenty-five men of Assault Unit Three as they burst through one of four main gates of the massive downtown Los Angeles liquid natural gas storage facility. The captain braced for the explosions—mines that the terrorists might have managed to put down in front of the gates—but they did not come. Thank God they had been able to respond so quickly to the crisis, less than an hour after the storage facility had been taken over, negating the terrorists' ability to entrench themselves.

As the men spilled into the compound, the sounds of automatic gunfire peppered the air. Riflemen posted in buildings across the street pasted the face of the storage facility's main administration building with a withering fire to support the four assault teams.

From the rooftop of the administration building a terrorist rose to spray the assault troops with a hail of Black Rhino shells that would shred their steel vests like paper. But before the hooded figure could even depress the trigger of his weapon, he was picked off neatly by a sharpshooter leaning through the slightly open door of a dark, hornetlike helicopter hovering in the night sky several hundred feet above the building. The man was hurled back by the force of the sharpshooter's bullets, and he cartwheeled over and over until he came to rest facedown, dead on the sticky tar of the roof.

Four more terrorists rose from their protected positions on the rooftop to deliver deadly fire. Three were gunned down instantly by sharpshooters in the helicopters. But for a moment the fourth man escaped the heavenly fire and was able to deliver a horrible payload of fifty rounds into the gloom below. Six of the assault troops were hit as they sprinted for the main storage area of the compound, where the great tanks of compressed liquid natural gas stood side by side—in essence, huge bombs begging to be ignited. A second later the terrorist on the roof who had momentarily managed to escape the fire from the helicopter was hurled backward, dead.

Through his night vision goggles the captain of Assault Unit Three could see the men of Units One, Two, and Four beginning to converge on the main storage area from their entry points at the other three gates. So-called friendly fire—as if any gunfire could be so termed—could be a problem. The men were acting mostly on adrenaline and instinct, and some of them might fire at anything now, despite the intense training they endured daily in preparation for a situation exactly like this one.

Suddenly the sound of a Diamondback rocket, a new handheld weapon developed by the Iraqis, pierced the air.

"*Cover!*" the captain yelled. He had not seen the missile's launch but recognized its eerie whine instantly. The men threw themselves to the asphalt, chest first, as the rocket sliced through the air above them. A moment later it slammed into the street beyond the facility's fence, detonating in a burst of fire. Deadly shrapnel flew forward with the momentum of the rocket, shattering the windows of buildings on the far side of the boulevard.

So they were not trained well in the missile's ways, the captain thought as he screamed at the men to push forward again. The terrorists should have made certain that the rocket struck the ground in front of the assault teams. Then the razor-sharp metal would have cut them to ribbons as the tiny pieces of scrap flew forward.

The men of Unit Two suddenly changed course and veered

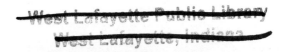

away toward the administration building, from which the Diamondback had been launched. Another brilliant burst of fire momentarily lighted a second-floor window of the building, and another Diamondback seared through the air. This time the weapon had better aim, and it slammed into the cement in the middle of the running troops. Seven men of Unit Four tumbled to the ground. Almost immediately the second-floor window from which the rocket had been launched exploded in a fireball. Grenades, hurled by the assault troops of Unit Two, blew out the window completely, leaving a gaping hole in the building. Three more explosions followed in rapid succession as the Diamondback rockets not yet fired by the terrorists were ignited by the grenades' explosion. Two hundred feet away the captain could feel the intense heat.

They were almost to their target. It was just yards away now. Sixty-six men, what remained of Units One, Three, and Four, came together at one end of the first mammoth storage tank; the men of Unit Two had entered the administration building to secure it after taking out the Diamondback launchers. As the troops reached the storage area, the captain of Unit Three spotted two terrorists through the darkness. They were kneeling at the far end of one of the tanks, a hundred yards away, trying frantically to attach something to the base of the structure. The captain could not see exactly what it was they were focused on, but he had a damn good idea. *"There!"* The captain pointed at the two terrorists and began to lead the rest of the men toward the targets. He knew the terrorists were hunched over a bomb that, if attached to the storage tank and detonated, would instantly incinerate most of downtown Los Angeles in a horrific fireball. What the hell were city planners paid for anyway? How could they leave this facility so naked and unprotected in this day and age?

The captain fixed his gaze upon the two terrorists as he ran, marveling in a way at their absolute devotion to task, their willingness to die so as to kill others. Just to make a statement. There would be nothing left of them if the tank blew. It is suicide, he thought. But they don't care if they kill themselves in the process. They have been brainwashed into believing that they will go to a better place when they are dead. How can we fight that dogma if they truly believe what they are taught? He pressed forward. There was no time to try to figure out the secrets of another man's religion at this moment. The bomb could explode at any second.

Fifty yards now. Close enough to fire. There is the chance that our bullets will ignite the bomb or the tank, but we must take that chance, he thought. There may be *no* time left now.

As the captain slowed to fire, one of the two terrorists pivoted toward the troops and unloaded the cartridge of his automatic rifle. Tiny bursts of white light spit from the gun he wielded. The captain went down, four bullets instantly paralyzing him below the neck. He fell heavily to the asphalt. With a huge effort he raised his head one last time and saw the two terrorists killed in a hail of fire. The Wolverines had won. Some had died, but they had saved the country's largest city from certain devastation. Then the captain tasted the blood filling his lungs, throat, and mouth, and his cheek fell back to the dirty asphalt.

3

Long dark hair fell carelessly about her delicate face in high-lighted layers, framing the perfect skin, deep blue eyes, thin cheeks, and pouty lips, which curled into quick, sultry smiles as the men in nearby seats flirted with her. And though most of her body was obscured from his view by the fawning admirers and the table behind which she sat, he had no doubt that the rest of this woman was as alluring as what he could see. Quickly he removed his gaze from her. His eyes had lingered too long in her direction.

From his position at the front of the amphitheater Mace scanned the ninety faces in the Columbia Business School classroom. Located in upper Manhattan, a short cab ride from the world's most famous money center, Columbia was perennially a top ten business school with its pick of bright, aggressive applicants. After two years of intense study most of them were graduated with seventy-five thousand dollars of debt, or more, and a piece of paper that claimed he or she was a master in the ways of business, which didn't amount to a hill of bean counters in the real world. But many of them were graduated with six-figure jobs too.

Those trying to land marketing positions with Procter & Gamble, Philip Morris, or any of the other well-known consumer product companies sat in the first row of the tiered classroom because they were obnoxiously enthusiastic and believed they could sell themselves to the professor more readily by being physically near to him. Those who coveted high-salaried jobs at McKinsey & Company, Bain, or other top consulting firms sat in the second row because here they were at eye level with the professor and believed they could be more convincing in the middle of the class, with the people, so to speak. The engineers sat in the third row because the other seats in the room were already taken when they arrived—precisely on the hour—and they didn't have time for mind games anyway. They were there to learn, not *just* for the diploma.

The sky deck, as the M.B.A. students affectionately nicknamed the fourth and top tier of the classroom, was typically occupied by the wolves who wanted to go to Wall Street after graduation. From the sky deck they could enter class discussions opportunistically and risk having their opinions attacked only from below, only from inferior positions, in which the other students had to turn uncomfortably in their seats to face them. In the sky deck they could prepare for their next class without being easily spotted by the professor. And from the sky deck they could also make fun of another's lame attempt to answer the professor's query without being obvious. The intelligent, paranoid, and painfully cynical occupants of the sky deck were the investment bankers of the future.

Mace knew a good deal about M.B.A. seating charts and M.B.A. career expectations because he had graduated from Columbia Business School only four years ago, prior to joining Walker Pryce's Real Estate Advisory Group. Perhaps his Wall Street career was progressing better than those of his former classmates because he hadn't followed tradition and occupied sky deck seats. He had sat with the engineers in the third row—and learned something.

With practiced indifference Mace made eye contact with each of the students in the top row. He moved slowly from face to face as they chatted with one another so that when his gaze again came to the beautiful woman, it would not appear obvious that he was staring at just her. Not until the student on which he was focused stole a glance in his direction, as each did, would Mace move on to the next individual. One reason he was sacrificing two nights a week to teach this semester's real estate finance class was that Walker Pryce would be a step ahead of the other New York investment banks in recruiting Columbia's top prospects. So it made sense for him to try to remember their faces before the official recruiting season started in another three weeks at the beginning of February.

The class was packed because the students knew that was why he was here: to find out who the best prospects were. Down deep, each of them, even the budding consultants, harbored fantasies of being an investment banker. The money was simply too good.

Finally Mace's gaze made its way unobtrusively back to the woman. He watched her eyes move seductively as she glanced noncommittally at each of her admirers. He watched her face break into smiles that gave the appearance of sincerity and pushed the men to fawn over her to even greater degrees. Then suddenly he realized that she was staring back at him from the top row of the classroom. It was not the sly glance the others had stolen. There was no attempt on the woman's part to hide her intentions as the others in the room had tried to do. She simply stared straight at him.

Mace met her gaze for a few seconds; then his eyes dropped to the nameplate that stood before her in the groove at the front of the tabletop. Rachel Sommers. The name seemed vaguely familiar. He searched his memory quickly but came up with nothing. Slowly he looked back up the baggy knit sweater until he was again staring into the dark blue eyes. Her full lips broke into the smile he had seen before, but this time she tilted her head slightly to one side, acknowledging his reconnaissance.

"All right! Settle down." Charlie Fenton, dean of Columbia's business school, rapped his scuffed pipe on the lacquered dais. "Now!"

Immediately the hum of thirty conversations evaporated. Mace smiled as he watched the tall silver-haired gentleman peer out at the faces. So Charlie hadn't lost his touch. He could still silence a roomful of arrogant M.B.A. candidates with a rap of that pipe.

Charlie liked to think he could quiet a room so quickly because he was naturally commanding. In truth the respect he garnered from the student body was a direct result of his high-level Wall Street contacts. Charlie Fenton knew the senior officers and partners at every bulge bracket firm on the Street, and he could jumpstart a career for a Columbia student at one of those firms if he so chose, a career that could make you a multimillionaire.

"That's better." Dean Fenton paused another moment for effect, then pointed at Mace with the hand holding the pipe. "This is Mace McLain. He is a vice-president at the firm of Walker Pryce & Company, one of Wall Street's elite investment banking establishments." Dean Fenton said the last few words with an aristocratic, nasal accent, which conveyed a subtle dislike. Despite the fact that Fenton sincerely treasured his Wall Street contacts, he also enjoyed making himself appear to the students to be an outsider, though Fenton's mansion was located next door to that of a Goldman Sachs partner in Darien, Connecticut.

"Mace is a member of the club," Fenton continued, his voice still full of mock contempt, "which isn't necessarily a good thing to be. He works sixteen hours a day seven days a week. He eats Chinese food and pizza for dinner and *cold* Chinese food and *cold* pizza for breakfast." Dean Fenton paused for the appropriate titter from the audience, then resumed. "He camps out on a sofa at work four nights a week and knows more about the inside of most major airports around the world than you and I know about the inside of our homes."

Mace shook his head and smiled. Fenton was right.

"Oh, sure"—Fenton went on—"he makes lots of money, probably owns a condominium in an exclusive Upper West Side building, and gets to work and socialize with some of the most interesting and intelligent people in the world." The room was deathly silent as the M.B.A. candidates listened with capitalistic intensity. "But I bet that condominium on the Upper West Side doesn't have a stick of furniture in it except for a mattress, a beat-up dresser, and an unused exercise bike because he hasn't had a minute to think about furniture since he moved in. And those people he deals with can be pretty damn difficult. I'm sure you'll agree with me that the sacrifice isn't worth the money." Fenton turned toward Mace. "Mace, how many first-year associates did Walker Pryce hire last year from the nation's top business schools?"

Mace glanced around the room at the hungry men and women who hadn't had real jobs in almost two years. It was difficult not to smile. Charlie was doing such a superb job of softening them up. It was the reason Lewis Webster, the senior partner at Walker Pryce, wanted Mace to teach this class. When Charlie finished the introduction, every person in the classroom would be falling all over himself to be hired by Walker Pryce. "We hired thirty-three last year, Charlie."

"Thirty-three, thirty-three . . ." Fenton said the words to himself, as though lost in thought.

Here it came. As Webster always said, Fenton could sell ice cubes to Eskimos and down parkas to Jamaicans. It was beautiful the way he worked them over. And no other investment bank had this intimate opportunity to sell itself to the top M.B.A. students at Columbia because Fenton wouldn't allow it to happen. Only Walker Pryce was allowed to teach a semester-long class.

"And what was the average annual compensation of those thirty-three individuals, Mace?"

"One hundred and seventy-seven thousand dollars."

A gasp raced around the room.

"And what was the compensation of the top earner in that group, Mace?"

Mace shot a lightning-quick glance at Rachel Sommers. Her lips were pursed, and the blue eyes stared straight at him. "Two hundred and thirty-two thousand dollars."

Again an involuntary gasp shook each student.

Dean Fenton's gaze dropped to the scuffed tile floor, and he shook his head. "Twenty-seven-year-olds earning two hundred and thirty-two thousand dollars. My God, what is the world coming to, Mace?"

"Young people at investment banks work hard, Charlie," Mace responded. "They deserve to be paid for that work at whatever rate the market will bear."

The free market disciples seated in the four tiers before Mace nodded as if in a trance, as if they all should make $232,000 their first year out of business school.

Dean Fenton let out a long sigh. "I guess so. It just seems so out of whack with reality." He shook his head again, then continued. "Well, enough talk about compensation. This is real estate finance, and Mace McLain is your teacher when he doesn't have a deal stranding him in Los Angeles or London"—Fenton's voice became suddenly paternal—"although I do have assurances from his senior partner that he will make every attempt to be here, or else . . ." Fenton raised a silver eyebrow at Mace, who nodded in agreement. "All right then, I'll leave you alone." And he was gone, out the swinging door at the side of the room.

Immediately Mace removed his suit jacket, laid it across the small black table standing next to the dais, and began. "Okay, let's get started. Who here can tell me about IOs and POs?"

No one raised a hand.

"Come on, people, unless you've never heard of the *Wall Street Journal*, you know about IOs and POs."

Still no one volunteered. No one wanted to engage the investment banker who stood before them with four years' experience in the industry.

Mace gestured randomly at a curly-haired man in the third row and read his nameplate. "I'm going to have to cold-call Mr. McDuffy over there unless someone volunteers."

McDuffy threw both hands in the air and gazed skyward as

though seeking divine intervention. The action evoked a gush of nervous laughter from the class.

"The terms *IO* and *PO* refer to interest only and principal only strips of mortgages." The laughter subsided quickly as McDuffy's prayers were answered. All heads turned toward Rachel Sommers. Her voice was confident. "Several years ago investment bankers began pooling large numbers of similarly structured mortgages and then selling securities backed by these mortgages to public investors. Subsequently, to broaden the investor market further, they stripped the interest piece away from the principal piece and sold them separately." Rachel folded her arms before her as she finished.

Mace stared at the young woman for a few moments. So she was beautiful *and* bright. "Excellent." He nodded at her, then glanced around the class. "Somebody please tell me what a REIT is."

The spell had been broken. Rachel had calmly jumped through the fire and come out the other side unscathed. Hands shot into the air.

"Yes, Mr. uh . . ." Mace could not read the nameplate of the dark-haired man in the back left corner of the sky deck.

"Jensen." The man prompted Mace, pointing down at his own nametag.

"Yes . . . Jensen. Go ahead."

Jensen rambled for several moments about real estate investment trusts and their tax advantages vis-à-vis typical investment structures. Mace allowed the man to continue speaking for a short time, but his explanation was neither as succinct nor as accurate as Rachel's discussion of mortgages. Finally Mace put him out of his misery. "Thank you, Mr. Jensen."

Aware that Mace was not impressed, Jensen stopped in mid-sentence.

"By the way, there's a large REIT in trouble out in California. Anyone know the name?" Mace asked.

The class was silent.

"Come on. It hasn't been front-page news anywhere, but it's been in the second section of the *Wall Street Journal* each of the past couple of days." Mace scanned the students.

Again there was only silence.

"A prerequisite for any good investment banker, for any business person at all, is to read the *Journal* every day, religiously. You've got to know what's going on in the—"

"The name of the REIT experiencing trouble in California is the East Orange Limited Partnership."

Mace glanced up at the speaker, but he had already recognized the voice. He smiled at Rachel for a few moments. "You seem to have all the answers, Ms. Sommers."

Rachel did not respond.

"That's exactly right, Eastop." Mace used the nickname the traders had given the REIT. A name neither Rachel nor the rest of the class could have read in the *Journal*. It demonstrated that he was on the inside and they were on the outside.

"There's an outfit in Cleveland, a big outfit, that's about to have trouble also, and once that story breaks, Eastop will be a memory. The firm in Cleveland *will* make it to the front page." Rachel offered this comment unprompted.

Mace stared at her. There were only two big REITs in Cleveland, and as far as he knew, both were on solid financial ground. At least they had been the last time he had checked several weeks ago. He smiled up at her as she stared back down at him from the sky deck, not showing the slight consternation he felt at this revelation. He had recently recommended that a good client of Walker Pryce invest in the limited partnership interests of one of the firms. "And what is the name of that firm?"

Rachel's expression turned into the sly smile. "Mr. McLain, you wouldn't really expect me to give you that kind of information, would you?"

A chorus of whistles and jeers filled the room immediately. The prospective M.B.A.'s suddenly sensed that the investment banker might somehow be exposed in the Cleveland situation, and they were enjoying their classmate's advantage vicariously.

Mace McLain nodded at Rachel Sommers, then broke into a wide grin. Perhaps Walker Pryce had just found this year's top prospect from Columbia Business School.

Two hours later Mace was sitting in Dean Fenton's office. It was expansive, piled high with hundreds of business textbooks, which rose like small skyscrapers toward the ceiling, creating miniature cities on the floor and the assorted tables furnishing the office. On the walls were the monuments to Fenton's career. Diplomas, honorary degrees, and awards covered the plain white paint. On the front of his desk were several pictures. They faced strategically from his seat and toward the visitor. In them he was shaking hands with recognizable business types. Warren Buffett, the CEO of Berkshire Hathaway; Stanley Gault, the CEO of Goodyear Tire; and Lewis Webster, the senior partner of Walker Pryce.

Mace watched as Fenton attempted to end the telephone conversation. He was probably on the phone with a Wall Street executive. They constantly contacted him for advice.

Finally Fenton hung up. "These late nights are going to kill me." He winked at Mace from behind the desk.

"Charlie, you love having these guys run to you for your opinion." Mace smiled.

Fenton waved a hand as if all the attention were a pain in the neck. "So how was your first day in the classroom? Did you see anyone you liked? Anyone Lewis Webster will want for Walker Pryce?"

Mace eyed the picture of Fenton and Webster sitting before him on the desk. "There was one," he acknowledged.

Fenton smiled. "Let me guess: Rachel Sommers."

Shadows made by the flames of the fireplace on the far side of the office played on Mace's face. He could not mask the grin that tugged gently at his mouth. "Maybe."

The dean laughed. "I thought I saw you look in her direction a few times as I was introducing you."

Mace shook his head, but the grin would not release its hold on him.

"And if I'm not mistaken, I think she was busy looking at you when you weren't looking at her."

Mace forced the smile from his face. "Charlie, my interest in Rachel Sommers is purely professional."

"Sure, sure." The dean leaned back in his chair unconvinced.

Mace ignored Fenton. "You told me beforehand that all the best finance prospects are in that class. As far as I'm concerned she is head and shoulders above anyone else in there. Plus, another woman at Walker Pryce always helps our little ratio problem."

Fenton nodded.

"So tell me about her, Charlie." Mace paused. "It sounds crazy, but her name seems familiar."

"It ought to be. She was the subject of a *Wall Street Journal* article a couple of weeks ago. You know, the middle column of the front page where they try to do a human-interest story or something other than hard financial news."

"Of course. I remember now." Mace sat up in his seat. "She runs some kind of small equity fund for the school, and it has outperformed all the stars at Fidelity and Vanguard."

"Yep. Those guys say it's easier for someone like Rachel with a relatively small amount of money to exhibit strong returns for a while when they've got so much to manage, but I think that's hogwash. They're just jealous. We give the finance club ten thousand dollars at the beginning of each school year to manage. It provides the students with some real-world experience, as opposed to managing some sort of paper portfolio using imaginary money in portfolio theory class. At the end of the year we donate what's left in the fund to charity. Usually it isn't much. But Rachel's been chief strategist the last two years, and things have been different."

Mace was extremely interested now. No wonder Rachel had

known about the REIT in Cleveland. She was in touch with the market constantly. And she had probably made some very strong contacts along the way, contacts that could prove useful to Walker Pryce. "What's her background?"

Fenton laughed caustically. "That's where she might run into a problem. Her blood isn't exactly blue, and that's usually a prerequisite for employment at Walker Pryce."

"That doesn't matter as much anymore. You know my story, and that didn't seem to bother them."

"You were a special case."

"I think she is too." He hesitated. "Where is she from?"

"She's from across the East River in Brooklyn. Her family's pretty poor. She went to Queens College after attending public school, then picked up a job on the government bond desk at Merrill Lynch as an assistant. Somehow she made her way into the analyst program there. Now she's here on the strength of recommendations from her bosses at Merrill. I think they'll want her back when she's finished here at Columbia because Merrill's not quite as concerned about lineage as Walker Pryce. They seem to think she's pretty smart. And you know how deadly a woman can be on Wall Street when she's smart and beautiful."

Mace rolled his eyes. He knew. "Everyone will want her."

Fenton shrugged. "Maybe. Anyway, I decided to let her into Columbia, even though there was some question of how she'd pay for all this."

"She's paying for it just like everyone else, by borrowing," Mace said.

"Yes, but a lot of these other people have mommies and daddies with money who'll cosign the loans. It wouldn't matter if hers cosigned or not. They've got nothing." Fenton paused. "But she's current so far." He stopped speaking for a moment and brought a hand to his chin. "Enough about Rachel Sommers. How are you doing, Mace?"

"Oh, I keep on trying, Charlie, but there's a long list of smart people out there, you know?"

Dean Fenton did not respond. That was true. There was a long list of smart people out there. And Mace McLain was right at the top of it. Now in his fourth year at Walker Pryce he was generating enough income for the firm that he was almost forcing Lewis Webster to name him a managing director, the last step before making partner, despite the unwritten rule at Walker Pryce that no one made MD until at least his seventh year. He might even make partner before the mandatory tenth year. "You're being modest."

"Am I?"

Fenton laughed. "Yes."

"Thanks." Mace said the word sincerely but paid little attention to the compliment as he watched the flames. He was concentrating on Rachel Sommers. He wanted to know more about her, much more.

The phone on Fenton's desk rang and interrupted Mace's thoughts. The dean picked up the phone. "Hello. Of course." He leaned across the desk and handed the receiver to the younger man. "It's for you. It's Webster's secretary."

Mace shook his head as he took the phone. Walker Pryce's senior partner was going to drive Sarah Clements, his executive assistant, to an early grave. It was after ten o'clock, and the woman had probably arrived at the firm by eight this morning. But Webster was a workaholic; therefore so was she. "Yes, Sarah?"

"Mace, I'm sorry to bother you, but it's important. Mr. Webster needs to see you first thing day after tomorrow. Eight o'clock sharp. And please don't mention this meeting to *anyone* else. He will be meeting with just you."

"Did Webster say what the subject of the meeting would be? I'd like to prepare."

"No, he didn't."

Mace nodded. Of course the old man hadn't mentioned any details about the meeting. He would simply expect Mace to be perfectly conversant in any topic on which he chose to focus. That was Webster's style. He expected that from everyone at any time. "All right."

"I'm glad I caught you," Sarah said in her maternal tone. "Thank you for keeping your schedule so up-to-date on your computer calendar."

"You're welcome. Good night, Sarah." Mace handed the phone back to Fenton. So the senior partner wanted to see him. Alone. He had worked with Webster on several transactions, but always along with another partner. Never alone. "Don't mention the meeting to anyone else." Sarah's words. This could prove interesting.

It was late when Rachel slipped into Columbia's library, and the tables in the great room were completely unoccupied. Everyone was at home sleeping or at an East Side bar drinking. Coming here at this hour was silly, she thought. She laughed to herself. Screw it. Live a little. God knows, you deserve it.

"We'll be closing in a half hour," an elderly man yelled from behind the front desk as Rachel moved through the doors.

She waved calmly at the man as she made her way toward the back of the stacks of books but said nothing. This wouldn't take long. She hoped.

"Hi, Chad." Rachel smiled as she leaned into the communications room, a small space off the main library floor furnished only with several on-line information systems—Lexis/Nexis, Telerate, and Bloomberg, all a good M.B.A. candidate needed to get ahead. Unfortunately Chad Maddux, a fellow second-year M.B.A. student and the only other person in the room at this late hour, was using the system she wanted, the Bloomberg system.

Chad turned in the seat positioned in front of the screen. His expression brightened immediately. "Hi, Rachel." He leaned back and ran long fingers through his shaggy black hair. It was a student's haircut, screaming of irresponsibility.

Rachel nodded at him. "You better get that mop clipped pretty soon. Interviews begin in a couple of weeks."

Chad began to stretch, groaning as if he had been cramped over the terminal all evening. His biceps flexed obnoxiously under the short-sleeved T-shirt.

It was all for her benefit, and she knew it. Men were so predictable.

"What are you doing here at this hour, Rachel?" Chad finished stretching and brought his hands to rest on his thighs. His gaze focused momentarily on her chest, trying to determine the shape of what lay beneath, but he was unable to do so because of the baggy sweater she wore.

"I've just got to analyze a stock for the portfolio," she lied, "and this is the only time I've got." She noted the direction of his gaze.

Chad snorted. "You and that portfolio." He shook his head. "Oh, well, I guess if I had a front-page *Wall Street Journal* article written about me because of a portfolio, I might watch it like a hawk too."

"Chad, I really need to use the Bloomberg terminal for a few minutes before the library closes." She was becoming impatient. "Would you mind terribly?"

"On one condition."

"What?"

"I get to walk you home."

"Sure." She smiled at him. It wasn't a bad idea to have a male escort walk you home at this time of night in New York City. But if he expected anything at the end of the walk, he would be disappointed. "That would be nice."

Chad rose to give her the chair.

"Would you be a sweetheart and get me a Diet Coke?" Rachel asked. "I'm really thirsty." The soda machines were outside the library, so it would take him a few minutes to run the errand.

"On my way." He was out the door immediately.

Rachel turned toward the Bloomberg terminal and made her

way quickly into the who's who section of the system. Her fingers flew over the keys. She did not want Chad Maddux to see her true objective. That was why she had sent him for the drink. "Come on." The system seemed to be taking longer than normal.

Finally it was prepared for her inquiry. She typed the letters carefully, M-C-L-A-I-N, and then pushed the enter button. The screen filled with McLains. Abigail, Adam . . . She scrolled down. Mace William McLain. Immediately she moved the cursor to his name and pushed the enter button again. Instantly his image filled the screen. He was dark like Chad, with jet black hair, but he seemed infinitely more mysterious. She stared at the gray eyes, sculpted cheeks, and a half smile. She laughed and shook her head. The technology available today was incredible. Anything you wanted right to your computer monitor. Even Mace McLain.

Rachel paged down through the system. She was looking for one thing. She swallowed and felt the flutter in her stomach. God, this was silly. She was acting like a teenager, but she couldn't help herself. She had to know. There it was. At least as of six weeks ago, the last marked update of his biography. Marital status: single.

"I didn't see a ring on his finger in class tonight." The voice came from behind her.

Rachel spun in the seat and was instantly face-to-face with Chad. Her eyes narrowed, but she said nothing.

Chad handed her the Diet Coke. "Of course I'm sure you noticed that too."

4

Bob Whitman, president of the United States, hurried after several members of his staff down the narrow corridor toward the White House press room, his attention riveted to the pad on which he had scribbled brief notes just minutes before. He would read the hastily prepared statement, answer only a few questions from those reporters he knew to be unfailingly amicable toward his administration, then get to Camp David as fast as possible. The decision was controversial. There was no doubt. And after almost seven years as the country's chief executive he knew that the best strategy in a situation such as this was to drop the bomb with little warning, make a quick getaway, then watch the dust settle from a safe distance. He drew in a long breath as he made the last turn toward what he knew was a packed house.

"Mr. President."

Whitman glanced up from the notepad as the vice president, Preston Andrews, slipped between members of the entourage until he stood directly before the president, blocking his path to the press room. Whitman's eyes narrowed. He had hoped to avoid this confrontation until after the Camp David vacation, until after the dust had at least begun to settle. But this announcement was going to have a dramatic impact on the vice president. So the fact that Andrews would try to stem the tide even as Whitman was going into the press room to make the announcement came as no surprise. The president gathered himself. "Yes, Preston." He made his irritation obvious.

Andrews paid no attention to the tone. "Mr. President, are you really going to give the CIA permanent responsibility for fighting domestic terrorism?"

"Yes." Whitman was curt. The decision had been made and would not be altered.

"You could have at least let me know that the decision had been made."

"There wasn't time," Whitman said matter-of-factly.

"But Malcolm Becker is their leading candidate." Andrews lowered his voice. "He's already a lock for the Republican nomination. All this attention you're giving him might push him over the top in the November election."

"That's a gross exaggeration."

Andrews ignored the barb. "You're killing our party, not to mention me."

The president rolled his eyes. "This has nothing to do with the party, or you, Preston."

"It has everything to do with me!" the vice president whispered intently. "And it isn't right either. The FBI should maintain responsibility for domestic terrorism."

Whitman glanced around at his aides. They were becoming nervous at this unanticipated roadblock. His focus returned to Andrews. "Did you see what Malcolm Becker's Wolverines did to those people out in Los Angeles yesterday?"

The vice president swallowed hard, then nodded.

"That city could have been incinerated, but it wasn't. Because of that fighting force, because of its capabilities." Whitman's face became grim. "Do you remember a little problem in Waco and that other one up in Idaho? Remember how well our domestic law enforcement officials reacted in those situations?"

Andrews grimaced, remembering the fiascos.

Whitman moved closer to Andrews until their faces were just

inches apart. "Can you imagine the FBI or the ATF going into that L.A. facility against terrorists armed with high-tech weapons when they couldn't even take a facility that was occupied mostly by shot-gun-toting civilians without blowing everyone inside up?" The president shook his head, then set his jaw. "I said I was going to give Becker and his people at the CIA a chance. I gave them that chance, and they have performed extremely well. The world is a different place now, Preston. We need Becker and his experience. Even if he is a Republican." Whitman paused to draw in a long breath. "I know some of my fellow Democrats will be appalled by this decision. They'll say I'm not being faithful to the party in an election year. That I'm giving the other side's best hope a shot in the arm. That I'm giving Becker free publicity, a forum from which to launch his campaign. The whole nine yards. But I don't care. I have to make the best decision possible in this situation, one that isn't polluted by politics. A decision that is in the best interest of the people's safety." Whitman touched the vice president's arm.

Andrews glanced up from the floor into the president's eyes.

Whitman smiled at the vice president. "Don't worry, Preston. You are going to be the Democratic nominee, and you are going to defeat Malcolm Becker this November in the general election. You are going to succeed me in the White House."

Andrews hesitated. "But the investigation," he whispered. "Does this announcement mean you are going to give up your investigation into misappropriation of funds at the CIA? I—"

Whitman held up his hands to interrupt. "When I get back from Camp David, we will revisit the issue. I promise. Everything will be all right." He glanced around at his entourage. "Ready?"

The aides nodded back uncomfortably. The president was now four minutes late to the briefing. They hoped the press wouldn't read anything into that.

"Let's go." Whitman brushed past Andrews and moved confidently into the glare of the press room lights.

The vice president turned to watch Whitman move to the

podium. "I wish I had as much confidence as you do," he said softly to himself.

Whitman climbed the platform at the front of the room and was met by Malcolm Becker, director of the Central Intelligence Agency. Cameras popped and flashed as the two men shook hands before the podium bearing the presidential seal. Preston Andrews gazed at Becker as the man smiled for the press. He detested Becker more than any other human being in the world.

The long table stood beneath the arched ceiling of the Partners' Room on the thirty-eighth and top floor of Two Wall Street, the headquarters of Walker Pryce & Company, one of the Street's oldest investment banks. The powerful firm traced its origin to the Civil War and the underwriting of bonds for the Union to support its effort in winning the conflict. The table was surrounded by comfortable leather chairs, in which the partners of the esteemed firm had sat at the end of each fiscal quarter since 1912 to review their good fortune, 1912 being the year Walker Pryce had purchased what was then considered a skyscraper on the northeast corner of Wall Street and Broadway across from Trinity Church. A thick Persian rug covered the floor of the large room, and oil portraits of prosperous-looking stern-faced men hung from the dark green walls. Small alcoves lined the walls of the rooms. They were furnished with handsome upholstered chairs and provided the partners—and only the partners because no other members of the firm were allowed in the Partners' Room upon pain of employment termination—with a haven from the constant barrage of telephone calls from clients and other people at the firm.

At the end of the year when the rankings of the top securities underwriters were published, Walker Pryce was consistently among the top five in the league tables. It also boasted a highly respected Mergers and Acquisitions Advisory Department and several trading groups that moved with lightning speed when they identified an opportunity—or, better, still, an arbitrage. As a result of its financial prowess, the firm had netted more than a billion dollars in profits before employee bonuses in each of the last three years.

Most of the high-profile investment banking firms that had begun the twentieth century as partnerships were now publicly held or had been swallowed up by larger financial entities. Morgan Stanley, Salomon Brothers, First Boston, Kidder Peabody, and Lehman Brothers all had forfeited their partnership status in favor of the larger pools of capital available to a public firm. Even Goldman Sachs had sold a large piece of its equity to the Japanese. While being public enabled them to access more diverse funding sources, which improved their competitive positions, forfeiting partnership status also had one very steep downside: profits had to be shared with the public stockholders.

Walker Pryce had managed to remain independent, and as a result, its partners were wealthy beyond most Americans' dreams. Of the firm's seven thousand employees, only one hundred were partners. It might take fifteen years to achieve this position—at a minimum, ten—but once this status had been achieved, the partner's financial security was assured, as was his family's for generations to come. Depending upon his tenure with the firm, a Walker Pryce partner might be worth between fifteen and three hundred million dollars, the figure Lewis Webster was rumored to have amassed.

But remaining independent was becoming increasingly difficult, even for Walker Pryce. The demand for more and more capital to fund growth was ever-present. Investment bankers in all areas of the firm constantly pounded the table for more money to fund transactions, and as older partners began to retire, draining funds from the firm's reserves, giving in to the allure of the public market seemed inevitable.

Lewis Webster sat at the head of the table, the seat traditionally reserved for the senior partner of the firm. He was the nineteenth senior partner in Walker Pryce history, and when he stared back over his shoulder at the portrait of Harley Walker, the firm's founder, hanging above the room's mammoth hearth, he dared

convince himself that no senior partner in the history of Walker
Pryce had ever faced as difficult a situation as the one that loomed
before him now. The partnership was totally divided on whether
or not to forgo 152 years of independence, while an individual bent
on ultimate power was wielding his authority to force Webster and
Walker Pryce into a terrible risk. But true to his nature, Webster
would turn this situation into a win—at least for him. He was a sur-
vivor, and he would sacrifice anyone to achieve his objective.

Polk and Marston entered the Partners' Room through the
doorway at the far end of the room. Together Polk, Marston, and
Webster made up Walker Pryce's executive committee. They alone
were responsible for major decisions involving the firm. They were
few in number for such an important committee, but it was the
number specified in the original charter and bylaws, and the men of
the partnership were unwilling to alter those time-honored documents. Besides, the small number of executive committee members
was in keeping with the entrepreneurial culture of the firm. Important decisions could be made efficiently and without fanfare.

Webster heard the hinges of the ancient door creak as it closed.
He turned away from Harley Walker's portrait and watched the
other two approach. Graham Polk was head of Sales and Trading,
responsible for client trading, distribution, and principal positions
Walker Pryce took in specific securities. Walter Marston was the
top investment banker, responsible for originating debt and equity
issues as well as for all of the firm's advisory activities. Polk was
short, fiery, overweight, and suffering from stomach ulcers. He
rarely wore his suit jacket, and when he did, it usually did not match
his pants. Marston wore perfectly pressed, expensive suits and
looked ten years younger than his fifty-two years. The two men detested each other, rarely agreeing on anything simply as a matter of
principle. Each believed himself responsible for Walker Pryce's
huge profits, believed the other's activities to be a drag on earnings,
and constantly accused the other of attempting to encroach on his
turf. This discord was acceptable to Webster because it caused both

men to push their people very hard to prove that their areas were the most valuable to the firm's earnings and because by default he could always count on one of them as his ally. The bylaws clearly stated that the executive committee needed only a simple majority to adopt a measure. Webster watched them carefully as they approached. He needed at least one of them very badly tonight.

"Good evening, Lewis," Marston said as he sank into the chair to Webster's right. He glanced around the huge space. It was dark except for the soft glow emanating from two green-shaded lamps in the middle of the table. The feeble light cast strange shadows into far corners of the large room.

Polk grunted something unintelligible as he took the seat to Webster's left. He placed a large glass of milk on the antique table-top and began to roll up his shirtsleeves.

Marston snorted and shook his head at Polk's lack of social grace.

Polk stopped rolling up his sleeves momentarily. "You got a problem, Marston?" He spoke like a platoon sergeant on maneuvers, quickly and with a sense of purpose.

Marston leaned forward. "Yeah, I've got lots of—"

"Gentlemen, that is enough." Webster's whispery voice cut through their differences immediately. Some called it the death whisper because the eerie quality in the low tone killed other people's sentences in mid-word. Ten years ago Webster had battled throat cancer and won; however, it had left him unable to speak normally. But true to his nature, Webster had turned this disadvantage into an advantage. "Mr. Polk, please use a coaster." Webster nodded at the glass of milk.

Polk retrieved a coaster from the middle of the table immediately, straining as he leaned across the wood. He placed the glass on the coaster, reseated himself, then turned respectfully toward Webster, as did Marston. They both feared him intensely, just as the rest of the partnership did.

Webster did not have a physically commanding presence. He was thin and of average height. His slim face made him appear almost malnourished, the skin drawn tightly into deep crevices beneath protruding cheekbones. His head was bald except for a halo of gray hair above his ears and at the nape. Unlike any other partner, he wore a closely clipped beard, the color of which matched his gray hair. His eyes were dark brown, almost black, and they seemed half hidden below dark eyebrows. He was not imposing, yet he intimidated people immediately.

Webster ran Walker Pryce with an iron fist. In the early days of his nine-year rule as senior partner there had been attempts at insurrections when people took exception to some of his unilateral operating decisions. Then they had been called to his office for one-on-one meetings, and suddenly their criticisms had ceased. Rumors began circulating that Webster maintained files on each partner, files filled with incriminating evidence he had somehow obtained and used to influence those threatening insubordination. But no one who had been called to a one-on-one meeting with Lewis Webster had ever revealed what had taken place there.

"I appreciate your coming here at such a late hour this evening." It was well after eleven o'clock. "I have something of extreme importance to discuss with you." Webster spoke slowly, enunciating each word carefully. "It will have an immense impact on the firm." He paused and looked at each man in turn.

They looked down into their laps, away from Webster's glare.

"As you are aware, our capital requirements seem to grow each day." Webster continued. "Both of you want more money all the time for your departments. Let me assure you, I don't have a problem with these capital requirements. You both have performed admirably over the last three years, and the firm has achieved outstanding success as a result."

Polk and Marston nodded but did not look up. Webster rarely meted out compliments, and their personalities did not allow them to receive accolades easily.

"But at the end of this year another seven men will retire, and our total annual payment to retired partners under our payout schedule will reach almost two hundred million dollars. We are generating very little new cash at all from our one billion dollars in profits after accounting for three hundred fifty million dollars of employee bonuses, provisions for the partners' taxes, and the two-hundred-million-dollar payout. It would seem that our only alternative would be to end a century and a half of the partnership and take the firm public." Webster's low whisper had become almost inaudible.

Polk's and Marston's eyes remained transfixed on their laps. They were aware that Webster wanted Walker Pryce to stay independent at all costs. But it would not matter. Polk, Marston, and a slim majority of the other partners wanted to go public, and they would ultimately be victorious. The opportunity was too appetizing. They would be able to cash in some of their stock immediately in the initial public offering, and the third-party investors would probably pay a whopping premium just to be able to buy the shares, just to be able to say they were Walker Pryce shareholders. Even Lewis Webster would not be able to stem this tide.

"So you both agree on this matter?"

Polk and Marston glanced across the table at each other, and their eyes quickly narrowed, their disdain for each other obvious. But they nodded silently. Despite their desire to disagree, their greed eclipsed their pride. The equity markets were performing well. If Walker Pryce was able to go through the registration process quickly, the partners might be able to cash out at a truly remarkable multiple, given the firm's outstanding performance over the last three years.

"Yes, Lewis," Marston said quietly.

Polk grunted his assent softly.

Webster brought a hand to his face and stroked his beard. He had been afraid of this. Normally Polk and Marston would have disagreed just to disagree. He would have had an ally, and Walker Pryce could have remained independent. But greed was too strong a unifying factor in this case. "You both know that I want very much for this firm to stay out of public hands?" he whispered.

"We do know that," Polk replied. His tone was subdued but firm. "However, we think in the long run it will be best for Walker Pryce to go public. It's what the majority of the partners want."

"But it's not what I want!" Webster pounded his bony hand on the table as he stood.

Polk and Marston jumped in their chairs as though they had suddenly touched an electrically charged cable. Webster was not prone to violent outbursts, and they looked up at him in shock.

Webster pointed a gnarled finger at Polk, who swallowed hard. "This firm has produced record profits each of the last three years"—his whisper filled the vast room—"because of decisions I have made, because of risks I have taken."

"But, Lewis"—Marston's voice was soft—"it's the best thing for the—"

"Don't interrupt me, Walter!" Webster snarled, turning toward the firm's top investment banker.

Polk wiped his forehead. He was thankful that Marston had distracted Webster's attention away from him. He retrieved the glass of milk and finished it in several huge gulps.

"I want a chance to speak, an opportunity to put forth a plan, an alternative to going public. I deserve that chance."

Polk and Marston glanced across the table at each other. Both had limousines waiting for them on Wall Street in front of the building. But Webster was the senior partner, so they would accommodate him.

"All right, Lewis," Marston said.

Slowly Webster sat back down in his chair. "Thank you so much, gentlemen," he said sarcastically. "As I said, I have an alternative to going public. I want to raise a large fund, a billion dollars in size. Maybe two. Walker Pryce will seed the fund with fifty million and manage it day to day, generating some nice operating fees on an ongoing basis. But more important, we will receive a substantial share of the profits, much greater than our relative share of the investment."

"Like the funds put together by the leveraged buyout firms in the late eighties," Polk said, staring at his empty glass. He said the words halfheartedly. He wasn't interested; that was obvious.

Webster nodded. "Exactly."

"What would this fund invest in?" Marston picked at his fingernails. He too was not interested in the discussion but was simply playing out the string, allowing Webster to enjoy a last fantasy before he and Polk slammed the door shut.

Marston eyed the old man. Perhaps as part of going public, the partnership should take the opportunity to ease Lewis Webster out of an active management role and into the beginning of retirement. Webster was almost sixty-three and clearly showing the signs of his age. Marston shot a glance at Polk. One of them would succeed Webster, and the struggle would be titanic. He would begin lining up support tomorrow.

"The fund will invest in Manhattan real estate and common stocks. I firmly believe that Manhattan real estate as a whole is grossly overvalued and that the Dow Jones and the S & P 500 averages are much too high as well. I strongly believe that in the near term both the Manhattan real estate market and the shares traded on the Exchange are going to suffer significant devaluations. I want to be ready to take advantage of the devaluations when they occur. Once the corrections take place and the prices have bottomed out, we will buy heavily with money from the fund." Webster paused. "I therefore propose that we raise nine hundred and fifty million from third-party investors immediately, in addition to the fifty Walker Pryce will commit, and leverage the fund's equity by borrowing another one billion dollars on top of the equity so that we have a total of two billion to play with. Then we sit back and wait for the corrections to occur before we dive in. We should make several billion in excess of our investment in a very short time. That would be plenty of money for us to fund growth into the twenty-first century. And we wouldn't have to go public." Webster's gaze moved slowly in turn to each man. His head was angled forward, and his dark eyes burned.

Marston stared back. "You can't be serious, Lewis."

"I am absolutely serious."

Marston shook his head. "There are huge risks in raising and managing a purely speculative fund of the size you are proposing. If we didn't earn the kinds of returns you are talking about, we could end up negatively affecting our mainstream asset management business, at which we make a pretty penny. Worse, a slip up in a speculative fund might inhibit our ability to go public. At the very least we wouldn't get as good a price from public investors. No, Lewis. We should forget about this fund idea and go public at the earliest possible moment. That is my decision, and there is no room to negotiate with me." Marston leaned forward over the table triumphantly, as if he had actually wrested control of the firm from the senior partner at that exact moment.

Webster turned his dark gaze upon Polk. "Is this your decision as well, Graham?" Webster's whisper seeped through the deathly silent room.

Polk swallowed hard as his eyes flickered back and forth between Webster and Marston. Webster would require that both he and Marston record their vote, and the partnership would have access to that record. If he voted with Webster, the other partners would see that he had not voted for what the majority wanted, and when the day came for Webster to step down—and that day would come sooner rather than later—Marston would remind the others that he had voted to go public and that Polk had voted with Webster. If he didn't stand up to Webster now, Marston would end up controlling the firm because the others would vote for Marston as senior partner at that point—hands down.

Polk shifted in his chair. He did not like the fire he still saw burning in Webster's eyes, but there was no choice. Polk took a deep breath. "I have to agree with Marston," he said quietly.

Webster nodded once slowly, then leaned forward toward Polk. "Are you absolutely certain of your decision?"

"Yes." Polk did not hesitate this time. So the partnership would die. He glanced over Webster's shoulder at Harley Walker's portrait. Sorry, old man, he thought, but it couldn't be helped.

"Fine." Webster's voice was even. "I'd like you both to take these home with you tonight and glance through them at your leisure." From the floor Webster picked up the two thick brown packages that the man in the hotel had given him and slid them to Polk and Marston respectively. He smiled widely, as if he were giving out Christmas presents. "But I would caution you. You probably want to open them when you are alone."

Marston's triumphant expression faded from his face. He picked up the package from the tabletop. "What the—"

"Don't bother opening it now, Walter. I'll give you a little sample of what's inside." Webster's whisper was gentle, almost soothing. "Let's see. It seems that for years now you've been making millions from a venture you own most of down in Argentina. But you haven't been reporting this income to the Internal Revenue Service. The ownership structure is very complicated, and it isn't immediately obvious that you actually own any of the stock or that you've ever brought money back to the States so that it would be subject to U.S. taxes." Webster's voice developed an eerie quality. "But the records in your package prove conclusively that you do own ninety-five percent of the venture and further prove that you have repatriated funds to yourself here in the United States, a total of almost twenty million dollars. You're looking at fifteen to thirty years in a federal penitentiary. The Argentine authorities would probably be interested to know that you've been ducking taxes down there as well."

Webster turned purposefully toward Polk, who clutched his package against his chest. "Graham, you've been playing with lots of little ten-year-old boys out at that private home in Staten Island, haven't you? You've had to pay quite a bit to do it too, but that's your business. Anyway, it's all on the videotape in your package. Nice graphic footage of your interludes. Shove that into the VCR at your Upper East Side apartment and show it to your co-op neighbors. If you don't, I will. But I won't stop with your co-op neighbors, you can rest assured of that. Every partner here will see that tape. And so will the New York City Police Department."

It was Webster's turn for triumph. In thirty seconds he had destroyed them both.

Marston started to say something but stopped. There was nothing to say.

"I'll expect your votes on my desk at eight o'clock tomorrow morning. We *will* remain a partnership for at least another two years, and you *will* give me full authority to begin immediately raising the fund I described earlier. Is that clear?" Webster smiled.

Marston and Polk nodded as if in a trance.

"Very well, you may go."

The two men rose unsteadily, grasping their packages of influence.

"One more thing, Marston," Webster said.

The two men stopped and looked back.

"I will be taking Mace McLain out of your Real Estate Advisory Group." Webster smiled. "He's the brightest man at this firm, and I'll need him for the fund. He will no longer report to you."

Marston nodded wordlessly. Webster could have said anything at this point and he would have agreed.

Webster's eyes fell to the empty glass left on the mahogany table. "Learn to pick up after yourself, will you, Polk?" Webster smiled. "You certainly have quite a few dirty little habits, don't you?"

Quickly Polk retrieved the glass. Then he and Marston melted from the room.

Slowly Webster turned his chair toward the huge fireplace and the portrait of Harley Walker. He smiled again. Perhaps this would work out well after all. Perhaps it was as the man had said. In the long run they all would come out of this much stronger than before. And it beat the hell out of that lice-infested cell waiting for him at Leavenworth.

Far below the bell of Trinity Church began to toll midnight.

5

He was a soldier, though his uniform was not that of a regular army. As a soldier he followed the orders of his commanding officer to the letter. Because as a soldier, if he stopped to question authority, he could be dead in the next instant. The bullet could find you in that moment of insubordination. It was that simple. Alive or dead: which did you want to be?

Sweat poured down Slade Conner's face as he crouched in the jungle at the edge of the remote dirt runway. The Honduran night was hot, steaming with humidity, and he had not yet fully cooled down from the arduous task of sledgehammering forty-two steel rebar rods into the narrow runway so that they protruded eighteen inches from the dirt's surface in six neat rows of seven bars each, as he had been ordered to do.

Slade flicked a mosquito from his cheek. He had never questioned the order, but as he scoured the night sky, while in the middle of dense foliage twenty miles from the nearest town—a town which was really nothing more than a ragtag group of shacks at the edge of a mountain stream—the shred of doubt that he had been trying so hard to ignore since leaving Washington four days ago began to worm its way into his thoughts again.

"Damn it!" Slade smacked at another mosquito, this time digging into the back of his neck, rolled the dead insect's carcass into a neat ball against his skin, then pinched it between his thumb and forefinger and brought it before his face. Even at a distance of only a few inches he could barely discern the bug's shape on his fingertip. The night was too dark for him to see clearly even to his hand. That was good. It meant that the pilot of the small plane would never see the truck hidden beneath the vines and leaves. More important, he wouldn't see the rebar on the runway until it was too late.

Of course Slade didn't really care about the pilot. Killing a drug runner was of no concern to him. Drug runners were the scourge of the earth. It was the person who was supposed to be accompanying the pilot on this flight that concerned Conner.

The plane was on its way from the jungles of Colombia to a small airstrip east of Lopeno, Texas, loaded down by a cargo of cocaine with a street value of more than twenty-five million dollars. Though the drug lords had recently become more brazen and diverse in their methods of flooding the United States with the drug, most cocaine still entered the country in two- and four-seater planes. The one being used tonight was a smaller craft and would refuel at one of two airstrips deep in the Honduran jungle before continuing its flight toward the United States. At least that was what his information indicated.

Above Conner a large branch suddenly snapped and crashed noisily to the jungle floor ten feet away. Instantly he stood and reached for the flashlight that fitted snugly in his wide leather belt, then thought better about pulling it out. He did not want to take any chances on giving away his position to the plane. He was also confident that the cause of the branch breaking was not human. He had scoured the terrain several times this afternoon and this evening and was certain no one was in the vicinity. The only road into the airstrip was an old logging path, which he had mined in several places. The branch must have broken under its own weight or that of an animal.

Slade stared in the direction in which the branch had crashed to earth and listened. He thought he discerned a slight rustling that he had not noticed before. A snake? The constrictors down here were big and could easily snap a branch under their great weight during an evening hunt. He hated snakes. Poisonous, non-poisonous, it didn't matter. He had attempted to lose this phobia through therapy, by holding a variety of snakes with the help of trainers at the Washington Zoo, but nothing had worked. Slade's right hand dropped to the handle of the 9 mm pistol wedged deep into the holster strapped to his thigh.

Suddenly, out of the corner of his eye, Slade noticed the blue landing lights illuminate. There were ten of them embedded in the dirt runway to guide the pilot onto the ground at night, and he had been careful not to sledgehammer the rebar into the runway near them. Slade's pulse accelerated. They were close. The pilot would have turned on the landing lights from the plane.

Slade moved through the tangle of bushes and vines, farther from the edge of the short airstrip, farther from where the branch had come crashing to earth only moments before. He wanted no part of the snake—if that had been the cause of the disturbance.

At first the sound of the plane's engine was nothing more than a high-pitched hum, as if a mosquito were circling close to his ear. But the hum grew steadily louder until the plane roared overhead just several hundred feet off the ground. It moved over the field and into the distance. So the pilot was being careful, Slade thought. He wasn't landing on his first pass. Slade wondered if the pilot had landed at the other strip first, twelve miles away, and found the empty tanks from which he had siphoned the fuel yesterday. If the pilot had found the empty tanks, he might be suspicious.

Slade pressed himself behind a huge tree as the plane passed low over the field again. There might be heat-sensing equipment on board, and though the heat Slade generated could easily be that made by an animal, he wanted to give those in the plane no reason to make any alternative plans. As the plane buzzed past again, he leaned from behind the tree trunk and watched the craft's orange lights disappear over the treetops. His heart pounded beneath the perspiration-drenched khaki shirt. Again he felt for the 9 mm, this time for a different reason.

The sound of the plane's engine faded to almost nothing, then began to increase in intensity again. The men were landing this time. He could feel it. They were probably low on fuel and late, and though somehow they sensed danger, they had no choice but to come to earth here. Slade leaned farther out from behind the tree, his fingertips clinging to the rough bark as he stared at the treetops, waiting for the light of the small craft to reappear. Beads of salty sweat dripped from his forehead, stinging his eyes. He rubbed the droplets away quickly, then looked back up at the tree-tops. As he did, the lights of the plane appeared, descending quickly toward the waiting blue landing lights.

Don't let them see the rebar. His heart felt as if it would ex-plode as it pounded in his chest. Don't let them see it.

The rubber tires clipped the second line of rebar, shearing off one landing support rod immediately. The plane immediately pitched forward, giving the pilot no time to react to the unexpected impact. The forward-mounted propeller bore into the dirt, spew-ing great clumps of sod and gravel into the air until the blades snapped and shot away from the fuselage. The two passengers were hurled against the windshield and then against the ceiling of the fuselage as the plane flipped over onto its spine and skidded on its overhead wings through the next line of rebar, which tore at the aircraft's delicate skin like razors.

By the time what was left of the plane had come to a stop against the fifth line of rebar, Slade Conner was almost halfway down the runway, flashlight gripped tightly in his right hand, the light bobbing wildly before him as he sprinted. "Don't blow, baby! Don't you blow on me!" Slade whispered as he tore down the airstrip, following the light, dodging the few rebar rods still stand-ing and the debris littering the ground. He needed to identify the passenger's body, and a fire might render him unrecognizable. He had been given various markings all over the individual as means of identification, but if the body hadn't been thrown from the plane, he would have to stay in this place until the flames burned themselves out, and that might be dangerous. Fire would attract attention, even in this desolate place. And if the body were burned too badly, he would have to open it up to make the identification. That was a task he did not relish.

Slade slowed down as he neared what remained of the craft. He sniffed the air but detected no fumes. So the plane had been *very* low on fuel, and the pilot had had no choice but to land. He switched off the flashlight, got down on his knees, crawled twenty feet to the right, then listened. If one or both of them had somehow survived the crash, he did not want to present an easy target. He squatted motionless for two full minutes, listening for any sounds of human life, but there was nothing.

Finally Conner began to creep toward the plane. As he did, he became aware of the plastic bags strewn about, some of them still full of the illicit payload. The drug lord would be mildly irritated at the loss, but there were other planes, many more pilots, and tons more cocaine. It was the loss of the passenger that would cause his fury. Because the passenger, if he was indeed on the plane, had enabled the drug lord to smuggle safely many more tons of cocaine into the United States than his competitors by providing important information regarding the identity of undercover agents and advance warning of raids and by alerting the drug lord to the timing and location of aerial night patrols. The passenger had done these things for a share of the profits. That was what Slade had been told.

The plane lay on its back, lodged against the rebar line. One wing had been neatly torn away from the fuselage, as had the stabilizer, but the passenger compartment appeared intact. Slade took a deep breath, then slowly rose to his knees and peered in through one of the cockpit's side windows. The glass was completely gone except for a small ridge of jagged edges around the window frame. He took another deep breath, then switched on the flashlight. He could only pray that the passenger had been on board and hadn't been thrown from the plane during the crash.

But there had been no need to worry. Carter Guilford, the senior field agent for all South American operations of the Central Intelligence Agency, lay faceup on the ceiling of the cockpit. His right arm had been completely severed from the rest of his body at the shoulder, and blood covered his face, but Slade recognized him immediately anyway. A CIA agent gone bad: that was what his commander had said, and it seemed he had been accurate. Here was Guilford, eyes wide open yet unseeing, lying amid the remains of the cocaine he had been helping transport and next to the dead pilot he had been abetting. "Obey your commander." They were words to live by. There had been no reason to question. Guilford was a renegade agent. The only other explanation for his presence on the flight was that he was working undercover, but that was impossible. CIA people as senior as Guilford did not work undercover. They were too easily recognized and were too great a loss to the agency if uncovered. Hell, Guilford was only a few rungs below Malcolm Becker, the director of the CIA.

The window of the plane was wide enough for Slade to crawl through. He did so slowly, careful not to cut himself on the jagged glass around the frame. He stared at Guilford's open eyes as he inched toward the body. How could anyone turn against the country this way? How could he so blatantly forswear the people's trust and the oath to uphold and protect the safety of the nation? Avoiding the blood trickling along the spine of the plane toward the tail, Slade slid next to the body. He checked the outside pockets of Guilford's suede jacket, found nothing, then searched the inside pockets.

The date book was small, three inches by six, made of black leather, and trimmed with gold at the corners. Slade rested the flashlight on the ceiling of the plane, then leaned down and flipped through the pages in the glow of the bulb. His business was intelligence, so he was naturally drawn to such an article as this that might reveal much about the man. Suddenly he stopped, flipped back several pages, and stared at the entry. It made no sense. The commander had told him nothing that hinted of this second treason, only of his crimes of aiding and abetting the drug lord.

Slade's eyes narrowed. A meeting, already to have taken place according to the book, between Guilford and Preston Andrews, vice president of the United States. Malcolm Becker and Preston Andrews despised each other and agents were never to meet with the vice president alone, yet here was the appointment in Guilford's date book. Recently in Bogotá, according to the entry. It made no sense. Was that what this whole incident was really about?

Slade shook his head. There was that worm again, slowly but relentlessly boring its way into his brain. He had to stop questioning. The commander was above reproach. Wasn't he?

6

The office decor seemed more appropriate for a man running a stodgy nineteenth-century bank than for one about to steer the Street's most progressive investment bank into the twenty-first. Modern financial hardware was not to be found in the room. There were no on-line systems, no computers, no fancy telephone banks, nothing indicative of the technoinformation age that had overtaken the financial world.

The office walls were painted dull gray. From them hung ancient fox-hunting prints in heavy, well-worn frames. The room's furniture, including a huge dark wood rolltop desk in the far corner, would have looked natural in a museum exhibit. Everything was old, including the typewriter sitting on the credenza beneath the window overlooking the beginning of Wall Street, which was just outside Walker Pryce's front door. The office even smelled ancient—musty and slightly stale. J. P. Morgan would have felt at home.

Mace had been to this office only a few times in his four-year career at Walker Pryce, so he hesitated in the hallway and took in the scene for a moment. The office was out-of-date, that was certain, but somehow it was still impressive. Finally he knocked on the open door.

Lewis Webster glanced up from the papers on the desktop to

Mace. "Are you quite finished gawking at my office?" he asked in his unfriendly, gravelly whisper.

So the old man had known Mace was there the entire time. Webster didn't miss a trick. He might look a little feeble, but looks could be deceiving. Mace did not respond directly to Webster's confrontational tone. It was better to ignore the old man's barb than to respond. "Marston said you wanted to see me."

"Yes, come in. Close the door behind you."

Mace walked slowly through the doorway into the large room and closed the door.

"How is Marston?" Webster asked.

As Mace sat down in the chair, he thought he detected the hint of a smile cross Webster's thin lips but could not tell for certain. Webster rarely smiled. "He's fine." But Marston hadn't seemed fine. Usually the man was focused and energetic. Since yesterday morning he had been preoccupied and lethargic, unable to assist effectively with several large transactions other vice-presidents in the Real Estate Advisory Group were attempting to close. Marston's problems didn't affect Mace, however. Mace closed his own deals.

"I'm glad to hear that," Webster said.

Mace brushed a tiny piece of paper from the pants leg of his conservative chalk stripe suit. "Lewis, what did you need me for?" In business matters Mace was terse and direct. His ability to earn money was limited only by the hours in the day, so he made the most of them.

Webster stiffened slightly. He was unaccustomed to anyone but another partner addressing him as Lewis. Even some of them addressed him as Mr. Webster. "I want to enlist your assistance on a project I am pursuing."

Mace nodded but said nothing. Though he did not have daily contact with the man, he had been in enough meetings with Webster to determine that the older man seemed suddenly uncomfortable.

"It is an extremely important project for Walker Pryce." Webster continued. "One that I believe will enable the firm to remain independent, one that should enable us to maintain our partnership status and not have to access the public market."

Mace inhaled slowly but exhibited no reaction to this piece of news. Like all good businessmen, Mace was adept at gathering information both from clients and from members of his own firm, and he knew that a majority of the partners wanted to go public. Now. This project had to be a blockbuster for Webster to be able to convince the others of the executive committee—Marston and Polk—to forgo the public equity markets at this point and remain a partnership. "Tell me about it."

"I want to raise a large pool of money we will use to invest in Manhattan commercial real estate and shares listed on the New York Stock Exchange. Walker Pryce will manage to fund and seed it with fifty million dollars of the partners' capital."

"How big a fund are you talking about?"

"At least a billion."

Mace stared at Webster. A billion dollars. That was big. Even for Walker Pryce.

"And I want to leverage that billion dollars of capital by having the fund borrow another billion on top of the equity from commercial banks to give us a total of two billion to invest." Webster went on. "Walter Marston, Graham Polk, and I all believe that the markets are extremely overvalued, that we are headed for some very big corrections in these markets, severe downward movements in real estate and stock prices, and we want to be ready when that happens. When the crash hits, we'll wait for the prices to hit the trough, then buy cheaply and enjoy the spoils when values go back up again—as they always do."

"A classic vulture fund," Mace said.

"Yes." Webster's voice was almost inaudible.

Mace nodded. Prices *were* too high. But in the investment world it was almost impossible to predict a correction accurately.

Just when all the pundits thought values would dive, they would spurt up. And vice versa. But if they raised all that money and the fund didn't work because prices didn't dive, it wouldn't be a good thing for his career. The investors, who had been looking for sky-high returns and had instead received very little, would be hot. Word would get out that he had been responsible. Webster wasn't going to take the heat. That was certain. Of course, Mace thought. He was the fall guy in case the fund tanked, an insurance policy. "But, Lewis, our own economists on the twenty-third floor aren't predicting any kind of severe downturn. They aren't pressing the panic button." Mace attempted to substantiate his lack of enthusiasm.

"Economists." Webster sneered. "Ask them for someone's telephone number, and if they don't know it, they'll estimate it for you. Toilet paper is of far greater value than an economist. The only reason I maintain our economic department is that as such a high-profile firm we have to have one."

Mace didn't agree. Walker Pryce's economists were extremely talented and had provided him with an immense amount of highly accurate information. But that wasn't a battle he was going to fight at this moment. "All the same, I think it would be a huge risk to bet the firm's future on the success of a fund like that." Mace swallowed hard. He could tell that what he had just said wasn't what Webster wanted to hear.

Webster nodded thoughtfully and stroked his beard. "Mace, how old are you?"

"Thirty."

Webster smiled. "In your four years at Walker Pryce you've performed very well. Fifty million dollars in fees last year as a vice-president if I'm not mistaken."

"That's correct."

"Quite a remarkable accomplishment for such a young man." Webster snickered. "There are forty-year-old managing directors walking around here who didn't generate even two million in fees last year, let alone fifty."

Mace nodded. He knew where the deadwood was.

Webster shook his head. "It's gotten to the point that as long as you are managing director and can fog a mirror, we pay you over a million dollars." Webster paused. "Mace, what did we pay you last year, all in?"

"Eight hundred and fifty thousand."

Webster shook his head again. "Not enough. You should be a managing director. At least."

"Sounds good to me." Mace grinned at the old man.

"It's just that we have these unwritten rules at the firm. You know, a minimum of seven years at the firm to make managing director, a minimum of ten years to make partner."

Mace glanced out the window again. The old man was a master manipulator.

"Youngest managing director in Walker Pryce history. In its *history*." Webster whispered the last few words again loudly for effect. "How does that sound?"

"It sounds very good, Lewis." Mace answered the question immediately, but his voice was flat. He did not like being cornered.

"As senior partner I can guarantee you that title, Mace. Within six months. If you help me with the fund. I need your contacts in the real estate business and your ability to see value in the equity markets. I can guarantee you the title and an annual compensation of two million, minimum. You know you'll make partner in short order after that, and you will have the satisfaction of knowing that your work enabled this firm to remain a partnership. So that someday you will know how it feels to be a partner at the most prestigious investment bank on Wall Street."

Mace did not respond.

Webster pushed forward. "As an old man I can tell you that success or failure in life depends on a few very important decisions. And playing for the right team. This is one of those decisions,

Mace, and I'm the captain of the team you want to play for." He paused. "If you aren't with me, you are against me."

Since his childhood Mace had been analytic, gathering pertinent information with respect to a decision he was facing, then making the best decision based on that information. But sometimes the information available wasn't enough to resolve the issue and you simply had to go with your gut. Now his gut was telling him to reject Webster's plan and go back to the Real Estate Advisory Group. But then he'd be playing for the other team in Webster's eyes, and as long as the old man held on to the senior partner spot, he'd never make managing director.

It shouldn't happen this way. It wasn't fair to have to be caught up in a political maelstrom. He ought to be able to work hard, make the firm a great deal of money, and be compensated appropriately. But life wasn't always fair. He was well aware of that. "What would my role be?" he asked quietly.

Webster's eyes danced. He had struck a nerve, as he had been certain he would. "Chief investment officer. I want you to target Manhattan properties in which the fund might invest. The profile of the target properties will be simple: large, prominently located commercial office buildings that are on shaky financial ground. I'm sure you know about a few of those."

Mace nodded. Half the real estate world was constantly on the brink of bankruptcy. It was always that way, no matter how strong the economy was. Real estate buyers consistently attempted to use as much debt and as little of their own money as possible to fund a purchase, putting a huge cash-flow burden on the property in the form of debt service. A small hiccup in rental income, and cash flow wouldn't meet interest expense. Any extended cash-flow shortfalls, and the owner would have to run for bankruptcy protection and look for the best price offered for the building as a way out of his mess.

"Begin negotiating with the owners of those properties and with the mortgage holders as well. Just open a dialogue, nothing more than that to start with. Visit them, or invite them here for a nice lunch. But clear the property with me first."

"Okay." Mace inhaled slowly. That would be easy enough. People were always willing to listen. And for the right price any piece of property was for sale. Investors were not sentimental. Not the good ones anyway.

"Start researching the stock market for undervalued shares too. I realize that's a kind of open-ended project, but you're smart. You know where to look for value. You can use a couple of associates from the Mergers and Acquisitions Advisory Department to do the grunt work. I'll call Renenberg, the head of M & A, myself and inform him of your requirements. But don't tell the associates why you need the research."

"Of course not," Mace said cynically.

Webster ignored Mace's tone. "Finally, and in the strictest confidence, I want you to begin talking to your contacts at the large New York commercial banks about committing loans to the fund. Talk to banks that specialize in lending to real estate and equity funds. We might need quite a few institutions in the syndicate to raise a billion dollars for a blind pool, and it may not be easy to rope them in."

Truer words had never been spoken, Mace thought. Opening the discussions wouldn't be difficult. He knew all the senior people in the real estate areas of the big New York commercial banks. Getting them to commit to a loan would be another story. "Where are you going to find the fund's equity, Lewis? The billion dollars that will support the bank loan." Mace folded his arms across his chest defiantly.

"I'm going to a select few of the wealthiest U.S. families."

"Why? Why not go to the institutions? That's where we have our best relationships."

"I want to keep this fund quiet. Very confidential. I don't want others to know what we are doing. Institutions would blab this thing all over the Street."

"How many families do you intend to go to?"

"Eight, ten at most."

Mace grimaced as though he were almost in physical pain. "Old-family money is hardly high-octane cash. I mean, they'll take some risk, but do you really think you'll circle a billion-dollar fund with ten families? That's a hundred million dollars a family. I know you're talking about some pretty well-hung people, but still—" Mace hesitated, his silence conveying his doubts. "And I can't help you there. I don't know those people. I know a different kind of investor. I know the institutions: the insurance companies and the pension funds."

"I have that angle covered," Webster said.

"Really? I didn't know you were buddy-buddy with those people. Usually we go to the institutional market."

Webster coughed and rearranged several papers on the desktop in front of him. "I'm not familiar with those people either, the families, I mean. But you'll have help from someone who is."

"Help?" That sounded mysterious.

Webster stared directly at Mace. "Yes, help. Do you have a problem with that?" The old man's whisper became confrontational.

Mace pushed out his lower lip. "No, no problem."

"Good."

"Who is this person?" Mace wanted to know.

"Someone from the outside."

"Oh." That was interesting. Walker Pryce rarely went outside the firm for a project like this. It rarely went outside the firm at all, except to hire junior people. "Have you already made an offer to this person?"

"Not formally. I wanted your opinion first."

Mace nodded. That was good. It demonstrated a respect he appreciated. "When do I get to meet him?"

Webster coughed again. "First of all, it's not a he—it's a she—and you will meet her tomorrow afternoon."

Mace grinned. "I see. Well I don't mind a female subordinate. I'm an open-minded guy."

"She won't be your subordinate, Mace. She's coming in at the managing director level." Webster was matter-of-fact. "She will report directly to me, and you will report to her. And only to her. As of this moment you are no longer a member of the Real Estate Advisory Group. Marston is in agreement with this." Webster paused. "Of course you will have direct access to me also. But I want this woman informed of everything you are doing. I want her in every meeting you are in."

Mace touched his lip. He had nothing against having a woman as his boss. His problem was the fact that he would have a boss at all. For the last two years he had operated almost independently. He had been free to originate and close his own deals with a minimal amount of interference. And that system had worked very well. Now he would have reporting responsibilities again. And who knew how controlling this woman might be? He stared at the old man. "Isn't it unusual to bring someone in from the outside like this? Someone who doesn't know Walker Pryce?"

"First of all, she has excellent contacts with wealthy families as a result of previous experience. Second, this fund will be independent of the firm except for the involvement of you and me. And third, if she does need help with the ways of Walker Pryce, I expect you to give her any help she needs. Is that clear?"

"Perfectly." That was one thing about Webster. You always knew where you stood with him and what he expected of you.

"Good, then I believe that's all we need to discuss at this moment. You can begin putting together your list of real estate targets. Wait until tomorrow to contact the associates in the M & A group. Give me a chance to speak with Renenberg first. I'll have Sarah call you tomorrow with the names of the associates you can use."

Mace rose to leave. The meeting was over. That was clear. He wasn't happy with what had transpired, but the opportunity to argue with Webster was slim—and slim was out of town.

"One more thing, Mr. McLain."

Mace turned back toward Webster.

"Tomorrow I want you to move down from your office on the thirtieth floor to the seventh floor. We'll be able to keep this project much quieter there, away from the others. I'll make certain that you have all the computers and on-line systems you need. I know how much you like having technology at your fingertips." Webster said the last few words as if they left a bad taste in his mouth.

"Fine." Mace turned to go. As he reached the door, he stopped and turned back. "Lewis?"

Webster glanced up from his papers. "Yes?"

"You know that I've been teaching a real estate class at Columbia Business School."

"Yes."

"I've identified a woman in the class I think would fit in well here at Walker Pryce. She's extremely bright and—"

"Rachel Sommers." Webster cut Mace off in mid-sentence. "That's who you are talking about, isn't it?"

Mace nodded. "Yes, but—"

"I've already talked to Charlie Fenton. He told me that you two had a discussion about Miss Sommers. I've already had Sarah schedule a full day of interviews for her next Monday. Take her to lunch, and make certain that she will accept our generous request to interview here at Walker Pryce. And make sure she's for us."

Mace stared at Webster. The man always seemed to be one step ahead of the game.

"It's been a long time, Mace," Slade Conner yelled above the music blasting from the speakers over the bar of Poor Richard's, a popular watering hole at the South Street Seaport frequented by Wall Streeters. The bar was one of a collection of pubs, restaurants, and shops in a three-story pavilion overlooking the East River, just north of the downtown financial district.

Mace smiled, pushed his mug of beer against Slade's, then took a long drink of the amber liquid. After a few moments he lowered the mug and spoke directly into Slade's ear so as to be heard over the music. "Let's move to the back, where the noise isn't as bad."

Slade nodded in agreement.

Slowly the two men made their way toward the back of the room, carefully picking a path through the mass of bodies crowded around the bar area. Just as they reached the edge of the congestion, a blond woman in a short red dress caught Mace's hand.

"Wanna dance?" she screamed above the music.

Mace smiled quickly. "Sorry, not now. Maybe later." He squeezed her hand gently, then let it go and continued his attempt to break out of the pack.

Finally the two men reached a spot against the back wall where they could hear each other more easily.

Mace took another sip of beer and shook his head. "You sure you want to stay here, Slade?"

"Absolutely." Slade was watching a group of three women dancing together on the small dance area. They moved easily and seductively to the beat of the bass, without male accompaniment. "Oh, yeah, I'm sure I want to stay here."

"You said you wanted women and music when we talked on the phone. This is the best place I know of downtown for that combination."

"It's perfect," Slade said, not taking his eyes from the three women.

Mace smiled and took another sip of beer. Slade's sexual appetite could not be satisfied. It had been that way since Slade had come to the orphanage in Plymouth, Minnesota, at age thirteen, and Mace supposed it would always be that way. Slade had been the first boy in their age-group at the home to have the audacity to walk up to the counter of the local 7-Eleven and purchase a *Playboy* magazine, then successfully smuggle it into the orphanage dormitory. He had also been the first of their crew to "do the deed"—at fourteen, after a mixer with a local girls' orphanage. At least he claimed to have done it.

Mace watched him watch the women. Slade was not tall, under five feet eleven inches in his leather cowboy boots, but he was extremely muscular. His neck was that of a lion's, his arms were those of a blacksmith, and his legs tree trunks. And his physique was not just a facade. He was strong. He always had been. Mace had seen Slade pull a drowning cow from the deep waters of the Minnesota River when they were just sixteen—by himself. He had also seen Slade in a fight, when they were seniors in high school. The fight had lasted all of twenty seconds, but the other boy, who had made the mistake of inciting Slade, had stayed down on the ground for at least five minutes before groggily crawling away. Slade did not anger easily, but once he was aroused, about the only way to stop him was with a firearm.

After high school they had gone to the University of Iowa to play football together, Mace the quarterback and Slade the hardworking offensive lineman who never made the spotlight. But that hadn't mattered to Slade. The only thing that mattered to him was that they played four years of football together. He had protected Mace so that Mace could make the big plays and garner the media attention while he remained in the shadows. He was one of the most loyal and team-oriented individuals Mace had ever known.

Upon graduation Mace had gone to New York to work for Chemical Bank before attending Columbia Business School, and Slade had gone into the Marines and become a heavily decorated soldier. Now he was in Special Services or something. He was not forthcoming about his work.

Mace stared at the long blond hair flowing over the back of Slade's maroon turtleneck and grinned. They saw each other infrequently now, but they were such good friends that there was no period of discomfort old acquaintances sometimes felt before the familiarity returned.

"Like that, huh?" Mace gestured at the women.

"Yeah." Slade nodded vigorously.

"So, tell me about yourself. What's going on?" Mace asked.

Slade's gaze lingered several seconds longer on the women. Then he turned toward Mace and grinned, revealing two lines of crooked teeth, which had never been touched by braces. Braces were extras the orphanage could not afford. "I could tell you what's going on, but then I'd have to kill you." He turned back toward the women.

Mace laughed. It was the standard military response Slade gave every time Mace attempted to pull the cover back just a little.

The impression Slade made upon a first-time acquaintance was that of a gentle, plodding blond bear. He was quiet, rarely used words of more than three syllables, and did not seem to have many strong opinions. A nice enough man, but one who probably wouldn't be able to find his way out of bed in the morning without directions. It was not an accurate assessment. Slade was extremely bright—enough to maintain a straight A average in electrical engineering all four years at Iowa. And bright enough to be on special assignment for the United States government somewhere in the world, though Slade would never specify exactly what or where the mission was. That was another of Slade's special qualities: he yielded no secrets.

Slade took his eyes from the women. "What's going on in your world, Mace? Hell, you've got a much more interesting life than I do."

Mace sincerely doubted that. "Well, I've got a new job as of this afternoon."

"You've gone to another firm?" Slade asked incredulously. "I thought you were going to be at Walker Pryce until the day you died."

Mace shook his head as he finished the beer. "No, I'm still at Walker Pryce. I'm just taking on some new responsibilities there."

"Oh." Slade seemed relieved. "What kind of responsibilities?"

Mace hesitated. He shouldn't say anything. But Slade hardly cared about Wall Street. And he would never tell anyone if Mace told him not to say anything. "It's highly confidential."

Slade rolled his eyes. "You say that all the time."

"Yeah, but I *mean* it this time."

"Okay. I understand. I'm not going to tell anyone. So go ahead. Tell me what's happening, Brother." Brother was a nickname Slade had used for Mace since grade school. They were that close.

Mace glanced around to make certain no one was listening. "We're going to try to raise a pool of money from several wealthy families and invest it in Manhattan real estate and common stocks. We think there will be large downward corrections in the values of these assets in the near future. We'll wait until the values drop sufficiently, then buy. It's called a vulture fund."

"A what?" Slade's face twisted into a strange expression.

Mace smiled. "A vulture fund. If prices of real estate and stocks drop significantly in a short period of time, there will be a lot of unhappy people. People who are worth a lot of money one day and then suddenly, poof, the next day they owe more than they have. Those people will be putting guns to their heads or jumping out of windows because they can't meet loan payments and margin calls. We'll circle for a while, and then, when things get really bad, we'll come in and feed off the carnage. We'll offer cents on the dollar for properties that would be worth a great deal more than that in a stable economic situation. But people will accept our offers because they'll want to get some cash in a hurry. Then, when prices rebound, we'll make lots of money."

Slade shook his head. "A vulture fund. You investment banking guys crack me up. You're almost as quick with a joke as you are with your hand in someone else's pocket."

"Just making sure the markets are efficient. That's the job. Someone has to do it." Mace winked at Slade.

"Oh, yeah. Tough job. Put together a buyer and a seller and make millions. My heart bleeds for you, Brother. Let me tell you about tough jobs."

"I wish you would." Mace raised his glass toward his friend.

Slade smiled the wide, toothy grin and brought his glass to Mace's. Mace had almost pulled the cover back. Slade finished the glass of beer, pulled it away from his lips, and wiped his mouth with the back of his shirtsleeve. "So how big a pool of money are you going to try to raise?"

Mace glanced around again. "A billion dollars."

Slade's eyes widened. "Jesus Christ! That's a lot of money."

Mace continued to smile but said nothing.

Slade laughed and turned back toward the crowd. "My buddy. Mr. Wall Street." He nodded at a waitress, signaling for her to bring two more beers.

"Tell me what's going on in your personal life."

"I could, but then I'd have to kill you," Mace joked.

Slade broke into another grin, then turned his gaze once again toward the group of women dancing in the middle of the floor. The group had increased from three individuals to five and seemed in desperate need of male participants.

Within the hour the man would be deep in discussion with one of those women, Mace thought, telling her whatever was necessary to be able to climb into a taxi with her at the end of the evening. Mace had to get back to Walker Pryce. There was a great deal of work to do if the fund—Broadway Ventures LP, as he and Webster had christened it—was going to make it off the ground.

Slade watched the five women. As he did, he wondered if Malcolm Becker's request that he make contact with Mace had anything to do with the billion-dollar vulture fund Mace was now involved with.

*   *   *

The ring of the private office telephone Webster had reluctantly installed last week suddenly pierced the serenity of the late evening. In the first moment its shrill noise reached his ears, a flood of emotions rushed through him. He knew the identity of the caller instantly. Only one man had this number: the man in Washington.

Webster's eyes narrowed, and his head tilted forward at the second ring. He did not want to answer. He wanted to close his eyes and have it go away. The man in Washington. The fund. Mace McLain. The telephone. All of it. Just go away. The man was calling more often now as the conspiracy was falling into place, as Webster was constantly being squeezed more tightly in the snake's coils. And the increasing frequency and intensity of the calls were beginning to tear him apart.

At the third ring Webster glanced out the large window into the darkness of Wall Street. There was nowhere to run, nowhere to conceal himself. Even with all his money. *Because* of all of his money. The man would find him if he ran. That was clear. And when the man found him . . . Webster shuddered at the thought of what had been threatened. Finally he drew in a deep breath and reached for the receiver.

7

The engineer sipped coffee from the steaming cup, careful not to burn his lips as he watched the security guard clean the .30-caliber rifle. The guard was a retired New York City policeman, living off a generous pension plan and what he earned here at the Nyack Nuclear Generating Facility. It probably wasn't a bad life, thought the engineer, to which the guard's burgeoning belly attested.

The guard stopped cleaning the gun for a moment and reached for the half-eaten huge Danish lying atop wax paper on the metal desk. Cheese and fruit dripped from the side of his mouth and onto the blue uniform as he bit into the pastry.

"Damn it!" The fat guard reached for a wad of paper towels lying next to the wax paper.

The engineer smiled and looked away toward the black waters of the Hudson River flowing relentlessly southward, far below the lookout tower. The sun's first rays were just beginning to break through the morning clouds well to the east, and the engineer could barely discern the outline of a tugboat as it churned north against the current. He sipped again from the mug, which he held with both hands. The mouth of the Hudson and New York City's harbor lay not more than twenty miles to the south.

He took a deep breath. The engineer enjoyed winter mornings up here on the lookout tower after a long graveyard shift in the

control room of the huge two-thousand-megawatt electric generating facility. He closed his eyes and leaned back. Perhaps he
would stay up here for a while before heading down the long stairway to ground level. It was quiet, and he might be able to catch a
little shut-eye before heading home to his wife and children.

"How was the shift, Mr. Wilson?"

The beautiful brunette walking toward him on the beach in
nothing but her bikini evaporated from the engineer's daydream.
He rubbed his eyes for a moment, then opened them and focused
in on the old guard, who was busy cleaning the gun again. "Fine,
Liam. It was fine."

"Any problems?" Liam asked.

"No." Wilson sat up in the chair and took another sip of coffee.
It was clear that Liam wasn't going to allow him to return to the
woman on the beach.

The security guard rubbed a rag lovingly over the rifle's shiny
black barrel. "Mind if I ask you a quick question, Mr. Wilson?"

"No, Liam. Not at all." Wilson liked the guard. He was a
simple man who came to work every day and did his job. No fuss,
no muss. As it should be.

"I feel kind of silly." Liam placed the gun on the desk, then
smiled sheepishly.

Wilson eyed the guard. "Christ, Liam. You aren't going to
ask me where babies come from, are you?" he said, teasing the
older man.

"No! Of course not." The guard was instantly embarrassed.

"Good. Well, I can probably handle any other question you
might have, so fire away." Wilson eyed the rifle and sort of wished
he'd used a better choice of words.

Liam paused. "It's like this. I mean, I come to work here every
day at this nuclear plant, and I really don't know how it works. I
know it generates electricity for New York City—"

"All of the city's needs by itself," Wilson interjected.

"Uh-huh." Liam nodded as if he were having a hard time

believing what Wilson had just said. After all, New York City's population was approaching eight million people. "Well, I'd kind of like to know how it works."

Wilson smiled at the security guard. It was commendable for a man to want to know more about his workplace. "Sure, okay," Wilson said. "You've heard the other engineers and me talk about the nuclear core, right?"

"Yeah, of course."

"Well, that's where most of the action takes place. The core is filled with water, and when we move the fuel rods into place from the—"

"Fuel rods?" the guard interrupted.

Wilson nodded. "Yes. Long bundles filled with pellets of uranium. From the control room we can automatically move these rods into place in the core, and when we do, a nuclear reaction begins, like when you strike a match and it bursts into a flame, generating heat. The nuclear core is pretty much the same concept, except on a much bigger scale. The nuclear reaction generates tremendous heat, in excess of two thousand degrees, which boils the water in the core pretty quickly and turns it to steam. The steam moves through pipes leading from the core to the turbines. As the steam moves the turbines, they begin to turn, thereby generating electricity. Pretty simple, huh?"

The guard seemed unconvinced of the operation's simplicity. "So then that steam from the core is filled with radiation?"

"Yeah." Wilson lowered his voice. "Yes, it is. Lots of radiation. If you came into contact with it, you'd be a very unhappy camper."

The guard glanced out the window of the lookout tower at the steam rising from the two massive cooling towers.

The engineer followed his gaze, then began to laugh. "No, no, Liam." Wilson knew what the man was thinking. "That steam is coming from the water we pump in from the Hudson River to cool the steam coming from the turbines, to condense it into water again so that it can go back into the core and be reheated. The steam coming from the towers doesn't have a lick of radiation in it."

Liam gazed at the cooling towers for a few minutes. "Must get pretty damn hot in the core."

"Incredibly hot."

"How do you cool it down in there?"

"There are rods we can move into place that are called control rods. They are made of boron. Inserted into the core, they interrupt the nuclear reaction, and the core cools down."

The guard stared at the engineer. "What if the control rods don't work? What if they don't move for some reason?"

Wilson stared back at Liam. "We send you in there to see what the hell the problem is."

Liam did not laugh. "Seriously."

Wilson inhaled deeply again. He had explained the basics of the Nyack Nuclear Generating Facility hundreds of times to people who didn't understand how it worked. There were thousands of ways the conversation could go, yet the discussion always seemed to end up here: at the meltdown question. Yet Nyack had never experienced a serious accident in its twenty-year operating history. A few small things here and there, which were to be expected, but nothing major.

People didn't realize how much they were saving on their electric bills because the Nyack plant was nuclear. If they had known, they wouldn't ask so many questions. "Nuclear power is one of the safest means of power known to man. And it is cleaner and infinitely more efficient than coal or oil."

"But what if the control rods don't work, Mr. Wilson?" Liam asked the question a second time. He wanted an answer.

The engineer gazed at the old security guard over the coffee mug. "We run for the hills."

Liam swallowed hard. "Huh?"

Wilson continued. "You could think of it like a car engine when the cooling system fails and the radiator explodes. Like when you're on the highway and you see steam shooting out from beneath a car's hood on a hot summer day. It's the same principle really. Pressure builds up until something gives and the core is violated."

"Violated?" Liam didn't like the sound of that.

"The core explodes or simply melts through the containment vessel surrounding the core. Either way, radiation is released into the atmosphere."

"And that would be dangerous."

"Radiation makes you grow ten fingers on one hand, if it doesn't kill you first." Wilson sipped from his coffee mug and glanced south toward the city. "It gets on buildings and into the water supply. A big dose of it can make a place uninhabitable for a long time." He said the last few words quietly.

The guard nodded. He wished he hadn't asked about the plant. Coming to work would never be as easy again. It was true what people said: ignorance *was* bliss.

Wilson turned away from Liam and stared out the window. People were always assuming the worst about nuclear power plants: that these plants were constantly just minutes away from blowing sky-high and raining deadly radiation down on everyone living within a hundred miles of the explosion. It was so ridiculous. Far away on the horizon he could see the World Trade Center towers soaring skyward from lower Manhattan.

The dark man with the thick black mustache stood on the ridge, cracking sunflower shells between his teeth, watching the men rappel quickly down the sheer face of the quarry on the long ropes. He smiled as he removed several delicious seeds from their casings with his tongue, spit the empty shells into the West Virginia snow, chewed the seeds for a moment, then swallowed them. The men were ready. Very ready. The training had been difficult—already they had lost two men during exercises on these cliffs and in the abandoned mines. But it had been worth the trouble. They were a machine now, having weeded out those who might have failed in their duties during the attack. They were a strike force no ragtag group of ex-policemen could ever hope to delay, let alone stop.

They would overpower the defenses of the target the way the

panzers had overpowered Poland. It would be that easy. He laughed aloud as he thought about the poor assholes at their posts, drinking coffee and eating doughnuts. Most of them wouldn't even know what had hit them. They wouldn't have time. The fires of hell would open up before them for a few brutal seconds, and then they would be killed, mercifully. It would be that fast. A turkey shoot. Conventional rifles and fat bellies against high-tech weaponry and trained assassins. It didn't add up. It wasn't fair. It was just as he wanted it, just as the man in Washington wanted it.

Vargus—what he was calling himself for this mission—yelled to his second-in-command at the base of the cliffs. The other man nodded, then screamed at the men, who immediately began pulling themselves back up the cliffs by the long ropes. Vargus stuffed another handful of sunflower seeds into his mouth. The men, hand-picked by Vargus from the best pools of talent Syria, Libya, and Iraq had to offer, had dedicated themselves with vigor to this mission, though of course they did not yet know what the target was. But they knew it was high-profile, and they knew the attack would be launched against a U.S. installation. And they had been told that this would not be a suicide mission, that the powers controlling the mission intended to get them out once the ransom was collected. They were too talented a pool of men for the powers to lose.

Vargus laughed. They had bought the explanation so easily. He was the only person who was going to get out alive. All the others would be killed. Each and every one of them except him. It was all part of the plan, the master plan every detail of which even he was not privy to.

Vargus gazed up toward the top of the cliffs. Several of the men, the best ones, were almost there already. He would have to undergo intense plastic surgery right after it was over. The doctors would actually lift his face off and sew a new one on. They would rush him right to the hospital after the attack because time would be of the essence. The powers in the Middle East would understand quickly what had happened: that they had been stung. They wouldn't understand exactly how, but they would figure out that he, Vargus, was responsible. And they would send death squads for him. Immediately.

After the surgery the man in Washington would move him to another destination to convalesce. In fact he would probably be moved several times to ensure his safety. There would be incredible pain and suffering for a few weeks during the recovery, but once it was over, he would be free to slip away forever with no fear of being recognized. There would be no questions asked. He would enjoy the spoils of war for the remainder of his long and happy life. Twenty-five million was the price they would pay. That would buy several mansions, several boats, and all the beautiful women he could possible lure into his bed. Twenty-five million dollars. He was worth every penny.

He turned and began to trudge back toward the main buildings, inhaling the clean, crisp West Virginia air as he moved through the four inches of new powder that had fallen overnight. His eyes narrowed as he passed a small shed on the periphery of the compound. He paused and stared at the wooden door. They still needed to dispose of the bodies of the lost hikers he and his second had murdered. He considered checking on the bodies for a moment, then dismissed the idea and kept moving back toward the main buildings. It was a detail, something he would take care of later.

8

From the raised level at the back of the large room Rachel watched the dark-haired woman lead Mace through the crowded restaurant. Rachel took another sip of wine. She rarely drank at all, never during the middle of the day, but this was a special occasion.

Through the curved glass Rachel watched the hostess guide Mace the long way from the maître d's stand to the table, past the bar and the checkroom. The woman flung her waist-length hair over her shoulder each time she glanced back at Mace to make certain he was appreciating her sensual walk. The hostess smiled and chatted with him, something she had not done with any of the other men she had guided through the restaurant. He smiled back at her politely, but Rachel was glad to see that he was not overly impressed with her, as the other men had been.

Rachel took another sip from the wineglass and counted the heads of the women who turned as Mace moved past their tables. "Swaggered past their tables" was a better description, she thought. Not the swagger of arrogance or insecurity, just the stride of a man who gave the impression that he could remain calm in any situation, no matter the chaos around him.

"Hello, Rachel." Mace's natural smile broadened as he saw her. He glanced quickly down at the wineglass, but his expression did not change.

When he came to the table, he took her hand gently, but she could feel the restrained strength in his grip as it wrapped around her delicate fingers.

The hostess's demeanor receded to its former state of boredom as she watched the greeting. She placed the menus on the table as Rachel shot her a smug look. "Your waiter will be right with you," she said.

"Thank you," Mace said, without taking his eyes from Rachel. God, she was even more beautiful up close.

"Certainly." The hostess flashed him one more desperate smile, which he did not notice, and then she was gone.

"Hey, this looks like a great place. A good choice on your part." Mace motioned back toward the restaurant. "A couple of associates down at Walker Pryce told me the food here is fantastic."

"Carmine's has some of the best Italian food in the city. And the portions are huge." Rachel pointed at the large menu high on the wall. Her lips curled into a quick smile. "Somehow I figured you'd much rather go to a place that has good food and lots of it than some fou-fou place where you get a piece of steak the size of a quarter and a strip of asparagus as your entrée."

Mace's gray eyes caught her glance. "You know me well."

No, but I might like to, she thought. She laughed to herself. Usually men did not affect her this way. At Columbia she could have any man she wanted. But she paid little attention to them. She was at Columbia to learn, not to be distracted by men who presented no challenge. Mace was different. "Well, sit down and take your coat off."

Mace did not hesitate, hanging his suit coat on the back of the chair.

"I like your suspenders." She nodded at the colorful straps which crossed the blue pin-striped shirt at his broad shoulders.

"Thanks." He laughed as he looked down at them. "It's a long way from the Plymouth orphanage." He sat as he spoke.

"What's that?" she asked quickly.

"Would you two care to hear about our specials?"

Rachel and Mace glanced up at the tall waiter holding a small pad before him. Rachel wasted no time. "This gentleman needs a drink. We'll wait on the specials," she said firmly.

"I'll have one of those." Mace pointed at the wineglass before Rachel.

The waiter nodded and was gone quickly. He realized that his presence was not appreciated and was experienced enough to know that in this case his tip would probably be inversely related to the amount of time he spent at the table.

Rachel leaned forward. "What did you say before the waiter interrupted?"

Mace allowed himself to gaze again at her for a few moments before answering. She was so fresh. Her hair fell gently about the soft, smooth skin of her face. When she smiled, a dimple appeared in her right cheek. She had perfectly shaped, full lips, and her slightly gravelly voice was terribly sexy.

"Mace, what did you say before the waiter came?" Rachel persisted.

He snapped out of his daydream. "I said I was from Minnesota originally. Plymouth, Minnesota. It's about twenty miles northwest of Minneapolis. Actually I was born downtown, but I grew up in Plymouth."

"That's not what I meant. You said something about an orphanage."

"Oh." Mace stretched out the interjection in mock surprise. "You're interested in my time at the Plymouth Home for Wayward Boys."

"Yes." Her eyes were riveted to his.

The waiter interrupted again, this time with Mace's glass of cabernet. He placed the wine on the table quickly and retreated without a word.

Mace picked up the glass, swirled the contents for a moment, then drank. He nodded. "Not bad." He took a deep breath. "My mother had me when she was sixteen. She was poor and didn't have any way to support me, so she gave me up for adoption, but no one wanted me. Fortunately the good people at the Plymouth home took me in." Mace took another sip from the glass. He had remembered Charlie Fenton's comment about how poor Rachel's family was. The bit about the orphanage had been an awfully forward thing to slip into the conversation so early, but he had researched her background thoroughly and thought she would relate quickly to his experience. If Walker Pryce was going to win her services, it was going to have to do so on the strength of something special, of something different. She would have to feel comfortable with the people with whom she would work. All the other firms were going to offer her tons of money too.

Mace had now taught three classes of the real estate course and was convinced that Rachel was the star of this year's graduating class at Columbia Business School. He wanted to make certain that she came to Walker Pryce. With a face as beautiful as hers and the brains to match, she could be responsible for winning quite a few financing mandates very quickly in her investment banking career. And he would be a direct beneficiary of her capabilities.

His background was sinking in, and it was having the desired effect. He could see it in her eyes. So his gamble had worked. For an investment banker, being a good psychologist was an asset.

Rachel gazed back into the gray eyes. She had never seen eyes that color. They were mesmerizing. She tried to think of something to say, but he was making her nervous simply by sitting at the same table with her. She hadn't felt this way in a long time. It was wonderful.

"Enough about me, let's talk about you," Mace said. "Do you have any brothers or sisters?"

Rachel leaned back in her chair without responding to his question.

So she didn't want to talk about her background yet. He saw it in her body language. Well, that was fine. He wouldn't push it.

"How is the Columbia fund going? I spent some time on the Bloomberg machine and pulled up that *Wall Street Journal* article on you. Very impressive."

She looked back at him and smiled. "Thanks." Rachel played with her silverware. "We work hard to ensure the fund's strong performance," she said.

He liked the way she used the word *we*. It indicated that she was probably a team player. That was good. She would fit right in at Walker Pryce. That was if she could keep the wolves at bay. All the younger men at the firm would want to see her crash and burn right away because they would immediately see her great potential. If Rachel were able to develop confidence in herself, she would accelerate past them quickly because the older partners would prefer her around them to another obnoxious young man wearing flashy suspenders. "*We?* I understand it's your show."

"There are several people involved in the management of the fund." Rachel took another sip of wine.

"But it's your show. I talked to Dean Fenton about it. He says the charities to which Columbia donates the proceeds are going to be very unhappy when you are graduated."

"They'll get over it." She smiled quickly, then became serious. "I've been lucky and had several good small cap stock picks." She said the words matter-of-factly as she watched the waiter deliver a heaping plate of pasta to the table next to theirs. As she watched the man serve it, she wondered what Mace was thinking. What was the true motivation behind this lunch? Did he want a quick trip to the Marriott Marquis just a few blocks away for a roll in the sack? Was that why he had called to arrange this meeting? Or was this really an honest recruiting lunch?

"You're very talented, Rachel. I think you would fit in well at Walker Pryce. I want you to come down to Two Wall Street, our headquarters, and meet some people."

Immediately her eyes dropped to the tablecloth. "I doubt I'd fit in very well at Walker Pryce. I'll probably just end up going back to Merrill Lynch. They have already sort of made me an offer."

So she was scared of that blueblood, aristocrat crap. "Don't be put off by the firm's stodgy reputation, Rachel. It's just a spin the other firms on Wall Street market to turn people off about us. Look, I know that you're from a tough part of Brooklyn, and you probably think you wouldn't be accepted by people—"

Her eyes flashed to his.

"—but your background wouldn't be a problem." He'd played all his cards now, and there was no turning back. But from the sound of it, there wasn't much time left, so there was no reason to be coy. "The firm has changed a great deal in the last few years. Look at me, for God's sake."

"Yeah, look at you." Her lips broke into a wide smile, and she brought a hand to her face. It had spilled out spontaneously.

Mace ignored her comment. "Merrill Lynch is an excellent firm. I know a lot of people over there in the real estate group. But it's not Walker Pryce. You'll earn more money faster at Walker Pryce, and more important, you'll be able to work on a wider variety of projects."

Rachel tilted the wineglass back and finished it off. So the lunch was purely for professional reasons after all. He respected her for who she was and not for what was beneath the clothes. She should be happy. Shouldn't she? Wasn't respect what she should want from him?

"Rachel, a full day of interviews has already been arranged for you at Walker Pryce on the basis of what I've seen of you in real estate finance and what Dean Fenton has conveyed to our senior partner, Lewis Webster. We want you to come down on Monday. I suppose you'll have to miss a few classes at Columbia, but believe me, it will be worth the time."

She heard him speaking, but the words barely registered. Her thoughts were a million miles away. Mace was probably earning three-quarters of a million dollars a year, if not more, and he probably went out with a different runway model every night of the week—that is, nights he wasn't running an important board meeting. She was a business school student from a poor family in Brooklyn, New York. How could she possibly have thought Mace McLain's interest in her might be anything but professional?

Mace glanced at the beautiful face and then away. Her expression projected an obvious inner strength and a desire to succeed. The fire of motivation burned brightly in the gleaming blue eyes. But in those eyes there lay a hint of vulnerability too. "So can I tell Webster you'll see us?"

Rachel hesitated a moment. "Yeah, sure. What the heck?" She did not look at him as she spoke.

9

obin Carruthers stood naked before the full-length mirror of her bathroom in the Doha Marriott. She did not like what she saw. The whirlwind trip through Saudi Arabia, Jordan, Kuwait, Bahrain, and now Qatar had taken its toll. Puffy bags had formed beneath her eyes, red blotches had appeared on the pale skin of her face, and her body seemed to be sagging in all the wrong places. Minimal sleep, bad food, and no exercise. A wonderful combination for a forty-three-year-old woman trying to remain at least somewhat attractive for just a little while longer.

The vice president's official visits to foreign countries—other than Europe—were a terrible pain in the ass. But as his chief of staff and longtime trusted adviser, she simply had to accompany him on a tour as important as this one. The election was now less than a year away. The presidential campaign was entering its most critical state, and Preston Andrews viewed this trip to the Middle East as a major opportunity not only to plaster his photograph all over the papers back home but also to put some distance between himself and his only real competitor for the office of the president, Malcolm Becker, director of the CIA, an opportunity to gain some ground on a man he viewed as an unworthy opponent.

Robin cupped her breasts with her hands and pushed them up. There had been a time years ago when they had maintained this lifted position all on their own. Not now. She had never been pregnant, but gravity and time had worked just as effectively to make them sag. Robin removed her hands and watched them fall to their natural state. "Ugh." Was she still attractive? She primped her auburn hair for a moment. Rumors of late-night trysts between the vice president and her—rumors that had run rampant during the early days of his term and were completely unfounded—had faded away in the past two years. Perhaps that was the best indicator of all that her appearance had deteriorated. No one would believe the rumor now because no one would believe that the vice president might want her anymore. She glanced into the mirror one more time. Her body hadn't really gotten that bad.

Quickly Robin removed the soft full-length cotton robe from the hook on the back of the bathroom door and slipped into it. She moved out of the bathroom and padded across the thickly carpeted living room of the beautiful suite until she reached the sliding glass door leading to the balcony. The door moved easily to the side, and she stepped from the living room into the darkness, walking across the cement of the balcony floor in her bare feet until she reached the railing, where she leaned against the iron and stared into the Arabian night. From her twenty-fifth-floor perch Robin could see several green and red lights twinkling far out in the darkness. They were running lights of oil tankers, churning constantly north and south on the Persian Gulf, full of oil for export or on their way to take on another hold of the black gold.

She laughed as she lighted a cigarette and inhaled deeply. People had started awful rumors about Preston and her in the early days of his term as Bob Whitman's vice president. About how she and Andrews would purposely schedule long international trips for weeks at a time to get Preston away from Sandra, his wife. About how they always stayed in adjoining suites on these trips. And about how they had actually been caught in bed together on several occasions. Robin inhaled again. None of the rumors was true. They were typical Washington intimidation techniques. She had worried terribly the first time she had heard the whispers and wished that people would stop. Now she vaguely wished the rumors would resurface.

Robin checked her watch: five in the morning. She had better touch base with Preston one more time before she turned in for a few hours' sleep. No doubt he was awake. The man seemed never to need sleep, a prerequisite for any top politician. At two o'clock he had seemed adamant about not needing her for the rest of the night, but that meant nothing. He expected her to check in constantly.

She stepped back into the suite and locked the sliding glass door—a silly precaution since she was protected by at least fifty Secret Service men on the roof above her suite, in the hallway just outside the living room door, and on the floor below them—then moved toward the short hallway connecting her suite to the vice president's. Robin tiptoed down the dark hall, then tapped on the vice president's door lightly. Without awaiting a response, she pushed the door open and leaned into the room.

Preston Andrews sat in the far corner of the living room with his back to Robin. Sitting next to him was a dark man, with bushy black hair and a thick black mustache that she could see only because the man was turned in his seat toward Andrews. They were huddled close together, muttering in subdued tones. This was strange, she thought. She knew Preston's schedule like the back of her hand, and he had nothing on the docket until noon—a boring luncheon with one of the emirs. So what was this man doing here at five in the morning?

"Preston?" Robin moved into the suite without closing the door to the small hallway after her.

The vice president rose instantly, obviously surprised by her entrance. He turned toward her as he stood, smiling nervously. The other man seemed to bend down in his seat so as not to be seen. Or was it simply her imagination?

"Robin, Robin. I thought I told you to go to bed." The vice

president spread his arms as he reached her and enveloped her in a huge hug.

She felt him guiding her gently but firmly back toward the door through which she had just entered. "Who is that man, Preston?"

Preston kissed her gently on the cheek. "Do you know how beautiful you look in that robe?"

"Like Miss America, I'm sure." She turned to try to catch one more look at the dark man sitting in the chair as Preston opened the door and pushed her back toward her suite. "Who is that man?"

"Don't be surprised if I finally try to crawl in bed with you tonight, sweetheart. We need to validate all those rumors sometime."

Robin stared at him in shock. "Preston?"

"See you soon." He smiled at her as he closed the door in her face. For a moment Andrews stared at the door he had just shut. He was breathing hard. Then he turned and gazed at the dark man sitting in the living room of his suite. It would be light soon. They needed to finish this quickly.

10

Frigid February gusts whipped empty paper cups, gum wrap-
pers, and old napkins up off the black pavement into chaotic
frenzies, as frigid economic gusts sometimes whipped Wall
Street traders into chaos on the New York Stock Exchange, just
down the block from the Walker Pryce headquarters. Mace dodged
several pieces of flying paper and slipped into the backseat of the
stretch limousine, nodding at the elderly driver, who stood stiffly in
his long dark coat, holding the door open against the cold wind.
The old man had been waiting for Mace in front of Walker Pryce
for the last half hour and was not happy because twice he had been
forced to move the huge limousine at the request of one of New
York's men in blue. The door slammed shut as Mace relaxed into
the deep leather. He rubbed his hands together quickly, then passed
them through his dark hair.

"You look fine."

Mace turned slowly to his right to face the woman sitting on the
backseat beside him. Darkness had overtaken Manhattan an hour
before, but several lights glowed softly inside the limousine, and he
could see her quite well.

"In fact you look more than fine." Her voice was smooth.

"Mace McLain." He extended his hand toward the woman.

She responded slowly, smiling demurely at him before gently
putting her hand in his. "Kathleen Hunt."

Her hand seemed very warm, almost as if her body temperature were running slightly above normal. Mace glanced down. Her fingers were long and thin and uncluttered by jewelry. Her nails were perfectly manicured, painted dark red. His eyes moved back up to hers.

"Mr. McLain, we are headed to Columbia Business School, is that correct?" The driver's nasal voice emanated from a speaker positioned above the limousine's small television set.

"That's right." He attempted to release the woman's hand from his, but she held on for a moment longer before letting go. "Take the West Side Highway." He glanced toward the woman. She smiled again, then turned away from him and gazed out the tinted window at the entrance to the Bank of New York at One Wall Street.

"Thank you." The speaker clicked once, and the static, which had been coming through the speaker with the man's voice, was gone.

This wasn't going to be easy, Mace thought.

"Mace . . ." the woman said. "That's an interesting name."

Mace turned back toward her as the limousine began to move slowly forward. "I'm an interesting guy." Immediately he regretted the remark. After all, none of this was her fault. She was simply being opportunistic. Still, he felt she wasn't necessary, and he did not have time for an extraneous level of management.

"So I understand."

He inhaled heavily. "Look, I'm sorry I kept you waiting, but I got caught in a meeting that went longer than I had anticipated."

"Not a problem." She nodded at the tiny television. "I spent this time with Peter Jennings. He's kind of an interesting guy as well."

Mace ignored her comment. "It's too bad we had to meet this way, on a limousine ride up to Columbia Business School, but my schedule has been extremely full. This is the first free time I've had in several days, what with trying to close two deals before jumping into this fund idea of Webster's."

"I think it's kind of a nice way for us to get to know each other. We'll have a beautiful view of the Hudson River and the lights from the boats as we drive up the West Side Highway." She tilted her head back and played with her earrings.

Mace watched her adjust the tiny gold chains hanging from her lobes and wondered if all this civility was just an act designed to engender initial feelings of goodwill or if it was a sincere attempt to lay the groundwork for a strong working relationship. He rubbed his chin. She was older than he, probably in her late thirties. He judged her to be this age by the faint lines at the corners of her mouth. But the age lines did not detract noticeably from her beauty. She was an attractive woman, he had to admit, and she did not fit into the female professional mold of pumps, pearls, and panty hose. Long blond hair cascaded loosely down her neck, onto a fashionable black sweater, violating the Wall Street rule that a woman's hair be worn off the shoulders. The knee-length skirt clung sexily to long legs that appeared to be well maintained, probably with regular visits to the gym, he thought. Her legs were not imprisoned in stockings, which he found sexy. Her face was thin, and she wore an unusual pair of clear-rimmed glasses that seemed to enhance her facial features. Although it was difficult to determine accurately as they sat in the limousine, he decided that she was probably tall, perhaps five-eight or more. Being tall himself, Mace liked tall women.

"So you are going to raise a billion dollars for Lewis Webster's little fund, for his bold foray into the vultures' world." Mace folded his hands on his lap. He wasn't going to warm up to Kathleen Hunt too quickly. He was going to make certain that she knew where he stood.

"I take it you aren't one hundred percent behind this idea." Her voice gave away no irritation at his cynical tone. "Lewis told me that you weren't completely convinced that Walker Pryce ought to be raising this fund."

Her voice was naturally soothing, like a steamy shower or a hot cup of coffee after a long walk on a snowy winter evening. He made a mental note to remember not to be mesmerized by it.

The limousine moved into the Battery Park Tunnel. Mace watched the lights lining the tunnel walls flash by as the vehicle picked up speed. He had to be careful. First impressions were lasting impressions, and despite his reservations about the fund, the reality of the situation was that this woman was his superior and would probably report any insubordination directly to Webster. "I think it's a big risk for the firm. Let's just say that."

"No risk, no reward," she said.

"Mmm." The limousine broke out of the tunnel into the Lower West Side of Manhattan. "Look, I'm sure you've got great credentials and you believe we are going to be wildly successful with the fund, but I think the partnership really had its collective heart set on going public and cashing out at a big multiple now. Therefore you, *and I,* for that matter, have a tough row to hoe. If the fund works, we'll be heroes. If it doesn't, we'll be looking for work elsewhere."

"Uh-huh." She seemed to be mulling over Mace's comment. Suddenly she pointed out the window. "Hey, isn't that the Downtown Athletic Club?"

Mace leaned toward her side of the limousine and glanced out her window. "Yes, it is."

"That's where they award the Heisman Trophy each year to the outstanding college football player, right?"

Mace nodded, wondering what the connection was.

"Herschel Walker won the Heisman in 1982."

"Yes. How did you know that?" Mace smiled despite himself.

"Walker played running back at the University of Georgia, and I'm from Georgia. I used to love to watch him run the ball. I'd go to the games on Saturday afternoon with my boyfriend and a bunch of friends. We would tailgate and drink, then go into the stadium and watch them play between the hedges. Those were good times." Her voice was wistful. "You were an excellent football player in college, Mace." She said the words offhandedly, in the same faraway tone.

Mace's eyes raced to hers, but he said nothing.

"You passed for over two thousand yards your senior year and threw for fourteen touchdowns." She continued. "Not quite Heisman statistics, but certainly more than respectable. You tried out for the Minnesota Vikings as a free agent, but it's hard to make a pro team when you aren't drafted," she said sympathetically.

So Kathleen Hunt could use research systems too. Well, that was great, but it wasn't going to raise them a billion dollars. He had to admit that it was a nice touch for her to go over his college football statistics.

"You're from Georgia?"

"Yes." She laughed as she turned toward Mace.

"But you don't have an accent."

"How far do you think I'd get on Wall Street with a thick southern accent?" She broke into a heavy Georgia drawl.

"Not very far." Mace acknowledged what she was saying. She was smooth, with an answer for everything. *Engaging* was the word people used. Easy, Mace, he told himself. Don't give in so easily.

The limousine moved past the World War II aircraft carrier *Intrepid*, now a floating maritime museum at the Forty-sixth Street pier. "Who will you go to for the money?" he asked. He wanted some answers before they got to Columbia.

She leaned her head in one direction and passed a hand slowly through the entire length of her golden hair. "Very wealthy families here in the United States."

"Specifically."

"You're very persistent."

"I thought I was 'interesting.' "

The woman smiled at Mace. Lewis Webster had warned her about him. He was not a man to be taken lightly or to be easily manipulated. Her demeanor became serious. "I'll go to the Rockefellers, the Mellons, the Basses, the Stillmans, Sam Walton's family, the Koch family, and Bill Gates . . . to name a few."

Mace whistled cynically. "You certainly seem to move in the right circles. Do you really know those people?" He was unconvinced.

"In most cases I know at least one family member or their advisers."

"How?"

"In the mid and late eighties I worked at Kohlberg, Kravis & Roberts. Some of those families were KKR's biggest investors, and I met them there. In 1989 I moved to LeClair and Foster in San Francisco, and I developed more investor contacts there. More wealthy families. They like to buy companies quietly."

KKR. LeClair and Foster. Those were players, real players. Mace leaned against the door as the driver guided the limousine off the highway and into the Upper West Side of Manhattan. It would not be long now before they'd arrive at Columbia. "And you think your relationships with those people are strong enough to raise a billion-dollar fund to speculate on Manhattan real estate and Big Board stocks?"

She leaned forward and touched his knee. "I know they are."

Mace grinned. "And just what makes you so confident?"

"How about this? I've already got preliminary commitments from some of those families for two hundred million. You see, I've been working on the fund for a couple of months. Lewis didn't tell you everything, did he?"

Mace swallowed hard. Two months? Two hundred million dollars already? "No, I guess he didn't." So all that crap from Webster about waiting until Mace had a chance to talk to this woman before hiring her was just that—crap. Webster had hired her without the slightest input from him. Still, she claimed to have preliminary commitments for two hundred million dollars already. If that were true, it would be big. Because raising a fund was like a snowball rolling down a hill. Once it had developed critical mass, it would keep rolling of its own accord and grow larger and larger as it rolled.

The limousine came to a gentle stop in front of Columbia Business School, but Mace continued to stare at her for a few moments. He did not know any of those wealthy families. His investors consisted mostly of professional money managers who couldn't be counted on to keep their mouths shut, undoubtedly how Schmidt at Morgan Stanley had found out about and almost destroyed the WestPenn short line railroad transaction. But families were different. They worked in the shadows. They didn't like the market to know what they were up to. And they seemed to have a ton of cash that they could put to work quickly—without having to deal with investment committees. Mace stared at her. He wanted to like her. After all, they were going to be working together very closely, at least for the foreseeable future. But it wasn't that easy. She had come into Walker Pryce on day one as a managing director without putting the work into the firm he had. If Webster had promised him two million and his managing director title, Webster had probably promised her five million and partnership status. If she could pull this thing off, he was probably looking at the first female partner in Walker Pryce history.

"Well, it was nice to meet you." Mace leaned forward and reached for the door handle, not bothering to wait for the driver to open it. "I'm sure it will be interesting working with you. The driver will take you wherever you want to go."

"I'm going with you."

"What?" Mace glanced back over his shoulder at her.

She grinned seductively at him. "I want to watch you work. And after you finish teaching class, we're going to a late dinner so that we can begin mapping out strategy with respect to the fund. I'm going to have a billion dollars for you to invest pretty soon, so we'd better get to work as soon as possible." The driver opened her door, but instead of stepping out, she leaned closer to Mace. "And my friends call me Leeny. It's short for Kathleen."

"Leeny? Leeny." Mace said the name twice, as if he were trying to become used to it. "That's an interesting name."

"I'm an interesting woman." Leeny winked at him, then turned and took the driver's hand as he helped her from the car.

Rachel leaned back in her seat and checked her watch. Five after seven. Mace McLain was late for real estate finance. It was the first time since the class had begun several weeks ago that this had happened, and somehow she felt vaguely offended, as she had when boys had promised to call in high school at an exact time and then hadn't.

The noise level in the room was loud as students discussed job offers, other classes, and the cold February weather that had enveloped New York City over the past few days. Everyone in the classroom except Rachel was happy about Mace's irresponsibility, ecstatic for each minute they didn't have to face the investment banker, who had turned out to be somewhat of a ballbuster. He asked difficult questions and expected accurate, well-prepared answers in return. And he expected a significant amount of class participation from everyone. No one could hide from his eagle eye.

"All right, all right. Party's over." Mace moved into the classroom quickly, smiling broadly, aware of the unanimous disappointment suddenly filling the air.

The class groaned as one.

Rachel sat up and smiled. Her anger at Mace's tardiness dissipated immediately. She had prepared tonight's case extremely well and was looking forward to the class discussion, a discussion she anticipated dominating by the end of the two-hour session as the material became more complex and the others faded away, unable to understand exactly where she was going with her line of comments, unwilling to risk trying to stay with her in uncharted territory for fear of saying something stupid.

"Okay. Get your notes out and let's get going." Mace's voice echoed throughout the large classroom. As the students looked away from him in unison for a split second to pull out and arrange their notes, Mace nodded subtly in her direction.

Rachel nodded back. As she did, she felt a rush of relief at the fact that he had appeared. She'd been afraid that Dean Fenton was going to walk through the door at any moment and inform them that Mace would be unable to appear tonight because he had been called to some exotic port of call on a deal. Everyone in the class would have erupted into a loud cheer, except for her. Now they were all irritated and she was happy. Too bad, she thought.

Rachel watched Mace. Perhaps she was beginning to enjoy these classes a little too much. She swallowed. No, there was nothing wrong with what she felt. For the first time she realized that she was actually looking forward to her interviews next week at Walker Pryce, particularly her meeting with Lewis Webster. Mace was right. She was good enough to be accepted at Walker Pryce. She was good enough to be accepted anywhere. In today's world her family background was irrelevant. She laughed. He had given her so much confidence.

Suddenly Rachel's body tensed and her smile disappeared. The tall blond woman who had just moved into the classroom was not a student or a professor. Total enrollment at Columbia Business School barely exceeded five hundred people, and almost everyone knew one another, at least by sight.

Leeny Hunt moved to Mace, placed a hand on his shoulder, and whispered something into his ear as he arranged several papers on the black table at the front of the room. Catcalls arose from the classroom's male contingent.

Mace glanced quickly at the men making the noise, then automatically at Rachel. Rachel looked instantly away from Mace to the desktop, where it was safe.

"Enough, enough." Mace raised both hands above his head. "Settle down."

Just as order seemed about to be restored and the classroom became quiet again, one of the more obnoxious marketing majors in the front row, Jake Levin, a large ex-college baseball player, hooted one more time. The class burst into laughter at Jake's bravado. Even Mace could not keep the smile from his face. Finally, after several moments, the noise subsided.

Mace shook his head at Levin. "Christ, Jake, one would think it had been a long time since you had seen a woman."

Jake paused for a moment, considering how far to push the exchange. Finally he smiled mischievously. "It's been a long time since I've seen one like that!"

Again the class burst into applause, and several of the men close to Jake elbowed and pushed him.

Slowly, as the class settled down for a second time, Leeny began moving toward Jake. As she neared him, the class became quiet until finally as she stood directly before him, hands on her thin waist, the room was completely silent. Her eyes were merely slits as she stared down at him. Very carefully she brought her right forefinger to her tongue, wet it, then leaned over and touched her forefinger to Levin's shirt. Every eye in the class was riveted to Leeny's finger as it slid away from Levin.

Slowly a sly smile crossed her face. "Look at what I've done," she said in a husky voice. "Now I need to take you right home and get you out of those wet things."

For a moment Levin stared at Leeny openmouthed. Then he brought both hands to his chest and slumped back into his seat. The class erupted for a third time as Leeny took several sexy steps away from Levin and back toward Mace. As she reached Mace, she grabbed his hand. Mace simply shook his head and smiled as every person in the class continued to cheer. Every person except Rachel Sommers.

11

Frantically the two terrorists attempted to attach the explosive to the huge natural gas tank even as the Wolverines bore relentlessly down on them. Finally, when the Wolverine captain slowed to kneel, one of the terrorists suddenly wheeled about and released a burst of ammunition from his automatic rifle at the approaching troops. White fire spit from the gun, and instantly the four bullets tore through the captain's body. He fell, paralyzed from the neck down, but managed to lift his head to watch both terrorists go down in a hail of Wolverine fire. Then his cheek dropped to the pavement, the last breath of life close at hand.

"Turn it off," Malcolm Becker said quietly, nodding first at Willard Ferris and then at the wide screen in the far corner of the large office.

"Yes, sir." Ferris pointed the control at the television and the screen went blank. The sounds of screaming voices stopped. "If I do say so myself, sir, I think it was a stroke of genius to put that camera on top of the unit captain's helmet before the Wolverines went in there." Ferris snorted with excitement and self-adulation. "God, I love watching that tape."

Becker stared at the little man. They called Ferris Rat Man at the CIA because of his pointed nose, his scraggly mustache, which in a way resembled rodent whiskers, and his long, curved front teeth, which were constantly in view, a result of his thin, arching upper lip. Becker knew that Ferris was not particularly popular with the others of his staff at CIA because Ferris was a whiny, pushy nag. But the Rat Man was a damn good administrator and loyal beyond question. The director's word was law at the agency, and the law was that Ferris was to be obeyed, if not respected. The two men had been together since Becker's days in Vietnam, and they would stay together until hell froze over.

"What a performance." Ferris continued. "Those guys neutralized the terrorists in minutes, without any problems."

"Incompetence," Becker murmured.

"What?" Ferris asked.

Becker rubbed his eyes. "The terrorists should have been able to blow the tank in the time they had. They were incompetent. We were lucky."

Ferris snorted. "Was it luck that you had a contingent of Wolverines actually stationed in Los Angeles? No way. That was careful planning. You have the Wolverines in Los Angeles, New York, and Chicago because those are primary targets. Within an hour the wolverines were on site. Actually *on-site*. If they'd had to come in from another part of the country, maybe the terrorists would have been able to mine the area and detonate the bomb. Response time: that was one of the keys. The fact that your men were victorious wasn't luck."

"Mmm." Becker liked the sound of that.

"I love that tape," Ferris said. "It gives you a good feeling about America. I really think we should show it at your inauguration ball."

"You think so, do you?" Becker smiled slightly. Ferris was absolutely convinced that Becker was going to be the next president of the United States, and Becker liked that kind of enthusiasm. He appreciated people who exuded confidence, who believed that anything could be accomplished as long as the proper resources and commitment were brought to bear by the right people. Becker knew that the only way to win a tough battle was to have a positive mental attitude. Positive things happened to positive people. This was the gospel according to Becker.

"I do," Ferris said loudly.

"And what do you think, Major Conner?" Becker turned toward Slade Conner, who sat in a wooden chair near the television they had all been watching, arms folded across his chest.

Slade flexed his hand as he considered the director. Becker's head was massive, seemingly the size of a bull's. His dark hair was closely cropped, and as a result, the blue veins of his scalp were clearly visible. Becker's nose, eyes, and ears were also large, over-sized even for his huge face. These monstrous characteristics helped him a great deal when he appeared on television because they made him seem very tall, as in fact he wasn't. To augment further the powerful image he naturally projected, every day Becker wore his regular uniform of the United States Army, the branch of the service he had commanded before being named CIA director by President Whitman during his first term five years ago.

Becker was a man of conviction and action. He made decisions quickly and acted decisively after consulting with his most trusted advisers. Sometimes he agreed with the consensus, and sometimes he did not. But once the decision was made, he never wavered, never second-guessed himself. He was fiercely loyal to those who were loyal to him and cutthroat to those who betrayed him. He did not mind a different opinion from his own during the decision-making process, as long as it was conveyed directly to him and not behind his back and as long as it was delivered with respect. But once a decision had been made, Becker required absolute commitment to the cause. No second-guessing and no backstabbing. If he uncovered such, you were gone. He was ruthless that way.

He did not mind sacrificing a few good men to achieve an objective either. His army training had long ago purged him of any lingering guilt with respect to ordering young men into combat. Becker considered dying for one's country to be an honor of the highest degree, especially when that country was the United States of America.

Malcolm Becker was aggressive, direct, and demanding. But despite Becker's fierce nature and stony countenance, Slade knew of the man's caring side. He knew of Becker's deep devotion to the men who served under him and to their families. He knew of Becker's commitment to those less fortunate than he through his diligent charity work. Those who didn't know Becker well and hadn't seen these gentler sides of the man described him as mean-spirited, as a callous, shallow man. Certainly he was aggressive, direct, and demanding, as the director of the Central Intelligence Agency of the United States had to be, almost by definition. Protecting the United States of America was no game. But Slade had seen the softer sides since his appointment to Becker's personal staff six months before. The softer sides did not shine through often, but they were there if you looked long enough and hard enough. It was what made this thing so much more difficult.

Slade smiled. "I agree with Mr. Ferris, General Becker. You should play that tape at your inauguration. There'll be a lot more hawks there that night than doves."

"I like it when people agree with me." Becker pounded his heavy fist on the desk, smiling back at Slade.

"Let's be analytical, Chief." Ferris piped up again. Chief was Ferris's nickname for Becker, and he was the only one allowed to address Becker that way. For everyone else it was General Becker or sir.

Becker leaned back. "Okay. I like it when you're analytical, Willard."

"Fine, yes, well, look at it this way, Chief. You've got the Republican nomination locked up. The convention this summer will be nothing more than a formality. There's Morgan, the senator from Texas, and Cain, the governor of Connecticut," Ferris said. "But they aren't really players. They have regional support, but that's about it. They don't have the national appeal. Not the way you do. Other than Morgan and Cain, there's no one."

Becker nodded as he reached into his top drawer for a beloved Monte Cristo cigar.

"So then we have to think about the Democrats." Ferris continued.

Slade watched Ferris. He was becoming more excited as he spoke, excited at the prospect of becoming chief of staff to a president of the United States. Slade glanced toward Becker, who was already taking his first puff from the Cuban. He wondered whether Becker would levitate Ferris to such a position in the event he did win the position he so coveted or turn to someone with a bit more sex appeal in this age of image. Loyalty might have its limits even for Malcolm Becker.

"It seems pretty obvious that the Democrats will nominate the vice president, Preston Andrews. The polls show him well ahead of any of the other Democrats. And you will crush Andrews in the general election."

Becker inhaled slowly, then exhaled until his lungs were clear. For several seconds Becker held the burning cigar before his huge face, considering it carefully. "The Monte Cristo Churchill," he said, "the most popular cigar in the world." He turned to Slade. "Did you know that John F. Kennedy waited to enforce the Cuban embargo until he could import a lifetime supply of these things for himself and all his friends?"

"No, sir, I didn't." Slade smelled the faint aroma of the Monte Cristo for the first time. Though he did not smoke, the scent was mildly pleasing.

Becker nodded. "Oh, yes." He laughed. "That's how the world really works." Becker turned back toward Ferris. "Willard."

"Yes, Chief."

"Let's not mention that civilian's name in here again if at all possible. Mr. Andrews is our enemy."

"Yes, sir." Willard used the more formal address of sir as his eyes dropped to the carpet.

Becker inhaled again from the cigar. "It's just that I detest the man. He has been after President Whitman for five years, since I started here, to cut CIA funding, and he has clearly never been an advocate of the Wolverines." Becker nodded at the television screen.

"I think 'not being an advocate' is a nice way to put it," Ferris said, sneering. "It must have crushed him when those people took over that gas storage facility in Los Angeles and the Wolverines responded so effectively."

"Yes, and we have Major Conner to thank for the success of the Wolverines," Becker said, turning again toward Slade and nodding.

Slade nodded back. Five years before, at the direct request of the newly appointed director of the CIA, Slade had transferred from the Marines to take charge of a new counterterrorist task force that Becker wanted to initiate. In response to stepped-up instances of terrorist activity within United States borders—the World Trade Center bombing, the Oklahoma City bombing, a car bomb explosion on Pennsylvania Avenue just outside the White House, and the takeover of a Chicago hotel in which a contingent of U.S. senators were staying—President Whitman had secretly directed Becker to form the antiterrorist attack group because of what the president grudgingly agreed was total ineptness at the higher echelons of the domestic law enforcement agencies. In turn Becker had tapped Conner to select, train, and lead the elite strike force to be known as the Wolverines.

Initially President Whitman had wanted to allow the FBI to maintain responsibility for reacting to domestic situations. But Becker forcefully argued that the FBI was not equipped or trained to handle the kind of high technology firepower a crack terrorist squad would employ, that as an ex-commander of the U.S. Army he, and therefore the CIA, was in a much better position to guide the Wolverines. Just as important, Becker reasoned with Whitman, most domestic terrorist plots would originate in countries unfriendly to the United States, in countries in which the CIA was operating. The CIA would have better information about who was involved in an attack, about the strength and profile of the attackers, and so on. Again, the CIA was therefore in a better position to handle the attacks. Ultimately Whitman had agreed to a trial period. The L.A. situation had pushed the president over the edge.

Setting up, arming, and training the Wolverines had been an extraordinarily expensive proposition, and Vice President Andrews had been one of Becker's most outspoken critics, citing the tremendous cost of the Wolverine Project.

For several years the project did appear to lack merit. Billions of dollars seemingly poured into a bureaucratic black hole. There were no terrorist incidents on U.S. soil. Bashing Becker for the Wolverine Project became popular with his enemies. But three months ago extremists had attempted to take over simultaneously the control towers at each of New York's three major airports—Kennedy, La Guardia, and Newark—so that they could watch fuel-starved planes actually drop from the night sky onto New York City unless they were given what they wanted. Then the L.A. attack had occurred. In both cases the Wolverines had used the latest high technology weapons, superior training, and old-fashioned bravery to eradicate the terrorists quickly without the loss of a single civilian life.

Now Malcolm Becker was the toast of Washington, as well as of every small town and large city from the Atlantic to the Pacific. He was appearing on the front pages of major newspapers and magazines around the globe, and he appealed to the American people. He was a throwback, a cool, tough John Wayne type who wasn't going to allow gun-toting foreigners to come into *his* country and disturb *his* way of life. He conveyed a no-nonsense, take-no-prisoners attitude that played well. He was a tough negotiator and cool under fire. A man completely convinced that his views were the right ones, a man who seemed to be able to lead not only the CIA but the country as well. Becker was a man on a mission, a man who would stop at nothing short of the presidency, and would do anything to get there. Slade was well aware of that.

Now he was a member of General Becker's personal staff

because of the Wolverines' success. The man remembered his friends. There was no question about that. "Thank you, sir."

"No, thank *you*, son."

Slade glanced back at Becker. The man had never before called him son. Suddenly he felt a sense of devotion to the man as he never had. But he must bury that feeling. It was all business, he reminded himself.

Slade smiled. "You know, General, what you need is one more terrorist attack here in the United States, another situation like the one in Los Angeles. That would put you over the top." Slade thought he noticed a subtle exchange between Becker and Ferris but wasn't certain.

"And can you arrange that for us?" Ferris asked, showing the full length of his upper front teeth as he smiled.

Slade chuckled and held up his hands. "I'm just saying that with respect to the campaign, it would be strategic to have another situation like that. I hope you don't infer from my comment that I would actually *want* to see that happen. I still know many of the men in the Wolverines, and I would never want to wish them into battle." Slade paused. "I still feel guilty for not having gone into the L.A. facility with them."

"Nonsense!" bellowed the general. "You're much too valuable to go in there. Leaders cannot be lost during battle. That is one of the first rules of warfare." He sucked on the cigar for a moment, then pointed it at Slade. "Another situation like Los Angeles, huh? That would be nice. Slade, you're starting to think like a politician."

"That's a little scary," Slade said.

The three men laughed for several seconds, and then there was a short, uncomfortable silence.

Finally General Becker drew in a long breath, then coughed. "Well, unfortunately another terrorist attack is something far out of my control. I can't sit around and wait for a battle. I've got to take my battle to Mr. Andrews." Becker paused. "Speaking of which, Willard and I have got some work to do, Slade."

Slade understood the implication. "Yes, sir." He stood, saluted, and moved to the door. Just as he was about to close the door, he turned around and leaned back into the office. "Sir?"

Becker glanced up from the desk. "Yes, Major?"

"There was something you said you needed to speak to me about."

"Oh, yes. I'll contact you later today. At your office. You will be there?"

"Yes, sir." Slade saluted again and was gone.

"What was that all about, Chief?" Ferris asked.

Becker did not respond immediately. His gaze was focused upon a bank of tiny television monitors standing together on a small table next to the desk. He stared at one of the monitors until Slade Conner had finished speaking to the general's secretary and exited the outer office, then turned his attention back to Ferris. "Nothing, Willard."

There was something there, but Ferris decided not to push. The general maintained his own agenda sometimes. It was better for people not to ask questions. Even the chief of staff.

Becker crushed the half-finished cigar into a large glass ashtray on the desk. "Always stop smoking a cigar at the halfway point, Willard. Even if it is a Monte Cristo. The smoke in the last half of any cigar will kill you. That's where the bad stuff is." Becker removed another cigar from the desk drawer and put it in his mouth but this time did not light it. "Did the president send over the new budget figures?"

Ferris hesitated. Suddenly the elation of the tape and the discussion of Becker's run for the presidency faded away. He had been dreading this moment. But as Becker's chief of staff he had to address the issue even though it was so sensitive.

"Willard?" The general's voice rose.

"We have received the figures," the Rat Man said quietly.

"And?"

"And the information isn't good."

"What does 'not good' mean, Willard?"

Ferris could hear the tension rising in Becker's voice. "The memorandum, directly from the president's desk, says that our budget will be cut over the next three years: two billion the first year, then three and five in the next two. It says these numbers are preliminary and could increase after further review."

"What?" The general stood up behind his desk.

"The memorandum cites a study that projects that annual interest expense on the national debt will exceed four hundred billion dollars by the year 2000 unless significant government spending cuts are made. It says here Whitman has decided that raising taxes is out of the question, not even an option. So he will concentrate on the spending side. Apparently Wall Street has told him in no uncertain terms that something must be done about the deficit or it will tag him with the catastrophe even if he's already gone from office. That's the spin from the staff office anyway. Obviously he doesn't want Wall Street pinning the deficit on him, not even if he's out of office. He wants his place in history secure."

"Ten billion dollars?" The general brought one mammoth fist down onto the desktop. The glass ashtray flipped over completely, spilling its contents and coming to rest upside down. But Becker took no notice.

"It gets worse."

"It gets worse? How can it get any worse?" Becker stared down at Ferris from behind the great desk.

Ferris gazed up at the massive head. The veins of the huge scalp began to bulge and pulsate beneath the crew cut, and the brown eyes seemed to be drilling holes into him. He had seen the general's volcanic temper only a few times in their thirty years together, and he did not want to see it now. Oftentimes the bearer of bad news, even if he was only the bearer, could be punished as severely as the individual responsible. Ferris took a deep breath. "It says here that Whitman wants a full accounting of all expenses related to the Wolverines since the inception of the program. He refers to several maximum expenditure levels to which you and he agreed at the beginning of the project." Ferris paused and looked up at the general slowly. "Chief, we are well over those maximums."

"*I know that!*" Becker leaned on the desk with both hands. His right palm came to rest on a cigar ember that had been spilled from the ashtray and had not been completely extinguished. Slowly he stared down at his hand, gritting his teeth. "Andrews," he whispered. "That bastard Andrews is behind this."

Ferris nodded. "Probably."

"He's trying to manufacture or expose financial improprieties here at the agency to offset the financial problems at his family's business." Becker's eyes flashed to Ferris.

Ferris glanced up at the general. "What problems at his family business, Chief?" Was this something else he was not privy to?

The general hesitated. He had not meant to convey this piece of information to Ferris yet. But there was no holding back now. Willard might become suspicious if there was no explanation this time. Willard was a suspicious man by nature. "It has come to my attention that Preston Andrews's family business, the multibillion-dollar Andrews Industries, manufacturer of a wide variety of vehicle component parts used by the Big Three in Detroit, is in deep financial trouble."

"I read the *Journal* and the *New York Times* every day. There has been no mention of any financial problems at Andrews Industries in either of those papers."

"The company is privately held. Just a few members of the Andrews family own shares. There is no public stock. And as a result, there are no third-party shareholders and no Securities and Exchange Commission scrutiny of the company's financial statements. They don't even tell their banks what is really going on."

"You're serious?"

"Absolutely."

"How did you get this information, Chief?" Ferris glanced at the door, wondering if Slade Conner was somehow involved.

Becker and Conner had seemed to clam up when he came in the room, but he had thought then that it was simply his imagination. Now he wasn't so sure.

The general's eyes narrowed. "I don't give away sources, not even to you. You should know that by now."

Ferris nodded. That was true.

"I will tell you one more item that you may find even more amazing, Willard."

Ferris looked up.

Becker smiled slightly. "Carter Guilford, the man we lost in Honduras several weeks ago . . . "

"Yes." Ferris leaned forward and shook his head. "A shame. I'm glad it hasn't become public that he was working with the Ortega drug cartel. It would be very difficult for his wife and family."

Becker disregarded the comment about Guilford's family. "I think I know where his cut of the profits was going."

A strange expression clouded the Rat Man's face. "You don't mean . . . " His voice trailed away.

The general nodded gravely. "Information points to the unsavory fact that Guilford was working with Vice President Andrews. It appears that some of that money from the cartel may have ended up at Andrews Industries, after Guilford had taken his share, of course."

Ferris gazed at Becker in amazement. "What?"

Becker's eyes narrowed. "Preston is panicking. He can't have a financial crisis at his company exposed just before the campaign begins. The press would have a field day. So he's taking money from a drug cartel to save his ass. He's willing to do almost anything to fund his campaign and keep the problems at the company quiet. And that includes using drug money."

Ferris swallowed hard. What Becker was saying seemed incomprehensible. But the general did not make such accusations lightly. Not even when the other person was his mortal enemy. He was too honorable a man.

12

A nd how was your day, Miss Sommers?"

Rachel eyed Lewis Webster as he sat hunched behind the old desk staring back at her from beneath dark eyebrows. It had been a grueling day. Her first interview had started at nine this morning with a bombastic partner named Sherman Stevens, who was perhaps the most egotistical human being she had ever met. For the first ten minutes of the meeting the man had gone on a raving monologue about his accomplishments at Walker Pryce, about his brilliant and aggressive style of investment banking, and about his beauty queen wife, who, to judge from the large picture of her sitting on his credenza, would have been lucky to have been allowed into the Westminster Dog Show at Madison Square Garden. Rachel had tired quickly of his inane garble, so she had crossed her legs at one point during the monologue—she had worn an old blue business suit for the day of interviews, and the skirt fell slightly farther up from the knee than was typically acceptable—as she sat across from him on the couch of his office, bringing her left leg over her right very slowly, lifting the leg higher than was necessary. For a split second Sherman's gaze had slipped downward, an almost imperceptible shift of his eyes. But from that moment on he had wanted to know all about her. It wasn't a move she was proud of, but the meeting was not supposed to be about him.

From Stevens's office Rachel had gone on to meet two associates in the Mergers and Acquisitions Advisory Department and a vice-president on the government bond desk, with whom she had gotten along with exceedingly well; they had talked mostly of her experience on the Merrill Lynch trading floor, in which he seemed most interested. Then there had been lunch with Mace and the head of Human Resources in a small, formal dining room with all the amenities, including four forks on the left side of her place setting that she had skillfully manipulated at exactly the correct moments, as the Human Resources director dutifully noted. After that she had interviewed with three more partners and two managing directors.

She had been peppered with questions about her background, both business and personal; about her studies at Columbia Business School, including her rank in class; about her ability to be a team player; about her ability to be an entrepreneur; about deals she had worked on at Merrill Lynch; and finally about her resolve to do whatever it took to close a deal—whether that meant pulling three all-nighters in a row or taking the red-eye back to New York's Kennedy Airport from a Seattle deal at two in the morning, then running across the airport to jump on the Concord to work on another transaction in Paris without so much as a shower in between flights. She had dealt with the usual interview routines: the good cop/bad cop, the partner who kept taking telephone calls until she requested that he ask his secretary to hold calls until they were done, and even the subtle pass from the partner who looked like a movie star. Now it was seven o'clock, and she was exhausted, but she wasn't about to let Lewis Webster see that.

"I'm doing very well, thank you. I just wish all my days were this easy." Rachel smiled at the older man evenly.

Webster rubbed his beard for a moment and smiled back although it seemed more like a grimace. His eyes moved slowly from her face all the way down to her shoes and back up again. His gaze lingered at her hemline, but she sensed that he was deriving no pleasure from the long look at her short skirt. He was simply registering the fact that it was too short, made of a nonnatural fiber, and slightly frayed in one spot.

"Walker Pryce is a demanding place to work, Miss Sommers," he whispered.

"I'm very confident that I can—"

Webster held up a hand. "I'm not through."

Rachel cut off her words in mid-sentence. The whisper sent a cold shiver down her spine.

Webster continued. "Many of the people at this institution, with whom you would be interacting on a daily basis, come from privileged backgrounds. You do not. That might create hostility between you and those people." He paused and smiled slightly. "Some of them will want to tell you about how wealthy they are . . . all the time."

"My turn now?" Rachel asked politely.

Webster's grin faded. "Yes."

"I can handle anyone." She said the words calmly, but her eyes flashed. "Most of the students at Columbia are upper-middle-class, at least. Personally I think most of them are as soft as Sherman Stevens's belly." She paused to allow her remark to sink in. "Envy makes people hungry. I've got enough envy inside me to choke a Rockefeller. I want what you and many of the others here have: financial security. Growing up poor is no fun, and I'm perfectly willing to be very upfront about that. I will work hard, very hard, to be financially secure. As a result, you will benefit."

Webster moved a hand to his mouth, then back to his lap. "Walker Pryce has no female partners and only two female managing directors—one in Personnel and one on the trading floor. You want to come into the Corporate Finance Department, where there aren't *any* women above the rank of vice-president."

"I don't care." Rachel said the words coolly. "I like a challenge."

The intercom on Webster's desk buzzed. He reached forward stiffly. "Yes, Sarah."

"Ms. Hunt is here to see you."

Instantly Rachel's and Webster's eyes met.

"Send her in," he whispered through the black box. "I'm sorry, Miss Sommers. I'm going to have to end the interview now. I need to see this lady immediately." He rose from the chair and gestured toward the door without offering Rachel his hand. "Someone from Walker Pryce will get back to you in the next few weeks."

Rachel nodded as a lump rose in her throat. This did not sound like a man falling all over himself to hire her. She stood, nodded a quick thank-you to Webster, and moved away from him. As she neared the door, it opened suddenly and she came face-to-face with Leeny Hunt.

"Good evening. I'm Kathleen Hunt." Leeny offered her hand.

Rachel took the other woman's hand. So Mace and this woman were working together. Well, wasn't that great! "Rachel Sommers."

An expression of recognition suddenly crossed Leeny's face. "Oh, you're the ace from Columbia, the one running the fund for the business school that the professional money managers are all hot and bothered about. Don't worry about them, Rachel; they're just jealous." She released Rachel's hand and glanced at Webster. "You'd better sign this one on here at Walker Pryce quickly, Lewis. Otherwise Goldman or Morgan will have her, and you'll look very foolish in about three years."

Webster grunted and sat down in his chair.

Leeny turned back to Rachel and smiled. "Don't worry about him," she said softly. "He's just a grumpy old man. He acts tough because he has to. But Mace adores you. He can't stop talking about you. As I understand it, you're one of Walker Pryce's can't miss kids."

"Thank you," Rachel said.

"You're welcome. Sorry I interrupted the interview."

"It's all right." Rachel smiled, then walked quickly out of the office into the hallway beyond.

When Rachel was gone, Webster pointed at Leeny. "Close the door," he ordered.

Leeny pushed the huge door shut, then turned and moved toward Webster.

"How goes the money-raising business?" His tone was not friendly.

"Fine," she said nonchalantly.

"What does that mean?" Webster was immediately exasperated.

"It means that it isn't going to take me very long to raise fifty million dollars from the wealthy families I've been talking to. Not long at all," she hissed. Leeny became suddenly angry, her frustrations at his constant harassment bubbling to the surface from nowhere. And the guilt she was beginning to feel needed an outlet.

"Easy, Ms. Hunt." Webster understood the strain and the need to release it. It wasn't that he cared about her personally. He did not at all. But he had to have her remain stable so that she could complete the critical task to which she had been assigned.

Leeny ignored Webster. "I mean nine hundred and fifty million dollars of the money for the damn fund are already raised for me. Fifty million from Walker Pryce and nine hundred million from Washington." She still sounded on edge. "When the families hear that the fund already has commitments for that much money, they fall all over themselves to tell me they can't wait to put money in too. They'll figure with that much money already raised and Walker Pryce as the sponsor, it must be a good deal."

Webster nodded. "Good."

"Any idiot could do this job," she said.

"You're wrong."

"No, I'm not." She gazed at Webster for a moment. He was a scary-looking man, she thought, like death warmed over. "Is it really necessary for us even to involve outside money? The families, I mean. Why don't we just do it all with money from Washington?"

Webster shook his head quickly. "No. We must have independent money to provide credibility. It might be crucial to be able to prove to people that we have outside investors in Broadway Ventures someday. I hope it never comes to that, but if it does, we will be very glad for the money you are raising. We will be very glad for your talents." He rarely dispersed compliments because he did not find it as self-satisfying as others did. But it was necessary to do now, to make her feel good.

"It could turn out to be risky too." Leeny shook her head.

Webster's eyes narrowed. "When will you have definite commitments from the families? When can you have the money in the fund's account?"

"I could have fifty million in the fund cashed and ready to go by tomorrow," she said, but she was exaggerating.

"Good."

"But if I actually had the money in the till that fast, then old Mace might smell something rotten on Wall Street, mightn't he? And we've got to make it look as if this whole thing weren't rigged, don't we? As if the deck weren't stacked. You do your part; I'll do mine. Don't fucking sweat it, old man."

"Mace isn't going to smell anything." Webster's voice was icy. He did not appreciate Leeny's impudence or her foul language. "Except your perfume. He knows this deal means his managing director title and a lot of money."

"You think Mace McLain is really that easy to fool, don't you?" Leeny pulled a pack of cigarettes from her dress pocket.

"No smoking in here," Webster said quickly.

"Oh, right, I forgot about your little throat problem." For a moment she considered disregarding him and smoking anyway, then shoved the pack back in her pocket. Webster was much closer to the man in Washington than she, and if the man was willing to risk lending himself nine hundred million dollars from a government account—even if it was just for a few weeks—he probably wouldn't hesitate killing someone if Webster said that person was becoming a problem. Even over a pack of cigarettes.

Webster motioned toward Leeny with a gnarled finger. "No, I don't believe Mace can be easily fooled. But he can be led away from things that matter so that being fooled doesn't even become an issue. Which is where you come in again."

Leeny smiled grimly. "Yes, my baby-sitting job. I bet I'm the best-paid au pair in Manhattan. And I'm legal. Sort of." She laughed.

"Yes, you are the best-paid baby-sitter in Manhattan," Webster whispered immediately. "And you'd better act like it. I don't want Mace McLain going anywhere without you other than to the men's room. And if you feel you can get there too without causing suspicion, I would be relieved." He raised an eyebrow at her.

"No pun intended, right?" She thought she noticed an evil smile flicker across his face.

Webster shrugged, and the slight smile passed from his face. He did not have much of a sense of humor.

"You know, Lewis, Mace is a very attractive man," Leeny said. "Not just physically."

Webster glanced up at her. He didn't like the sound of that. "Ms. Hunt, if you are thinking of falling for Mace McLain, I wouldn't suggest it. He probably won't be with us for very long."

"Do you mean he won't be with Walker Pryce, or do you mean 'with us' more generally?" she asked.

"You figure it out. You always seem to have all the answers."

Leeny looked away. Webster disgusted her. But for better or worse they were partners, united by their past criminal endeavors, as yet unproved by anyone who wanted to prosecute them—at least through the court system.

Webster leaned back in his chair. "So how is our friend in Washington manipulating you, Ms. Hunt? What brings you into this mess so agreeably?" The sinister smile returned to his face.

Leeny did not answer, but her mind raced back to the numerous leveraged buyouts she had been a part of at LeClair and Foster. How she had known beyond all doubt that a specific stock's price would double the next day once the offer to purchase had been announced in the *Journal* and the *Times* and how many times she had taken advantage of that inside knowledge. She laughed sadly. She thought she had hidden her tracks so well. "I've got to get going." Webster did not respond, but as she turned and moved toward the door, she could feel his eyes boring into her back.

The air outside Webster's office seemed cool and refreshing, and she leaned back against the closed door and breathed it in. Her hands were wet with perspiration. God, he turned her stomach every time she was with him. But there would be no avoiding him as this thing came closer to its conclusion. In fact there would be more contact. Leeny dug a hand into her purse. Where was that vial? It was the only thing that kept her going now. There it was. Thank God. She wondered if they knew about this little habit. They seemed to know everything else.

Mace looked up from his desk and smiled at Rachel standing in the doorway of his office. "How did it go with Webster?"

Rachel moved into the room, tossed her purse and folder onto a chair, then collapsed onto the long couch. "I don't know, Mace. He's such a—such a—"

"Jerk." Mace finished the thought.

"I could think of a couple of other words that would be a little more descriptive."

Mace smiled. "As Lewis is the first to admit, he skipped congeniality class."

"I don't think so. I think he went, but he failed."

"What did he tell you?" Mace asked, closing the file on his desk.

"He said someone from Walker Pryce would get back to me in a couple of weeks or something." Rachel picked up a copy of the latest *Business Week* from the table at the end of the couch, flipped through it quickly, then placed it back on the table. "I don't know what to think."

"He didn't say to forget about Walker Pryce. He says that to nine out of ten business school students who walk into that office. And only about one in twenty applicants who go through here even gets to his office. The other people you interviewed with must have had great things to say about you. You should feel good."

"Oh, I feel great. Ten straight hours of interviewing. Ten straight hours of having to listen to egomaniacs stroke themselves, of having men stare at my legs and of making sure I am using the correct fork at the correct time so that Fred Forsythe, head of Human Resources, won't think I'm a social outcast." She glanced at Mace. "I've never felt better."

"So you noticed Fred watching you at lunch?" Mace's grin became wider.

"You were watching too, buddy boy." She used an angry tone but could not help smiling back at Mace. "Besides, the whole thing is rigged. The only reason everyone is being so nice to me here is that you are pulling strings."

Mace shook his head. "If you must know the truth, Rachel, I can do only so much. I'd like you to think I have that kind of influence down here, but I don't. I can get you in the door, but that's as far as it goes. The rest is up to you. The reason you were invited to Webster's office at the end of the day was that every person with whom you interviewed liked you and thought that you would make a strong contribution here at Walker Pryce. That's the way it works. That's why you waited outside Forsythe's office after your last scheduled interview. He was talking to all the people you saw today to see if they thought you should continue the process before he sent you to see Webster. It's a partnership here. Everyone has an equal vote."

"I'm sure some votes are more equal than others."

Mace did not respond to her comment. "You saw some very tough people today, people who know all about the fact that you aren't from a privileged background and don't care."

"Webster did. He told me all about how I should expect people to look down on me if I came here."

"He was just trying to be difficult. That's his job."

Rachel brushed a dark thread from her white stockings. "I met Kathleen Hunt." She tried to seem uninterested, but it was difficult.

"Oh?" Mace folded his arms across his broad chest.

"Yes. Actually she's the reason my interview with Webster ended. When Webster heard she was waiting outside his office, he all but fell over himself to kick me out. He's almost as bad as you are."

"What are you talking about?" Mace's face took on a strange expression.

"You and Ms. Hunt were definitely flirting with each other at class last week. You seemed to enjoy her corny little bit with Levin." Rachel tried to make her voice seem airy and nonchalant.

"Do I detect a hint of jealousy?"

"What?" Rachel looked at him incredulously.

Mace smiled. "You sounded a little jealous."

"Oh, sure. I'm jealous. I'm just out of my mind with jealousy." She paused. "My God, you've got some ego, Mace McLain."

"Do I? Well, right, why would I think you might be jealous?" He was pushing her because she ought to be vulnerable by now. Ten hours of interviews ought to be enough to break down her defenses, and as a result of her vulnerable state, he might be able to find out something useful here. Like how she really felt about him. He had seen that look on her face the other night at Columbia as Leeny had come back toward him after playing with Levin, the look of a lost deer. But it might have been his imagination. It was unfair to do this to her now, but he wanted to get to her true feelings. He wanted to know if there was really anything there. Mace leaned back in the chair and stretched. "Leeny's nice . . ."

"Oh, it's Leeny, is it? Not Kathleen?"

Mace smiled. "She likes Leeny better. And she is attractive, I'd have to admit that. I mean, anyone would think she was pretty, right?" He was pushing.

Rachel shook her head. She wasn't going to be pulled into a competition. "Sure," she said blandly. He was trying to goad her, to make her explode for his own satisfaction, and she wasn't going to give him the pleasure of seeing her affected.

"I just wish I didn't have to work so closely with her," Mace continued.

Rachel sniffed and picked up the *Business Week* again. That didn't sound good. "What do you mean?"

"It's a new project Webster has me working on with her. That was why she came to class the other night. We were discussing it on the way up to Columbia; then we went to dinner afterward to do some more planning. I was going to have her stay in the limousine I took up to school while I taught class, but she said she wanted to see me work." Mace grinned. "I'm not sure what that meant. Maybe I'll find out at some point."

Rachel ignored most of what he said. "What project?" She felt her pulse quicken. She didn't want to ask, but she couldn't help herself. If Leeny and Mace were going to be working together all the time, she wanted to know.

Mace didn't answer right away. "I'll tell you about it if you come to dinner with me."

"Tonight?"

"Yes." Mace glanced at his watch. It was almost eight o'clock. "In fact we should go right now. I've got to be up early in the morning. I've got a seven o'clock breakfast meeting, and then I have to catch a flight to New Orleans." He said the last sentence almost to himself, as if making a mental note as he spoke.

"Are you traveling by yourself?"

Mace glanced up from his watch. "Um, no."

"Going with your new business partner?" Rachel's tone was sarcastic.

Mace nodded.

"Well, have a great time. I've heard New Orleans is kind of dark and mysterious, a very romantic city." Rachel rose from the comfortable couch.

"Hey, where are you going?"

Rachel retrieved her purse and folder from the chair. "Back to Columbia."

"What about dinner?"

"I'd better get some studying done."

"No. I'm not going to let you go back to Columbia yet." Mace moved out from behind the desk. "You're coming with me."

"Oh, I am, am I?" Rachel stopped in the doorway of his office and looked back at him over her shoulder, then turned slowly toward him as he moved to her.

He stopped before her and smiled broadly. "Yes, you are. No books for Rachel Sommers tonight. I'm kidnapping you."

"It's gorgeous, isn't it?" Rachel whispered.

Mace nodded but said nothing.

From the Brooklyn Heights Promenade—a wide brick-paved walkway running for perhaps a half mile along, and several hundred feet above, Brooklyn's waterfront—one was afforded a tremendous view of the downtown Manhattan financial district across the East River from this most western point of Long Island. Lights ablaze, the huge skyscrapers rose into the darkness of the New York night like the cabins of a mammoth ocean liner at rest in port. On a hot summer night the promenade would have been crowded with people enjoying the sight, but tonight the walkway was almost deserted.

"Are you warm enough, Rachel?" Mace turned toward her as he leaned against the railing.

"Yes, I'm fine." She had not noticed the cold temperature at all since leaving Walker Pryce's Wall Street building. A slight breeze blew her hair gently across her face, and she withdrew a hand from the pocket of her long coat to brush it away. She glanced from the soaring buildings down to the dark water moving far below. "I hope the interviews went all right today." Her voice was soft.

Mace smiled at her. "I'm sure they went fine. I have a lot of confidence in you. I bet you knocked them dead." His tone was filled with strength.

"You're nice, Mace." She turned her head away as she finished the sentence. It was a forward thing to say, and though Rachel wanted to look in his eyes to judge his reaction to the words, she could not force herself to do so.

"Thank you," he said, still smiling. "But I have to tell you, there are probably one or two women around who might disagree." It was a subtle warning, almost subconscious in its delivery.

"No, I mean it." Her voice was far away. "It's really great of you to help someone like me." Somehow it was easier to be so forward outside the office.

Mace drew himself up, and his face twisted into an expression of mock irritation. "What is that supposed to mean? Someone like you. What are you talking about?" He knew exactly what she was talking about. But she couldn't think that way. She couldn't consider herself inferior in any way if she was really going to make it in the Wild West show that was Wall Street. She had to develop a strong self-confidence, bordering almost on arrogance. If there was any doubt in her own mind, everyone else would doubt her too. And they would attack her unmercifully, like a pack of hungry dogs.

Rachel glanced back toward the lights of lower Manhattan and shook her head. "I gave Webster the old 'I can handle anything' speech but I don't know, Mace. Maybe I can't. Maybe I don't belong in the Walker Pryce world."

"Nonsense. That's ridiculous." Mace's voice was gentle but firm.

Rachel laughed cryptically. "You should see where I live, Mace. It's not a ghetto. I don't mean to imply that. My dad worked very hard all his life to provide my family with a good home. But it isn't an estate either. Far from it. If the partners at Walker Pryce saw my home or met my parents, they'd laugh. You probably would too." She looked back down into the water.

Another gust of wind blew Rachel's long dark hair across her face again. Instinctively Mace reached to brush it back. The reflex surprised him.

She turned toward him as his fingers touched her cheek. They were standing very close to each other now.

"That's not what I'm about, Rachel. I wouldn't laugh. You know that." His voice was filled with compassion. He knew what she was going through. "But I won't lie to you. There *are* people at Walker Pryce who are extremely impressed with themselves and their family trees and who like to tell you about it and remind you that you aren't one of them every chance they have. I heard it quite a bit when I first joined the firm, believe me." He stared straight into her glistening eyes. Then a slight smile edged across his face. "But nobody ever said you were going to like everyone you worked with, particularly on Wall Street. The thing to do is to use those kinds of people at Walker Pryce and let them think the whole time that they *are* superior while you earn a million dollars a year. Let them use all their contacts to help you make that money. Just because you work with them doesn't mean you have to socialize with them."

Rachel shook her head. "It's just that when I think about it sometimes, I'm intimidated by all that wealth and heritage and four forks at lunch stuff. I'll embarrass someone at some point. I know it."

"You will never embarrass anyone." He took her hand in his.

She glanced away. "You've really put yourself out for me, Mace. Most of all, I wouldn't want to embarrass you."

"Hey, I just told you. You will never embarrass anyone."

Rachel gazed up at him. He was so sure of himself. She searched his eyes for several seconds, wondering if all this support might have another agenda, hoping it did. She moved slightly closer. Perhaps she should push the moment to find out what was there, to see if there was anything romantic.

She could be the one, Mace thought. Sometimes he had these convictions early on in a project, or a deal, or a relationship. He knew that this relationship could be very right. He didn't have to go through a long, drawn-out process to make certain. And Mace sensed that the feelings were mutual.

He glanced into her eyes quickly and then away. It was wrong. He had to bury those feelings. She should not be distracted now. She was so close to having all the hard work he knew she had put in over the last several years pay off. So close to making it out of a place she was not particularly proud of. Just as he had made it out when he had been accepted to the University of Iowa. Out of the orphanage, a place he was not proud of.

She would have to redouble her efforts if Walker Pryce actually did make an offer and she accepted it. Her time wouldn't be her own again for several years. She would have a multitude of bosses, all wanting her time, all confident that their task was the most important one. Partners, managing directors, vice-presidents, and senior associates at Walker Pryce would be at her desk constantly, pestering her twenty hours a day to finish projects. The pressure to produce and perform would be intense. But the potential payoff was huge. The last thing she would need at that point would be Mace, distracting her from that possible payoff.

But it wasn't so easy to disregard his feelings. He glanced into her eyes one more time and then against his will began to lean forward toward her lips.

Rachel felt her heart begin to beat strongly as she became aware that he was going to kiss her. Her legs went weak, and she squeezed his hands tightly. As his lips neared hers, she closed her eyes. It was going to be wonderful.

But his lips did not touch hers. Instead at the last moment he kissed her gently on her cheek and withdrew. Her eyes fluttered open as she realized what had happened. She stared at his face, trying not to give away the deep disappointment coursing through her body.

Mace took a deep breath. "We'd better get going. I've got that early meeting and then the flight to New Orleans. And I'm sure you've got work to do too."

Rachel nodded slowly. She did have an immense amount of work, including case preparation and a complete review of the Columbia Business School stock portfolio. But she wasn't going to be able to concentrate on anything now. That was for certain.

13

Everyone who is anyone and works in the New York financial world *lives* in Connecticut or Westchester County and commutes to and from the city daily on the trains of Metro North. These trains all converge at Grand Central Station, in the heart of midtown Manhattan. So the Grand Hyatt, above the station, is the perfect meeting place. Everyone who is anyone has breakfast there at least once a month.

Every morning Hyatt management accommodates the power brokers with a beautiful setting in which to move and shake. The bountiful buffet is decorated with huge bouquets of gorgeous flowers and an ice sculpture of a particularly well-known Manhattan building. The forks, knives, and spoons are sterling silver, the tablecloths linen, and the waiters white-gloved. And a small bowl of Special K, barely enough to fill a few tablespoons, costs eight dollars.

From his seat in the dining room Mace identified the chief executive officers of three Fortune 500 companies, listening to what looked like their personal bankers as they stuffed their faces with eggs benedict or eggs with bacon or sausage, all of which was being paid for by their corporate shareholders. Corporate executives made almost as much from their fringe benefits as they did in salary, bonus, and stock options.

"Your banker friend is late." Leeny's smooth voice reached Mace's ears.

"He'll be here." Mace checked his watch: seven-ten. "Bankers are usually late. It makes them feel more important." He put a hand to his mouth to hide a slight yawn.

"Sorry I'm not more exciting company," she said lightly.

"Leeny, I'm sorry. I don't know why, but I didn't sleep very well last night." Mace knew exactly why he hadn't slept well last night. The cause had been Rachel Sommers. He hadn't been able to stop thinking about her.

"Well, I hope you aren't really tired because it's going to be a long day," Leeny said.

"I know. What time is our flight to New Orleans anyway?"

"Nine o'clock out of La Guardia." Leeny sipped on a glass of freshly squeezed orange juice.

Mace checked his watch again. "We need to leave here by eight o'clock at the latest."

"And who exactly are we meeting in New Orleans? Don't tell me." Leeny pulled a date book from a pocket of her leather briefcase, leaning against a leg of the table. She leafed through the book until she had reached today's page. "Oh, yes. Bobby Maxwell. Tell me about him while we have some time."

Mace smiled. "Bobby Maxwell, one of the most colorful real estate men you'll ever meet, or ever want to meet, for that matter." Mace glanced at Leeny. "He's loud, obnoxious, and considers himself quite a lady's man. He'll be all over you. I guarantee it."

"You will protect me, do you understand?" Leeny's voice rose unsteadily. "Remember, I'm from Georgia. I know about those so-called southern gentlemen," she said sarcastically.

Mace raised an eyebrow at her. "That's right, you do."

Leeny finished her orange juice. "What is so special about Mr. Maxwell? Why are we going to see him?"

"Oh, he owns a small piece of Manhattan real estate called the

Trump Tower. And eleven other commercial buildings on prime Manhattan sites."

"What?" Leeny leaned over the table toward Mace. "I thought Donald Trump still owned the Trump Tower."

"No. Maxwell paid three hundred million dollars for the building last year, when the Donald needed money to build that new casino out in Las Vegas. Of course part of the agreement when Maxwell bought the building was that its name remain the Trump Tower. So everyone thinks Donald still owns it. Despite what people may say about him, Trump's a pretty good deal maker. But Maxwell didn't care about the name thing. People on the jet set circuit know he owns it. That's all he cares about. What the jet-setters don't know is that Bobby put up only about three percent of the money for the purchase. The rest came from several large insurance companies in the form of high-coupon bonds. Lewis Webster wants me to target prominent properties on shaky financial ground. This one fits the bill pretty well. Maxwell won't want to talk about the Trump Tower today. He's still in love with the fact that he owns it, so that one's off the list. But he's got some other Manhattan commercial properties that are on prominent spots and aren't doing so well. He'll be only too glad to talk about them. He won't like our prices, but he'll talk. And if Webster is right about a correction in Manhattan real estate prices, Maxwell will be on the phone to us in a New York minute about the Trump Tower and all his other properties as well. That three percent equity cushion of his will evaporate very quickly in a panicked market."

"I take it you know so much about Bobby Maxwell's Trump Tower deal because you put it together for him."

"Well now, little lady, you catch on pretty doggone fast." Mace did his best Georgia drawl.

"Yes, I do." Leeny paused as she reviewed the date book. "Tell me one other thing, Mr. McLain."

Mace had been watching one of the CEOs at a table near them, but the use of his last name caught his attention, and he turned to Leeny. "What's that?"

"My date book says we take a ten o'clock flight back from New Orleans tonight. Why so late?"

"Our meeting with Maxwell isn't until three in the afternoon. We'll be lucky if we're done with him by six. The ten o'clock flight was the next one out."

"If our meeting isn't until three, why are we leaving so early?" Leeny asked.

"The next departure after the nine o'clock flight for New Orleans doesn't leave until one this afternoon. That would be too late to make it to his office by three."

"If we take a ten o'clock flight home, we won't be landing at La Guardia until about two in the morning New York time."

"So?" Mace glanced back at the CEO.

"So why don't we stay in New Orleans this evening as opposed to killing ourselves to get back? We'll eat Cajun food after the meeting, then catch some music at this little out-of-the-way jazz club I know about down there. We'll do breakfast at Brennan's in the morning and catch a nice civilized flight out of New Orleans around eleven. We'll even be back in New York tomorrow afternoon in time to get some work done. How about it? It will give us a chance to get to know each other a little better." Leeny winked at him.

Mace laughed. Funny, it had never even occurred to him to stay overnight. Get in, get out. As fast as possible. He was conditioned to think that way. Get one deal done and get on to the next one as quickly as possible. That had been his mind-set since graduating from Columbia. Sitting in a jazz club, you might miss a transaction and therefore miss a big fee. He smiled at her. Of course you might have some fun sitting in a jazz club too. That was something he hadn't had much of lately. He allowed his eyes to roam for a few moments. She seemed particularly beautiful this morning in her silk blouse and ankle-length black skirt. "Well, I—"

"Mace! God, sorry I'm late." John Schuler waved at Mace and Leeny as he moved slowly through the crowded dining room. Schuler was on the short side, balding, and suffering from a growing middle-age girth so common among men of his years, that restricted his movements as he tried to make his way through the cramped room, tightly packed with tables and chairs.

Mace and Leeny stood as he reached the table.

"Hello, John." Mace shook Schuler's hand, then gestured toward Leeny. "John, this is Kathleen Hunt. She is a newly hired managing director at Walker Pryce." Mace forced himself to specify Leeny's title. It was protocol at Walker Pryce to introduce a superior by title.

Schuler was immediately impressed and took her hand. "It's very nice to meet you, Ms. Hunt."

"It's nice to meet you too, John." Leeny smiled coyly at him as she spoke.

Mace took note as Leeny held on to Schuler's hand a moment longer than she should have, just as she had done with him when they first met in the limousine. She was good. That was certain. The little hand maneuver would probably be good for at least a few hundred million, and the slight southern drawl that had crept into her tone from nowhere would probably be good for more. But she hadn't asked John to call her Leeny. That was interesting.

Schuler coughed self-consciously. "I'm very sorry to be late. The train was delayed."

"Not a problem." Leeny smiled warmly. "Please sit down."

The three of them sat, and at once their cups and glasses were filled with coffee and orange juice by two young waiters.

"John, we've got to catch a plane this morning, so I'm going to get right to the heart of the matter." Mace watched as Schuler pulled a large biscuit from the linen-lined wicker basket and began covering it first with butter, then with raspberry jam.

"Fine," Schuler said as he took a huge bite of the biscuit.

Mace eyed Schuler while the banker chewed. His cheeks filled up like a chipmunk's as he pushed more of the biscuit into his mouth. He was not a person who made an overpowering first impression, but he was a solid corporate banker who knew his way around his institution—and knew how to get a deal done. Mace turned to Leeny. "As I mentioned to you, John is an executive vice-president with Chase. He runs all domestic lending for the bank, which includes real estate lending and loans to financial institutions, such as funds like the one we are raising. He has been with Chase for almost twenty-five years, and if there is a person who can get this deal done, it's John."

Schuler nodded as he grabbed another biscuit.

Mace continued. "I've done a number of transactions with John and people who work for him since coming to Walker Pryce. Some of the deals might have seemed risky at first blush, but John saw through the risks, and all the deals have ultimately turned out quite well."

"Mace has made me look like a star," Schuler said as he chewed.

"He's good at that." Leeny glanced seductively at Mace over the rim of the cup as she sipped the hot coffee.

"Anyway." Mace began again, turning back toward Schuler. "Here's the deal, John. Walker Pryce is going to be raising a fund to be known as Broadway Ventures Limited."

"How big will it be?" Schuler put down what remained of the second biscuit and wiped his mouth with his napkin.

"We are looking for a total subscription of a billion dollars."

Schuler whistled. "That's big even for Walker Pryce. What's the use of proceeds going to be? What will you do with all that money?"

"We're going to buy Manhattan real estate and Big Board equities," Mace answered, "which is confidential."

"Of course." Schuler waved a hand in front of his face. "Those types of assets are kind of pricey already, don't you think, Mace?"

Schuler placed his elbows on the table and folded his hands in front of his face.

Mace glanced quickly at Leeny, then back at Schuler. "We think we know where there are some values." Mace did not want to convey specifically Webster's theory about the value corrections in the markets. That would smack of speculation, and speculation scared bankers to death. Even good ones like Schuler.

Schuler laughed and turned to Leeny. "If anyone else had said that, I would have told him they were crazy, right to his face." He inhaled slowly. "But Mace has proved me wrong several times. And I know that Walker Pryce doesn't do anything on a wing and a prayer." He pushed the biscuit around on the plate. "Where will you get the money, the billion dollars of fund equity?"

"That's her job." Mace nodded at Leeny.

Leeny placed one elbow on the table, rested her chin in the palm of the hand, and leaned toward Schuler. "Walker Pryce will seed the fund with fifty million, but we'll get the balance from wealthy U.S. families. In fact we already have preliminary circles for almost three hundred million."

Mace glanced at Leeny quickly. That was news. It had been only two hundred just a few days ago. How in the hell could she be raising money that fast?

"Well, I can see why Walker Pryce brought you in at the managing director level, Ms. Hunt. That's very impressive." Schuler sipped his coffee, then looked at Mace. "And of course you want me to persuade Chase to lend you money on top of the billion of equity at some ridiculously low interest rate so you can leverage the fund, buy more stocks and property, and make even more money as their values go up."

"That's what I like about you, John. You get right to the point." Mace patted Schuler on the back.

Schuler grinned wryly. "Of course, if the total value of the investments you make drops below the amount of my loan, I'm screwed." His face became serious. "How much do you want to leverage the fund?"

"One to one," Mace answered right away. "We want a billion dollars of bank debt on top of the billion in equity so that we have a total of two billion to invest."

Schuler moved the coffee cup from his lips quickly and began to sputter. "One to one? In the nineties, Mace?" Schuler stared at Mace incredulously. "You want me to arrange a billion dollars of bank financing on top of a billion dollars of equity for a fund? And I suppose this will be a blind pool; you will want to have very few restrictions from the banks on what you can invest in."

Mace nodded solemnly.

Schuler shook his head. "That will be tough in today's market, Mace. Even for you and Walker Pryce. I could probably get you five hundred million pretty quickly, given the fact that Walker Pryce will be the sponsor and that you personally are involved. Maybe seven-fifty. But a billion? It will be difficult to convince the powers that be at Chase to do that."

"But Mace told me that you *are* one of the powers that be at Chase, John." Leeny slid her left hand smoothly across the linen tablecloth until it reached Schuler's. She squeezed his pudgy fingers for a moment, then pulled back.

Schuler smiled at her nervously. He wanted her to be impressed, but he did not want his career at Chase to grind to a halt at the executive vice-president level either. He had designs on a higher office. But he also realized that by committing to work on the project, he would see a great deal of this alluring creature over the next few weeks and perhaps beyond. Suddenly an image of his overweight credit card–guzzling wife flashed through his mind. He might never have a chance like this again. And the woman's eyes were telling him that she might be willing to relax her morals a bit to get this money.

"So, what can you do for me?" Leeny tossed her head gently to one side. The blond tresses tumbled about her shoulders in waves. It was enough to push Schuler into the abyss.

Mace chuckled to himself, marveling at her work.

"Let's say I could commit Chase to underwriting a billion dollars of bank debt, what would I get in return?" Schuler played with his silverware.

An underwriting commitment of a billion dollars. It was unbelievable, more than Mace could have hoped for. He had mentioned the one-to-one ratio simply as an unattainable opening salvo to establish one endpoint to the range, however ridiculous that endpoint was, as any good negotiator would start a discussion, with the hope that Schuler might ultimately see his way clear to saying he could underwrite perhaps half a billion dollars. But here was Schuler essentially committing Chase to a billion over breakfast. Schuler's reaction was due in part, as he had said, to the fact that Walker Pryce—and Mace specifically—would be managing the fund. But Mace knew that Leeny's little toss of the hair might have been just as important. Incredible, he thought. The real world.

"The base pricing on any amounts outstanding will be Chase's cost of funds plus three percent." Mace's voice was calm. "For any amounts committed to but not outstanding, the banks will receive seventy-five basis points—three-quarters of one percent. And if, as you say, Chase commits to underwrite a billion dollars, you will receive an up-front fee of two percent."

Schuler raised both eyebrows. "That's pretty rich."

"Yes, but we think you deserve it. And we want to get this done fast." Mace said the words firmly. Webster had already committed to the bank pricing two nights ago. In fact he had suggested it, to Mace's shock. Usually Webster didn't like to pay banks much of anything.

The waiter approached the table, pad in hand. "May I take your orders?"

Mace glanced at his watch. It was just after eight. "I'm afraid not, my good man," he said as he stood. He shook Schuler's hand. "I'm sorry, John, but Leeny and I have to catch a plane for New Orleans. You understand."

"Of course." Schuler rose from his seat as Leeny stood. He was obviously disappointed as he glanced at Leeny, wishing now that he hadn't been so arrogant as to keep them waiting. "I'm very sorry I was late. I'm so rude," he said.

Leeny smiled as she took Schuler's hand. "Not to worry. I get the feeling we'll have plenty of time to find out more about each other in the near future. I'm looking forward to working with you, John."

Schuler hesitated for a moment. "Yes, as I am with you." Schuler glanced at Mace. He had fallen into the web, and now there was no escape. Leeny might as well have had loan papers for Schuler to sign on the spot.

Mace turned to the waiter and pressed a crisp hundred-dollar bill into the young man's hand. "Please bring our friend whatever he would like for breakfast. And could you bring him the *New York Times* while he waits? He's probably already read the *Journal*."

Schuler nodded and laughed. "Very perceptive, Mr. McLain."

"I'll be in touch tomorrow, John." Leeny waved as she and Mace headed for the door. "We need your commitment as soon as possible."

Schuler nodded again vigorously. "I'll start working on it as soon as I get back to the bank. By the time you land in New Orleans there will be an entire team put together to work on the deal." He watched longingly as they moved away from the table.

"Great," she called back over her shoulder.

As they reached the maître d's stand, Mace leaned toward Leeny. "They should call you the barracuda."

Leeny touched Mace's elbow lightly and laughed. "They do." But she wasn't laughing inside. Schuler disgusted her, almost as much as she disgusted herself for agreeing to be party to this. He was a horrible little man. But Webster had made himself very clear: do what has to be done. She turned away from Mace, and her expression soured.

* * *

Nothing Mace could have said would have prepared Leeny for Bobby Maxwell. He was a study in contrasts. Wild contrasts. His fire engine red hair stretched in a neat ponytail down the back of his smartly cut Armani suit jacket to a spot in the middle of his shoulder blades. His Sierra Club membership hung on his office wall next to a neatly framed picture of himself holding open the mouth of a huge alligator he had just shot somewhere deep in the Louisiana bayou. The small Confederate flag stood on one corner of his desk, and a picture of him shaking hands with leaders of the local NAACP chapter on the other. And Leeny was certain that somewhere sprinkled in his deep southern accent she could hear a harsh Brooklyn *er* every few moments.

"You want to do what, Mace?" Maxwell's voice was terribly loud, even in normal conversation.

Mace stood before the huge window of Maxwell's grand office, fifty floors above the streets of the Crescent City, staring out at the Mississippi River stretching southward to the Gulf of Mexico in the fading light of the early evening. "I want to buy your Lexington Avenue property in Manhattan for a hundred million dollars. The office building at the corner of Lex and Forty-seventh Street."

"Make me laugh again, Mace McLain. Say that one more time. Come on, please. It's been a long time since I've laughed really hard, a long time since I've heard a good joke. One as good as that anyway."

Mace turned away from the window and toward Maxwell. His voice was even. "I'm serious, Bobby, a hundred million."

Maxwell slapped his knee and screamed with delight. "And I thought you were a serious man, Mace." Suddenly he swung his snakeskin boots from the desktop to the floor, leaned over the desk, picked up a World War II grenade standing next to his Confederate flag, and flung it against the far wall.

Leeny, who had been eyeing the grenade carefully since entering the office, hunched over quickly as the weapon struck the paneling

of the far wall with a sharp crack. Leeny's sudden movement caused
her eyeglasses to fall to the thick shag carpet.

"You thought that was real, didn't you, sweetheart?" Maxwell
asked. "She thought it was real, Mace." Maxwell laughed again
loudly as Leeny bent over to pick up the glasses.

But Mace wasn't laughing. He was frustrated with the conversation. They had discussed each of Maxwell's Manhattan properties, except Trump Tower, and Maxwell had howled at the offering
price Mace had mentioned for each property, as Mace had suspected Maxwell would. The prices were low, in some cases just
above the value of the mortgage Maxwell had on the property. But
the offering prices were Webster's. Mace had tried to convince
Webster that Maxwell wouldn't be interested, but Webster hadn't
cared. Let Maxwell laugh, the old man had said. It will be bluster.
Because when the crash hits, Maxwell won't be laughing anymore.
That attitude was fine for Webster, who could sit in his ivory tower
in Manhattan, worth three hundred million dollars, and still live
like a king for the rest of his life even if the crash never hit and
Broadway Ventures wasn't successful.

It was different for Mace. If the fund failed, Mace would have
to return to the advisory side of the financial services business. And
his contacts, people like Bobby Maxwell, might not take him seriously anymore.

Maxwell shook his head. "Oh, Mace, you know I love you for
that Trump Tower deal. I really do. And I want to repay you for it,
over and above the fee I already gave you. But I've got a reputation
as a tough negotiator to uphold."

Suddenly Mace picked up his suit coat from the table in front
of the window and moved to Maxwell's desk. "I'm sorry to have
troubled you today, Bobby." Mace turned to Leeny. "Come on,
let's go."

Leeny stood. She needed no urging to leave this office.

"Aw, c'mon, Mace. Don't be upset with me. Stay awhile longer.
Look, come up twenty million on the Lexington Avenue property

and I'll accept. It'd still be a low-ball offer, but I'll be a sweetheart. 'Cause I love you." Maxwell rose from his reclining leather desk chair. "Tell you what, I'll treat you both to dinner. First I'll drive you out to my place in the swamp, and we can show missy here how to hunt alligators at night with a flashlight." Maxwell gestured toward Leeny. "You ever hunted gators?"

Leeny shook her head quickly, then crossed her arms over her chest instinctively.

"It's a lot of fun. I'm telling you. When we're done hunting gators, we'll have the help grill us up some food. After that you and I can take a little walk. There'll be a nice moon out tonight, so there won't be a problem seeing the snakes. We'll leave Mace behind at the mansion while we go down by the water. At that point maybe I'll even accept just a fifteen-million-dollar increase on Lexington Avenue."

Mace stepped in front of Leeny. "Thanks, Bobby, but we've got a plane to catch."

"Damn." Maxwell scratched his head, trying to think of a way to keep Leeny around for the evening.

Mace grabbed Leeny's hand and pulled her toward the door. Several moments later the elevator door closed, and they were alone in the car as it began to descend.

Leeny shook her head and laughed. "That's a hillbilly if I ever saw one."

"Don't kid yourself." Mace watched the numbers over the doors light up as the car sped downward. "He's worth almost a billion dollars."

"What?" Leeny looked at Mace incredulously.

"Yes, ma'am." Mace imitated Maxwell for a moment. "Funny thing, though."

"What's that?" Leeny asked.

"If real estate values declined about ten percent, he'd be broke. Bankrupt. Out of business." Mace shook his head. "But now he's the king. It's the power of leverage, Leeny. It's what makes this country great. If a nobody like Bobby Maxwell can just convince a bank to make him a loan, he can become a billionaire overnight." As he finished speaking, the doors of the elevators opened to the massive lobby of the Maxwell Building, the tallest skyscraper in New Orleans.

In just twenty minutes Mace and Leeny were sitting in a table at the rear of Blue Note Heaven, a popular French Quarter jazz club. Mace rolled up the sleeves of his white dress shirt as he watched the band, then picked up the cold glass of beer, touched it to Leeny's, and drank. It tasted so good. After a few moments he put the glass down and began to attack the heaping plate of steamed spiced shrimp that lay before him. He had not eaten since consuming a small plate of fresh fruit on the plane this morning, and suddenly he realized that he was famished.

"Hey, save a little for the rest of us, Mr. McLain."

"Sorry, Leeny." Mace dropped the shell and legs of another shrimp into the waste bowl at one corner of the table, dipped the orange and white meat into a smaller bowl of hot sauce, popped the creature in his mouth, then pushed the plate toward Leeny. "I'm starving."

"That's obvious." Leeny picked up a shrimp and began to peel it. "It's nice down here, isn't it?"

"Yes." He wiped his hands with a napkin. "So you haven't told me yet why you left your job at LeClair and Foster. You must have been earning quite a bit of money. And in San Francisco no less."

Leeny sighed. "Are you going to make me dredge up bad memories?"

"Didn't get along with the partners, huh?"

"It had nothing to do with the firm. I was enjoying my job very much."

Mace smiled at her. "Then it must have been a significant other problem."

"Oh, you checked up on me, did you?" She raised her eyebrows at him. The divorce had nothing to do with anything, but if he wanted to think that it was a factor, then fine, she would play along.

"Wouldn't you expect me to? You checked me out. I mean, with the technology available today it's kind of stupid not to take the five minutes and learn everything you can about someone." Mace paused. He wanted to know more about the reason for her departure, and she was not being forthcoming at all. Still, there was no reason to push her and ruin what was becoming a very enjoyable evening. "Say, what do you look like without your glasses on?" he asked.

"Wouldn't you like to know?" Her face broke into a sexy grin.

"Come on, take them off." Mace took another sip of Dixie beer.

"I take my glasses off for only one reason, Mace."

"What's that?"

"Why don't you call up my ex-husband and ask him?" she asked calmly.

"Oh, I get it." He laughed, then let out a long breath.

"What's the matter?"

Mace shook his head. "We wasted a whole day coming down here. Maxwell isn't going to sell, not at our prices. We've got to convince Webster to come up about ten percent."

"Forget about it for now," she said quickly. "Have some fun."

Mace glanced at his watch. "It's almost time for us to get out to the air—"

"No way." Leeny grabbed Mace's wrist and stood up. "Come on!" The band had just broken into a fast song with a driving bass beat, and the dance floor of the small club was fast filling with half-drunk revelers.

"No, I'm a terrible dancer," Mace yelled back as the music became louder. "Really."

"Come with me!" Leeny wasn't going to take no for an answer. That was clear from her expression.

Mace grabbed the mug of beer on the small table, downed its remaining contents, then allowed himself to be pulled into the mass of gyrating bodies. He was not one to make a spectacle of himself, so he needed as much alcohol in his body as possible.

For the next half hour he spun Leeny from one end of the floor to the other during the faster songs and felt her move seductively against him to the slower ones. Finally, when neither could take any more, they moved back to their table and collapsed into their seats.

"Oh." Leeny touched her chest as she picked up the gin and tonic glass in which the ice cubes had melted to tiny crystals. "And you said you weren't much of a dancer. I should have known. After all, you were an athlete in college."

Mace smiled. She was sexy, smart, and one heck of a dance partner. He kept trying to tell himself that it wasn't a good idea to get close to someone he worked so intimately with, that he shouldn't be attracted to her. But not being attracted to her was becoming more difficult by the minute.

Leeny pulled him into the hotel room, put her hands behind his neck, and kissed him deeply. Mace did not resist. Her mouth tasted wonderful, wet and warm. She nuzzled his neck, began to unbutton his shirt. "See." She was breathing hard as she worked. "I told you it would be a good idea to stay the night." She pulled his shirt apart and slid her hands over his chest as she kissed his neck.

Mace leaned back against the wall as Leeny grabbed his shoulders. God, it felt so good. Suddenly he picked her up by the waist and rotated her slowly so that she was suspended in the air against the wall, her face at his. She pulled her skirt up to her thighs so that she could wrap her legs around his body, biting his ear gently as he supported her. "Jesus, it isn't any effort at all for you to keep me up here, is it?" She could feel the power in his torso.

"No." He stopped and stared at her in the light streaming in from the door, still slightly ajar. "You're like a feather." She was too. She seemed to weigh nothing.

"Mmm. Don't stop what you were doing to me. Keep going."

Again she kissed him, this time sliding her right hand down his body to the belt buckle of his pants.

But Mace continued to stare at her in the dim light. This wasn't what should be happening. "Stop." He allowed her feet to slip to the floor.

"What? Stop what?"

"This. We need to stop what we are doing." Mace breathed deeply. It took every ounce of willpower in his body to say the words.

"No, I won't stop." She began to sink to her knees in front of him, but he caught her by the arms and gently pulled her back to her feet. He was still feeling the alcohol. It would be so easy to let her do what she wanted to do, what he wanted her to do. But they had to work together, and he knew that most of the time men and women did not work together effectively once they were involved. "It's not that I don't find you attractive."

"Then what's the problem?" She touched his cheek gently.

"We have to work together. I think that might become difficult. We'd try not to let it affect us, but at some point it would end up becoming a real problem."

"It wouldn't be a problem for me," she whispered.

Mace laughed softly. "No, it probably wouldn't. You seem to have the ability to handle anything in stride. So let's blame it on me."

"One night. No more after that. I promise. And I would never mention it again."

He breathed deeply again. She was making this so difficult.

Leeny rubbed his chest gently with the back of her hand as she stared up at him. Then she took a slow step backward toward the large bed and began to undress, never allowing her eyes to leave his. Mace watched her seductively remove each article of her clothing, his eyes riveted to every silky stretch of skin that became exposed as the skirt, blouse, and lingerie dropped from her body. Finally she stood before him naked, her hands resting on her upper thighs as she smiled coolly at him. Her fingertips moved almost imperceptibly against her skin as he stared, and then her back stiffened and her eyelids closed for a moment, as if she were deriving an immense amount of physical pleasure just from the slight movement of her fingernails against her thighs.

Leeny slowly moved toward him. She placed her hand on his shoulder while she removed her clear-framed glasses and placed them on the bureau. "As you probably guessed, this is the one thing I take my glasses off for," she said demurely. She took his face in her hands and kissed him on the lips, sucking his lower lip gently into her mouth for a moment. He could feel her breasts rub against him as she kissed him. How could he resist this?

"I can't wait any longer, Mace. With or without you, something's got to happen," she said in a low voice. With that she moved away from him, crawled slowly onto the bed, then turned and lay on her back facing him.

Mace watched as she ran one hand slowly through her hair and allowed the other to move sensually over her breasts and then down past her stomach. It was too much for him. He could resist no longer.

In seconds he had stripped off his clothes and moved onto the bed with her. They kissed tenderly for several moments, and then she moved beneath him. She did not want to wait any longer. Her hand closed about him and gently tugged until he was poised above her.

Mace gazed into Leeny's eyes. He had almost forgotten how intoxicating this could be. "Leeny, I can't give you any kind of commitment."

She gazed back at him, running her ankles slowly against the backs of his calves, then up to his thighs. The action caused him to enter her partially and automatically her back arched, thrusting her breasts up against Mace's broad chest. "Don't talk," she whispered. "I don't want to talk right now. I just want to enjoy you."

"Webster, is Ms. Hunt keeping a close eye on Mr. McLain?"

"Very close," Webster whispered into the phone. He hated

these calls, which were coming much more often now as the deadline approached.

"I'm worried about McLain. From everything I've been able to learn, he's a very bright man. He could uncover what is going on."

"I would know if he were aware of anything and would tell you immediately. And I presume you would take the necessary action."

"I would," the other man said. "But the problem is that your main source of information is Ms Hunt. And we cannot have full faith that she will remain impartial."

"You think she might tell him what she knows?" Webster was incredulous. "Surely she would realize that she was signing both their death warrants."

"I think she might come to find him attractive and be swayed by that."

Webster hesitated. He thought back to the day in his office when she had alluded to the fact that Mace was an attractive man. "I don't think she would be that stupid."

"Just the same, I don't want Mace McLain around any longer than he needs to be. When will he have things in place with the banks, the target properties, and the stocks such that we won't need him anymore? When will he become expendable?"

"Not much longer. A few weeks at most."

"Good."

Webster could hear the other man's satisfaction through the phone. "I really don't think there is any need to worry. But if it makes you feel better, have someone follow him for the last couple of weeks."

"I might. Still, I don't want to risk making him suspicious."

"No, you don't." Webster took a deep breath.

"There is one more thing before I let you go." The man changed the subject.

"Yes?"

"They will need more money in West Virginia soon."

"Oh?"

"Yes. Next week all of the money from here will have made it to the account at Chase. When all nine hundred million dollars has gotten there, I want you to put in the fifty from Walker Pryce, then send a million down to the people in West Virginia at the Charleston National branch in Sugar Grove. Don't wait for Ms. Hunt to close out the fifty million from the third-party investors."

"All right."

"It should be the last time we need to send them anything. Do you understand?"

"Of course." Webster wanted the conversation to be over.

The other man coughed into the phone. "When will Ms. Hunt have the other money? The fifty million."

"She tells me that should be closed out very soon, within two weeks."

"Good."

Webster hesitated. "Will you tell me before you sic the dogs on McLain?"

"Why would you want to know?"

Webster swallowed. It wasn't that he cared about Mace. For all he cared they could chop Mace up and feed him to the sharks when this was all over. He just wanted an early-warning system for himself. He didn't trust them at all. Why should he? "So that I can tell you whether or not he really is expendable."

"I'll make sure to ask." The voice was defiant.

"All right." Webster could only imagine that this was what it must be like to deal with the Mafia. You never felt comfortable. You never felt anything that even came close to comfortable. You just felt fear.

"Good-bye, Lewis."

"Good-bye." Webster's hand shook as he hung up the phone.

Slowly Mace came out of a deep sleep and toward consciousness. He was still groggy, but somehow he had an eerie sense that something wasn't quite right. He rubbed his eyes for several moments, then opened them. In the gray morning light seeping through the thin slit between the drawn curtains, Leeny's face began to come into focus. She was kneeling beside him on the bed, her face just inches from his, staring intently down into his eyes. She did not blink. She did not move at all. She simply stared at him.

"Leeny?" Mace quickly gained full consciousness. "Are you all right?"

She did not respond, nor did she move, remaining statue-still as she continued to stare into his eyes.

"Leeny!" His voice rose, and he brought a hand to her cheek.

Instantly her face moved away from his hand. For several more seconds Leeny stared at him. Then she rose from the bed and slowly walked to the bathroom without a word.

Mouth agape, Mace watched as the bathroom door closed behind her.

Leeny flipped on the light, then leaned over the sink and stared into the mirror. She was a high-priced whore. That was what this amounted to. Nothing more, nothing less. That was what she had become.

Without removing her gaze from the mirror, she reached for the small makeup bag lying on one side of the sink. Her hands shook violently as she dug through the bag's contents until she found the prescription. She withdrew the small vial from the bag, removed five of the tiny green pills, and popped them in her mouth. It wasn't fair what they were making her do. It was hell what they were making her do. How could she have fallen so far so fast?

14

Vice President Andrews gazed out into the gathering darkness from the thirty-sixth floor of the downtown Detroit office building that served as the headquarters for Andrews Industries. He exhaled slowly as he looked over Lake St. Clair, a huge black shape far below him. Things were bad. Andrews Industries— the firm his great-grandfather had founded eighty years ago to supply component parts to the budding auto-manufacturing industry, a firm that had grown in the intervening years to its present five billion dollars in annual revenues, a firm that had enabled the family to live an idyllic lifestyle for eight decades—was in dire need of a large cash infusion. And so was he. He had already spent every penny in his personal accounts on the election campaign. He had planned simply to pull cash out of the company at this stage to fund his bitter battle against Malcolm Becker, as his 30 percent ownership stake allowed him to do. But now he couldn't because the firm was bleeding red ink everywhere. The corporate coffers, which for years had been so full of money that the dividends seemed endless, were suddenly bone dry. This disaster could not have happened at a worse time.

Andrews sneered. Becker. He detested the man. Becker was an opportunist, nothing more. An egomaniac who had gotten lucky with the Wolverine Project and taken advantage of the instant fame that came with its successes to lay claim to the highest office in the land, the office of the president.

Becker didn't know how to run a country, especially one as complicated as the United States of America. Becker knew how to run an army, how to obtain sensitive information, how to be director of the CIA. That was where he should stay: across the Potomac River at the CIA. Andrews chuckled as he thought of Becker hosting a dinner for another country's head of state. It would be ghastly. The man would probably belch and unhitch his belt over dessert.

How in the world was Becker funding his own campaign? Becker's family had limited financial resources. They were blue-collar types, people who might have even worked on the assembly line at one of the seventeen Andrews Industries manufacturing plants around the United States. They couldn't be providing the money. The CIA job certainly didn't pay very much, even at the director level—nowhere near what he needed to fund a national campaign. And Becker had not yet raised a huge pot of cash from backers. That was clear from the digging Andrews's people had done.

So where was Becker coming up with the money to pay for all that television advertising that depicted him as the tough American, the man other governments would cower before? Andrews' eyes narrowed. He was fairly certain he knew. The money was coming from CIA accounts. It was the only answer. This use of government money was completely illegal, but Becker's assistant, the Rat Man Ferris, guarded those accounts so carefully that it was impossible to find out what was going on in them. Still, Andrews was going to find out. He had finally convinced the one man who had the power to unlock them, the one man who could run roughshod over Ferris, to do so: Bob Whitman, president of the United States.

After months of discussion Andrews had finally convinced Whitman that to judge from the size of the Wolverine force and the type and number of weapons purchased for it, Becker must have far outspent the budget he had agreed to for the project at its outset. If that was the case, if Becker had overspent on the Wolverines, he was using money budgeted for other CIA initiatives to fund the Wolverines. Not that Andrews really cared if in fact that was what Becker was doing. All he really cared about was that if initial irregularities were uncovered, the audit of CIA accounts would increase in scope, and the government accountants might discover that Becker was using CIA money to fund his presidential campaign—and probably for a host of other personal reasons as well. If that were uncovered, Becker would be gone from the presidential race, and he, Preston Andrews, would sweep to victory because there was no one else to challenge him.

After all the discussion the president had finally sent over a request for accountability to Becker, along with a serious reduction in the CIA budget. Andrews tried to hold back a smile as he gazed into the Michigan night. He only wished he could have seen Becker's reaction to the memorandum. It would take some time to get into the accounts. Becker and Ferris would stall. But they could hold out for only a few months as long as he and Robin could convince the president to keep pushing. The election was nine months away. That was too much time for Becker to hold out against a president pushing for answers.

He would get Becker. He would continue closing in on Becker until he exposed what he strongly believed was going on across the Potomac at the CIA. Unless Becker somehow found a way to cover up the overspending on the Wolverines. Andrews pressed his hand against the window. Never underestimate Malcolm Becker. The cardinal rule.

"Nice night, isn't it?" Robin Carruthers stood next to Andrews, looking down on the city lights with him. She smiled, then turned from the window and took a seat at the conference room table.

Robin was a wonderful woman, as loyal as they came. Bright, capable, and fairly attractive. She should have settled down with someone long ago, but she had sacrificed everything for him instead. "Yes, it is," he said softly. He moved away from the window and to the seat next to her.

She nodded. "So how are you, Preston?"

"All right, I suppose."

"You seem lost in thought."

Andrews took her hand and patted it gently. He gave her the huge friendly grin that could light up a room. She called it his candidate smile. "I'm fine," he said smoothly. "I'm just a little worried about Andrews Industries. And I'm worried that Becker might find out about the problems here." He smiled again. "But I'll be fine."

Robin took his hand in hers as she had done many times before and began massaging it. The rubbing motion relaxed him. "Do you really think Becker could find out about the problems here? After all, it's a private company."

"He's a spy, isn't he? Supposedly the country's best. He's paid to get information on people like me for the country. There's no reason he can't do it for himself every once in a while. I bet he's already had people through here *and* the accountants' offices. Or he's going to have people go through them. He's very thorough, our friend Mr. Becker."

"Yes, he is." Robin stared at Andrews as she rubbed the skin between his thumb and forefinger. Preston was movie star handsome: tall, dark blond hair that never seemed out of place, perfect teeth, perfect skin, which seemed permanently bronzed, and many different smiles ranging from sincere to mischievous, a smile for every situation. Quite a package. And he was cool under fire. Those smiles weren't just a veneer.

"He'll leak the information to the *Wall Street Journal* and the *New York Times*, and they'll have a field day with it." Andrews continued. "He'll say I can't run my own business; how can the people elect me to run the country? He'll probably try to find improprieties here to show that not only can't I keep my own house in order, but I can't be trusted either. That I steal from my own family, so certainly I'd steal from the people. Or worse."

"But there's nothing to find."

Andrews stared at her for a few moments. Robin was so trustworthy. But she was still a little naive, even after seven years in Washington. However, that naiveté worked to his advantage. He could make her do things other, more cynical people wouldn't. "No, there isn't anything to find," he said firmly. "But Becker might try to manufacture something, to create improprieties out of thin air."

"You'll be fine." She continued rubbing his hand.

"I'm glad *you* have confidence." He glanced down at her hand. "That feels good."

"That's the idea," she said softly without looking up. "Perhaps you need to hire some extra security help around here and alert your accountants to increase theirs too."

"Perhaps." Andrews paused. "What I really need is to get hold of the CIA account records on the Wolverines."

"So that we can see if he's using CIA money to fund his campaign." Robin finished the thought for him. They had been over it many times, and it was almost reflexive for her to say the words.

Andrews laughed. "I've got to stop thinking about that. It's going to drive me crazy."

"Hello, Mr. Vice President." Bob Howitt, president of Andrews Industries, moved into the room. His eyes focused on Andrews' hand as it moved stealthily away from Robin's and then flashed to Andrews' face. "It always seems a little strange to call you Vice President." Howitt laughed uncomfortably. He had been running the company for the family over the past six years and was on the hot seat because of its financial difficulties. "Heck, I remember when you were in college. I was just starting out here. The company was barely five hundred million dollars in sales back then."

The vice president and Robin rose to meet Howitt. The two men quickly shook hands. "You remember my chief of staff, Robin Carruthers." Andrews motioned toward Robin, disregarding Howitt's stab at nostalgia.

"Of course. Nice to see you again, Robin." He took her hand quickly, then let it go.

"Yes." Robin smiled politely. Howitt was short and thin with few distinguishing physical features. She had met him several times before and remembered that he had looked much younger than his fifty-five years. Now he looked as if he were seventy. The family must be raking him over the coals for what was going on, she thought.

"Please sit down, Bob." The vice president's voice was firm, almost unfriendly as he and Robin retook their seats.

"Yes, of course," Howitt whispered as he slid into the chair next to Andrews.

Andrews wasted no time. "How bad is it, Bob?"

Howitt smiled nervously. "No small talk, huh?"

"No." Andrews crossed his arms over his chest.

Howitt made a clicking sound with his teeth as he opened a notebook he had brought into the conference room and laid it across his lap. He rubbed his chin as he scanned the pages. "We are bleeding approximately a million and a half dollars a day in cash, Mr. Vice President. We have drawn almost one-point-four billion dollars under our two-billion-dollar bank facility, and by the end of the second quarter, by June 30, we will have broken several covenants in the loan agreement. We'll also be fully drawn by then unless things get better. All two billion of the bank facility will be outstanding. June is four months away. That seems like a long time, but it will get here faster than we think it will."

"Are the bankers asking questions yet?" Andrews asked.

Howitt shook his head. "Not yet. Not tough questions anyway. They've gotten a look at the preliminary numbers for last year. Those numbers aren't too bad. We sold a couple of small divisions before year-end to raise cash, and we were able to book some capital gains to offset the operating losses as a result. We told the bankers that the operating losses were simply the result of restructurings in several divisions. Bankers seem to buy into the restructuring thing pretty easily as long as it happens only once in a while. But there isn't anything left to sell now. The numbers for the end of this year's first quarter will be pretty grim, the bankers probably won't buy the restructuring thing again, and according to the loan agreement, we have to make those first-quarter numbers available to them by May fifteenth. They'll start asking the tough questions then. In fact they'll probably go ballistic. They won't be able to take any action until we actually break the covenants in June, but they'll be pretty unhappy. Unless of course the family is willing to put some equity money into the company to pay back their loans. Then they'll get happy very quickly."

"How much would the family have to put in?" The vice president's eyes narrowed.

Howitt coughed. "The chief financial officer informs me that the banks will probably require about five hundred million dollars of fresh equity. But they'll ask for a billion. A billion-dollar repayment would cut our annual interest expense by almost a hundred million dollars a year. With some layoffs we might be able to stop the bleeding and break even by the end of next year." He said the last sentence quietly.

"A billion dollars, Bob?" Andrews' voice rose unsteadily. "You must be kidding. I need to take money *out* of the company to fund my campaign, not have to put money *in*. A *billion* dollars? That would be three hundred million dollars to me." The news was not unexpected. Howitt had been telling Andrews that the picture was bad for more than a year. But it was still tremendously unsettling to hear the actual number. Three hundred million.

Howitt swallowed. "I know, I know." He glanced at Robin. "And we here at the company appreciate what you've done over the past year to help out."

Robin glanced quickly at Andrews. What did that mean?

"Look, we're working hard to turn this thing around." Howitt continued.

"Work harder." The vice president's voice was ice cold.

"It's just this damn power train recall at General Motors. That's costing us five hundred thousand a day, and there's nothing we can do about it."

"When will the recall be over? When will you have replaced all the defective parts?"

"Another month."

Andrews gritted his teeth. Howitt had gone to GM too fast with the new power train design. Much too fast. He had told him not to go, but Howitt had gone anyway. Now they were paying the price. He was seething inside but did not let it show. "Fine. Here's what you are going to do, Bob. You are going to keep the bankers at bay. Don't pay too much attention to them. If you do, they'll know something's up. Just keep them away from the books. Do whatever you have to do, but don't let them hear about the fact that this company is bleeding one and a half million dollars a day."

"Yes, sir." Howitt looked at Andrews meekly. He knew what Andrews was thinking. "Do you anticipate that the family will be able to put anything into the company?" He did not want to ask the question, but he had to. The banks would ask, and he had to have an answer.

The vice president shook his head, then glanced at Robin. "Not right away. We are"—he paused—"exploring several different avenues."

"Such as?" Howitt wanted to know exactly what that meant.

"I am going to be meeting with investment bankers in New York very soon. They may be able to help us. They may be able to raise us quite a bit of long-term money."

"Who?" Howitt perked up suddenly. He had been trying to persuade Andrews to allow him to go to the New York moneymen for months, but Andrews would not hear of it. The vice president was petrified that if a couple of people on the Street found out about the company's financial difficulties, the news would be on Bloomberg the next day. Andrews had made it clear that he didn't trust investment bankers. He knew that they would release the information to the press because that action would force the company into naming an adviser, and then the firm that won the advisory mandate could begin accruing its huge fee immediately.

"I am meeting with *the* most senior person at one of the top firms on Wall Street." Andrews thought of the strange-looking man who headed Walker Pryce & Company for a moment. He could not be too specific, but he had to tell Howitt something. The vice president did not want him jumping ship at this point. By all rights he should fire Howitt now. At this meeting, for God's sake. But then the Street would hear that Howitt had been canned and that a new president of Andrews Industries had been named. And the sharks would start smelling blood. That was something that could be disastrous. So Howitt was insulated from harm, ironically as a result of the problem the man had caused himself, Andrews thought.

"Who?"

"Stop with the whos, for Christ's sake. What are you, a damn owl?" He wanted to deflect Howitt away from the question.

"I'm sorry, I just want to see this thing get better."

"We all do." Andrews used a soothing tone. "Trust me, Bob."

"Of course, sir."

"Bob, I want you to start laying people off. Nothing major, just a couple of hundred people here and there. No one here in Detroit and no one at our plants in the small towns. Nowhere that would have a big impact on the economy or in big enough numbers to attract attention. We want no press. None at all. I realize we have never enforced layoffs before, but at this point we have no choice. We have to conserve cash. Do you understand?"

"Yes." Howitt's eyes dropped to the table.

"Well, what are you waiting for?"

Howitt rose, shook the vice president's hand, and moved slowly toward the conference room door.

Andrews rubbed his forehead. A billion dollars to the family. Three hundred million to him. He could feel a headache coming on.

Robin took his right hand and began to massage it again. It would be a difficult flight back to Washington.

"You are certain Schuler will come through with the commitment from Chase?" Webster's eyes burned.

"Almost," Leeny murmured quietly.

"Almost isn't good enough." Webster's awful voice knifed through the air. "We need that commitment as fast as possible. We must be certain Schuler gets us that money."

"I'm doing everything I can do." Leeny was becoming exasperated.

"Are you?"

"Yes," she said firmly. She knew what he was driving at, and the thought disgusted her. Mace McLain was one thing. But the little Chase banker was another.

Webster pointed a long yellow fingernail at her. "I want you to do *absolutely* everything you can do to get the money. Do you understand me?"

She stared at him evenly but said nothing.

A smile slowly enveloped Webster's face. "I'd hate to have to relay the fact that you weren't giving your all for the mission."

Leeny turned away from Webster. She hated him so much.

Vargus watched Tabiq, his second-in-command, as the other man pulled on his gloves. It was cold in the tiny cinder-block–walled office, and they both wore heavy coats. But it was nothing compared with the cold outside. The mountains of West Virginia had been hit with a horrible cold spell. In the past two days the temperature had not risen above ten degrees Fahrenheit.

"What are you saying?" Vargus asked gruffly.

Tabiq hesitated. Vargus was not one to annoy. He would choose his words carefully. "The men have been training hard. They are ready."

"Yes." Vargus increased the intensity of his voice. He sensed insubordination, and there could be none of that.

"How much longer will it be?"

"Are the men becoming impatient? Is that why you are here?"

Again Tabiq hesitated. "A few have asked questions. And you know as well as I that if a few have asked, they all are wondering."

Vargus reached for the bag of sunflower seeds on the small desk. His eyes narrowed. "You tell them it will not be long now." He pushed a handful of seeds into his mouth. "And give them tomorrow off."

Tabiq nodded, then rose from his chair. That would help, but it wouldn't stop all the grumbling. He turned to go.

"One more thing, Tabiq."

Tabiq turned back toward Vargus. "Yes?"

Vargus broke into a toothy grin. "You know those boxes in the shed where we've stored the two bodies?"

"Yes."

"It's twenty cases of vodka. Let them at it tonight."

It was Tabiq's turn to smile. Vargus always had an ace in the hole. Always.

15

ace held open the front door of One if by Land, Two if by
Sea, the popular Greenwich Village restaurant. Rachel moved
smoothly past him through the doorway and into the venerable
dining establishment. He had picked her up a half hour ago in the
limousine and was looking forward to this dinner immensely. Not
only because he had some very good news for her but also because
he had missed her. Broadway Ventures was beginning to consume
him, as he knew it would, and he hadn't had any time to talk with
her, even after class the last few times. Tonight would be a wonderful evening in many ways. He had that feeling.

"Thank you," Rachel said, pausing only long enough at the
doorway to touch his chin with a fingernail.

Mace smelled her subtle perfume as she passed by him. It was
pleasing, and he breathed again, this time more deeply.

Rachel began to remove her ankle-length winter coat, but
Mace moved quickly behind her, taking it by the shoulders, moving it down and off both arms simultaneously.

"You certainly are a gentleman, Mr. McLain," she whispered
over her shoulder.

"Not always." He winked at her.

"What does that mean?"

"Oh, nothing." Mace handed Rachel's coat to the woman who
would check it, then stopped, shook his head, and smiled. She wore

a stylish black dress, cut off the shoulders. It ended well above her knees and clung sexily to her body, accentuating her figure. Sheer black stockings covered her toned legs, and she wore a pair of black suede high heels to match the stockings. Her hair, worn up, revealed the soft skin of her delicate shoulders. "Why do you hide all this underneath those baggy sweaters and jeans you wear to class all the time?"

Embarrassed, Rachel brought a hand to her face to hide a smile. "Can we please get to the table?"

The maître d' led them to a small, cozy table in the back of the room, away from two large parties near the front. It would be quiet here, and it was the table Mace had requested. The man held Rachel's chair, then put the menu and the wine list down at the other place setting for Mace.

"Thank you," Mace said as he slid into the comfortable chair.

The maître d' nodded. *"Bon appétit."* And he was gone.

For an hour and a half they ate, drank, and talked. Rachel did not ask Mace if there was a special reason he had called yesterday and insisted upon the meeting, as he had termed it on the phone, and he did not volunteer a reason or tell her why the "meeting" had become dinner. They did not discuss business or anything remotely related to it. They exchanged details on each other's backgrounds. They exchanged philosophies. They talked politics and religion, and though they did not agree on everything, it did not matter. They were having too good a time.

"Now, tell me about this new project you are working on," Rachel said, finally bringing Walker Pryce into the conversation, "the one you mentioned to me in your office the other day. You said you would tell me about it if I went out to dinner with you." She smiled. "Here I am."

Mace hesitated. It might not be a good idea to tell her too much about the fund.

She reached across the table and touched his hand gently, sensing his hesitation. "I'm trustworthy. You know that."

Of course she was, he thought to himself. She conveyed her sincerity so easily. "Well, okay. But I can't tell you too much."

She nodded and folded her hands before her.

For the next several minutes Mace explained in vague terms the nature of Broadway Ventures—its size, scope, and general objectives.

Rachel listened intently, interrupting to ask several pointed questions during his explanation. When he finished, she shook her head. "I shouldn't be criticizing Lewis Webster because I guess he can decide whether or not to hire me, but the fund seems risky."

Mace pursed his lips several times before answering. "It could work. It could work very well in fact, and Lewis Webster has an uncanny ability to predict swings in markets. That's one of the reasons he is senior partner. But if you noticed hesitation in my voice, I wouldn't deny it. Of course Lewis Webster can make or break my career too. He gave me a direct order to help him on this. So I don't have much of a choice of whether or not to be involved, do I?"

Rachel smiled. "No, I guess not." Her expression slowly changed. "What is Leeny Hunt's role in all this?" She did not want to break the mood, but she had to know.

Mace ignored the hard edge to Rachel's tone. "Leeny is in charge of raising the equity money."

"Can't you do that?"

Mace shook his head. "Webster wanted to raise the money from wealthy families to enable us to keep the whole thing very quiet. I know the institutional money in this country, not the family money. Which reminds me. I shouldn't be telling you any of this."

"You know I won't say a word." She hesitated. She knew she would be pushing with the next question. "Which families?"

"The Stillmans out of Pittsburgh, the Bass brothers, Sam Walton's family, the Rockefellers, and several others."

"That's it?"

"There are others."

"How many others?"

"I think she said she was going to about eight families in all. Maybe ten."

"Just ten? That's all? She's going to raise a billion dollars from ten families?"

Mace nodded.

"That will be difficult."

Mace shrugged. "She's already got circles for three hundred million dollars of it."

Rachel leaned back in her chair. "How much are the Stillmans going to invest?"

"I don't know exactly. She's been pretty closemouthed about it all. But I would say she's expecting a minimum of a hundred million from them. Maybe even two."

"No way," Rachel said quickly. "I know one of their portfolio managers very well as a result of this fund I run for Columbia. The Stillman family's limit is fifty million dollars in any single fund."

Mace shrugged. "I don't know what to tell you. Maybe they are making an exception in this case." What Rachel was saying made sense. Everybody had limits imposed to ensure diversification and as a mechanism to protect against fraud. He didn't have an answer. "Look, Leeny has a good track record. She worked at KKR and then LeClair and Foster. She checks out. And what difference does it make as long as the money is there?"

Rachel crossed her arms over her chest, pouted for a few moments, and then smiled. "I'm sorry. I'm making too big a deal out of it." But she couldn't help herself. Leeny Hunt was the competition. She had sensed that about the other woman in the classroom and in Webster's office. Leeny had attempted to be nice, to come off as a friend. But she had been *too* nice.

The waiter quickly cleared away the plates from the main course. When he finished, Mace leaned back in his chair and stared at Rachel. Her eyes shimmered in the glow of the candlelight.

They were having an even better time than he had anticipated. He shook his head. It was such a shame.

"What are you smiling at?" Rachel's voice was soft.

Mace shrugged as he sipped his coffee. "A very beautiful woman." The red wine had increased his ability to be direct with her—and his desire.

"Thank you." Rachel was not unaware of her beauty. She glanced into her lap and then slowly back up at him. The wine had affected her exactly as it had Mace.

"Yes, a very beautiful woman"—Mace began again as he put down the coffee cup—"who is about to begin a very lucrative career on Wall Street."

She looked at him curiously. There was something strange in his tone. "What are you talking about?"

He leaned forward over the white linen tablecloth. "The results have been tabulated, and the verdict is in."

Rachel leaned over the table as well. "Will you please explain yourself?" But she knew what he was about to say. A thrill coursed through her body.

"Fred Forsythe, head of Human Resources, asked me yesterday to inform you that Walker Pryce will be making you an offer of employment as an associate in our Corporate Finance Department." Mace paused. "A very generous offer, I might add." He glanced about the tastefully decorated restaurant. "I thought this might be a nice atmosphere for you to hear the news."

Rachel reached across the small table and clasped his left arm with both her hands. Her fingernails dug into his skin. "You jerk," she whispered. "You made me wait this entire time before you told me." But she could not hide the smile enveloping her face.

Mace took her hands in his. "But now we have something to celebrate." He glanced at his watch. "If I had told you at the beginning of dinner, you might be over the excitement by now, and then you'd tell me that you have to go home to watch over that portfolio of yours. Now I can keep you out a little longer, ply you with more wine, and get your acceptance to our offer in writing tonight so you don't have a chance to call the other places and get them to up their offers."

"You can keep me out as late as you want," she whispered.

"What?"

"Nothing. I need more wine." She took her hands from his and reached for her still half-full glass. Her knees were weak.

"Do you want to hear specifics, or should we wait?"

Rachel shook her head. "I don't want to wait. Tell me now."

Mace took a sip from his glass, then replaced it on the table. Suddenly his expression turned solemn. "First of all, you must keep every detail of your offer completely confidential. We are not like other firms, which make equal offers to all their first-year people. You will be the highest-salaried first-year associate at the firm. And if you perform up to expectations, you will earn the highest bonus as well."

She gazed at him over the glass. The highest-paid first-year associate at Walker Pryce. At Walker Pryce, where the blood was as blue as blue got. It was incredible.

"You must keep all this completely to yourself. Do you understand?"

She nodded, but she could barely focus on him.

"Okay." He lowered his voice. "Well, your annual salary will be one hundred thousand dollars. And you have the opportunity to earn up to twice your salary in bonus in the first year, which I have no doubt you will do. Of course that multiple will increase quickly after the first year. You could be earning as much as half a million dollars by your third year, maybe more. It really depends on how badly you want it. Of course we will formalize all this in a letter."

Rachel felt tears welling in her eyes. A half million dollars. She thought of the struggle and sacrifice of the last ten years: of Queens College, then Merrill Lynch, and now Columbia; of how she had enjoyed almost no social life at all since high school. But now all the sacrifices seemed worthwhile. Her life was finally coming together. She would never have to worry about money again.

Neither would her family. They had suddenly crossed over the line into the world of the haves, and she was the catalyst. Little Rachel. The strange one who liked to read the stock page of the newspaper, not the style section, as her older sisters did. Her family would not believe it, but she would show them the letter from Walker Pryce, and they all would begin crying together. Even her stepfather, who, since marrying her mother when Rachel was four, had worked his entire life at the welding job on the docks, earning barely enough to keep a roof over their heads and food on the table. He had steadfastly supported her when the others had laughed at her dreams. He had been there for her every step of the way, and she would never forget it.

"Are you okay?" Mace was smiling at her. He understood what she was feeling. The world had suddenly changed radically. Anything was attainable now.

"I'm fine." Rachel picked up her napkin and dabbed her eyes for a moment. "Stop smiling at me." She threw the napkin at him.

He caught it easily. "I take it you will accept our offer."

Of course she would. It was well more than Merrill Lynch was offering her to return to its sweatshop. And it was Walker Pryce. But those weren't the only two reasons she would accept the offer. She leaned over the table again. She had to ask. It was time. There was no reason to wait any longer. "What about us?" Her voice dropped to a whisper.

Mace stared into the azure eyes. What about us? He had thought through that question so many times today, anticipating the fact that he would have to come face-to-face with his feelings as well. What if their relationship did not work out and there were bad feelings between them? She would be uncomfortable from the first day she walked through the Walker Pryce front door. What if it did work and she spent too much time doting on him and ignoring her work? What if she didn't achieve the big bonus, and *then* they broke apart? That would be an even bigger disaster. But he cared. He paused, torn between the alternatives. But the answer was clear. He couldn't do this to her.

"Us?" he asked innocently. He saw the terrible hurt in her eyes immediately. It was cruel, but there was no other way. This was for the best. She would thank him later. Working at Walker Pryce was the opportunity of a lifetime for her, and she had to stay focused.

"Yes, us."

"I don't know what you mean, Rachel."

She shook her head slowly, unable to comprehend. "Look, I'm not an idiot. I know there's been something going on between us. I've felt it. I know you have too." Her eyes pleaded with him. "I mean, tonight was wonderful. And you said you wanted to keep me out late."

"I want to make sure you join Walker Pryce. You are our number one recruit. It's a big win for me if you join." He looked at her evenly. "My stock at the firm goes way up if you join." This was so difficult.

"So this is about your stock at the firm going up? But I thought . . . I was sure . . . I . . ." She turned away. The words had spilled out into the open, and now she regretted them. She could see in his face that there was nothing there for her. He had simply been a friend, but that was all. "I'm sorry."

"Rachel . . ."

"No. God, I've acted terribly. You have made a wonderful offer of employment to me tonight, and look how I've acted."

Mace felt a sharp pang in the pit of his stomach. He wanted so badly to make her understand. Perhaps it was worth a try. "Rachel, you are a beautiful woman, and I would love to—"

"No." She stood up. "I'll be back in a minute. I need to freshen up."

"Of course." Mace stood immediately and helped her with her chair. He watched her move away quickly toward the front of the restaurant, then sank back down into his chair as she disappeared around the corner. He had not wanted to hurt her. He had wanted to tell her the truth, about how much he cared. But this way would be far better for her in the long run. He refilled his wineglass and took a long sip.

Leeny had been waiting in the small doorway of the apartment building across Barrow Street from One if by Land for three hours. It was a tiny street snaking through Greenwich Village, the lower Manhattan neighborhood that was so different from any other part of New York City. But Leeny did not care about the aesthetics of Greenwich Village at this point. She was concerned about Rachel Sommers, who was becoming a problem. Mace had begun to develop that look in his eyes when he talked about her, and that was becoming more and more frequent now. Rachel was the reason Mace had kept his distance from Leeny since the night in New Orleans. Leeny had no doubt of that.

Men usually could not resist Leeny's beauty and charm. Most of them were like the sniveling little banker John Schuler. They fell all over themselves in an instant to be with her. If she wanted it to happen, it happened. She had that kind of power over men. She had been able to lure Mace into bed as well, right on schedule. He had whispered the words about no commitment as he had moved against her body in New Orleans, but confident that she could make him want her constantly, she had discounted the words. But it hadn't happened that way. Mace hadn't mentioned the tryst once.

He was supposed to have fallen for her by now. At least that had been the plan. So that she could keep a very close eye on everything he was doing, particularly as they neared the end of the project. The man in Washington was disappointed. That was how Webster had put it. Disappointed that she could not lure Mace McLain into a tawdry relationship. Disappointed that Mace had not moved in with her, or she with him. Disappointed that she was not an accomplished enough whore. She slammed her fist against the brick wall of the doorway. Wasn't that what it came down to? Being a whore.

Leeny felt her throat tighten. Don't think of it from that perspective now. You are simply acting out of self-preservation. She glanced at the restaurant door. An elderly couple had emerged, but there was still no sign of Rachel or Mace.

She had advised Webster not to extend the offer of employment to Rachel. It would only ensure that Rachel remained in the picture. But Webster had overruled Leeny. Rachel had impressed everyone she had seen during her day of interviews at Walker Pryce. Everyone had recommended that the firm extend this woman a job offer immediately. Mace knew that. Rachel had to be extended an offer.

Suddenly the restaurant door swung open, and Rachel stepped onto the sidewalk. Leeny moved back into the shadows of the garden-level doorway, waiting for Mace to appear. To her surprise Mace did not appear right away. Rachel looked up and down the street, then waved to a cab waiting a half block away. The cab roared to life and squealed up the block to meet her. Rachel threw herself onto the backseat and the hack sped away.

Leeny moved slightly out of the shadows. What the hell was that all about? Mace should have given her the offer, and after three hours of drinking Rachel ought to have been happy. They should have left together arm in arm. They should have gotten in that cab together. Her lip curled involuntarily.

Several minutes passed, and the door opened again. Again Leeny moved back into the shadows. Mace stepped onto the sidewalk beneath the streetlamp and looked up and down Barrow Street several times. Finally his shoulders slumped, and he moved back into the restaurant.

Leeny leaned back against the brick. Rachel had ditched him at the restaurant. That was the only explanation for what she had just seen. She smiled. Perhaps he had pushed himself on to her a little

too obviously after making the offer. Perhaps he had linked the job
to a night of sex, and Rachel had reacted fiercely, storming out.

Leeny let out a long breath. This was certainly a positive devel-
opment for the project. Still, she would follow Mace wherever he
went tonight, just to make certain he didn't rendezvous with his little
student at some point.

The ether-soaked rag wrapped tightly around Liam's face
pressed hard against the old guard's nose and mouth. He awoke
immediately from his fitful sleep and attempted to break the viselike grip of his attacker as soon as he realized where he was. But his
efforts proved futile. The chemical rushed into his nasal passages as
he sputtered and coughed, weakening him instantly, rendering him
incapable of breaking free of the man's powerful hold. The ether
did not work quickly, but the attacker was incredibly strong
and did not release the wet rag from Liam's face for a full minute.
Finally the guard's eyes fluttered shut.

The invader let Liam's body fall gently to the floor of the guard
tower, then secured his hands behind his back with a length of ny-
lon rope and stuffed the ethered rag into his mouth. Next he
moved to the window of the tower, pulled his flashlight from his
belt, and flicked it on and off three times into the pitch-black
night.

Immediately the assault team began pouring into the compound. The front gate of the Nyack Nuclear Generating Facility
had already been neutralized, and as the men headed for the front
entrance of the huge building, they realized that what they had
been told over and over—that the defensive force of old cops had
no chance against them—was absolutely true. Dressed in black
from head to toe, the invaders did not hesitate when they reached
the main doors. As they burst through the door, they sprayed the
three men dressed in the neat blue uniforms behind the desk with a
splattering fire. The guards fell backward over their chairs to the
floor.

Two of the attackers moved quickly behind the desk and threw several switches, opening the huge metal doors and allowing them access to the entire nuclear power plant. There were many places they could have gone inside the massive structure, but they had only one target: the brain of the building, the control room. Once they controlled the brain, they could do anything they wanted to the body.

They rushed down the hallway, following their leader toward the control room, running almost in unison, the floor tile cracking beneath their thick boots. Suddenly they turned right, then just as sharply left into another hallway. A technician emerged from a doorway. She did not even have the chance to scream before she was gunned down in a murderous fire.

Down one flight of steps and around another corner. Two more people, this time off-duty engineers, were gunned down. One reached for a general alarm as he staggered against the wall, but he was pasted with another volley of fire before his fingers could reach the button. He collapsed to the floor.

Around one more corner, and they were in front of the huge, highly polished stainless steel control room doors. The doors were locked, but the leader had a special password, one only he and five other people in the world knew, that would gain them entrance into the brain. The leader entered the long string of numbers—twenty-six digits in all—into the lock in perfect sequence. If he had not, if he had missed one number, four extra bars inside the great doors would have slid automatically and smoothly into place, preventing entrance into the control room by anyone for twenty-four hours. There were no second chances with the password. No one could have entered or exited, but the people in the control room would have been safe. More important, so would the facility.

If the leader had entered a wrong number, in addition to the bars sliding into place, four things would have occurred instantaneously. A piercing alarm would have screamed through the control room, alerting those inside that a wrong sequence had been entered into the lock and that unwanted intruders might be just outside the door. Another alarm would have gone off in the Nyack Police Station and at the Fifty-fourth Street precinct in Manhattan, alerting the authorities to the danger. Finally the control rods in the nuclear core would have slid into place automatically, shutting off any nuclear reaction in the core for twenty-four hours. All these things happened instantly unless the string of twenty-six numbers was entered absolutely correctly or the people inside the control room opened the doors.

Slowly but steadily the massive stainless steel doors opened, the gears humming as they strained to move the several tons of metal. As soon as the doors were far enough apart for a man to fit through, the attackers began spilling into the brain. In a matter of seconds twenty of them had moved into the space just inside the doors, securing the room that controlled every important aspect of the facility. They stood there for several moments, rifles pointed menacingly at the unarmed engineers. The engineers did not move. They did not dare to. The room—dark except for the blue, green, red, and yellow lights that flashed from the gigantic control board— was still, except for the heavy breathing of the attackers.

After what seemed like several minutes, the man in charge of the control room on this graveyard shift, Richard Steele, began moving toward the leader of the assault troops from the far side of the large room. Steele moved with a sense of purpose mixed with agitation.

Finally he reached the man who had opened the doors with his twenty-six-digit combination, grabbed the man's rifle, then turned and sprayed the control room with paint canisters, screaming loudly as he fired. The other engineers in the room, as well as the attackers, ducked as the tiny pellets splattered the walls. In seconds the clip was spent, and he hurled the gun to the floor. It clattered against the tile until it slammed into the base of a central processing unit.

"God damn it!" the little man screamed at the top of his lungs again. "I keep telling them that the security around here isn't worth shit! But they won't listen to me." The words echoed in the huge room. Slowly Steele turned toward the attackers' leader, who was removing his black ski mask. "We've got to do something," Steele whispered.

Jim Dolan, the off-duty senior engineer at Nyack who was acting as the terrorist leader in tonight's simulation, nodded at Steele. "Yes, we do." It was all he could say.

John Schuler moved quickly on the park side of Central Park South, across Fifty-ninth Street from the New York Athletic Club, the collar of his long winter coat pulled up about his face, the brim of his hat pulled down over his eyes. He had not taken these precautions as a result of the winter cold, but for quite another reason.

It was stupid, he thought as he walked east toward the opening into the park. No, insane. He was an executive vice-president with one of the biggest banks in the world, with a good chance of attaining an even higher title—members of the board had expressed this belief to him in the past year—and here he was sneaking around New York City like some hoodlum. But he had never known a woman as beautiful as Leeny Hunt, and she was making herself available to him.

Fear and exhilaration flashed through Schuler's body as he turned left and ducked through an opening in the stone wall into the park. He followed the narrow asphalt path for fifty feet, then turned right down a set of stairs toward a lonely pond tucked into the southeast corner of Central Park. The path became dark as the streetlights disappeared. Tall trees rose on either side of him, blocking out all but only the tops of the tallest buildings on Fifty-ninth Street. He could barely hear the sounds of the cars now. He was alone. It was amazing how desolate Central Park could become just a few feet inside the stone wall surrounding it on this side of the park. Schuler slowed his pace. It would not take long to make contact.

"Coke, smoke, anything you want." The whisper startled Schuler. It came from beneath a large pine tree to his right.

For several moments Schuler focused on the tree until he could make out a lone figure leaning against the trunk. Finally he nodded at the figure. The man pushed off the tree and moved over the thin snow cover toward Schuler. Schuler caught his breath. If this was a cop, it would all be over quickly. His career would explode like Fourth of July fireworks, for everyone to see, splashed all over the business and society pages of the *New York Times*.

The drug dealer stopped several feet in front of Schuler, eyeing him through the gloom. "What you want?"

Schuler swallowed. "Cocaine. Can you help me?"

Schuler saw the other man's white teeth as he smiled at Schuler's request. "Don't you worry, my man. I've got all the help you need."

16

M alcolm Becker and Willard Ferris sat smugly in the large red
leather chairs in front of the vice president's desk. This wasn't
going to be easy, Andrews thought. The president had directed Andrews and Becker to coordinate an award ceremony to
honor several Wolverines who had performed with exceptional
bravery in the Los Angeles incident. The purpose of this morning's
meeting was to begin planning the event. The ceremony was something that should have been arranged by assistants on each staff.
This meeting shouldn't have had to occur. But the president had
called Becker to inform him of the intended proceedings with respect to the Wolverines, making it clear that Andrews was to be the
host of the event, and Becker had required this face-to-face meeting
to set the agenda.

Robin sat in a chair to the side of Andrews's desk. The vice
president tried to elicit some sort of subtle response from her but
received none. Her face remained impassive.

Andrews rubbed his eyes. He knew why Becker had required
this meeting. As always there was a hidden agenda with this man.
But Becker was about as subtle as the Washington Monument, and
therefore few things about him could truly be termed hidden. It
was all part of his direct, take-no-prisoners attitude that seemed to
play so well with the general populace, but that would go over like
hillbillies at a black-tie ball with the Washington establishment if

Becker were actually elected president. You didn't get things done in Washington with a direct, can-do attitude. You got things done by scratching the right person's back while he scratched yours. That was why it was called politics.

If Becker were elected, four years of gridlock would ensue. But of course the American people didn't understand that. They actually believed that an outsider could get things accomplished here. Andrews shook his head and laughed as he continued to rub his eyes. They were so naive.

"What's so funny, Preston?" Becker asked. His tone was stern.

"Oh, I was just thinking of a good joke I heard yesterday, Malcolm." The vice president stopped rubbing his eyes and allowed his hands to fall to his lap.

Becker leaned forward in the leather chair. "I don't have time for jokes, Preston."

Andrews nodded. "I forgot, you're the man with no time for anything but saving the country from every evil empire on the face of the planet. A joke might hinder your ability to solve all the world's problems by tomorrow."

Becker inhaled through clenched teeth. "I'm doing a pretty good job of that from my office over at the CIA. But I can't solve *all* the world's problems until I move into the White House. Which ought to be in about another year."

Ferris snickered.

Andrews smiled the candidate smile. He was not going to be dragged into a verbal sparring battle. He would try to remain above that.

"Perhaps we should begin planning the award ceremony for the Wolverines." Robin broke in. She turned toward Ferris. "You were going to bring a specific list of the men who are to be honored at the—"

"We'll get to that, missy," Becker interrupted. He grabbed the huge lobe of his right ear with several fingers and pulled it a few times.

Andrews watched Becker play with his ear. He had seen that action several times in previous meetings, and it always seemed to precede a provocative comment.

Becker pointed at the vice president. "I want to know who or what is really behind the memo I received from President Whitman the other day."

"What memo?" Andrews asked evenly.

"Don't play coy with me, Preston." In a show of disrespect, Becker refused to address Andrews as Mr. Vice President, just as Andrews refused to address Becker as General. "The memo outlining cuts in the CIA budget over the next three years. The memo that requests a full accounting of all expenditures on the Wolverines since the program's inception."

"Oh, that memo." Andrews could have claimed ignorance of the memo, but he didn't. He wanted Becker to know of his involvement, that he could play his own mind games with opponents.

"Yes, that memo," Becker growled. "I want to know why you put the president up to it."

"Who says I put the president up to it?" Andrews glanced at Robin with a slight smile. "Did you tell Mr. Becker that I did that?"

Robin shook her head innocently.

"I say you did." Becker was exasperated.

"Oh," Andrews said quietly. He stared at Becker for a few moments, waiting.

"So why did you put Whitman up to it? I want to know."

Andrews' expression became serious. "I'm not saying I did put him up to it." No one ever admitted anything in Washington, even if he was filmed doing it. "But let's look at why the president might want some accountability." He broke into the anonymously aggressive mode all polished politicians used to attack an opponent. "We know that the president is under pressure to cut government spending, and we know the president has a whole legion of cost accountants working for him over at the Office of Management and

Budget. Let's just say they started putting together some rough estimates on what the CIA has spent on the Wolverines, and the president became concerned when he looked at the numbers: concerned that the CIA was spending too much on the Wolverines and not enough on other things; concerned that the Wolverines had become too much of a pet project for someone at the CIA; concerned that in his drive to attain the Oval Office he might be compromising the country's security as a result." Andrews paused. He was becoming too animated. He had to maintain his composure. He did not want Becker to see how personal this had become.

Becker's eyes narrowed. It was time to turn the tables. He was burning up inside, but he managed to begin quietly. "And let's suppose that somewhere high up in the president's administration there was an individual who had designs on the White House himself. Who thought he was going to have a clear path to the Oval Office after his president finished two terms. Who thought there were no real rivals to a position he covets so much he will go to any length to attain it. Any length." Becker said the words ominously.

As if by reflex, Andrews moved back in his chair slightly. Robin noticed the small movement.

"Then on the horizon a challenger appears," Becker continued. "At first this challenger doesn't seem to be a real threat. But his popularity grows. Suddenly the two men are in a dead heat, but the challenger has the momentum. Seems to me that person in the administration might have an ax to grind. Seems to me he might go sniffing around where he has no business sniffing."

"Trying to find something that isn't there." Ferris finished the anonymous rebuttal.

Andrews swallowed hard. The blood pounded in his brain. He shouldn't say what he was thinking. They were playing a political war game, one in which Becker was proving to be a worthy adversary. So far neither had broken any rules of engagement. They had tested each other, and he should leave it at that. Let it settle back to a benign discussion of the award ceremony. But there was always a time in a battle when one of the players stepped up the level of competition just to see what the other had, and as controlled as Andrews was, he was nothing if not competitive.

Andrews began to speak, then stopped. Always think before you speak. Always take that last second in moments such as this to make certain you are committed to what you are about to say. Becker had come here for battle. He must have known what Andrews would say, so he must be holding something in reserve. Let it go, Andrews thought.

But he couldn't. "The president might wonder how someone was funding his campaign too." The words hung in the office air for several moments. It was a calculated risk. It was something Becker might not have been expecting, and it might throw him off stride. Andrews was playing his hand for all to see, but sometimes that was the best strategy. Sometimes a frontal assault like this so totally devastated the other player that he wilted and left the game quietly. Now Becker knew that Andrews was not just looking for mismanagement of funds at the CIA. He was looking for fraud. The stakes had been raised immeasurably.

Robin coughed, and Ferris moved uncomfortably in his chair. But Andrews and Becker continued to stare at each other steadily. Hatred permeated the room.

Becker forced a smile. "People might wonder about that person in the president's administration too. If they gave it half a thought."

Andrews felt his pulse quicken. What the hell did that mean? Suddenly he thought about his rule never to underestimate Becker. Had he? "What are you talking about?"

Becker inhaled slowly. "People might wonder how he was funding *his* campaign." His voice was calm.

Robin squeezed the arm of her chair. She wanted to break in. But that would make it appear that she was defending Andrews directly. The rules of this engagement did not allow for that.

Andrews said nothing.

"Sure, he and his family are supposed to have huge personal net worths," Becker went on.

"More money than God," Ferris said with a sneer.

Becker chuckled. "Yes, more money than God. But things are not always as they appear." He paused, waiting for Andrews to blunder in, to defend himself so vehemently in the process that he indicted himself.

But the vice president said nothing. He was polished at the game as well. Even under direct enemy fire.

"His family's huge business might not be performing as well as people think." Becker continued. "In fact it might be in the *shitter*." His normally loud voice increased even further in its intensity as he emphasized the last word of the sentence. He turned to Robin. "Please excuse me, Ms. Carruthers." He was too polite in his apology.

Robin showed no emotion, but inwardly she bristled.

"The company might be bleeding badly, so badly that simply funding the campaign became secondary. A more pressing concern might be a corporate bankruptcy. Worse still would be a personal bankruptcy. And that could be a real possibility if someone had too much of that massive net worth tied up in the company, and if a man saw his fortune and his political future crumbling before his eyes just as he was about to achieve the highest office in the land, he might be willing to do almost anything to save himself. Almost anything."

Andrews sat silently, wondering how much the man knew and how much was simply a guess on his part. But the reality was that he knew *something*. "Of course, if that company were privately held, it would be very difficult for anyone to know the truth about its financials." It was a lame response. Andrews knew this, but he had to say something.

Becker waved a hand in front of his face. "Of course it would be." He and Ferris exchanged a well-rehearsed glance.

Andrews did not want this to go any further. "Yes, well, this is all interesting speculation, but I think we ought to get back to reality." The vice president pulled his chair to the desk, a subtle signal that the discussion was over and they needed to get to work.

"There's just one more thing, Preston." Becker pulled his earlobe again vigorously. Suddenly the veins beneath his short scalp hair became quite visible.

Andrews glanced up at the adversary. He didn't like the way Becker was pulling so hard at his ear. "Yes?"

"The CIA lost a man down in Central America recently, down in Honduras," Becker said, "a man named Carter Guilford." He shook his head and made a sad face. "A terrible story really. Carter was a good man with a nice wife and a beautiful family. I met them several times. But somehow he lost his way. He died in a plane crash on a remote jungle runway alongside a drug runner, a member of one of Colombia's most powerful cartels."

"What has this got to do with anything?" Andrews' jaw was set. The man was relentless.

Becker ignored the question and went on. "Our sources tell us that Guilford was working with the cartel, providing them with highly sensitive information about the efforts of the CIA and the Drug Enforcement Agency to stop drug running. The information allowed the cartel to avoid law officials and to ship much more cocaine into the United States than any other cartel. They paid him a lot of money for the information. A lot of money. Some reports we have put the payments to him at as much as two hundred million dollars. The actual amount could be more. Of course we can't find the money anywhere."

"So what?" Andrews hissed.

"Well, I know how Guilford was able to get information about the CIA's activities to stop the drug runners, but I don't know how he got information on the DEA. They are very secretive, almost as secretive as we are."

"I don't get the point." Andrews swallowed.

Becker hesitated for several moments. "It's just that we were able to recover some of Guilford's personal effects from the crash. One of those items was a notebook, a date book." Becker hesitated again. The office was deathly still. He gave his ear one more giant tug. "There was an entry in it about a meeting with you a short time ago."

Robin's gaze shot to Andrews. What was that about? She was breathing quickly. She knew this man Preston Andrews, didn't she? He was beyond reproach, wasn't he?

Becker scratched his head. "Preston, aren't you heavily involved with the Drug Enforcement Agency? Hasn't that been one of your pet projects, as you like to call them, during your tenure as vice president?"

Andrews stood. "Get out." He did not raise his voice. "Now. My staff will organize the ceremony for the Wolverines."

Becker, Ferris, and Robin stood also. Becker nodded. "Okay, I guess we've worn out our welcome now," he said, smiling at Ferris. He began striding toward the door with Ferris in tow. At the doorway he turned back toward Andrews and Robin. "Preston"—his voice dropped—"don't fuck with me." Without another word he and Ferris were gone.

Andrews stared at the empty doorway. He was livid, but somehow he maintained his composure. He could not let Robin see him explode. If she did, she might suspect something more than she already must, and he needed her now more than ever.

He tried to clear his mind but couldn't. Obviously Becker was going to come after him with everything he had or could manufacture.

Slowly Robin moved from her chair to a position directly in front of Andrews' desk. She leaned over it, placed both hands on the polished wood, and stared into Andrews' vacant eyes. Finally he focused on her. "I want to know who that man was in your room at the Doha Marriott," Robin said. "And I want to know now."

Andrews stared back, eyes not blinking. He said nothing.

*   *   *

"Good afternoon, Kathleen." John Schuler rose as Leeny and Mace entered his large office. He moved out from behind his desk to greet them as his secretary closed the door. "I appreciate your coming over." Schuler took Leeny's hand gently as they came together in the center of the room.

Leeny smiled slyly. "It's no problem, John," she said in her honey-smooth voice. "You have no idea how far I'm willing to go for a billion-dollar underwriting commitment from the Chase Bank." She paused. "By the way, please call me Leeny."

Mace glanced up quickly, as if a warning bell had just gone off.

Schuler nodded, hoping he correctly understood the implication of how far she might go. "Yes, well, good." He let her hand go slowly, then shook Mace's hand. "Hello, Mace," he said brusquely.

"Good afternoon, John." Mace laughed to himself. He could only imagine what thoughts raced through Schuler's mind as Leeny implied how far she might go for a billion dollars from Chase. Mace had seen that desirous leer pass over the little man's face for a moment. It didn't matter anyway. Leeny wouldn't actually go to bed with this runt of a man. She'd make him think she would, but she wouldn't actually do it. She didn't need to.

"Would you care for some coffee?" Schuler motioned toward the tray positioned in the sitting area of the office. On it were two pots of coffee, soft drinks, and snacks.

"Thank you, John. I think I will," Leeny said. She and Schuler moved toward the refreshments.

Mace did not go to the tray, but instead moved to the office window, which overlooked the East River and Brooklyn beyond. It was a gorgeous, cloudless February afternoon. The sky was a deep blue. The color of Rachel's eyes, he thought, as he looked across the river toward Brooklyn. Perhaps that was where she had gone after leaving him at the restaurant. Perhaps she had headed home to Brooklyn to forget about him. He had called her apartment at Columbia several times over the weekend but received no answer. And he did not know how to reach her in Brooklyn. The four

Sommerses listed in Brooklyn claimed not to know a Rachel when he had called.

Across the river the mass of buildings stretched toward the horizon as far as he could see. What an idiot he had been. He should have explained the situation to her and treated her like the mature adult she was. There was just one problem with that. If he had started to explain to her how he really felt, he would not have been able to resist trying to initiate a relationship with her. He suddenly realized how truly attracted to her he was.

Mace turned away from the window. Schuler and Leeny seemed to be standing just a little too close together as they poured coffee, and they seemed awfully comfortable as they conversed. It wasn't possible. It was simply his imagination. She would never do that to close the deal.

Schuler moved slightly away from Leeny when he noticed Mace watching. "Why don't we sit down?" He motioned toward the long couch and chairs of the office sitting area.

Mace nodded, and the three sat down, Schuler and Leeny on the couch and Mace in one of the chairs.

"So, John, you called us." Leeny put her coffee cup down on the end table as she waited for the liquid to cool.

"Yes." He began in a deep executive vice-president voice. "I wanted to bring you up-to-date with respect to Chase's consideration of underwriting the billion-dollar revolver for Broadway Ventures." He spoke directly to Leeny, as if Mace were not even in the room, not wanting to miss a moment looking at her beautiful face, not wanting to miss any reaction she might have to what he was saying.

Mace smiled. Schuler had gone off the deep end. He was trying to sound official, trying to maintain some mystery about whether or not the bank would commit to do the deal by starting off with the "bring you up-to-date" routine. But he was completely under Leeny's spell.

"And?" Mace prompted Schuler.

Still Schuler did not glance in Mace's direction. "I have discussed this opportunity thoroughly with our chairman, our president, our EVP of credit, and the head of syndications." He paused. His expression was serious.

"Well, don't keep us in suspense, John." Leeny reached across the couch and touched Schuler's knee.

"I think that after a lot of discussion we are ninety-nine percent of the way there." Schuler broke into a huge smile.

Leeny brought her hands to her mouth, then grabbed Schuler's leg again. "Oh, my God, that's wonderful. You are incredible."

Mace noticed the Georgia accent creeping into her voice again, the "southern belle, oh, aren't you an incredible provider, I'll do anything for you" accent.

Schuler's hand fell to Leeny's for a moment, then away. "There are a few more details to discuss."

"Of course, of course," Leeny gushed.

"Any drawings under the facility will be contingent upon a minimum of a billion dollars' worth of equity subscriptions being signed and executed." Schuler continued. "And the money being in the bank. I know sometimes you investment bankers don't make the investors actually put cash in the account. But in this case we would require that it would all actually be there in the account before we would lend a dime." He seemed slightly uncomfortable as he said the last sentence, as if he expected a problem with this requirement.

"Why, certainly, we'd expect nothing less in this case," Leeny said.

Mace did not miss Schuler's glance toward her hands, and for a moment the thought of her stretched out beautifully before him on the large bed in the New Orleans hotel room flashed through his mind. Then he remembered how she had been staring at him in the morning as he had awakened, how she had moved to the bathroom and back without a word, how she hadn't mentioned the episode once, as he hadn't either.

Schuler relaxed at her reaction, as if a great weight had been lifted from his shoulders. "But all that being said, I think we will probably be able to commit to this transaction sometime tomorrow." He hesitated. "If there aren't any unforeseen problems."

"I can't imagine there will be." Leeny's accent was becoming thicker by the word.

Poor man, Mace thought. Schuler really thinks he is going to get something from this beautiful creature.

"Well, as I said, there are a few details to attend to. I'd like to go over them now."

Mace and Leeny nodded.

For the next hour they discussed the bank's concerns and how best to structure the transaction so that not only would Chase be able to sell the paper to other banks and reduce its billion-dollar exposure quickly, but the terms and conditions would as well meet Walker Pryce's criteria and allow Mace and Leeny to do what they wanted to do without being unduly restricted.

Finally, after the last point had been hammered out, Schuler leaned back on the sofa. "I think we can live with all that." He groaned as he stretched. "But I can't guarantee anything until tomorrow." He smiled at Leeny.

Mace checked his watch: almost five o'clock. He needed to get back to Walker Pryce to review some of the stock valuations the two associates from the M&A Department had come up with. And he wanted to try Rachel again. He hoped she had gotten back from class by now. "I think we'd better get going, Leeny." Mace rose from the chair.

Leeny glanced quickly at Mace, then at Schuler. "Oh." She hesitated for a moment. "Why don't you go ahead back to Walker Pryce without me?"

Mace paused. Schuler had reached for what had to be a very cold cup of coffee and was burying his face in it. "Okay. But I thought we were going to go over the stock valuations from the associates."

"Right, well, bring them on the plane with you tomorrow. I'll look at them then."

Mace hesitated. "Do you want me to have the driver swing by your place and pick you up on the way to the airport tomorrow morning?" He suddenly realized that she was going to give Schuler what he wanted, and for no reason. She must have known that Schuler was going to get this deal approved. It probably already was approved, for Christ's sake, and he was just holding back. All of Schuler's bluster about not knowing for certain until tomorrow was just that: bluster. She didn't have to do this.

Leeny shook her head quickly. "No, I'll meet you at the gate."

He watched her for a few moments. She seemed sad, despondent almost. "Are you sure you want to do that?" He tried to force the real meaning of his words into his tone. "You don't have to."

She gazed back at him for several seconds before answering. "Yes, I do," she said, the picture of the man in Washington clear in her mind.

17

"Good afternoon, the Stillman Company." The woman's pleasant voice filtered softly through the telephone to her ear.

Rachel was tired, and the gentle voice seemed so soothing. It was one of those voices that could put you to sleep in an instant. "Is Bradley Downes there?"

"May I tell Mr. Downes who is calling?"

"Yes, it's Rachel Sommers."

"Just a moment, please."

The line clicked and was silent for several moments. Rachel enjoyed the silence. She didn't like the way most places played music or had you listen to news while you were on hold these days.

As she waited for Downes, she considered the tiny studio apartment that had been her home for the last two years. It was barely big enough for a bed and a sofa. Not anymore, she thought. The letter from Walker Pryce had been delivered this morning by messenger. She smiled sadly. Mace felt something for her. He had to. But he was holding back for some reason. Maybe that reason was Leeny Hunt.

"Rachel?"

"Hi, Bradley." She used her softest voice and his full first name because she knew he liked that. And she needed information. Bradley was one of several portfolio managers who looked after the huge net worth of the Stillman family of Pittsburgh, one of the

wealthiest families in the country. The family's worth was esti-
mated to be in excess of four billion dollars.

Rachel had met Bradley Downes in New York at an analyst
presentation she was attending to hear about a stock she had put
the Columbia fund into. He was there representing the Stillman
family, which also owned shares of the company, a significantly
greater amount than Columbia's. They had become friends during
a break and spoke once or twice a month now by phone. Bradley
had asked her out several times when he came to New York City,
but she had politely declined each dinner invitation, citing her heavy
load of schoolwork for her Columbia classes.

"How have you been?" Downes' voice was instantly animated.
Usually he was the one calling her. So this was an unexpected
pleasure.

"Fine." She wasn't really fine. She hadn't slept more than a few
hours since she had left Mace at the restaurant.

"I'm glad to hear it." He spoke in a slightly snobbish Ivy
League voice, but he was nice enough. He had told her more than
once that he ought to be working on Wall Street, but that the Still-
mans had made him an offer he couldn't refuse out of Stanford
Business School five years ago. After all, he was from Pittsburgh.
"And to what do I owe this interruption?"

"Oh, I'm sorry, Bradley. I can call back if you're busy." He was a
pain in the ass that way, always making it seem as if he were so busy.

"No, no. What's on your mind?" The snobbishness diminished
noticeably.

"A couple of things. First I was wondering if you were going to
be in New York any time soon. I thought maybe if you were coming here, we could get together for dinner. I'm going to be graduating from Columbia soon, and I'd like to get your perspective on
the world since you've been out there for a few years and I've been
sitting in this protected academic nest. You know, the buy side versus Wall Street, Pittsburgh versus New York, that kind of thing."

It was sickening to make herself seem so naive, but at this point she had to do whatever it took.

"Great! It'll be on me." Downes was instantly excited. "I'd be glad to talk to you." His condescending air had disappeared completely now.

Rachel smiled. He would provide her the information without a problem.

"I'm going to be there next month for several days."

"Good, call me a couple of days before you come, and we'll make a definite date." She was careful to use the word *date*.

"Wonderful. I'm really looking forward to it."

"So am I," she said sweetly.

"Was there something else you needed?"

"As a matter of fact, there is." She hesitated for a moment. "I've been hearing about this new fund that Walker Pryce is putting together."

"You have, have you?"

Rachel could hear a hint of caution seeping into the man's voice. "Yes. It's called Broadway Ventures. Walker Pryce is looking for a billion dollars to invest in Manhattan real estate and stocks." She was direct and conveyed very specific information immediately. She needed to show him that she wasn't simply fishing for the basics. She had to show him that she might have some worthwhile information that he did not have, that she would be willing to trade.

"How did you hear so much about it?"

"I have my ways," she said sexily.

Downes laughed. "I bet you do. Yeah, okay. I've heard something about it."

"So Walker Pryce *has* contacted you?"

Downes hesitated. He sensed that he shouldn't be divulging too much information, but he also wanted a date with this beautiful creature. "Yeah, they contacted us."

"Was it a woman named Kathleen Hunt who called?"

Again Downes hesitated. "Yes, it was."

Rachel inhaled. This was the key question. Mace had said at dinner that Leeny was expecting to get as much as two hundred million dollars or more from the Stillmans. "How much is the Stillman family going to put into the fund?"

"That decision has not yet been finalized," Downes responded quickly.

"But you are going to invest?"

"Yes. But that's off the record. If somebody calls me up and says that Rachel Sommers has told them the Stillman family is investing in Broadway Ventures, I'm going to be angry." He tried to say the words lightly so as not to offend her, but he was dead serious. He had a good job, and he did not want to risk it.

"I'd never say a word, Bradley."

"Good."

"Is the amount you are looking to invest north of a hundred million?" Rachel asked firmly.

"*What?*" Downes began to laugh. "Are you kidding me?" Suddenly his voice became serious. "Did someone tell you that?"

"No, of course not."

He ignored her. "Because if they did, they are very much mistaken. We wouldn't do close to a hundred million in that fund."

Rachel was breathing hard. "Of course you wouldn't." Something was suddenly smelling funny on Broadway. Leeny was expecting at least that much from the Stillmans. Mace was certain.

"A hundred million." Bradley was laughing again. "Old man Stillman would have our butts on a silver platter. Hell, they'll be lucky to get ten from us. She was only looking for twenty anyway."

"Only twenty?" Rachel asked incredulously. That made no sense. Twenty was a drop in the bucket for a billion-dollar fund.

"Yeah. She said the thing was almost done and we'd be lucky to get in. I would have told her to go pound salt except that Walker Pryce is the sponsor. We want to maintain a very good relationship with them, so I'm sure the family will approve at least ten. But not much more than that."

Rachel hardly heard the last few words. The fund was almost raised, but Stillman would invest only ten million. It wasn't adding up. It would take forever to raise a billion-dollar fund with ten-million-dollar pieces, yet she said she had most of it already raised. Maybe that was just bragging, a story for the other investors so they would come in. "Bradley, have you ever dealt with LeClair and Foster?"

"You mean the investment bank in San Francisco?"

"Yes."

"Sure, a number of times." His voice became condescending again. "I have a very good friend who works there, a guy I went to Stanford with. We were roommates second year."

Rachel hesitated. She did not know Bradley Downes that well. If Leeny found out that Rachel was checking on her, it might present a difficult situation. Leeny might try to persuade Lewis Webster to rescind the offer of employment at Walker Pryce—especially if the Stillman family got suspicious as a result of Rachel's snooping around. "Bradley, did you know that Kathleen Hunt, the woman who is raising this fund for Walker Pryce, worked at LeClair and Foster?"

"No. But that's not surprising. It's a pretty big firm. I told you, it's my friend who works at the firm."

"Of course." She was committed now. She had linked Leeny's name to LeClair and Foster. "Could you do me a favor? Could you call your friend and ask him about Kathleen Hunt?"

There was silence at the other end of the phone.

Rachel held her breath.

"What's the problem?" Bradley asked slowly.

"Nothing, just routine." Rachel hoped her voice sounded normal. She was glad he could not see her face.

"That sounds as if you're with the SEC or maybe the New York City Police Department."

She laughed loudly. "You're too funny. I think dinner is going to be great."

"I hope so." His voice gave away his anticipation.

"So will you do it? Will you ask your friend about her?"

"Not going to tell me any more about why?" he asked.

"I'll tell you at dinner. But seriously it's nothing." Rachel could hear him breathing all over the other end of the phone.

"All right."

"Tell him to give me everything he can find, everything. And thank you. You are really nice to help."

"Don't mention it. Hey, do you like Le Cirque for dinner?"

"Who doesn't?" Suddenly a beep interrupted the line. "Oh, someone's calling, Bradley. I've got to go. Can you call me as soon as possible after you talk to your friend at LeClair and Foster?"

"Sure, sure."

"And you have the number here at my apartment?"

"Yes."

"Okay, bye."

"Bye."

Rachel heard Bradley put down the phone. Again the line beeped, indicating another call. Slowly she hung up the receiver. It was Mace. She could feel it. But she wasn't ready to talk to him yet.

Bradley Downes stared at the phone for several seconds after he hung up. A strange call. But he wanted Rachel Sommers. He hadn't told her the whole story about his contact at LeClair and Foster. The man was his best friend in the world. Downes smiled. Rachel was going to be impressed. If there was anything to know about this woman Kathleen Hunt, Rachel was going to know it. His buddy would understand and help in any way he could. Downes wanted Rachel to be very impressed at their dinner. Perhaps he would even spend his own money to upgrade to a suite at the Plaza that night.

18

I t was three o'clock in the morning, but Slade Conner could not
sleep. He sat on the edge of the bed, reading the anonymous
letter for the fourth time in the last two hours.

Dear Mr. Conner,

I need to tell you about Carter Guilford, former senior Central
Intelligence Agency field officer for all of Central and South America.
He was killed recently in Honduras, the result of a plane crash.

Guilford was working closely with the Ortega drug cartel of
Colombia. He was providing sensitive information to the cartel with
respect to the activities of the CIA and the United States Drug Enforcement Agency and their efforts to limit the flow of illegal drugs
into the United States—specific information on the identities of undercover agents, the whereabouts of border patrols, and the flight
patterns of DEA planes scouting drug runner aircraft. The information Guilford provided to the cartel enabled the Ortegas to ship significantly more cocaine into the country over the past four years
than any other operation. It also enabled them to identify and presumably kill at least eleven undercover agents, whose bodies have
never been found. His assistance translated into billions of dollars of
profits for the Ortegas, and they rewarded him for it with almost
two hundred million dollars.

The money Guilford was paid went directly into CIA accounts
and was used by Malcolm Becker to fund the Wolverines, an outfit

you are intimately familiar with. The Wolverines were well over budget—and in fact still are. Becker needed the drug money to cover his excess spending on the Wolverines. There was more money coming in, but Becker found out that Guilford was going to blow the whistle. He was going to reveal what was going on to a high-level contact in the Whitman administration. So I believe Becker had Guilford killed. I don't believe the plane crash in Honduras was an accident.

You must find the evidence directly linking Becker to Guilford's death. I will contact you again within two weeks.

Slade could not take his eyes from the page. "A high-level contact in the Whitman administration." His mind raced back to the entry in the date book he had pulled from Guilford's pocket: the meeting with Preston Andrews. But that was ridiculous. If all this were true, Guilford would never have written the vice president's name in a book. That would have been stupid. But then people did stupid things sometimes. Even CIA people. He shook his head. *Especially* CIA people.

He lay back on the bed. It might be Becker testing him. Perhaps he was supposed to bring this letter directly to Becker, at which point Becker would shake his hand and thank him for his loyalty.

Or it could be Ferris. Maybe the Rat Man didn't like old Malcolm as much as it seemed he did.

The most likely possibility was that someone else was guessing, probing to see if a nerve was struck.

Slade slammed a fist down onto the mattress. There was no way to determine anything about this letter, whether there was some grain of truth to it or it was simply a pack of lies. He needed more information about Wolverine accounts. And there was no way for him to determine whether Guilford really was working with the Ortegas because he didn't have strong contacts in Central

America. Poking around down there without knowing whom to talk to would get you killed very quickly.

"Damn it."

He couldn't do anything. All he could do was sit and wait. And he was a man of action. He hated waiting.

Leeny sat on the bed naked, her legs pulled up to her chest and her arms clasped around her shins. From over her knees she gazed at the light emanating from the crack beneath the bathroom door of the hotel room. Behind it John Schuler was doing something. Who knew what? Who cared?

She shook uncontrollably but did not cry. She was past the point of crying. For the last two hours Schuler had taken her every way he wanted. Every way he could think of, grunting like a pig each of the four times he had reached his climax.

She pulled her legs even more tightly against her chest and closed her eyes. She was a billion-dollar whore. He had promised mightily after each orgasm that when he arrived at the office in the morning, the first thing he would do was sign the letter committing Chase to a billion-dollar underwriting for Broadway Ventures and fax it over to her at Walker Pryce. She shook her head. The man in Washington would be smiling if he knew of the sacrifice she was making.

But it was worth it, wasn't it? Letting this runt have his way in exchange for a billion dollars. She had avoided certain jail time for her insider trading crimes, and when the project was over, she would be paid five million dollars and would run away and hide forever. Or maybe she would stalk the little banker behind the bathroom door first, kill him in cold blood, and *then* run away and hide forever—with her five million dollars.

Four times in two hours he had exploded. She had never seen anything like it. How could he keep this up? Yet he claimed to want more. She was not a religious woman, but suddenly she slid her hands together over her knees and began to pray to any god willing to listen that John Schuler might have a heart attack in the hotel bathroom.

Leeny kissed her knee gently. Steady, girl. Keep everything in perspective. A means to an end, that was all this was. Suddenly she thought of Mace. At least he had been forthright with her in New Orleans about his intentions. And he had been tender and gentle during their couplings. Schuler had manipulated her into bed, threatening to pull the deal if she didn't come to the hotel with him. He had exhibited no sensitivity during their sex, just wanton selfishness. She shook her head. The irony of it. She loathed the little man in the bathroom, yet she was helping him, taking his career to even greater heights. He would make millions off the loan to Broadway Ventures. And he was having her body every way he wanted, using her terribly. Against her will she had begun to care about Mace, yet she would in the end help bring about his death.

In the bathroom, Schuler stared at his phallus, fully erect again, and smiled. Cocaine, mainlined through a tiny straw as far down the opening of the shaft as possible, turned even a balding, overweight, middle-aged businessman into an accomplished lover for the night. Carefully he refolded the thin paper into its triangular shape, trapping the precious cargo inside, and hid it in the wicker basket full of complimentary toiletries. She would not be likely to use anything in there if she came to use this room.

He opened the bathroom door and without turning off the light moved to where Leeny sat on the bed. Gently he caressed her cheek for a few moments. Then slowly he took a fistful of her long blond mane and began to pull her to the edge of the bed.

"You're hurting me," she whispered.

But he did not stop until she was sitting on the edge of the bed. Then he slid several fingers beneath her chin and pulled it up until she was looking into his eyes. "You are exquisite."

"Thank you so much," she said hoarsely. How? she wondered. "Haven't you had enough yet?"

Schuler smiled down at her. "I could never get enough of you, Leeny." He caressed her cheek again. "Get down on your knees."

"John, it's four in the morning, and I've got to catch a plane in a few hours. Please let me—"

"Get on your knees." He interrupted. His voice was firm. "You wouldn't want me to reconsider the loan to Broadway Ventures, would you?"

"No," she said softly. Slowly Leeny slid from the bed to the floor, then turned so that her upper chest rested on the mattress. She felt Schuler getting down behind her. God, it was terrible. She felt him playing, touching. She closed her eyes tightly. Someone would pay for this. Then he was inside her. She grabbed the sheets and bit into the mattress. Someone would pay dearly.

Becker spoke on the phone to someone in Chile as Slade watched. The man had been like a father to him for the past five years, and he felt a deep affection for him. But ironically he did not trust him personally. How could he? Becker was the director of the Central Intelligence Agency.

Trust had become a relative beast to Slade Conner in his years of military service. You trusted people in certain ways but not in others. Malcolm Becker could be trusted to go to any length to protect the welfare of the country, but he could not be trusted with an individual's well-being. Becker would quickly sacrifice an individual for the sake of the whole.

The anonymous letter Slade had received this morning was in all probability a sham. Just someone attempting to worm his or her way into the most confidential records of the CIA, someone trying to find fire where there probably was none to find. It happened all the time, especially in this city. Washington was full of people who didn't care how they obtained information as long as they did. Washington was full of enemies.

Still, as he watched Becker complete the call, some of what was in the letter nagged at him. There were enough slivers in it to make him wonder.

Becker replaced the phone in its cradle. "Good morning, Slade."

"Good morning, General."

"How have you been?"

"Fine, sir."

"Good." Becker picked up the coffee cup and sipped at the steaming black liquid.

Every time Slade came here it was always the same. Good morning, Slade, how have you been and then a sip of coffee. The general's life was one master regimen. Discipline bred dynasties. Practice made perfect. Those were the general's credos.

The general replaced the cup on the desk. "You have always served me in outstanding fashion."

"Thank you, General."

"Slade, I won't beat around the bush. I need your special talents again."

Slade nodded. He had known that would be the purpose of the meeting as soon as he had not seen the Rat Man in attendance. "What do you need me to do?"

The general breathed deeply. The air made a whistling sound as it rushed in and out of his nostrils. "Our friend Preston Andrews is becoming a problem." Becker paused for a moment to gauge Slade's reaction to the mention of the vice president. But there was no reaction. It was one of Slade's special talents to remain completely impassive to any piece of information, and up until now Becker had appreciated the talent. Now he wanted to be able to read that face. "I need you to locate some information for me with respect to Andrews." Becker's eyes narrowed.

Inside, Slade breathed a sigh of relief, but he showed nothing to the general. When Becker had mentioned special talents, Slade had thought Becker meant Slade's ability to create deadly accidents. Loyalty to the general was one thing. Killing the vice president was quite another. Slade nodded.

The general nodded back. "So I have your cooperation?"

"Of course."

Becker smiled. Conner was a loyal man. The CIA needed more men like him, willing to do whatever it took. Becker leaned forward. "What I am about to tell you is top secret. Do you understand?"

"Yes, sir."

Becker hesitated for a moment, then began again. He used his stern commander's voice. "Mr. Andrews is trying to create a scandal here at CIA. He is trying to create something he can use to drag me down. He is doing this for a very good reason. He is petrified that I am going to beat him in this fall's election for the office of the presidency. So he is attempting to concoct a story to discredit me, so he can get me out of the race and win the election."

Slade's blood pressure ticked up slightly. The words in the letter came rushing back to him as he glanced at a picture on the office wall. "A high-level contact in the Whitman administration." The entry in Guilford's date book: Preston Andrews.

"Andrews has a dirty little secret. His family business, Andrews Industries, is going down the toilet. And I am led to believe that he may have misused funds at the corporation unbeknownst to other family members. There is the possibility that Andrews has committed serious fraud at the company in an effort to fund his campaign against me. But it goes even beyond that." Becker leaned farther over the desk. His eyes had become nothing but slits, and the blood vessels in his scalp bulged. "I have information that Andrews is somehow attempting to engineer a conspiracy of massive proportions, something that will generate huge profits for him, enough to bring his company back from the brink of disaster, fund his campaign, and more."

Slade swallowed hard. What the hell did that mean? He wanted to ask Becker how he had come upon this information, but he knew that was pointless. Becker would never say. "You want me to investigate him." Slade did not phrase the words in the form of a question.

"Yes. I want to know everything there is to know about the man. I've had my B team at work for a few months, but now it's time for the first string. I want you everywhere you can get. His family home in Michigan, his company, his accountants' office, his attorneys' office. Everywhere. I want exact financial information with respect to Andrews Industries, I want exact information with respect to his personal finances, and I want to know if there is any truth to what my contact in the Mideast has told me."

Slade raised an eyebrow. Contact in the Mideast. That was the credibility drop, the few words that were meant to legitimize his accusation of the conspiracy of massive proportions.

Slade eyed Becker. Perhaps he should have followed Mace to the financial world after college. Wall Street had seemed so useless and complex then. But it seemed so straightforward and simple compared with what he was involved with at this point. "Yes, sir. I'll get right on it." He stood and saluted the general.

19

L eeny, this is Roger Hamilton." Mace shook Hamilton's pudgy
hand, then guided him toward Leeny. "Roger is a senior vice-
president here at Maryland Mutual Life and the chief investment officer with respect to its entire mortgage portfolio. As you
know, Leeny, Maryland Mutual is the third-largest life insurance
company in the United States and also one of the largest long-term
real estate lenders."

Leeny gazed at Hamilton glassy-eyed. It was just ten o'clock in
the morning. That meant that horrible little banker John Schuler
had kissed her good-bye in the stark room of the Hotel Inter-
Continental only four hours before. A rough kiss she had forced
herself to endure, the kind of kiss she would have expected from a
fourteen-year-old. But she should have expected him to kiss her
good-bye like an inexperienced adolescent. He had made love all
night in the same fashion.

She had slept through the short early-morning flight from La
Guardia to Washington's National Airport and during the cab ride
from National to Maryland Mutual's downtown Washington
offices as well, not bothering to provide Mace with an explanation for her exhaustion. Fortunately he had not asked what
the problem was.

Finally Leeny gathered herself and focused on Hamilton's
obese face. "Good morning," she said hoarsely. She tried to smile

provocatively at the portfolio manager, who was obviously impressed with himself, but it was not in her now. She had actually considered calling Mace, after Schuler had finally left her, to tell him to go to Washington alone this morning, but she knew he might tell Webster that he had come here by himself, and that would infuriate Webster. She did not want to give Webster an excuse to become angry at her.

"Hello." Hamilton responded with a stiff, pompous accent, taking her hand as if it were a tedious chore.

She almost recoiled at the touch of his cold, clammy hand.

"Leeny has been primarily responsible for raising the partnership money for Broadway Ventures, but she will be involved on the investment side as well." Mace was playing his part well, making everyone comfortable, setting the stage. As usual, he was on his game: perfectly prepared, cool, and collected.

"I see." Hamilton seemed only vaguely interested.

She attempted to shake her hair sexily for him, to make herself more alluring, to play the part she knew she was expected to play. But it wasn't working. She wasn't feeling at all sexy. The image of Schuler on top of her over and over was still fresh in her mind, and Hamilton reminded her of Schuler: fat, balding, and useless. Hamilton was simply a taller, fatter version of the little Chase banker. With a pompous accent to boot. "How are you this morning, Roger?" Leeny took a halfhearted stab at being cordial.

"Fine." Hamilton pulled his dead-fish handshake from her grip and turned away abruptly, then solemnly moved behind his desk and sat.

Mace hesitated for a moment, wondering what in the world Leeny's problem was.

She shrugged quickly and turned away. When the shit began hitting the fan, she wasn't going to mind putting this arrogant investment officer through the meat grinder. He wasn't going to be so arrogant then. She could already hear him crying like a baby as he watched the value of his portfolio plummet before his eyes. He'd be begging her to take the mortgage paper off his hands.

"How big is the mortgage portfolio here at Maryland Mutual now, Roger? Did I hear it was thirty billion now? Is that right?" Mace glanced out the office window, toward the dome of the Capitol rising in the distance, before he sat down in one of the two chairs positioned in front of the desk.

Hamilton folded his arms across his upper belly as he sat in the desk chair. "Thirty-*two* billion." He sniffed.

Leeny moved to the other chair in front of the desk and sat. She could almost hear Hamilton begging her to buy the mortgage bonds—at any price. It would be sweet revenge for his insolent manner. In the end she would give him something for the paper, pennies probably, but not before inflicting great pain.

Mace nodded at the figure. "Impressive."

"Yes, it is." Hamilton was as impressed with himself as with the size of the portfolio.

Mace pushed himself to smile. The client was always right, he kept telling himself. Grin and bear it. "How is your wife, Shirley?"

Hamilton cracked his first thin smile since Mace and Leeny had entered the room. "Checked the prompt cards back at your office, did you, Mace?"

Mace shook his head. Shirley was a wonderful woman, warm and caring. Mace had met her two years ago at a closing dinner in Manhattan. They were there to celebrate the successful arrangement of financing, put together by Mace, for a gleaming new seventy-two-story office tower to be constructed in midtown for which Maryland Mutual had provided the bulk of the construction and permanent mortgage financing. So how did a man like Roger Hamilton snare a woman like Shirley? It was just one of those things in life that defied logic. "How is she?"

"She cooks, cleans, and takes care of the children, the kinds of things a woman ought to be doing with her day." Hamilton turned his face toward Leeny as he said the last few words but did not take his eyes from Mace.

Leeny felt her blood boil. She would bury this man. Alive. Up to his neck. Then smother his head with pollen and let the hornets loose. And watch him suffer.

Mace coughed once. Hamilton was an asshole. There was no denying that. But he controlled bonds with a face value of thirty-two billion dollars, a good deal of which was invested in Manhattan real estate. If Webster was right and property values in New York City really did take a nose dive, Broadway Ventures might be able to pick off a nice chunk of those bonds at a price well below their face value and then sell them at a tidy profit when prices re-bounded. "I'm glad Shirley's doing well. She's a nice woman. I re-member her telling me about her rose garden at the closing dinner for the Ames property." Mace smiled evenly at Hamilton.

Hamilton realized immediately that he had been upstaged, that Mace actually did remember his wife. He rubbed his face for a mo-ment. Suddenly he wanted to get on with the meeting. "So let me get this straight, Mace. Walker Pryce is raising a vulture fund be-cause it anticipates that real estate prices are going to plunge. Is that right?"

Mace nodded. He recognized where this was headed right away, but there was no way around it, and he had an answer prepared.

"And you wanted to come up here today to tell me about it so that when the crash hits, I'll sell you some of my bonds at a cut-rate price." Hamilton continued.

"Something like that, Roger." Mace grinned.

"So that you and your investment banking friends at Walker Pryce can buy back the same paper you sold to me. Of course you sold it to me at a hundred cents on the dollar and you'll buy it back from me at ninety cents. If I'm lucky." Hamilton rubbed his face again. "How much have I bought from Walker Pryce? Probably four billion of the thirty-two in the portfolio." Hamilton answered his own question. "Now you come here to tell me the real estate world is about to fall apart after you sold me all this stuff."

It was the classic conflict of interest all investment bankers faced, whether they were dealing in the corporate, real estate, or mergers and acquisitions market. Investment banking firms represented both buyers and sellers; this, by definition, created problems. When the chief executive officer of a company decided to sell stock to the public, he wanted his investment banker to obtain the highest price possible for the shares. But the investor—the individual or institution that ultimately purchased the shares—wanted to see the investment increase quickly in value, and that might not happen if the initial price was too high. In the end one or the other would not be happy. It was inevitable.

To make matters worse, the investment banker made money irrespective of the outcome. Firms like Walker Pryce took a hefty commission, sometimes as much as 7 percent of everything that was bought or sold, no matter where the share or bond price headed after the transaction.

Now Hamilton was not so subtly reminding Mace of the conflict. What held true for stocks held true for bonds as well, and Hamilton had a massive bond position.

Mace's expression turned serious. It was time to remind Hamilton that he and Maryland Mutual had been able to provide their policyholders with startlingly strong returns over the past five years directly as a result of Walker Pryce's advice. As quickly as Wall Street gave, it could take away. Wall Street was a tiny cartel; at most there were ten firms that consistently originated significant investment opportunities the size of which interested a Maryland Mutual. They were a tiny but powerful cartel. As strong as the OPEC oil cartel was, its influence over world economies paled in comparison. And if you irritated a member of the Wall Street cartel, or club, as its members preferred it to be called, your investment opportunities would dry up like a stream in the desert.

It was time for Mace to dust Roger Hamilton. "As you are well aware, Roger, investment bankers provide liquidity, opportunity, and the best advice we can to our clients. That's all we can do. We can't control the real estate market. You know that. It follows its own random walk. All we can do is bring you opportunities and be there when you need us." Mace spoke evenly but firmly. "Or not be there for you when you need us most."

Hamilton held up a hand. "Of course, Mace. Maryland Mutual is very pleased with the work Walker Pryce has done for us." He had heard the warning in Mace's last words.

Mace nodded. The understanding had been reached.

Hamilton smiled broadly for the first time. "I don't really think we're in for a correction in the real estate market anyway. If there is one, it will be slight, not enough to get excited about. Certainly not enough to raise billions for." Hamilton was a man who had to have the last word. It was simply his nature. And his comment and his unusually large smile were meant to convey the last word.

Mace ignored the missile. "If you don't mind, I have some questions about your portfolio. It's been a few months since I've gone through it with you, and I'd like an update."

"Okay," Hamilton said.

Suddenly the intercom on Hamilton's desk squawked loudly. "Mr. Hamilton?"

"Yes, Rose." Hamilton rolled his eyes as her voice crackled through the speaker.

"George Warner needs to see you for a moment."

Hamilton groaned as he lifted himself from his chair. "I'll be right back."

Leeny allowed her head to fall back as Hamilton exited the office. It was going to feel so good to crawl into her bed tonight and pull the covers up around herself. She would be asleep by eight.

"So what in the world were you up to last night?"

Leeny sat up with a start. She shook her head slightly, then straightened herself in the chair. "What are you talking about?"

"You seem a little"—Mace paused, then grinned—"off, shall we say?"

"It's that time of the month," Leeny responded immediately.

"Oh." Mace looked away quickly.

Leeny ran her fingers through her hair. That time of the month. It was the ultimate female cop-out, but it was effective. It could stop an unhappy boss in the middle of a tirade and a police officer about to deliver a speeding ticket. As long as the other party was male, it was successful 99 percent of the time.

"I thought maybe you had gone to dinner with Schuler," Mace said quietly.

She glanced at him. He was looking at something on Hamilton's desk. "No," she said firmly. "I talked to him for a while at Chase, then went home. Alone." She paused for a moment. "Why did you say that?"

"Oh, he called me at the office last night around eight o'clock from some restaurant to say that he had just gotten off the phone with his chief credit officer at Chase. The deal was approved last night. A billion dollars of bank debt underwritten by the Chase Bank. Can you believe it?" Mace shook his head as if he couldn't. "I was going to ask you if you had heard while we were on the plane, but you looked pretty tired, so I didn't want to disturb you." He paused. "Pretty soon we're going to have two billion dollars to play with, Leeny. I just hope I can do something with it. I hope your faith in me is justified."

But Leeny did not hear the last few words. Her vision blurred as the blood pounded in her head. Schuler had left the restaurant table at eight o'clock last night supposedly just to use the rest room. He hadn't been away from the table for long, so she had thought nothing of it. Apparently he had called his chief credit officer and then Mace in those few minutes, but when Schuler had returned, he hadn't mentioned a word about the calls. The little bastard. He had used her so badly. There hadn't been any reason to endure the torture. The deal had been done before she had gone to the hotel room with him. She felt tears welling up in her eyes.

"Are you okay, Leeny?" Mace touched her hand gently. Her skin was burning up.

"I'm fine," she said hesitantly. But she wasn't fine. She needed to get to a ladies' room immediately. She stood quickly and rushed for the door, clutching her stomach.

"Slade, this is Kathleen Hunt," Mace said, making the introduction. "She and I work together at Walker Pryce."

"Hello, Kathleen." Slade took her hand gently, then quickly let it go. He thought he recognized the woman, so he was careful not to look at her too long in case the context of his recollection was not favorable. Instead he glanced at her several times quickly, each time for less than two seconds because his training had taught him that if subjects became aware of you staring at them for longer than that short period of time, they instantly suspected that you were up to something and would pay careful attention to you. He did not want her to pay careful attention to him.

Kathleen Hunt. Kathleen Hunt. The name and the face were so familiar, but he could not place her. He cursed under his breath. He rarely forgot a name—or a face.

"Hi," Leeny said quickly. She was exhausted, and all she wanted to do was go home. But she could not let Mace out of her sight. Those were Webster's orders. Especially since they were in Washington.

As they stood in the reception area of Clyde's, a popular restaurant in the center of Georgetown, a young hostess waved at them from the center of the room. "Over there," she yelled, motioning toward an empty window table.

They moved quickly toward the table. It was just after noon, and the place was packed. They were lucky to have gotten a spot.

Mace held Leeny's chair as they got to the table, and she collapsed into it. She did not remove her sunglasses despite the fact that it was fairly dark inside the restaurant. She wanted to hide, to crawl under a rock and be forgotten. Her stomach was still queasy, and the smell of freshly cooked food was not helping matters. "What did you say you did, Slade?" She wanted to get her obligatory words in quickly and then fade from view.

"I'm an attorney." Slade winked at Mace. It was the safest response possible in Washington. There were thousands of law firms in Washington. If she asked whom he worked for, he could make up a name and she would never know the difference.

She nodded but showed no further interest.

Mace grinned. "Leeny is feeling a little under the weather."

"Oh." Slade glanced at her again. It was coming to him. He was almost there, almost certain of why her name and face were so familiar.

"I'm all right, really." But she wasn't. She needed to go to the ladies' room again. "I'll be right back." She rose to find the lavatory.

Mace and Slade rose quickly as well, helping her away from her inside position at the table. Slowly they sat back down as they watched her disappear toward the back of the room.

Slade tapped his fingers on the table. Almost. He almost had it.

"Pretty, isn't she?" Mace smiled broadly at his close friend. Slade never could get enough of the women. "I knew you'd like her. Unfortunately she's not doing that well today. I told her to go home ahead of me, but she—"

Suddenly Slade turned back toward Mace. He had not remembered everything about the woman, but he had remembered enough. He cut Mace off in mid-sentence. "If you ever need anything, call me. You know you can count on me."

Mace pulled back slightly. He had never heard that tone before. "What is that supposed to mean?"

Slade eyed Mace for several seconds; then his face relaxed. He did not want to alarm Mace. And he could tell him no more.

"Nothing. Nothing at all. Just remember to call me if you need anything. *Anything.*"

Mace nodded, still uncertain of the hidden meaning he had detected in the tone of his friend's voice.

Rachel had been waiting for this moment since leaving the restaurant last Friday evening. Waiting to see the handsome face and comforting smile, the confident walk and flashing eyes. Waiting for the warm feeling that took over her body instantly each time she saw him. She had ignored the telephone long enough. She knew he felt something for her. She had left him at the restaurant and remained beyond his reach for the last few days to make him realize in no uncertain terms just how much he felt for her.

Her breathing was short as she anticipated his arrival. He would stride through the door as he always did, focused on the black table at the front of the room. He would reach it, put down his leather briefcase, remove his coat and jacket and lay them on the table, then glance around the room for several seconds. He would look at everyone and everything in the lecture hall but her. Finally his gaze would come to her, as it always did. As his eyes fell on her, his expression would change subtly. Not enough for anyone except her to notice. And she would smile back at him, letting him know that everything was all right. They would definitely talk after class. Maybe it would be dinner. Maybe it would be even more. Perhaps by the end of the evening she would be where she really wanted to be: with him.

"Rachel, did you prepare the case pretty well?" Don Hammonds sat next to Rachel in the sky deck. He had not prepared the case at all and was worried that Mace would cold-call him to start the class because he had not yet been called on to do so. Hammonds was searching for a lifeline, and he knew Rachel was a good place to start looking.

"Yes." She slid her notebook across the tabletop toward Hammonds without taking her eyes from the door. It was almost seven o'clock, and there was still no sign of Mace.

"Thanks." Hammonds grabbed the spiral notebook and began taking copious notes.

Rachel did not respond.

Then her heart sank. Dean Fenton moved purposely through the door and to the dais next to the black table. The hum of conversation diminished at once.

He rapped his pipe on the lectern despite the fact that the classroom was already quiet. "Good evening." His face was sour. "Well, Mr. McLain has kept up a perfect record of attendance so far, so I suppose I shouldn't be too upset." He paused. "Mr. McLain has been unavoidably detained on a deal tonight and will not be able to make class. And we have no one else to teach the course tonight, so go home and study for midterms." With that he was gone, out the door and down the hall.

For several moments, until the class was certain Fenton was far enough out of range, they remained in their seats, quietly gathering papers together. Then they let out a huge cheer and slapped one another on the back. They were joyous at the prospect of not being embarrassed by a difficult question or asked to lead a discussion on some tough point of real estate finance. They all were excited. All except Rachel. As the class erupted around her, she remained still.

"Thanks, Rachel." Hammonds shoved the notebook back at Rachel. "Won't be needing that tonight after all. Thank God." He rose, picked up his knapsack, and was gone, with the others.

Rachel sat in her seat until everyone else had left the room. Then, slowly, she began gathering her things. Suddenly she was sorry she had ignored what had to have been Mace's calls.

"So, how was your friend Roger Hamilton?" Webster sat behind the antique desk in his office, looking out at Mace from beneath the dark eyebrows.

"As chauvinistic as ever, I imagine." Leeny cut in as she allowed herself to be swallowed up by the comfortable couch of Webster's office. "Although it's the first time I've ever met the man, I can't believe he has developed his complete lack of respect for women since you last saw him." Leeny glanced at Mace and then closed her eyes as she said the words. She hadn't wanted to come back to the office after the Washington excursion. She had wanted to go directly to bed upon their return. But Webster had left a message for them with Hamilton's secretary, instructing them to come back to Walker Pryce right after their plane had landed at La Guardia.

"Roger was just his normal self. He wasn't that bad."

"Not that bad?" Leeny became suddenly agitated. "He thinks it's a travesty women were given the right to vote. He's a Neanderthal."

"You're exaggerating." Mace grinned.

"He's a bastard," she said icily.

"Enough," Webster whispered sharply. He was not amused by their back-and-forth.

Mace glanced at Leeny. He had not heard that tone in her voice before.

"What was Mr. Hamilton's reaction to Broadway Ventures?" Webster asked.

Mace moved to a chair next to the sofa. "First Roger got irritated because I was telling him the real estate market was going to crash. Bad news for someone to whom we've sold billions of dollars' worth of mortgage bonds in the last two years. Then he told me it didn't really matter anyway because he didn't think much of our idea. He doesn't think the real estate market is going to crash."

Leeny could hear the frustration building in Mace's voice. He had expressed it to her several times in the last several weeks, as they had been snubbed over and over.

Webster ignored Mace's cynical tone. "Did you relay the prices Broadway Ventures would pay for his bonds? The prices I told you to relay to him."

Mace did not answer immediately.

"Did he?" Webster turned toward Leeny.

Mace's mouth opened slightly. Webster had gone off the deep end. Mace had generated fifty million dollars of fee income for Walker Pryce last year, and here was Lewis Webster, the senior partner, checking up on him with Leeny, who had barely been with the firm a few weeks. What kind of loyalty did this show? What kind of trust was this? "Lewis, I . . ."

"Did he convey the prices to Hamilton?" Webster's eyes bored into Leeny.

She despised Webster. Everything about him. "Yes. Mace conveyed the prices to Hamilton."

Mace turned toward Leeny. She could have told Webster the truth and probably been running the fund by herself. Yet she had come through for him. She had lied. He turned back to Webster. "Lewis, you have got to be more realistic about pricing. The prices for the properties you are setting are too low. And we haven't even talked about the share prices the two mergers and acquisition analysts have come up with. Every stock they have recommended as undervalued you have rejected. What's going on here?" Mace stood up and ran his fingers through his hair. He could no longer control himself. "You don't think the stocks the analysts have recommended are undervalued, so you must think they are overvalued. Right?" He was working Webster into a corner.

Webster shifted uncomfortably in the large chair but did not respond. He knew where Mace was going with this argument, and he did not want to go there.

"So if you think the stocks are overvalued, let's short them. Let's buy puts or sell calls." Mace moved slowly toward Webster.

"No." Webster stood slowly and leaned over the desk, resting both hands on the desktop. Suddenly he was sorry he had involved this brash young investment banker in the fund—even if Mace had already opened many doors for Leeny that neither she nor Webster would have otherwise known about.

Suddenly Mace sincerely regretted his failure to heed his gut reaction to this project when Webster had first presented it to him. Finally he turned and headed toward the door.

Leeny rose to follow him, but Webster's gaze froze her in her tracks. The door banged loudly behind Mace as he moved into the hallway.

"Where were you going?" Webster did not appreciate the fact that her first reaction had been to follow Mace.

She set her jaw. "Home, Lewis. I just want to go home." She moved toward the desk the way Mace had moments earlier. "Last night I did what you and that monster in Washington asked me to do." She was breathing heavily. "I've done everything that's been asked of me." The lump was forming in her throat again. "And all I want to do now is go home and go to sleep. And hope I don't have nightmares about how I compromised myself last night." She turned and began to walk toward the door.

"Stop right there." His whisper was menacing.

She wanted to keep moving, not to stop. To walk out the door of Webster's office and never come back. Webster could have her killed anytime he wanted. She had no doubt of that now.

"Has he really introduced you to twenty-five investors?"

Leeny nodded. She could hear by his voice that he was coming toward her.

"And do you have the complete list of stocks the analysts in the M & A department have come up with? And the stocks within that list Mace feels most strongly about?"

"No. He has that list."

Webster stood directly behind her now. He gazed at the long golden hair streaming down her back. She was beautiful. He had paid no attention to his urges for so long. He could only imagine what lay beneath the snugly fitting dress. But he no longer wanted simply to imagine. He wanted to know. "Mace McLain has almost outlived his utility. Do you understand?"

Leeny swallowed hard. So they *were* going to kill him. "Yes."

"It is critical that you watch him twenty-four hours a day now. I don't care how you do it, but you must. Otherwise we will put someone into this situation who can do this job correctly. Am I making myself clear?"

"Yes." Her voice was a monotone.

Webster drew in a long, deep breath.

Suddenly Leeny felt Webster's hands on her hips. She whirled to face him. "Don't ever do that again," she hissed. "Don't ever think you can touch me. I don't care if you can turn me over to the authorities for insider trading or if you can have me murdered. You can manipulate me any way you want except physically. I will never allow you to touch me, Lewis Webster."

Webster pulled back, then smiled wickedly and pointed at her. "Don't forget. Keep him in your sights at all times."

Leeny stared at the old man for several moments, turned, and walked toward the door.

The taxi crept slowly toward Mace from down the street. He watched curiously as it rolled to where he stood and then stopped. He had not hailed it. Smoothly the back passenger window dropped down. Leeny's beautiful face appeared.

"Hi, stranger," she said in a low, husky voice. "Need a lift?"

Mace smiled. It was cold out here, and he didn't really feel like walking the streets of lower Manhattan anymore. "Sure." He opened the door and slid onto the backseat next to her. "I'm glad you came along when you—"

But Leeny did not allow Mace to finish the sentence. Her soft hand moved to his cheek, and she pressed her thin body against him. Then her lips were on his.

Mace accepted her kiss. It was wrong. He shouldn't give in to this again. But he could not help himself. He slid his large hand through her hair and pulled her lips more tightly against his. She tasted so good, and he wanted this intimacy right now. He was frustrated with Lewis Webster, and the only other person who could understand what he felt was Leeny. Their tongues intertwined for several seconds in a passionate kiss.

"Where to?" The cabby sounded tough, Brooklyn all the way.

Mace attempted to answer, but Leeny would not allow him to pull away from her.

"Yo, I'm trying to make a living here. The faster you tell me where you want to go, the faster you can *really* get at it." The cabby was irritated. He was losing time, and somehow he didn't like the fact that the woman was all over the guy who had just gotten into the back of his taxi.

Finally Leeny pulled back slightly and licked her lips. They glistened in the bright neon lights of the Manhattan night streaming through the cab windows. "Maybe I want to do it in a cab," she whispered into Mace's ear.

He smiled at her. She was putting her full weight on him, yet he felt nothing.

"Hey, whose place are we going to? His or hers. Make up your minds." The cabby was angry now.

Leeny pushed her lips against Mace's ear. "Let's go to your apartment. Mine is a wreck."

He nodded. "Okay."

"Well?"

"Well, what?"

"Well, what's your address, silly?" She knew his address. She knew it by heart, but she could not give that fact away. He might be suspicious if she suddenly blurted it out.

"Oh, right." He had waited to give the man the address to see if she might respond, yielding a secret. "Eighty-second and Columbus."

"You got it." The cabby gunned the engine, and the taxi shot forward, pinning Leeny against Mace.

Again she kissed him deeply. Finally she pulled back. "You care about me, don't you?" she whispered.

Mace gazed back at her. "Of course I do."

Ten minutes later they reached Mace's apartment. As he turned into the room after closing the door, Leeny moved quickly into his arms. They kissed for several minutes in the dark foyer, and then Mace pushed her against the wall and moved his tongue against her neck. She arched her back as she felt his teeth and tongue working together on her soft skin. She moaned slightly. It felt so good. "Stop, Jesus. You're going to leave marks." But she dug her nails into his scalp, pulling him more tightly against her.

"No, I promise I'll leave dollars," he whispered.

"What?" She pulled back slightly. She was breathing hard.

"Nothing." He smiled at her. "Just a little banker humor."

She moved against him again. "You're a bad boy. You know I want you so much, don't you?"

"Maybe." He did not tell her how mutual the feeling suddenly was.

She kissed him again on the lips. "Fix me a drink, bad boy."

Mace eyed her for a moment, considering whether or not to honor the request. He wanted her right now. But of course the liquor might unleash any inhibitions. "All right. What will you have?"

"Scotch and water."

He nodded. "I'll be right back."

"Okay. I may not have as many clothes on when you get back. If that's okay with you."

Mace smiled at her again. "Not a problem for me."

They kissed deeply one more time. Then he turned and headed carefully toward the kitchen, through the darkness of the apartment.

He reached the wall outside the kitchen and flipped on the switch, bathing the space in light. He moved to a small cabinet next to the sink, removed a bottle of Chivas from it, and poured the scotch into a highball glass. He added some water. He reached into the refrigerator and pulled out a beer for himself, retrieved the glass of scotch from the counter, and headed back into the living room.

"Webster's such an idiot, isn't—" Mace stopped in mid-sentence. Leeny lay on the leather couch, fast asleep. He shook his head and chuckled. Of course. She was exhausted.

He took the drinks back to the kitchen, went to a hall closet, pulled down a warm wool blanket from the top shelf, moved back to the living room, and covered her with it. Her breathing had become regular. She was gone for the night. There could be no doubt of that.

Mace reached for the purse Leeny still clutched against her chest, pulled it gently away, and set it down on the coffee table in front of the couch. It was heavy. He laughed to himself. It was as if she were carrying rocks.

Carefully, with both hands, Mace removed Leeny's clear-framed glasses. He turned and held them up to the light coming from the kitchen. There seemed to be no prescription. The glasses seemed purely cosmetic. He shook his head and placed them on one corner of the table. Perhaps he just hadn't noticed the curve of the lenses in the darkness. Finally he covered her with the blanket, kissed her on the forehead, and moved toward the bedroom.

As she heard the door close, Leeny opened one eye slightly to make certain that Mace had in fact gone into the bedroom. When she was sure that he had, she rose and reached for the purse. She inspected it carefully. Thank God he had not opened it. If he had, he would have seen the small pistol.

Leeny dropped the purse to the carpet and lay back on the sofa. She was exhausted, but she could not give in to sleep yet. She was here on a mission, one she could not begin until Mace McLain was asleep. She breathed deeply. She hated this so much.

20

A t nine sharp the next morning Mace stepped out of the elevator onto the second floor of the Walker Pryce building, the
executive floor. At the far end of the corridor lay Lewis Webster's office. Mace drew in a deep breath. He needed to speak to
Webster about several things, not the least of which was whether
or not he still had a job.

He moved down the wide, high-ceilinged hallway, striding
quickly beneath the massive chandeliers. The hallway was lined
with sprawling secretarial workstations, equipped with all the latest
equipment. They were positioned immediately outside the huge
offices of the senior executives so that they could access their life-
lines to the outside world quickly if need be. The women who sat
at these desks protected the executives ferociously. They had been
with their respective superiors for years and were a key part of their
success.

Mace nodded to the ladies as he passed. They all were as well
known throughout the institution as the men for whom they
worked.

Usually Mace enjoyed coming to the executive floor. It oozed
power and reminded him of the preeminence Walker Pryce enjoyed and the respect it commanded throughout the world's financial markets. Inlaid cedar paneling covered the walls, filling the
corridor with the pleasant scent of wealth. Oil paintings hung from

the paneling, and each piece of furniture in the hallway—even the secretarial desks and credenzas on which stood modern computer and communications equipment—was an antique. Usually he would have moved slowly down the thick maroon carpet toward Webster's office, reflecting on the history of the venerable institution, but today he was preoccupied.

"Good morning, Mace." Walter Marston stood behind his executive assistant, dictating a letter. One hand gripped a strap of his brightly colored suspenders, and the other held a lighted fat cigar. Its rich smoky scent intermingled with the cedar aroma, adding to the atmosphere of conspicuous consumption pervading the great room.

"Good morning, Walter." Mace interrupted his mission for a moment and moved toward Marston to shake his hand. It was not a bad idea, anytime you had the opportunity, to kiss the ring of the man who would probably replace Lewis Webster as senior partner sometime in the next three years. Marston was a man who almost certainly would have a big part in determining when Mace would, or would not, become a partner, no matter what Webster said about single-handedly guaranteeing partnership status if Broadway Ventures was successful.

"You look a little distracted this morning, young man." Marston puffed on his cigar.

Mace smiled broadly and relaxed as he released Marston's hand. It was never wise to appear too aggressive at Walker Pryce. Mace had learned that in his first few months at the firm. Walker Pryce professionals were expected to maintain their calm at all times, to be what the partners called "conservatively aggressive."

"No, I'm fine," Mace said smoothly. "It's just that we've been working hard on Broadway Ventures, trying to put the thing together."

"Oh, yes, the fund." Marston sniffed.

Mace noticed a strange expression cloud Marston's face. It was almost as if the man found the mention of Broadway Ventures repugnant. But Webster had made it clear that Marston was behind the fund that day in his office.

"How is the fund going?" the older man asked stiffly.

Mace thought he detected misgivings in Marston's tone. So Webster had steamrollered at least this member of the executive committee into agreeing to the fund, maybe through one of those behind-closed-door meetings Mace had heard rumors of. He nodded. "Fairly well." He spoke in a restrained voice, in a tone that was meant to convey to Marston that he too was not convinced that Broadway Ventures was such a great idea. If the fund blew up, Mace wanted to be able to resurrect his career from the debris. Perhaps if Marston really did have misgivings about what was going on and understood that Mace's participation in the venture was not wholly voluntary, Marston would be forgiving after he had replaced Webster as the senior partner. Perhaps he would allow Mace to reenter the advisory side of Walker Pryce at that point. If the fund blew up for any reason, Mace knew that Webster would be torn apart by the partnership like some elderly lion on the African plain, and Marston would likely be the new king.

"What do you mean, fairly well?" Marston was suddenly interested.

"Well, all the money has been raised."

"You're kidding me." Marston exhaled cigar smoke.

Mace shook his head. "Two days ago Chase committed itself to underwrite a billion-dollar five-year revolver for the fund. The loan was to become effective once we had sold a billion dollars worth of partnership interests. This morning Leeny Hunt informed me that the last three-hundred-million-dollar interest had been committed to. We plan to close on all the money this afternoon. This afternoon Broadway Ventures will be completely operational and will have two billion dollars to invest."

Marston stared at Mace without speaking. Never had he thought Webster could pull this thing off. Never had he thought Broadway Ventures would raise so much money so fast. It defied explanation. He released the suspender strap from his left hand and rubbed his eyes. Webster was a hell of a businessman. Not likable but good, he grudgingly admitted.

"So now we have two billion dollars to invest." Mace dropped his voice as he continued. The walls had ears on this floor. "And nowhere to put it."

Marston nodded. That was the kicker. That little problem could still tank Webster if the senior partner was incorrect about a market correction. Still, he hadn't thought it would even have gotten to this point.

"Good morning, Mr. Marston."

The heavy Italian accent came from behind Mace. He turned to see who the speaker was. Moving down the hallway was Vincenzo, the elderly shoeshine man who had made a thirty-year career out of polishing the shoes of Walker Pryce executives.

"Good morning, Vincenzo," Marston replied cheerfully.

Mace turned back toward Marston.

Marston's face became serious for a moment. "Keep me informed of the fund's progress," he whispered.

Mace nodded.

The two men shook hands quickly. Then Marston turned and walked back into his office with Vincenzo in tow.

Mace smiled at Marston's secretary before continuing down the corridor toward Webster's office. That was good, he thought. Marston understood. He would have a lifeline if the fund blew up. But he would have to be very careful about what he told Marston. Webster would probably be furious if he knew that Mace was giving Marston information about Broadway Ventures. And Webster was still the senior partner.

Mace passed Graham Polk's darkened office. Polk spent most of his time in the middle of Walker Pryce's massive trading floor on seventeen. It only made sense. Polk had to be close to the action so he could make split-second decisions. But spending so much time on the trading floor meant he spent little time dealing with things political, and at the senior executive level political machinations were as important as making money for the firm.

Finally he reached Sarah Clements' workstation. "Good morning, Sarah."

Sarah glanced up from her computer, and her face broke into a wide smile. She liked Mace. Unlike many of the other young people at the firm, he was always pleasant. "Good morning, Mace."

Mace spent several moments making small talk, asking questions about Sarah's children, who were almost fully grown now. Finally he glanced toward Webster's closed door. "Is he in?" Mace nodded at the large door.

Sarah shook her head. "No, he's gone to Washington for the day. He was called away suddenly late last night." Sarah paused. "You should have just called down. I could have saved you the trip."

Mace smiled. "Oh, it's all right. I had to go down to the street anyway on an errand." It was an excuse. He had no errand to run. When he needed to see Webster, he never called. As standard operating procedure Sarah informed each caller that Webster was busy and would have to call him back. Unless Webster told Sarah to accept a specific individual's call, she deflected all of them this way. And it might be hours, or even days, before Webster called back, depending on who you were.

"He should be back in tomorrow."

"Washington," Mace murmured.

Sarah nodded. "Can you keep a secret?" she asked, leaning forward.

Mace gave her the hurt puppy dog look. "Of course I can."

"Okay. Well, you'll never believe who he's meeting with."

Mace laughed. "The president," he said.

Sarah shook her head solemnly. "No. The vice president."

The smile disappeared from Mace's face. She was absolutely serious. He could see it in her eyes. The vice president?

* * *

Rachel bent low against the chilly wind whipping across the street. She clutched the package from Pittsburgh tightly against her side. Inside the blue and orange envelope was information from Bradley Downes at the Stillman Company, information she had been nervously awaiting for several days. He could have easily ignored her inquiry about Leeny and not bothered to call his contact at LeClair and Foster, but he hadn't. He had followed through. Now every nerve ending in her body was on fire.

She had called Bradley yesterday, and he had indicated that he had just sent her the information via overnight mail service. He would not discuss the contents of the package with her on the telephone but made her promise over and over that she would never identify him as the source—except that he would confirm to Mace, and only to Mace, that Stillman had invested just ten million dollars in Broadway Ventures, not the hundreds of millions Leeny claimed she would get.

Rachel turned off the sidewalk toward the entrance of her apartment building. As she did, she paused and looked back over her shoulder. There he was again, the well-built man with the long blond hair, this time on the other side of the street, walking away from her. It was the third time she had seen him: yesterday on the street, a little while ago at the post office, and now. She stared as the man sauntered away. It was the same man. She was almost certain.

Another gust of wind swept across the street, nearly tearing the package from her grip. Rachel brushed the hair from her eyes and hurried to the front door of the building. She smiled at the blue-uniformed security guard as she passed through the second set of doors. He smiled back at her. Rachel gripped the package tightly even as she escaped the bluster outside. She could not wait to tear it open.

Even before the rickety elevator doors had fully closed, she had stripped open the package and removed the contents. Her eyes scanned the handwritten pages, then the typed ones. The elevator slowly climbed toward the fourth floor. Her breathing became shorter and her eyes widened as she sped through the information. Amazing.

The elevator stopped at the third floor, and the doors began to open. Instinctively she crammed the papers back inside the envelope. No one should see this.

An older gentleman holding a bouquet of scraggly flowers moved into the car. He smiled meekly at her, and she smiled back. He was headed for the top floor of the building, where all the spinsters lived, Rachel thought.

For a moment she wondered which woman he was courting, but her mind did not remain on the thought for long. She glanced down at the package in her hands. She needed to talk to Mace right away. He would want to see this.

Mace pushed through the door of his apartment, tossed his coat and jacket on the sofa, and headed toward the kitchen. He wanted that cold bottle of beer he had almost consumed last night with Leeny. On second thought, he didn't just want that bottle of beer, he needed it. It had been a long day.

Mace pulled the bottle from the refrigerator, popped the cap, and took a long, satisfying swig. Finally he pulled the dark brown bottle away from his mouth. He wiped his lips with the back of his hand and noticed the glass in the sink, the glass in which he had mixed the scotch and water last night for Leeny. He took another swallow of beer. She had still been asleep on the sofa when he had first come out of the bedroom this morning at six sharp to boil water for coffee, lying in roughly the same position in which he had left her after covering her with the blanket last night. But she had been gone when he emerged from the bedroom the second time after taking his shower.

Several more gulps of the beer raced down his throat. The bottle was already almost empty. Leeny had called him at Walker Pryce at eleven o'clock this morning to tell him that all

the Broadway Ventures partnership money had been raised, all
one billion dollars. It would begin coming into the Chase collection account tomorrow. And she told him that she would not be
in her office until sometime after lunch. She provided no explanation for her late arrival or for her abrupt departure from his
apartment that morning. She seemed distant on the phone and
still seemed that way when she finally arrived at the office
around three o'clock. She was a strange woman, he was coming
to find.

The empty beer bottle crashed into the trash can next to the
rarely used dishwasher. Quickly Mace opened the refrigerator
again, pulled out another beer, and headed through the apartment
to the second bedroom, which he used as an office. He wanted to
check his E-mail to see if the office had sent him anything since he
had left Walker Pryce forty-five minutes ago.

Mace relaxed into the comfortable captain's chair, adorned
with the University of Iowa insignia, in front of his desk. He
took another sip of beer, then flipped on the computer. As
it hummed to life, he gazed at the display. The virus detection
software flashed across the screen. Finally Mace leaned forward as the familiar figures at the end of the cycle appeared.
Suddenly, as he was about to start tapping an input sequence, the
computer began to scream loudly. He pulled back instinctively
as the intense beeping continued for a full ten seconds. His
mouth fell open slowly. Someone had turned on the computer
and accessed his files without his permission. The beeping
sound meant that someone had logged into his computer without entering the prescribed password. The computer could still
be used without entering the password, but Mace had installed
the warning just for fun. The salesman had pointed out that the
warning system came with the software he had purchased, so
why not use it?

Finally the alarm stopped, but still he did not move. Someone had accessed his files. And it was very obvious to him who

that someone was. There was only one person who could have done it. Sometime in the night Leeny had risen from the sofa and systematically rifled through the files he had stored on the hard drive and perhaps what he had on the wafer disks aligned in the small box next to the processing unit as well. But why?

21

Being here flew in the face of all the training. In the face of everything he had been taught to hold dear—like loyalty to your commander, obeying orders, and honor. But he had also been trained to understand that there might come a time when he had to disregard those things and act on his own. His experience told him that this was one of those times. Slade Conner slid the razor-thin lock pick into the office doorknob of James Franklin, a partner at the prominent Detroit-based financial accounting firm of Neel, Layer & Thoss. Franklin was the partner responsible for the Andrews Industries account. After several moments the door unlocked with a gentle click. Slade glanced both ways, but there was no need for caution; the place was dark and deserted. He smirked. If this had been New York or Los Angeles, the lights would have been burning brightly for the associates who wouldn't leave until two or three in the morning. He would not have been able to break in so easily. But this was the Midwest, where people valued things like time with their families. Those family values made corporate espionage a great deal less challenging.

He moved into the office, closed the door, pulled a flashlight from his jacket, turned it on, and surveyed the office. It was blandly furnished with metal and veneer. Everywhere there were stacks of papers: on the desk, the credenzas, and the several tables at the edge of the room, even on the floor. It looked like the remnants of a ticker-tape parade, for Christ's sake. Tax time was obviously fast approaching, Slade thought.

There was one spot in the office that seemed out of place with the chaos surrounding it: the center of Franklin's desk. Slade shone the flashlight on this spot from across the room. There everything seemed in order. Everything had its place. Including the envelope that lay in the very middle of the clearing, its lines exactly parallel to those of the rectangular desk.

Slade moved purposefully to the desk and surveyed the envelope under the arc of the flashlight. The front of the envelope was blank. But it was clearly meant for him. It had been left in this clear spot for him to find easily, just as his contact had written that it would be.

The person who had written the first anonymous letter had contacted him with a second letter, citing passages from the first letter to prove he or she was the author of both. Whoever had written the letter had somehow known—or made a damn good guess—that he was coming here, to the offices of Neel, Layer & Thoss, to look for information regarding Andrews Industries. The letter was very specific about how to enter the building clandestinely, about how to gain access to the Neel Layer offices, and in which office of the accounting firm the company financial statements of Andrews Industries would be waiting. The letter had included codes, camera locations, and the exact time of guard checks throughout the building.

Initially Slade had been convinced that the letter was sent to entrap him. He was certain at first that local or even federal law enforcement officers would be hiding on the premises to arrest him as he came through the door. Maybe someone on Preston Andrews' staff had sent the letter so as to link Malcolm Becker to a Watergate-like debacle and take Becker out of the election. But as Slade had performed his reconnaissance—watching the guards and trying the combinations during normal business hours when he would not arouse suspicion—he realized that the letter was truly meant to help him break in. If someone had been trying to set him up, one piece of the intelligence would have been false. One shred of information would have been deliberately delivered incorrectly—a wrong number in the code or a guard check time only minutes off—so as to trip him up, so as to cost him that one moment that in the end would nail him. But the information was accurate.

Even then Slade remained suspicious that the authorities would be waiting inside for him. Except for one other thing. The letter explained that contained in the envelope on Franklin's desk would be the latest annual financial statements for Andrews Industries, highly confidential documents exhibiting the financial position of the huge family firm, but that these financial statements would be inaccurate. The letter explained that the numbers had been fraudulently manufactured to show that Andrews Industries was strong and in solid financial shape. But really just the opposite was true. The company was actually incurring serious problems, but Malcolm Becker must not know this for certain. He must see the false statements and believe that Andrews Industries was flush with cash that Preston Andrews could use in his campaign. There was too much to the letter for it to be a setup.

Slade removed the neatly bound financial statements from the large envelope and leafed through the booklet quickly. He was not a financial expert, but he knew enough to see that the company these financial statements portrayed was performing quite well. And they were complete, right down to the partner's unqualified opinion. He slid the statements back into the envelope.

Slade switched off the flashlight and tucked the package under his arm, next to the package that contained the real statements he had located ten minutes ago in another office down the hall. These financials had not been so easy to procure. But the writer of the letters must have known he would go for the real statements as well.

He shook his head. The Rat Man. It had to be. Ferris must have realized that if Becker won the presidential nomination, he would leave his lifelong friend behind. Ferris just wasn't marketable enough to make the leap across the Potomac River to the White House with Becker. And this was the Rat Man's attempt to maintain his position in life. By somehow torpedoing Becker with the accusations in the first letter and now by making available these phony financial statements meant to confuse him, Ferris actually hoped to keep his boss out of the White House. Because he thought that the White House for Becker meant the end of the line for himself. It was the only explanation for all of this. At least the best explanation Slade could come up with.

Vargus shivered as he sat in the cold car. He watched the child playing gleefully in the snow. The front yard was illuminated by the lamp over the front step. He shivered again, involuntarily. America was too cold. Whether it was the backwoods of West Virginia or a suburban neighborhood of the Northeast, it was much too cold. At least in February. How he longed for the warmth of the Caribbean. But it would not be long now, he thought. Not long at all. And he would have all that money to play with to make paradise even better.

The swarthy man reached for the mug of steaming coffee sitting on the passenger seat beside him. He pressed the container to his lips, enjoying its warmth. The liquid passed over his tongue and down his gullet. It tasted so good, and it seemed to heat his entire body. He could not turn on the car because someone might become suspicious. Someone might notice the exhaust emanating from the pipe in the rear of the auto and come out of his abode to investigate. Then he would have to speed off into the night.

Vargus didn't care if someone took down the license number. The car was stolen, and the owner recently dead. So there was no reason to worry about a concerned citizen jotting down the six figures of the plate and reporting them to the police. By the time the police ever found the car or its dead owner, he would be long gone. But if someone somehow actually got a look at his face, that was another story. That might require another trip to the neighbor-hood for a much different purpose.

A pair of car lights appeared in the rearview mirror. Vargus leaned down onto the passenger seat until he was certain the other car had passed, then sat up again. The young boy was still playing in the yard.

He glanced at the lighted liquid crystal display of his watch. Al-most eight o'clock. Eight o'clock at night. Pitch-black. And the boy was outside building a snowman. By himself. The parents were not careful with the boy. That was good. Of course they had no reason to be careful with the boy. This was a quiet street in a quiet middle-class neighborhood. Vargus smiled to himself. In a very few days people would begin to be careful again. Young children would not play outside after dark. And they would never again play without parental supervision.

Suddenly the door of the small brick house swung open. The woman stood in the doorway, her arms crossed tightly over the thick sweater, calling to the eight-year-old boy. Even from this dis-tance Vargus could see the breath rushing out of her warm mouth and into the frigid night air, creating a mist before her face that slowly dissipated in the halo of light coming from the exposed bulb above her head. His eyesight was excellent. All his senses were ex-cellent. And he used them to their fullest potential.

The child did not come right away when his mother called, choosing instead to hide behind the snowman. The mother stamped her loafer on the cement step several times; still, the boy did not obey. Finally the woman moved back into the house, clos-ing the front door behind her. The young boy hid behind the snowman for a few more moments, assuming his mother would open the door and call again. But then the exposed bulb over the cement step went out, and within seconds the boy was banging on the door. Moments later it opened, and he disappeared inside.

Vargus smiled again. She thought she was teaching the little boy a lesson. In truth she was sealing his doom.

22

Printed on the single piece of paper in neat boldface type was a list of the real estate investors he and Leeny had visited so far, the specific names of equity and fixed-income money players he had targeted as the best prospects for the fund. Mace picked the piece of paper up off the desk. It was by no means a comprehensive list of his contacts in the real estate industry. But as far as equity investors went, the list represented the richest and most sophisticated ones. These were individuals and institutions that threw lots of cash around and threw it around aggressively, pushing financial leverage to the limit so that their return was as high as possible, so that the properties constantly teetered perilously on the edge of insolvency.

Mace cursed himself quietly. He should not have been so stupid. He should have been less generous with his Rolodex. Leeny had met them all in person now. She had direct access to them. And if she wanted to go around him for some reason, she could.

The buzz of the telephone distracted Mace from his thoughts. He glanced at the phone's display and saw that the call was coming from the receptionist's desk. "Yes, Anna."

"Mr. McLain, you have a visitor out here at reception."

Mace rubbed his cheek. He wasn't expecting anyone. "Who is it?"

Anna's voice dropped to a whisper. "She wouldn't say."

Mace hesitated. "Okay, I'll be right there." He hung up the phone, leaned back in his chair, and groaned. It was probably a messenger, carrying some kind of legal document, who had been given specific orders to give the package to no one but Mace. People were like that with legal documents sometimes. He rose slowly from the chair and moved to the office door. As he reached the doorway, he nearly ran into Leeny, just turning the corner to come into his office.

"Excuse me, Mace." She backed away several steps. They had actually touched for a moment.

"That's all right." Mace's voice was not as friendly as usual.

She glanced up at him quickly, noting the tone, and then away again.

Mace crossed his arms over his broad chest. It was eleven o'clock, and it was the first he had seen of her this morning, the first he had seen of her since discovering that at some point during the night she had spent on his couch, she had run through every computer file he owned—and probably everything he had in his desk as well. He said nothing, waiting for her to begin the conversation.

"Everything okay?" Leeny asked innocently.

She wore a short black skirt, a tight maroon blouse, and loftier-than-usual high heels. It was an outfit most women would not ever have considered wearing to work, particularly when their office was on Wall Street, he thought. But Leeny could carry it off somehow.

"Mace, is there anything wrong?" To the eye she appeared as calm and cool as usual. But her voice, usually soft and smooth, betrayed an atypical unsteadiness, something Mace had not heard before.

He shook his head but said nothing.

Leeny fiddled nervously with the small gold ring on her right index finger as she stood before him. It was terrible to hold a human being's life in one's hand, she thought, to play God. Suddenly she remembered fantasizing many times as a little girl about being God. About knowing things others didn't. About making people do what she wanted them to do. About causing pain. Now she realized how terrible being God really would be.

She glanced at Mace again and then away again. There was nothing more he could do for them. He had outlived his utility. And he didn't suspect a thing. There was nothing to indicate that he had the slightest suspicion of what was really going on or, more important, that he had communicated any suspicion to anyone. Nothing on the computer in his office here at Walker Pryce. Nothing on his computer at the apartment or in his desk at the apartment. He had been a good soldier, and now he would pay for it.

With one visit to Webster's office she would effectively put an end to his existence. Webster was pushing. He wanted to send the assassin to kill Mace. Because the men in West Virginia were ready to go. Because the man in Washington desperately needed the money. And because Mace had now become a huge liability, someone who might easily figure out what was really going on.

Finally she was able to meet Mace's gaze. He had to die. She had known that from the start. If he were somehow spared, he might figure it out, the whole thing. Then it all would come crashing down around them. She wouldn't collect her five million dollars, and she would end up in jail. So what was her problem? She looked deeply into Mace's steel gray eyes. She had begun to care about him. It was as simple as that. He had covered her with the blanket on the sofa of his apartment and given her the tender kiss on the forehead. It had been so long since someone had shown her that kind of compassion.

Leeny looked away from Mace and shook her head slightly. The conflicts were suddenly too deep. She could not make the pieces fit together as they should, and she felt herself beginning to shake. Perhaps this was what people meant by the term *nervous breakdown*. Perhaps she was in the middle of it right now and did not even realize. She hadn't realized it the last time.

"Where were you going?" She smiled at Mace, attempting to cover up the emotions within through an outward display of calm.

He nodded at the door leading from the inner offices to the reception area. "Down to the street to get some fresh air. I have something I have to get at the store." For some reason he did not want to tell her about the visitor.

"Which is it?"

"What do you mean?"

"Are you going to get some fresh air or do you have to go to the store?"

Mace did not respond immediately. She was a sharp character. "Both."

"And you were going to go in just your shirtsleeves. Without even your jacket? It's twenty degrees outside."

"I'm from Minnesota, Leeny. When it reaches twenty degrees in Minneapolis, summer can't be far away. At twenty degrees men start thinking about their golf clubs and women start thinking about their pool boys."

Leeny laughed. "Okay. Well, would you mind some company? I need to talk to you for a couple of minutes."

"That sounds ominous."

"No, it's nothing serious. I just have questions about some of the investors." She inhaled deeply. If he only knew how ominous his situation was. Perhaps she should tell him everything. So he could save himself. But the thought melted away as quickly as it had come to her. Save yourself, Leeny. No one else will. "It won't take long."

Mace nodded. "Fine."

Leeny began to walk back toward her office. "Just let me get my coat. I feel the cold more than you do. I'll be right back," she called back to him.

"Okay. I'll be at reception." He moved quickly to the door and pushed through it, then stopped abruptly. Rachel sat in one of the chairs next to the receptionist's desk reading a magazine.

For a moment Rachel continued to read. Then suddenly she became aware of Mace's presence. She dropped the magazine on the glass table in front of the chair and ran to him, stopping just short of where he stood. "Hi." She was full of enthusiasm, obviously glad to see him.

"Hello there." The door leading to the office area clicked shut behind Mace.

Rachel peeked at the receptionist, who was busy with a crossword puzzle. "I missed you," she whispered.

"I thought you couldn't stand me. You sort of left me holding the bag the other night, as they say. Kind of a strange way for a person who misses another to act. Wouldn't you say, Ms. Sommers?" He was being purposely formal.

"You didn't let me finish. What I was going to say was that I missed you at class the other night." She smiled coyly.

A hurt expression crossed Mace's face.

"I'm trying to apologize, Mace," she said.

He began to laugh. "I know. I'm just having fun. Hey, you'd better toughen up before you get down here to Walker Pryce."

Immediately she punched him in the arm.

"Ouch!" He grabbed his arm where she had struck him.

The receptionist glanced up at them for a moment and then back at her crossword puzzle.

Mace lowered his voice. "That hurt." But he was obviously enjoying himself.

"You big baby." Her whisper was tough, but her smile beautiful.

It had been only a few days since he had seen her, but it seemed forever since he had seen that beautiful smile. Suddenly he realized how much he had missed her. "What the heck are you doing here?" He stopped rubbing his arm and grinned at her. "Couldn't wait until tonight to see me, huh?"

Rachel rolled her eyes.

"You can't fool me. You just couldn't wait, could you?"

"You're too much." Her expression became serious. "I have to talk to you." She nodded at an envelope she held in her right hand.

"Talk away. Just don't hit me again."

Rachel shook her head solemnly. "I don't want to talk here."

"It must be serious. God, everybody has serious things to talk to me about all of a sudden."

She looked at him strangely for a second, not understanding. "It is serious. It concerns your partner."

The door leading to the offices swung open. Leeny almost bumped into Mace again as she came into the reception area. She stopped short, her gaze fixed immediately upon Rachel. "Hello." Her tone was cool, and she did not extend her hand, as she had done in Webster's office.

"Hi." Rachel was equally distant.

Immediately Leeny touched Mace on the arm. She watched as Rachel's eyes followed her fingers to Mace's shirtsleeve. "Come on, sweetheart. Let's go."

Rachel felt the heat rush through her body at the word *sweetheart*. Her eyes met Mace's instantly, but she could discern nothing from his gaze.

Leeny tugged at Mace gently. "Come on." She was persistent.

He resisted Leeny for a moment. Something was wrong. Two nights ago Leeny had manipulated her way into his apartment, baiting the trap with the possibility of sex, only to fall asleep, or perhaps fake sleep, he realized now, and subsequently steal into his home office and rifle through his personal affairs. Now she was calling him sweetheart in front of Rachel, something she had never done before. It didn't add up.

Leeny pulled at Mace again, this time more firmly.

He resisted again for a moment. As Leeny looked away for a second, he quickly held up three fingers and mouthed the words *Paul Revere*. Then he was gone, into an elevator and away from Rachel.

She ran a hand through her long hair, wondering what in the world he had meant, disappointed that he had given in to Leeny so easily. Then she began to smile.

* * *

"I thought this would be an appropriate place to meet," Mace said as he glanced around One if by Land, Two if by Sea, the restaurant at which they had eaten several nights before. It was three o'clock in the afternoon, and the place was all but deserted. There was only one other table of patrons in the room. "I wasn't sure you'd figure out my code as Leeny was pulling me away."

"I figured it out."

"Obviously. Of course we could have just waited another few hours until class tonight."

Rachel shook her head. "No. You need to see this right away."

Mace watched her for a moment. She was serious. He could see that. "Okay," he said softly. "What do you have?"

She hesitated. "First I want you to know that I'm really sorry about the way I acted the other night, leaving you here without telling you that I was going." Her voice was almost inaudible. "The offer you made me at dinner is really generous. I received the letter outlining the offer by messenger a couple of days ago. I really do want to work at Walker Pryce. I hope my behavior hasn't affected my opportunity to join the firm."

"No, it hasn't," he said convincingly.

A waiter began moving toward the table. Mace saw him. "Two coffees," he said forcefully. He did not want the man ruining the moment. He was going to lay out everything for Rachel, and he did not want to be interrupted.

The waiter thought about complaining at the small order, then shrugged and walked away.

"It was really immature of me." Rachel continued.

Mace shook his head. "No, I acted badly. I'm to blame. By the way, I did try to get in touch with you."

"I thought that was probably you." She smiled at him.

"You were there? And you didn't pick up the phone?"

"I had to teach you a little bit of a lesson." She smiled at him shyly.

Mace feigned disgust for a moment, then grinned again. She was something all right. "So here I am calling all over New York and you're sitting in your apartment ignoring me."

"All over New York?"

"Hell, yes. I even tried to call you in Brooklyn. But each of the Sommers' residences I called didn't know who you were."

"Of course not." She was still smiling.

Mace gazed at her. "What do you mean, 'of course not'?"

"The listing in Brooklyn is under my stepfather's name. Bond. Francis Bond. I kept my birth father's name, though I'm not sure why. He left my mother high and dry when I was two years old."

"No wonder I couldn't reach you," Mace whispered. "Look—"

"Mace," she interrupted him.

He stopped speaking.

Her fingers slid across the table and touched the back of his hand. "I know you were just protecting me against myself the other night. Walker Pryce is a tremendous opportunity. It's a chance for me to make something of myself. I've worked too hard to get where I am. I can't be distracted. I know you're right."

So she had figured it out on her own. He laughed to himself sadly. He was about to open up as he never before had, and she had short-circuited him. He wanted to tell her how much he cared. He had decided that they would just deal with the fact that they both worked at Walker Pryce if the time came to deal with it. Maybe he would move to another investment bank, so that she could stay at Walker Pryce, if that was what it took. The new job wouldn't be as lucrative as the one at Walker Pryce, but *lucrative* was a relative term on Wall Street. And what good was money without the one you wanted? Wasn't that what people said? But now he couldn't tell her. She had come to the right decision all on her own, and to tell her now that he really did want her would be completely unfair.

"I've worked very hard in the last few years." Rachel continued.

"But Walker Pryce will expect even more out of me. I have to be prepared to make the sacrifice."

Mace nodded solemnly. "You'll work twenty-hour days. You'll be in your office when all your friends are out having a good time. You'll hate it. But you'll make more money than you ever thought possible."

"I know." She withdrew her fingers from his hand.

Mace watched her fingers move across the table away from his. If they had started dating and a relationship had developed, they would never have seen each other anyway. It was better this way, but somehow it didn't feel better.

The waiter brought the coffees, then left without a word.

Rachel opened the overnight envelope lying on the table in front of her and removed several pieces of paper. She considered them for several moments before speaking. "Kathleen Hunt is a bad woman, Mace." Rachel looked at him evenly.

Mace recoiled slightly. "What?"

"I think there's a lot more to her than meets the eye."

Mace began to smile. "What's that supposed to mean?"

Rachel shook her head, reading his thoughts. "It's not that I'm worried that she's competition. I promise. I care about you, and I also care about Walker Pryce now that I'm going to be an employee in a few months."

Her tone confirmed to Mace that this was not some ploy to drive a wedge between him and Leeny. "What do you have there?" Mace pointed at the papers on the table in front of Rachel.

Rachel's voice dropped to a whisper even though there was no one near them. "Remember you told me that Leeny had worked at LeClair and Foster before coming to Walker Pryce?"

Mace nodded.

"I have a friend who knows some people at LeClair and Foster," she said.

"And?"

"And he talked to them for me. It seems that about a year ago three people in the San Francisco office of LeClair and Foster were indicted on insider trading charges."

"I remember reading something about that. But it didn't get a lot of press. It went away quickly if I recall correctly." Mace picked up his coffee cup and took a sip.

"It did." Rachel raised one eyebrow as if Mace had just hit upon a significant point.

Mace leaned toward Rachel. "Are you saying Leeny was involved?" His voice rose as he anticipated what Rachel was driving at. He shook his head. "I don't believe it. Lewis Webster would have had her checked out thoroughly before hiring her. He wouldn't have taken the chance. As important as this fund is to him, he wouldn't have knowingly exposed it to this kind of risk."

"Listen to me, will you?" Rachel's voice was firm.

"Okay." Mace held up his hands.

Rachel began again. "A year and a half ago LeClair and Foster was retained by the management of Northwest Rod and Steel, a manufacturer of specialty steel, headquartered in Seattle. It was a public company, and apparently the people there had gotten word that someone, a corporate raider type, was going to take an unsolicited run at them. So they decided to retain a financial adviser. They chose LeClair and Foster. The four-person deal team at LeClair and Foster did some sniffing around and determined that indeed there was a hostile buyer about to make a bid. As a defensive strategy they recommended to management at Northwest Rod and Steel that they execute a leveraged buyout quickly, that management partner up with some equity money and some banks and buy up all the shares from the public stockholders before the raider did. Management agreed with the recommendation immediately. LeClair and Foster arranged the financing within weeks and then announced the takeover. Just as the deal was about to close, as the tender offer made by management was ending, the corporate raider surfaced and announced his own, higher offer. LeClair and Foster couldn't get the money people on their side to go any higher, so the raider won. LeClair and Foster negotiated management contracts for their clients, were paid a huge fee for their work, and the deal was done. End of story, right?"

"Somehow I doubt it."

Rachel nodded. "A few months after the deal had closed a senior person at LeClair and Foster figured out that the people on its deal team had bought shares in Northwest Rod and Steel *after* management agreed to proceed with the leveraged buyout but *before* the tender offer for the shares was publicly announced."

Mace's face was grim. "A clear case of insider trading."

"Yes." She ran a hand through her hair. "The chairman of LeClair and Foster found out what had transpired and called the feds immediately without the deal team's knowing what he was doing. There was a quick investigation, and within days the feds had put together indisputable evidence of insider trading by the deal team. Subsequently three employees of LeClair and Foster were criminally charged."

Mace rubbed his eyes. This wasn't good information. In fact it was terrible information. Even if Leeny hadn't actually been convicted in the case, if she had only been indicted, it would probably still have to be disclosed to the Broadway Ventures investors. And they might have the ability to take back their money as a result. "Leeny Hunt was one of them, I assume."

Rachel shook her head. "No. She was the only member of the deal team not charged."

"Then what's the big deal?"

"The big deal is that my friend's contact at LeClair and Foster says that even though Leeny wasn't actually indicted, there was no doubt that she was trading on the inside just as the other three were, that she had done so on other occasions during other deals as well." Rachel straightened up in her chair. "I know you don't want to hear this because it presents you with all kinds of problems. But Leeny was definitely involved, Mace. She resigned from the firm a week after the charges had been brought against the other three and went into seclusion. Everybody figured that she had cut a deal with the feds, that she was going to testify at the trial and be their star witness. But she wasn't a witness. She wasn't charged, and she wasn't a witness. She just went away."

"What happened to the other three?" Mace asked. "I don't remember."

Rachel's eyes met his. "That's where the whole thing becomes even stranger."

"What do you mean?"

"The trial was proceeding normally, and suddenly the judge started throwing out all the evidence, saying it was obtained illegally. Finally the feds didn't have anything left, and the jury had no choice but to find the defendants innocent. They walked away scot-free."

Mace said nothing.

Rachel kept going. "The person at LeClair and Foster that my friend knows says there was no doubt that these people were trading on the inside *and* that Leeny Hunt was involved. The feds had them dead to rights. But it all went away. Mysteriously."

A car horn sounded outside the restaurant. Mace glanced out the window. "It's troubling, but what am I supposed to do? The people were tried and found innocent, no matter how strange it all sounds." Mace hesitated. "What's really troubling is that Webster didn't find this out."

Rachel tapped the cardboard envelope with her fingernail. "He would have *had* to have known all about this before hiring her. It would have been easy to find out during the process of even a superficial background check. For God's sake, my contact sent me old newspaper clippings from the local papers out there."

"I can't believe Webster would have hired Leeny knowing all that—even if she was never indicted." He shook his head. "Who is your contact?" His eyes moved to the sender area of the envelope, but the address had been inked out.

"I can't tell you."

He rolled his eyes. "What made you think to do all this investigating, Nancy Drew?"

"You told me that you thought the Stillman Company was going to invest a couple of hundred million dollars in Broadway Ventures."

Mace nodded. "Yes. So?"

"I spoke with a friend of mine at the Stillman Company, someone I met because of the fund I manage for Columbia." Rachel hesitated. "The Stillmans invested only ten million in Broadway Ventures, nowhere near what Leeny told you she was getting from them."

"Are you certain?" Mace felt a sudden uneasiness, an almost eerie sensation that something *was* wrong with Broadway Ventures, that Rachel was right.

"I'm positive. You can call him." She glanced down at the envelope. "It's all in here, Mace. The newspaper clippings. A memo from the person at LeClair and Foster, unsigned, of course. A copy of a LeClair and Foster senior management memo detailing the evidence against the four people, including Leeny Hunt, on the Northwest Rod and Steel deal team. And the name and number of my friend at the Stillman Company you can call to confirm the amount of the firm's investment in Broadway Ventures." Rachel stuffed the papers back in the envelope and handed it to him. "You can keep this. I made a copy for myself."

Mace took the envelope from her silently. There *were* too many strange things going on: Rachel's information; the fact that Leeny had broken into his computer; the odd look on Marston's face; Webster's absolute conviction that there was going to be a Manhattan real estate crash; Leeny's ability to raise a billion dollars *so fast*. But what could they all mean? Did they really mean anything at all? Even if Leeny had traded on the inside at LeClair and Foster and Lewis Webster had known all about it, so what? She had never actually been accused of anything. It was wrong to trade on insider information, but if the feds couldn't put together a case, who was he to say anything? So what if Leeny was lying about where the money for Broadway Ventures was coming from? The money was clearly in the account. John Schuler had inked the Chase deal, and he wouldn't have executed the loan documents without confirming the fact that all the partnership money was in the Broadway Ventures account at Chase. Mace shook his head. It was all probably meaningless, but he had to follow up on what she had given him. It was his nature. He already knew where he was going to start looking for answers.

"There's one more thing you should know," Rachel said.

Mace glanced up at her. He had been lost in thought. "What is it?"

"About ten years ago Leeny spent some time in a Montreal mental institution as a result of severe clinical depression. She still uses prescription drugs to control the condition."

23

Washington, D.C., like New York City, had been wrapped in cold since the beginning of February. But this day the nation's capital was enjoying a brief respite from the heavy overcoats, gloves, and scarves that were the normal outdoor attire for this time of year. Slade Conner moved slowly down the sidewalk next to the long Reflecting Pool, still frozen solid despite spring's first foray north. As he walked, he took care to avoid the growing reservoirs in the sidewalk, reservoirs supplied by the melting snow piled a foot high at the edge of the cement. At the west end of the pool Abraham Lincoln looked out sternly from his seat inside the huge marble structure that bore his name.

Usually he would have enjoyed the warm weather, which he much preferred to the arduous Minnesota winters he had endured throughout his youth. But today he could not enjoy himself. Today things such as conformity, following orders, and being the good soldier did not seem to make sense any longer. The maxims he had lived by for so long were coming under scrutiny, and he was suddenly distracted as he had never before been.

Malcolm Becker, hands clenched behind his back, walked beside Slade. Becker stared straight ahead as he moved, oblivious of the deep puddles on the sidewalk. His black leather military-issue shoes were soaked, but he did not seem to notice. His face was grim, and his eyes were fixed upon Abraham Lincoln, who grew larger before them with each step.

"What was it that you wanted to discuss, Slade?" Becker was the first to break the silence. "What was so important?"

Slade removed a pair of sunglasses from his shirt pocket and put them on. The sun, already low in the early-afternoon sky, was bright, and its rays reflected strongly off the melting snow.

Slade swallowed hard. It was not normal to question orders. It ran counter to all his training. If he had done this on the sands of Kuwait during the Persian Gulf War, he might have been killed in the instant he had hesitated. But there came a time when one needed to know why, to see the bigger picture.

Slade checked ahead and behind quickly. There was no one around them at this point. The conversation they were about to engage in required complete confidentiality; that was why they had left CIA headquarters.

Becker stopped walking, sensing Slade's discomfort. "What is it, son?"

Slade stopped and turned toward Becker. He summoned his courage. This was tantamount to mutiny. "General, why did I go to Honduras?" The real question was, "Why did you send me to kill Carter Guilford?" But there was no need to ask it that way. Becker would understand what Slade meant.

Becker did not answer right away. So the pupil had suddenly come of age. He was no longer willing simply to accept the orders of his superior. It was the natural process, and Becker had seen it occur many times over his long career. Now questions had to be dealt with directly and immediately or things could spin out of control. "Take off the sunglasses, boy." Becker took on the military voice, low and gruff.

Slade removed the dark lenses but did not bother to put them back in his shirt pocket. He just held them in his hand, which fell to his side.

Becker moved a step closer to Slade so that their faces were very close. He ground his teeth together slowly. "I told you that Carter Guilford was working with a Colombian drug cartel. He was giving them extremely sensitive information so that the drug runners could avoid detection on their flights into this country, and he was being paid very well for the information." Becker's voice became even lower. "He was keeping some of the money for himself, but he was funneling most of it to Preston Andrews so that Andrews could use it to stabilize his family business."

Slade's face remained impassive, but his mind spun. Becker was claiming that the money from the Ortega cartel was actually going to the vice president, the exact opposite of what the anonymous letter had indicated. There could be no doubt that money from the Ortegas had found its way to Washington. But now there were two very different stories on the recipient of the Ortegas' generosity. This was insane.

"Andrews was able to access information with respect to anti-drug-smuggling activities at the DEA, and Guilford, in his position as head of all field operations for CIA in Central and South America, had our side covered. Andrews approached Guilford a year ago, when his company started to experience troubles. He knew that Guilford needed money, and he himself needed money to prop up his firm. They were a perfect match. Guilford made contact with the Ortegas almost immediately, and it didn't take the Ortegas long to accept the deal. But now that's over. Now Andrews needs something else to help him make it out of his jam. And he's using the power of his office to do it." Becker paused for a second to allow the gravity of what he had just said to sink in. "Carter Guilford was a criminal, Slade. That was why I had you *kill him.*" Becker raised his voice to emphasize the words. Slade recoiled slightly, in an involuntary reaction to the word *kill.*

Becker saw the blink. It was time to slam the door shut. "Preston Andrews is a criminal too, Slade. But I can't have you kill the vice president of the United States. Much as I'd like to, that might create some problems. But I'll tell you something. The country would be much better off without him. The fact that he even has a chance to be president of the nation I love so much, a nation both of us have risked our lives for, sickens me." Becker shook his head. "That SOB went into the Coast Guard to get out of his tour in Nam. I didn't have all those high-level connections his daddy had. While I was in a foxhole being shelled by the Viet Cong, he was chasing salmon poachers off Alaska." Becker snorted his disrespect. "It's not that *I* need to be president. It's that I want someone other than *him* to win the election. I would gladly pull out of the race if I knew by doing so I could guarantee a victory for someone other than Preston Andrews. But that isn't going to happen. It's a two-horse race at this point. I'm the only one that can keep him out of the Oval Office."

"And you believe that he is trying to create a scandal at the CIA to discredit you." Slade's voice was hushed.

"Yes." Becker nodded in approval. The pupil was returning to the fold.

"Why have I been keeping an eye on Mace McLain and the young woman Rachel Sommers?"

Becker's eyes narrowed. So the pupil had not completely returned to the fold yet. "Because I have information leading me to believe that Preston Andrews is working with the investment bank employing Mr. McLain, Walker Pryce and Company. Andrews has had several meetings with the senior partner of the firm, Lewis Webster. I believe that Andrews has recruited Webster to help him conspire to keep Andrews Industries afloat now that the money from Colombia has dried up. I am aware that you know Mr. McLain. I wanted you to keep that line of communication open in case I needed it, so that Mr. McLain would not think it strange if you called him out of the blue." Becker hesitated. "As I recall, the idea to check up on Ms. Sommers was yours."

For several moments Slade stared at his commander. Then Becker's face blurred, and Abraham Lincoln came into focus far behind the general's right shoulder. What was he thinking? How could he have possibly questioned Becker? A man to whom he owed his career?

Becker inhaled slowly. "It is a difficult situation, son. I know that. But it will work out."

Slade nodded.

They began to walk again, back the way they had come, away from the Lincoln Memorial. The meeting was over.

"By the way, Slade, have you been able to get any information with respect to Andrews Industries? I know you've been to Detroit several times." His voice was friendly again.

Slade's thoughts shot suddenly to the two sets of financial statements still hidden in the desk at his apartment.

"John?"

"Yes?"

"It's Mace McLain." Mace spoke loudly. The traffic screaming by the Seventh Avenue public telephone made it almost impossible to hear Schuler.

"Oh, hello, Mace. What's all that noise? Where are you?"

"I'm in between meetings, John." Mace was short with the Chase banker. He was going to be late to Columbia if he didn't get going soon.

"Oh. Well, did you get the execution copies of the loan agreement for Broadway Ventures?" Schuler asked. "I sent them over this morning."

"I got them." Mace was quickly becoming exasperated. He had another, more important topic to discuss than the mundane paperwork related to the loan from Chase. Like most bankers, Schuler was nothing if not chatty, and sometimes it was difficult to break his momentum.

"You all must be pretty happy over there at Walker Pryce." Schuler snorted. "Two billion dollars to play with. It's incredible."

"We're happy all right, John." Mace got to the purpose of the call as the other man stopped to take a breath. "I need a favor."

Schuler took a sip from a glass of water. "Name it."

"I need some information on the investors."

"You mean the investors of Broadway Ventures?" Schuler asked.

"Yes."

Schuler took another sip. "I'm not trying to be flip or anything, Mace, but why don't you just call them up and ask them yourself? I assume you must know them pretty well. They're your investors after all. Heck, I don't even know who they are. I wasn't even allowed to see the subscription agreements. I thought all the secrecy surrounding investor identities was a little much, but Webster gave me an indemnification from Walker Pryce that the investors were all qualified, and that was all I needed. Funny, he usually doesn't give anything away to the banks, but he was happy to give me the indemnification this time." The banker chuckled to himself as if it had been a great coup to win the concession from the normally inflexible Webster. "I would guess with all the secrecy involved that there must be quite a few Swiss investors. All I know is that the money *is* in the partnership account. I'm not sure what I could tell you that you couldn't find out by calling your *own* investors."

It was a dicey situation, Mace thought. If he came clean with Schuler and admitted that he didn't know exactly who the investors were because Leeny and Webster had kept that information to themselves, he risked alarming the banker. That was something he absolutely didn't want to do. If Schuler sniffed anything askew, he might become worried and try to squirm out of the loan. And Webster would find out why Schuler was trying to back out, that Mace had been the cause. But if Mace skirted the issue, Schuler might call Leeny to try to find out what was going on.

A truck roared by, bouncing over several potholes. Mace pulled his coat tightly around his neck as the icy wind from the truck rushed over and around him in the dark. "Look, I'm just doing some standard checking on one of the investors." It was lame, but there was nothing else to say. He used a parental voice. "There's nothing to be alarmed about."

"What do you need?" Schuler didn't sound convinced that this kind of checking was so standard.

"I need you to backtrack the wires into the Broadway Ventures partnership account at Chase. Tell me where the money came from."

"You want me to check *every* wire?"

"Yes." Mace didn't flinch. "I don't believe there will be that many." It was a shot in the dark, but Leeny had raised the money very quickly. There couldn't be that many investors. The gnawing suspicion suddenly intensified. She had raised the money so damn fast.

"This is a little unusual."

"Are you saying you can't do it, John?"

"No, I can do it." Schuler hesitated. "Maybe you could just give me a little idea of what this is about."

"John, I have a quick question first."

"What's that?" the banker snapped. He was becoming annoyed at Mace's evasion.

"Leeny has seemed a little strange since that night I left her with you. Do you have any idea what her problem might be?" He needed Schuler to be much more accommodating, and he knew exactly how to make that happen.

"No." Schuler's tone was suddenly stone cold.

"Have you spoken to her since that night?"

"No. I thought I was supposed to deal only with you. That's what she told me anyway. That's why I've been working the documentation on the loan to Broadway Ventures through you."

That was crap. Leeny never would have told Schuler to deal only with him on the documentation. Schuler was lying. He had used her that night, and now he didn't want to talk to her. He probably hadn't even told her until afterward that the loan had been approved. That was probably why he didn't want to talk to her. The little bastard. It was time to make him sweat. "Did you two go out to dinner after I left your office that evening?"

"No, no. She stayed for a few minutes after you left, then left by herself. I went back to Connecticut. She said she had to meet someone."

"That's funny. I thought Leeny said that you and she went out to get a quick bite to eat after the meeting." He was fishing, but he was certain his bluff would bear fruit.

There was nothing but silence at the other end of the phone for a few moments. "I—I'm just trying to remember. It's been kind of hectic, you know," Schuler sputtered.

"Of course it has been." Mace's voice was soothing.

"Yes, now I remember." Schuler began again. "Sure. We did go out for a little while, but just for a quick dinner." Suddenly Schuler was panicked. He sensed from Mace's tone that Mace somehow knew more about the night at the Inter-Continental than he was letting on. And if Leeny found out that he had called Mace from the restaurant to tell him that the loan had been approved, she might begin to scream. If she was aggressive, she could make a pretty good case against him for sexual harassment. At the very least she could make things sticky for him in the Chase executive offices. "Damn it," he whispered.

The traffic was stopped for a red light, and Mace heard the expletive. He smiled. He could almost see the perspiration forming on Schuler's upper lip. "Everything all right, John?"

Schuler changed the subject quickly. "Fine. Listen, Mace, I'll be happy to check out the wire transfers for you." Suddenly he wanted to get off the phone.

"I need the information fast, John."

"You'll have it tomorrow."

"Thank you."

"Is that all, Mace?"

"For now."

"I'll speak to you tomorrow. Call me at noon."

"Thanks for your help, John. Oh, and I'm sure Leeny will be fine. Of course anything that's bothering her is clearly none of my business."

Schuler hesitated for a moment. "Of course not."

Mace hung up the phone. He smiled as he glanced at his watch. There was no way Schuler was going to call Leeny now.

He hailed a cab. Tomorrow he would get some answers and probably be able to put this whole thing to bed in short order.

Becker glanced up from the file lying open atop his desk as Slade entered the office. The air was full of cigar smoke. "Good evening, Major," he said gruffly.

Slade nodded. "Good evening, General."

"It's late." Becker glanced at his military watch. It was almost midnight. "What did you want to see me about?"

Slade stepped forward, held the folder before him for a second, then dropped it onto the general's desk.

Immediately Becker placed the cigar carefully down into the glass ashtray, picked up the folder, opened it, and removed the contents—financial statements of Andrews Industries. He leafed through them for a few seconds, then gazed up at Slade. Slowly his left eyebrow rose. It wasn't what he had expected.

24

We have the equity money, the bank loan, and a substantial list of investors. People and institutions with significant real estate exposures in Manhattan, all of whom you have met. What more can Mace do for us?" Webster asked impatiently. "When the project reaches zero hour, you will call the investors quietly. They won't even question why it isn't Mace calling them. They won't care. They'll just want to get out at that point."

There was nothing else Leeny could say that might buy Mace a few more days. Save yourself, she thought. "You're right, Lewis. There is nothing more he can do for us." The death warrant had been signed. "Everything is in place. We don't need him now."

A smile formed on Webster's drawn face. "Mace McLain always has been a cocky son of a bitch," the old man whispered. "I wonder if he'll feel as cocky when he's staring down the barrel of a gun."

She felt a chill race up her spine as Webster tilted his head forward and most of the dark eyes disappeared below the eyebrows. He was disgusting.

Webster smiled again. "The shame of it all is that he'll probably never really have the chance to look down the barrel of that gun. They are very efficient. He'll probably never even know what hit him. It will be merciful." Webster said the last few words as if he were disappointed, as if he wished Mace's last few moments did not have to be so merciful.

"Yes, I suppose it will be." Leeny did not know what else to say. It was terrible that Webster could dispose of someone this coldly. Mace had worked hard at Walker Pryce and made Webster a wealthier man. His only regret seemed to be that he wouldn't be a witness to Mace's execution.

"I suppose Mace's little friend Rachel Sommers will be disappointed when she finds out what has happened." Webster stroked his beard.

"What's that?" Leeny's eyes shot to Webster's.

He looked perplexed. "You didn't know?" he whispered.

"Know what?" She was trying desperately to keep her voice in control.

"About Mace and this Sommers woman."

"What about them?"

"They've been screwing like rabbits for weeks."

Leeny's hands began to shake. So Mace really had been using her. He was just like every other man she had ever known. He had said that he cared in the cab. But it was Rachel he really cared about. He had lied to her just as they all had. Leeny clenched her fists tightly to her body so Webster could not see her hands tremble. She could feel herself losing control.

"Are you all right, Ms. Hunt?"

"I'm fine," she said hoarsely.

Webster's eyes narrowed. "I think perhaps you had better give me a copy of that investor list. The one that shows who you and Mace have visited in the last few weeks." He paused. "Just so there are two copies. It is a very important list."

Leeny brought a hand to her mouth. Were they going to kill her too? Was that why Webster wanted the list? She felt her stomach beginning to churn. She needed to get out of this office immediately. "I'll go get it right now."

"Good."

Leeny opened the door of Webster's office and then closed it behind her quickly. For several moments she leaned back against the dark wood, breathing hard. It was as if the walls were closing in on her, as if the room were breathing too. She wanted to scream, but somehow she maintained control. She closed her eyes tightly, opened them again after a few moments, then brought both hands to her eyes to brush the tears away, smearing mascara over her cheeks as she did so because her hands were shaking so badly. Finally she pushed off the door and began to walk unsteadily toward the elevators.

Through the crack of his office door Walter Marston saw Leeny go, watching her closely until she stepped into an elevator and the doors closed behind her. He wanted to help her, to find out why she was so distraught. But he did not want to spend the rest of his life in jail. The Internal Revenue Service was sensitive about people who had evaded taxes on almost twenty million dollars of income. He had no problem saving himself rather than help another in this kind of situation. Besides, there probably wasn't any hope for her at this point. One could only pray that she would see that for herself and get out.

Webster smiled to himself as he gazed out the window onto Wall Street. He had no idea whether or not Mace was sleeping with Rachel. But he knew how severely the image of Mace and Rachel making love would affect Leeny. He laughed out loud to himself for the first time in years.

"Mace McLain."

"Mace, It's John Schuler."

"Good morning, John." Mace glanced at his watch. It was eleven-thirty. "I thought I was supposed to call you at noon."

"That was what we agreed on, but as it turns out, I've got a lunch to go to." Schuler paused. "And I've already got some information for you, so I figured I'd give it to you right away. So you didn't have to wait."

Schuler's voice sounded strangely subservient. But at the same time he sounded as if he would rather be doing anything else in the world but having this conversation. "What do you have?" Mace asked.

"It's a little odd, I guess," Schuler said. "Nothing that causes me undue stress. I don't think it does anyway." He was trying to make it sound as if whatever he had found in the Broadway Ventures account was not puzzling him, but his tone was unconvincing.

There was something wrong. Mace could hear it in his voice. "What is it, John?"

"I had my people follow back to their source the wire transfers that have come into the Broadway Ventures account over the last three weeks, the transfers that basically represent the partners' investments. It's usually a pretty quick process these days what with all the system checks the government people have put into place to follow drug money. Of course I have some fairly high-level friends at other banks who helped us when we couldn't trace things through conventional means. I used up a lot of favors on this."

"I appreciate that." Mace sensed he was about to hear something important. This wasn't going to be put to bed as quickly as he had initially anticipated.

"Well, maybe it's just coincidence, but the odds seem pretty long for just coincidence."

"What is it?" Mace was becoming impatient.

"Two things really. First, there are a total of fifteen wires going into the Broadway Ventures account over the last three weeks. Nine of them trace back to Capital Bank, the large commercial bank headquartered in Washington, D.C. There are some intermediate steps along the way, but the backtracking always leads to Capital Bank. Each of those nine wires was for one hundred million dollars. The others were much smaller. Five were for ten million, and one was for fifty million. The fifty-million-dollar wire was from Walker Pryce. The five ten-million-dollar wires all were sent by real estate investors I've heard of before."

Mace didn't hear the last of what Schuler had just said. Capital Bank. Mace was familiar with the institution. Suddenly he felt his skin crawl. There was something very wrong with the fact that nine hundred million of the billion dollars sent to the Broadway Ventures account at Chase had come from Capital Bank accounts. Why would all the money flow through that one bank in Washington? Schuler was right. It was too much of a coincidence. Mace remembered Webster's recent visit to Washington to see the vice president. Impossible. "You said there were two things regarding the wires. The first is that all this money comes through Capital Bank. What's the other?" Mace began to scribble furiously on a notepad.

"The other issue is that we can't go much farther back than Capital Bank, and we should be able to. The accounts behind the wires at Capital appear to be dummy corporations. No substance at all to them, just shells. But I can't find out how the money got into those corporate accounts at Capital. I've hit a dead end."

"Do you have the names of the corporations?" Mace asked.

"I have one. Pergament Associates. But I'll be damned if anyone here at Chase can find a real company in any corporate directory anywhere in the world by that name. We've checked our databases for both public and private companies. There is nothing by that name."

It was crazy. Five wires had come from all over the country, just as they should have according to the list of investors Leeny had rattled off to him. And one had come from Walker Pryce. But 90 percent of the money had come from accounts at one bank, a bank in Washington. That made no sense.

"There's one other thing, Mace."

"Yes, John?" Mace refocused on Schuler's voice. "What is it?"

"There is one wire transfer going *out* of the account already."

"Really?"

"Yes. It's for a million dollars. The money was sent to an account in a branch of a West Virginia bank. The bank is headquartered in Charleston."

"Which bank?"

"Charleston National Bank and Trust."

"Which branch of the bank did the money go to?" Mace was writing again. "The main one in Charleston?"

"No. The one in Sugar Grove." Schuler laughed. "I said one because I imagine Sugar Grove isn't a multibranch town for Charleston National."

"Where in the hell is Sugar Grove, West Virginia?" Mace asked as he continued to scribble on the notepad.

Schuler snickered. "I was kind of curious myself, so I looked at a map. Sugar Grove is a small town on the Appalachian Trail near the Virginia border. Apparently the town is in the middle of a big forest. The next town over is Nowhereville, and it's forty miles away."

Mace did not laugh at Schuler's attempt at humor. He was too busy writing and thinking.

"What do you think all this means, Mace?" Schuler sounded nervous. "I mean, I'm making a billion dollars available to you people right now. That figure represents a good bit of Chase's capital. I should have most of this facility sold to other banks pretty quickly, so I'm not really worried about my exposure level being a problem. But as an agent bank I have to be able to represent to the other banks we're trying to sell this paper to that what we've got here is on the level." Schuler was obviously concerned. "If there is a problem, my syndications people won't be able to sell the paper, and I'll be stuck with everything." He swallowed the last few words.

Mace could hear Schuler having a quiet coronary on the other end of the phone. Suddenly the banker had sensed that his world might be coming apart, and he was trying to keep himself together. "Everything is fine, John," Mace said smoothly. "I just need to check one thing. I'll get back to you tomorrow morning. In the meantime don't worry about your money. I'm sure we won't spend it all by then." Mace laughed loudly and confidently into the mouthpiece, attempting to restore Schuler's faith in the transaction. But it was difficult to be convincing.

"Please do call me tomorrow. I want to know what's going on." Schuler's voice was unsteady.

"I will."

"How is Leeny, by the way?" Schuler asked tentatively.

Mace tilted his head back. He had to keep Schuler's balls wedged firmly in the nutcracker so that he wouldn't call her. "All right, I suppose. She did ask me exactly when I had found out that the loan for Broadway Ventures had been approved by Chase."

"She did, did she?" Schuler coughed nervously.

"Yes." By now the banker was probably wishing he had never met Leeny. "She was acting kind of strangely."

Schuler hesitated. "She was?"

Mace smiled. "Yes." There was no way Schuler was going to call Leeny now. It would take a catastrophe for the man to summon up the courage to call her now if he couldn't find Mace. "I'll talk to you tomorrow, John." Mace hung up the phone without awaiting Schuler's response. As he did, he glanced at the notepad again. If only he could have been a fly on the wall for that meeting between Lewis Webster and the vice president of the United States.

The limousine moved slowly down Pennsylvania Avenue, away from the White House. Robin Carruthers glanced across the seat toward Andrews, who was staring out the tinted window at the late-winter afternoon. The sun had almost dipped below the horizon, and the back of the huge car was quickly becoming dark. As dark as his mood must be, she thought. The meeting with the president had not produced the results for which Andrews had hoped.

For a moment Robin considered reaching across the seat and

taking his hand in hers to console him. They were alone in the back of the limousine. No one would see her do it. But somehow she could not bring herself to make the gesture because a shred of doubt had finally invaded her thoughts after all these years of blind devotion. She had bought Preston's story about Becker's ordering Carter Guilford to make contact with the Ortega cartel, about Guilford's funneling money to the CIA to cover financial abuses at the agency, to cover Becker's fraudulent use of CIA money to finance his campaign. She had bought it all because she was completely dedicated to Preston Andrews.

Now the whole thing was starting to sound preposterous. After all, Becker was a war hero. He was a man who had cleaned up the agency when he first took it over, a man whose honor could hardly be questioned. "Above reproach" was how most people, even his enemies, described him. But she had bought the story hook, line, and sinker.

Now, because of that blind devotion, she had exposed herself to terrible problems. The anonymous letters to Slade Conner, written on Preston's orders, could be damning if it was ever uncovered that she was the author. Andrews had wanted to smoke out the director by seeing if one of his own people would turn on him. So he had made her write the letters to see if Conner would investigate the allegations on his own. Conner could go where they could not. It had been a desperate gamble, she now realized, one that had gotten them nowhere. Conner had taken the financials from the accountant's office, all right. But he had taken the real financial statements too.

Andrews was still confident that something would come of it, but she had lost all hope, and now she was paranoid that instead of investigating his commander, Conner was doing all he could to find out who had penned the letters. And he *would* find out, sooner or later. Conner was in the CIA, for God's sake. It was his job to find out who sent letters like these.

Suddenly the image of her sitting in a crowded committee

room, being viciously questioned by senators or representatives as Malcolm Becker looked on, flashed through her mind. Her body shook. She wanted no part of Malcolm Becker. But he would get to her if Slade found out that she had written the letters. All because of Preston Andrews.

She breathed deeply and looked out the window. All this she had done for him, and what had it gotten her? Nothing but the beginnings of an ulcer and about five new pounds on her hips thanks to the chocolate she had been stuffing in her mouth because of the terrible stress.

Smoothly the vice president turned from the window of the limousine. "Are you all right, Robin?"

She turned to meet his eyes. "Yes." Her voice was icy.

Andrews shook his head. "I really thought we were going to be able to push the president more quickly on getting the information out of the CIA."

Robin nodded slowly. "It certainly doesn't look as if he's going to be much help. He seems to be concentrating on the bigger picture." Her voice was a monotone, devoid of expression.

"He doesn't want to be caught in the middle of something where he might have to show some backbone, where he might have to make an enemy. We're just going to have to expose what's going on over at CIA ourselves. I think it's time for you to make contact with Slade Conner in person."

"*What?*"

"That's all there is left to do," Andrews said firmly.

Robin could not believe what she had heard. "Preston, I've done everything you've asked me to do. Up until now. I won't expose myself to any further personal liability that way. I just won't do it."

"I thought you were dedicated to me," Andrews said evenly.

She felt her blood pressure suddenly skyrocket. "Don't ever question my devotion to you." Her voice shook. She had never spoken to him this way. But after all the years of dedication she did not expect him to ask her to throw herself to the wolves. "I can't believe what you are asking of me."

"I can't believe you won't do whatever is necessary for us to win this campaign."

"I'll do whatever I think is in my best interest. For a change. Whatever is in the best interest of the country." She paused briefly, considering the words she wanted to say next. She should not say them. She should hold her tongue. But her temper boiled over. "One of us has to."

Andrews did not respond immediately. "What is that supposed to mean?" His voice was still calm, but there was clearly a storm brewing.

"It means, how the hell did you know about Carter Guilford working with the Ortega cartel to direct money to the CIA? Where did your information come from? Up to this point I've taken your word at face value. I'm not willing to do that anymore. I need confirmation. I need to know the full story."

Panicked by the questions coming at rapid fire from the one person he thought would never question him, the vice president quickly churned possible responses through his brain. "Carter Guilford came to me several months ago to tell me what was going on," Andrews said quietly. "Carter made contact with me through people at the DEA, although he did not tell them why he wanted to speak to me. He thought of me because of my work with the DEA. He was the one who told me about Slade Conner, that Conner was the honest one over there at CIA, not to trust anyone else at the CIA but Conner."

"Did you record your conversations with Guilford?" She was not going to be won over easily. He was too convincing. That of course was why he was a politician.

"No. I tried, but he played loud music while we spoke, making it impossible to record anything. We spoke only once, for a very short time. We were to meet again, but I think Becker somehow found out that he had come to me. As I told you, I don't think Carter's plane crash in Honduras was an accident, Robin."

It all sounded so convincing. But Preston could convince you that professional athletes weren't really money-hungry too, that they played simply for the love of the game. He could make anything sound convincing. It was his gift. "Why did you meet with Lewis Webster, the senior partner of Walker Pryce?"

How in the world had she found out about that? "How much longer does the vice president's chief of staff plan on grilling him?" Andrews' voice rose in intensity.

She could tell he was furious. The tipoff was that he spoke in the third person. But she didn't care. She wanted answers at this point. "As long as she wants to," Robin retorted. "Answer my question, Preston."

"*He* called *me*. He said he had heard that Andrews Industries was in trouble and wanted to offer his help. I had him come to Washington to assure him that my family's company was not in trouble and that at some point I would give his firm some business with Andrews Industries. Wall Street people are so damned greedy. Once I offered him the business, he went away quietly. But it was the right thing to have him come to my office and give him the full red-carpet treatment. It worked perfectly. I haven't heard a word from him since. The last thing I needed was a person like that telling the world I have personal financial problems. How he found out that the company was in trouble, I'll never know. He wouldn't tell me. But his figures were awfully accurate. I refuted them, of course, but I'd like to know where he got them."

Again, it sounded so good, but who knew if Preston was telling the truth now? He had mentioned just one meeting, but her information was that there had been several. "Why didn't you tell me you were meeting with Webster? After all, I'm your chief of staff."

"I'm trying to keep you as far away from it all as possible, Robin."

"How can you say that?" Her voice rose suddenly. "You just

asked me to contact Slade Conner in person. How much more involved can I be?"

Andrews did not respond. He simply stared at her.

"I have one last question," Robin said quietly.

"Just one, I'm sure."

She ignored his sarcasm. "Who was the man at the Doha hotel that night I came into the room? You still haven't told me."

Andrews glanced away instantly. He could not tell her. That had to stay as quiet as possible. For as long as possible.

25

The man was dressed as an electrician, but his knowledge of the profession was limited to a single vocational course he had taken in high school many years before. He put his ear close to the door and listened intently for several seconds for any sound from within. But there was nothing. He checked the number on the apartment door one more time just to make certain, then pushed it gently. He gritted his teeth as he pushed. It would have been so much better to have surprised the target on a darkened street or in a crowded subway station, but his employers wanted him dead immediately.

The door gave way silently. The assassin glanced through the crack to see if there were any lights on in the apartment, but all was dark inside. He slipped into the room, closed the door, and slid the tool he had used to pick the lock into his pocket. Smoothly he dropped to his knees, placed the already unzipped bag on the floor before him, and pulled out the loaded weapon. He stood up again and began to move stealthily toward the bedroom. He had been given a rough map of the apartment—complete with approximate furniture locations—but there was no need to be cautious as the light from the city, coming through the large window in the dining room, was adequate to guide him.

The assassin moved quickly toward the far door, the door to the first bedroom. Mace McLain lay inside asleep. It was after two in the morning, and the information he had been given indicated that Mace had stayed at his office until nine o'clock and then taken a car service back to his Upper West Side apartment. He was tired and would be going to sleep soon after he arrived home. That was the assassin's information. But he had waited until this late hour just to be safe.

It was almost over now. The target was as good as dead. The man hesitated at the door for a second. The gun gleamed in the dim light from the window as he brought it up to his face and reached for the doorknob. It was not a conventional weapon. It was a dart gun. But the dart was not filled with a sedative. The sharp projectiles held deadly poison that would paralyze the target within six seconds of skin penetration and stop the heart seventeen to twenty seconds later. McLain might manage to make it out of the bed and to the floor, but that would be about all.

Killing McLain wasn't going to be the problem. The problem was going to be getting his body out of the apartment building without being detected. They did not want his body to be found—ever—so McLain had to be killed here with no signs of foul play or a struggle and then moved to a place where the body could be disposed of properly.

The assassin silently turned the knob to the right, took three short breaths, and burst into the room. The bed was empty. Quickly he moved to the bathroom and then to the second bedroom. McLain was not in the apartment. The assassin's information had been wrong.

Gently but firmly Mace moved Leeny against the wall and then pressed his naked body against hers. The wall was slightly cool against the flesh of her buttocks and back, but the feeling was not displeasing since the room was extremely warm. Her hands massaged his muscular shoulders for a few seconds, then locked together at the back of his neck. For a few moments she stared into his gray eyes as the light from many candles flickered in the dark pupils. Then his mouth came to hers and their tongues met.

But just as Mace should have entered her, just as her legs should have been wrapping around him, he stepped back. She shook her head, not understanding.

Mace moved to the bedroom door and opened it. Rachel, already nude, moved into the room slowly from the darkness beyond, took Mace by the hand, and led him to the huge bed in the center of the space. She crawled onto the bed in front of him and lay on her back, motioning for him to join her.

Leeny tried to cry out, but the sound caught in her throat. She tried to move away from the wall, but somehow she could not. She could do nothing but watch as Mace moved onto the bed and began to make love to Rachel.

Leeny bolted upright in the bed, screaming as she came out of the dream. She breathed heavily for several moments, then became aware that her body was drenched with perspiration. The mattress was soaked.

"God. Oh, God." She gazed into the pitch-black of her bedroom, then leaned across the bed to the lamp on the nightstand and switched it on. Instantly the room was bathed in a comforting glow. But the image of Mace making love to Rachel was still with her. It was an image she could not erase from her mind.

Again Leeny leaned across the bed to the nightstand, removed four pills from the bottle—four times the prescription inscribed on the vial—and swallowed them all with one gulp of water. Slowly she put the glass back down on the table. It balanced on the edge for a second, then tumbled to the floor, smashing loudly into many pieces. But Leeny hardly noticed. Her eyes were transfixed on the red digits of the clock. Two-thirty in the morning. The assassin had finished his work by now. Mace McLain was dead.

Slade watched the woman fade into the darkness of the Georgetown campus; it was almost three in the morning. It had taken immense courage for her to come here. She must know that it would be his duty to report this treachery to Becker.

In the distance the lights of the old McDonogh Gymnasium shone brightly. What was he supposed to do? Robin Carruthers, chief of staff to the vice president of the United States, had just revealed herself as the writer of the two anonymous letters he had received. She had made incredible accusations against Malcolm Becker, his commander. And she had asked for his help. Slade laughed aloud. It was bizarre, the only word he could think of to describe accurately what he had just heard.

Slade turned and moved in the opposite direction from that in which Robin had gone. What the hell was he going to do?

The engine had been working hard for twenty minutes, the pistons roaring as the car slowly climbed the steep mountain, hairpin turn after hairpin turn. The smell of burning oil pervaded the inside of the vehicle, and the temperature gauge showed that the motor could not take much more. If it burned up now, help was miles away. The last remnant of civilization had been the old gas station at the foot of the mountain, and there had been no lights on inside.

Finally the car reached the apex of the huge mountain and began the long descent. The bright headlights peered through the night, illuminating little else but dense forest, huge mounds of snow—in places piled ten feet high at the side of the twisting, desolate road—and occasional whitetail deer, several of which had careened from the forest into the path of the oncoming car before bolting safely away at the last instant.

Mace sat hunched behind the steering wheel of the small car—he had rented it because he did not want to be conspicuous in the tiny West Virginia town by driving a sporty or large model—both hands firmly on the wheel in the ten and two positions, concentrating hard on the narrow, curving road. He was exhausted. The flight from New York City to Charleston hadn't left La Guardia until eleven o'clock, and it had been snowing as the plane had touched down in West Virginia. That had cost him more time; he had been barely able to do more than twenty miles an hour for the first ninety minutes on the road. He had considered staying in Charleston for the night but had ruled out that option. He did not have the time to waste. They would realize quickly that he was gone.

But the snow had finally ceased, and now it was simply a question of negotiating the mountains in this godforsaken part of the country and avoiding the deer, which seemed to be as plentiful as the homeless on the streets of New York City. The huge mounds of snow and massive pine trees flashed by. This place really was off the beaten track. For Christ's sake, he hadn't seen another car in the last ten miles. Mace inhaled deeply. It had to be coming up soon. At least it looked like it according to the map.

Then he saw a small sign just visible at the top of a large snow-drift. SUGAR GROVE: 6 MILES. Slowly he began to relax into the seat. He was almost there.

Suddenly he hunched forward over the steering wheel again, this time farther than before. Always play the fourth quarter stronger than the first three. Don't ease up with the finish line in sight. Finish strong. His eyelids felt like lead weights, but he was almost there, and there was an all-night motel waiting for him in Sugar Grove. He had checked.

Mace shook his head. This was probably a wild-goose chase. The wire transfer from the Broadway Ventures account at Chase to this little branch of the Charleston National Bank & Trust here in Sugar Grove in the middle of nowhere probably meant nothing. But he had to find out.

Suddenly a deer moved out from beneath several tall pine trees, surprising Mace. It was a huge, magnificent buck. The animal, seemingly unaware of the steel beast bearing down on it, moved slowly, directly into the car's path.

Despite the animal's slow progress, it appeared to Mace that the deer would make the other side of the road easily before the car hit it. But as it stepped across the pavement, the animal made the deadly mistake of turning toward the headlights of the car. It stopped, statue still, and stared into the bright lights. Mace slammed on the brakes instantly, but the tires did not grab hold of the roadway immediately, instead skidding on a large patch of ice.

At the last instant Mace released his foot from the brake. The car hurtled to the right, following the front wheels, barely grazing the buck's thick coat. Then Mace was past the deer, slamming his foot on the brakes again. Again the compact car skidded on the ice. Finally it slammed headlong into a huge snowdrift.

The car had not been traveling particularly fast at impact, and Mace was unhurt. But in the crash the car's engine had stalled. Mace put the transmission into park and attempted to restart the motor, but there was no sound. Several times he tried, waiting a few minutes in between, but the ignition did not respond. Finally he kicked the door open and got out. It was going to be a long walk.

He reached back inside the car, grabbed his bag, and turned to go. The deer, which had not moved as the car had skidded past it and into the snowdrift, suddenly dashed for the trees at the edge of the roadway.

"Damn!" Mace stepped back involuntarily. The animal had startled him.

It bounded quickly into the pitch-black forest. Mace listened for several moments as the animal crashed through the under-brush, the sounds of its progress growing fainter and fainter until he could no longer hear the animal. Now he became aware that there were no sounds at all.

Slowly he began to trudge down the icy road toward Sugar Grove. What would Leeny think if she knew where he was? What would *Webster* think? Well, they weren't going to find out. He would be back to New York City on Monday night, back to work first thing Tuesday morning, with a plausible excuse for his Monday absence and no credit-card receipts for them to find. He had withdrawn a significant amount of cash this afternoon to fund any unforeseen situation he might run into down here.

Mace shook his head. Rachel was right. Leeny had a lot of problems. Why had she been so interested this afternoon in exactly when he was going home? And if he had plans to go out tonight?

26

Sugar Grove was nestled in a remote valley of the ancient Appalachian Mountains. Tree-covered snowy peaks rose about the cluster of aging clapboard homes in every direction. It was a land the twentieth century had all but forgotten. Every other vehicle on the potholed streets was a mud-splattered pickup truck. All three thousand inhabitants seemed to be related or at least to know one another. And there were two of almost everything: two grocery stores, two hardware stores, two banks, two liquor stores, and two ancient movie theaters, still playing 1970s fare.

The Deliverance Motel, located directly across Main Street from Mabel's Truck Stop Diner, offered rooms with little more than a stiff mattress, a Bible, and an old black rotary telephone. To make a call from the ancient phone, a motel guest had to be connected to the outside world by the person on duty at the tiny front desk, who most of the time was Max Shifflette, the establishment's obese owner. The only modern amenity available at the motel was a mammoth wide-screen television in the lounge that offered ninety-two channels, thanks to a huge satellite dish positioned at the top of the highest peak overlooking the secluded settlement. The Deliverance Motel was a far cry from the five-star hotels of London, Paris, and Los Angeles to which Mace was accustomed, but when he tumbled onto the rickety bed at five o'clock Saturday morning after the six-mile walk from his stalled rental car, it had seemed like heaven.

"Another beer, Max?" Mace passed the half-empty twelve-pack of Coors to the motel's proprietor, who sat in an old wooden chair next to him. Mace had purchased the beer at the Piggly Wiggly, located next door to Mabel's. It was funny, Mace thought as he held the carton out for the other man. This little part of Sugar Grove was a lot like New York City in that all of life's necessities were available right outside his door, twenty-four hours a day.

"Don't mind if I do," Max responded quickly in a high-pitched voice with a thick mountain accent. He turned the can he was holding upside down, guzzled what was left, tossed it onto the frayed rug of the lounge, and grabbed the carton from Mace. With a huge paw Max removed another gold can, popped the top, and drank half the contents. He belched loudly as he finally pulled the aluminum from his lips.

Mace smiled to himself as he watched the man consume the beer. Max was a bear of a man. Six feet six inches tall and three hundred pounds if he was an ounce. His black hair was long and scraggly, as was his beard, and he looked as if he could have enjoyed a sterling career in the World Wrestling Federation. Mace had jokingly offered to be his agent in this endeavor, but Mad Max, as Mace had heard the young maid call the owner this morning, didn't want that. Max wanted to remain in Sugar Grove until the day he died, tending the motel five days a week, hunting black bear and deer the other two. That was life for Max, and he was satisfied with it. And there was something to that, Mace thought.

Suddenly the huge television's reception dimmed, and the tractor pull contest faded from the screen. "Damn it!" Mad Max finished off the beer and hurled the can at the screen.

"What's the matter with the reception?" Mace asked.

Mad Max dug into the carton he had carefully placed on his lap and retrieved another beer. "Oh, the satellite probably went on the blink. That or the company that operates it finally figured out that I'm pirating their signal."

"What?" Mace smiled at the man.

Mad Max took a swig of the beer, then turned toward Mace and smiled back at him widely, showing his protruding upper gum. "Yeah, my brother and I put that dish on top of the mountain a couple of years ago without really telling anyone."

"And the cops didn't do anything?"

Mad Max shook his head. "My brother's the sheriff."

Mace nodded at the motel's proprietor. "Of course."

"Now what are we gonna watch?" Clearly upset by this latest turn of events, Mad Max began flicking through the channels wildly. "Maybe some of the other channels will come in. Maybe we can find another tractor pull."

Mace checked his watch. It was a few minutes after seven o'clock on Sunday evening. He thought of suggesting *60 Minutes*, then thought better of it. "Max, tell me a little bit about Sugar Grove."

Mad Max put the remote down on a small table next to his chair, stroked his beard for a moment, and leaned back in the chair. He did not question Mace's desire to understand Sugar Grove's history because he simply assumed that a visitor would want to know about his town. "It was settled in 1866 by the black sheep of a Richmond, Virginia, family who didn't want to live with the Yankees after the Civil War. He figured they'd never find him here, and he was right. Not many Yankees find their way here. I'm kind of surprised you did. And I'm kind of surprised you're still here." For some reason Max found this last observation hysterical and laughed for several minutes before regaining his composure with a few large gulps of beer.

Mace did not ask Mad Max why he had found the observation so funny. He did not want to know.

Finally the proprietor went on. "In the early 1900s the big paper companies came calling. They provided the town with jobs and made the grandson of the town's founder a rich man. In the late 1940s the coal companies came, bringing more jobs and making the great-grandson of the town's founder a really rich man. But since the downfall of Richard Nixon, the country's last *real* president, Sugar Grove's fortunes ain't been too good. Twenty years ago the paper companies pulled out because they could get timber a lot cheaper farther south, and now the coal has just about run out. The town's population is around half of what it used to be." Mad Max shook his head sadly. "In another twenty years there won't be anyone left. Then my cousin won't have anyone to sell his groceries to." He took another gulp of beer.

"Your cousin owns one of the grocery stores?" Mace took a sip of beer too.

Mad Max hesitated. "He owns both of them. He owns both of the hardware stores too."

Mace nodded. So that was why prices didn't seem any different here from in New York. Mad Max's family was running a monopoly. "And *you* probably own the motel on the other side of town, don't you?"

Mad Max showed his expansive pink upper gum again. "Of course. And that garage where your car's sitting. My wife runs that. Which works out real good. Keeps her busy. That way I don't have to see her too much. Means I can go hunting more."

Mace laughed out loud. "My God, you all are modern-day robber barons." He smiled broadly at the mountain man.

The smile disappeared from Max's face. He wasn't certain what a robber baron was, but it sounded criminal, and he didn't appreciate the implication.

"I bet some branch of your family owns everything in Sugar Grove. Is that right?"

"Just about." Max nodded stiffly. He didn't understand why that would so interest this man from New York. Max popped another Coors. "So why are you here, Yankee?" He winked at Mace.

"Were you just passing through our fair town when your car broke down?"

"No, I wasn't just passing through. Sugar Grove was my destination. I was coming here for a few days. But I'm beginning to think I'll never make it out of here again. It's taken a little longer than I thought it would to fix my car's engine." Mace raised an eyebrow at Mad Max.

Max smiled. "I gotta keep you a few nights so I can make some money. As you can tell, we ain't doing a bang-up business here."

That was true. Last night there had been only two other guests, and tonight Mace was the only paying occupant. "In fact I had to be here until tomorrow anyway," Mace said.

"Why?" Mad Max sat up. Suddenly he was interested. "Why are you here?"

Mace eyed the other man for a few moments. "I work for the government. We are investigating one of New York's crime families."

Max leaned forward. Now he was interested. He had heard about these families. "You mean the Mafia?" he whispered.

Mace nodded solemnly. "We think they are laundering money through the Sugar Grove branch of the Charleston National Bank and Trust." It was an inane story, but Mace knew that "laundering" sounded official and that Max would have no idea what it meant and probably wouldn't ask to have it explained either.

"Oh, God, my niece works for that branch."

Mace glanced up from his lap. Bingo.

"Are the people at the branch in trouble?" Mad Max was suddenly concerned.

"No, no." Mace realized that the mountain man would be on the phone to his entire extended family with this news in the next two minutes if he wasn't careful. "No, it's nothing to get excited about. And I need your word that you won't say anything to anyone."

"Nothing." Mad Max swallowed. His eyes were wide.

"Max, what does your niece do at the branch?"

"She's a teller."

"Do you think she'd be willing to help me?" Mace asked right away.

Max hesitated for several moments before responding. There was something in the eyes that told the mountain man to trust Mace. "Sure. What would she have to do?"

"Nothing difficult. I just need some information on one account. She would have access to that information, I assume."

Max nodded emphatically. "She has access to everything over there. She's a senior teller." He paused. "There isn't any chance that anyone will know that she was involved, is there?"

"None."

"And I'm sure the government would be willing to pay for the information she would provide, wouldn't it?"

Mace's eyes met the mountain man's. So that was his angle. Mace chuckled. "Yes, it would." He did not bother explaining that if the government wanted information on an account, it could simply walk through the front doors of the bank and get it. When it came to money matters, there were no rights of privacy.

Mad Max nodded. "Tomorrow morning go to the bank and ask for Carol Shifflette. She'll be happy to help you."

27

M ad Max had exaggerated his niece's desire to be of help to what she thought was an agent of the United States government. The young woman's eyes, set far apart on her broad, freckled face, revealed her reluctance. Mace smiled at her from in front of the teller's window, but she did not smile back. "Carol?"

"Yes." The woman's voice was hushed. The branch was small and not crowded this early in the morning. Clearly she did not want her superior, a chunky man sitting at a desk not far away, to hear their conversation.

"My name is Mace McLain." Mace lowered his voice as well. "Your uncle Max Shifflette sent me to see you."

"I know." Carol seemed annoyed, as though she were repaying a favor she wished she had never been the recipient of. She glanced around nervously. "Give me the account number." Her red hair hung straight down both sides of her face, and Mace noticed that her upper gum protruded terribly during her infrequent smiles, just as her uncle's did.

Mace slid a piece of paper and a twenty-dollar bill beneath the dark wrought-iron bars separating them. "Could you give me four fives please?" he asked loudly.

The chunky man glanced up from his coffee and paper but only for a moment.

The young woman picked up the piece of paper—on which was

written the account number—slid it in the pocket of the floral-patterned dress, then made change. "Meet me at the Shell station on the corner of Main and Ridge in a half hour," she whispered through the bars, handing him the fives. "I'll be able to get away for only a few minutes, so if you're not there, you lose."

Mace smiled at the woman, but again she didn't smile back. She was not impressed with the handsome city slicker. He was doing something wrong. She had no doubt of that. But Uncle Max had instructed her to do this, and she did not want Uncle Max to tell her father that she and her boyfriend had been using the Deliverance Motel as their backseat for the winter.

"I'll be there," Mace assured her.

Twenty-five minutes later, as Mace stood in the dilapidated telephone booth in front of the Shell station with the receiver pressed tightly against his left ear, speaking to no one, he saw Carol Shifflette walking hurriedly up Main Street. She leaned forward as she walked to protect herself against the wind and cold. One hand was pressed against her chest, and the other held a lighted cigarette. In the hand pressed against her chest was a manila envelope.

Mace slammed the receiver down and moved out to meet her. The whole thing was probably a wild-goose chase, and here he was about to spend his own hard-earned money. Again. And for what? Probably nothing. But what the hell? He'd come this far.

The young woman saw him exit the telephone booth and moved quickly across the icy gas station asphalt to where he stood.

"Why didn't you wear a coat?" Mace asked, genuinely concerned.

She shook her head and shivered. "Then Mr. Griffith would have noticed I was gone. He checks the coatroom a lot." She glanced around. "Here." She thrust the envelope at Mace. "Three months of activity for the account number you gave me. Pictures of all the canceled checks. Everything. But there isn't much to it. I hope it's what you're looking for, whoever you are." She stared at him for a moment. "Or maybe I don't," she said softly.

"Don't worry," Mace tried to reassure her. "Here." He slipped an envelope to her quickly. Inside was a thousand dollars.

The young woman snatched the envelope and stuffed it deep into a pocket. "How much did you give Max?" she asked evenly.

"The same. Exactly the same." It was a lie. Mad Max had required five thousand dollars to set up his niece. But Mace wasn't going to tell her that. He glanced down at the pocket into which Carol had stuffed the envelope filled with the hundred-dollar bills he had withdrawn from his bank account before leaving New York, part of the twenty thousand he had withdrawn just in case.

"You want it back now?" The young woman suddenly moved both hands to the envelope as if protecting it. "You can't have it. I'll start screaming if you touch—"

Mace held up both hands. "All I want is that piece of paper that I passed to you at the bank. The one with the number of the account on it." Mace cocked his head to the side. "I don't want that floating around. Neither do you. I think you understand."

Wordlessly the woman reached to the bottom of the dress pocket, found the piece of paper, and handed it to Mace. Then she turned and began to walk quickly back down Main Street toward the Charleston National Bank & Trust. It was the easiest money she had ever made. That was why she was so worried.

"So you been staying at the Deliverance, huh?"

"That's right, I have." Gene Shifflette, owner of Gene's Food Market, stood before Mace on the loading dock at the back of the building. Gene was a carbon copy of Mad Max. He possessed the same protruding upper gum, the scraggly hair and beard as his cousin, the same paunch, the same distant look. If they stood side by side, one would have pegged them for twins or at the very least brothers, not just cousins. But perhaps the years of inbreeding here made a Sugar Grove cousin about as close to a brother as possible without being one.

"Move it on out!" Gene screamed at several boys who were unloading a truck at one of the four loading bays.

The boys could not have been more than ten years old. So that was how businessmen did it here: through monopoly pricing and thumbing their noses at federal child labor laws.

Gene shook his head. "Good for nuthin'. Where were we? Oh, yeah. So what do you need? Max said you wanted to ask me something."

"That's right." Mace felt for the manila envelope stored securely in an inside pocket of his down ski jacket. His thoughts raced to the records Carol Shifflette had given him showing checks written to Gene's Food Market, checks written over the last two months totaling almost a hundred thousand dollars.

"Whatcha got? Any friend of Max's is a friend of mine. Hey! Get your asses moving, boys!" Gene screamed at the young boys again.

"Mr. Shifflette." Mace's tone was insistent. It was Monday noon. Leeny would have noted his absence by now and had probably alerted Webster. If he was going to find out anything important, he had to do it now. If he weren't back by tomorrow morning, there would be lots of explaining to do to Webster. One day away from work could be easily explained at this point, but two consecutive days would present more of a problem.

"Yeah, what?" He turned back toward Mace.

"Look, I work for the government. I'm doing a very routine investigation, and I just want to ask you a few questions about some large checks written to you over the last few months."

Shifflette held up his hands immediately. "Hey, I ain't done nuthin' wrong."

"Mr. Shifflette, we know that." Mace used "we" to sound more official. "It isn't you that we're interested in. I called my counterparts at the Internal Revenue Service last night. You're clean."

Shifflette stiffened at the mention of the tax authority. "Of course I am. I'm a law-abiding citizen." He glanced furtively at the young boys straining to carry several heavy containers of meat. "Why don't we go in my office and talk about this?" He put a huge paw on Mace's shoulder and began to drag him toward the inside of the building.

Mace shook his head. "Not necessary. This won't take very long."

Shifflette stopped. "Okay." He paused. "Can you at least tell me what this is about?"

Mace glanced around. "My information shows that over the past several months you have been paid almost a hundred thousand dollars by—" He paused and began to reach for the manila envelope inside his coat. "The name escapes me. Let me just—"

"Don't bother," Gene interrupted. "I know who you're talking about. They come every couple of days for delivery." He laughed. "They're the only customer who picks up their stuff back here. They have to. There's so much of it. It's been good business. I hope it never ends." Shifflette shook his head. "They must be feeding an army, for cryin' out loud."

Feeding an army? The words echoed in Mace's head. "Can you tell me anything about them?"

Again Gene shook his head. "Nope. They place the next order when they pick up the current order. Same thing every time. Ground beef, potatoes, and vegetables. Pretty much the same order in the same quantity. That's about all I can tell you. I couldn't even tell you what they look like. Seems like a different person every time they come here. At least the times they've come and I've been out here."

"Nothing else you can tell me, huh?" Mace was disappointed.

Shifflette scratched his beard as he looked down at his clipboard. "Nope. But if you have something to ask them, why don't you talk to them yourself?"

Mace's eyes narrowed. "What do you mean?"

Shifflette glanced at his clipboard. "They're scheduled to make a pickup tonight at nine o'clock after the store has closed."

Mace inhaled deeply. The transfer had come from the Broadway

Ventures account at Chase to an account at the Charleston National branch in Sugar Grove, West Virginia. And now there were almost a hundred thousand dollars of checks written on the Charleston National account to a country grocer who described the orders placed by the payers as big enough to feed an army. He glanced around. Leeny Hunt was interested in his home computer. Lewis Webster had raised an improbable vulture fund. And there was an army in the hills of West Virginia. There were too many coincidences now, too many unanswered questions. It then hit him with the force of a freight train. He shook his head violently. No. It couldn't be that. Lewis Webster considered himself a god, but even he wouldn't try that. Would he? Mace's eyes flashed to the mountain man. "Where can I get some wheels? My car is in the shop."

Shifflette smiled. "I know it is. Sounds like it's going to be there awhile too. Real sorry about that."

"I'm sure you are." Mace suddenly considered the possibility that he had somehow crossed over a border into some foreign country, some twilight zone, in which he was being held hostage without really even knowing it. Perhaps he would never get his car back and have to continue to pay the forty-seven dollars a night to the Deliverance Hotel forever. "Wheels. Where can I get some?"

Gene Shifflette nodded at what looked like a junkyard through the leafless trees.

"What can I get there?" Mace asked.

"Mike will sell you the fastest motorcycle known to mankind."

Mace stared at Gene. "Let me guess. He's your cousin."

Gene smiled. "No. My father."

"I should have known," Mace said to himself as he jumped nimbly to the ground from the loading dock. Suddenly he turned back toward Shifflette. "Hey, Gene!"

Shifflette paused and looked back. "What?"

"Not a word to these people tonight. Do you understand that? If I want to talk to them, I'll make contact. Don't you say anything. Uncle Sam is watching."

Shifflette nodded. For a moment he thought about the thousands of dollars of cash receipts from the grocery store he wasn't claiming on his income tax return. He swallowed hard. Any kind of audit of his tax returns matched against his checking account would reveal significant inconsistencies to even the most junior accountant. He had been cheating so long now there would be no way to cover it up. He shrugged his shoulders. If they wanted to come to Sugar Grove, let them. They'd be sorry they came. "Not a word," he shouted at Mace, who was already moving through the woods toward the junkyard.

Mace moved slowly along the crest of a snow-covered ridge running parallel to the abandoned huge coal-processing plant, darting quickly from tree to tree. The rusting buildings, constructed on several acres of cleared land in the middle of the dense forest, were just a few hundred feet below him at this point but were still only barely visible in the early-morning darkness. Mace could not see his watch—he had brought with him a small flashlight but did not want to use it for fear of giving away his position to anyone who might be out there—but guessed it was nearly four in the morning. Built at the base of the western side of the mountain, the facility would not begin receiving any sunlight for at least another two hours. Fortunately the night was clear, and though there was no moon, he could still make out the larger shapes.

For several moments he stared down through the gloom at the vast complex below, then moved back into the woods, sat on a large stump at the edge of the tree line, and closed his eyes. He was exhausted. From the trees between the store and the junkyard he had watched the large truck pick up its payload of food from the loading bay at Gene's Food Market exactly at nine o'clock last evening. The two men had worked silently, moving the boxes from the raised platform at the back of the store and into the cargo area of the large vehicle quickly. Then they had jumped into the cab of the truck and roared off. He had followed the truck from a safe distance on the used dirt bike Gene's father had sold him yesterday afternoon.

The truck had moved out of town in the opposite direction from that in which he had entered Sugar Grove Friday night and climbed at a snail's pace into the mountains south of town. At times the pace had been so slow it had been difficult for Mace to maintain his balance on the motorcycle. At those points he had simply pulled the dirt bike to the side of the winding road and allowed the vehicle he was following to make several minutes' headway, fearing that the men in the truck might become suspicious of the persistent single headlight in their rearview mirror.

Mace was very certain now that there was a reason Leeny Hunt and Lewis Webster had not allowed him to be privy to the identities of the investors. A reason that most of the money coming into the Broadway Ventures account at Chase had originally passed through Capital Bank. A reason that Leeny had been able to raise the money for the fund so quickly. A reason that the insider trading trial of the LeClair and Foster investment bankers had quietly gone away. He was certain there had to be a unifying factor for all these things. They weren't just unconnected coincidences. But he didn't know what that factor was. He had suspicions but no proof. However, the truck, or wherever it was going, might be able to confirm his suspicions. Unless the men in the truck detected him.

Big enough to feed an army; Lewis Webster's absolute certainty that the Manhattan real estate market would crash; Leeny Hunt's interest in his apartment computer: All these thoughts had raced through his mind as the wind whipped past the helmet he had purchased at one of the town's two hardware stores that afternoon.

Halfway up the third mountain, twelve miles south of town, the truck had suddenly veered right onto a dirt road. The two men had hopped out of the vehicle, locked shut a gate behind them, and continued on. Seeing no other option—the dirt bike would make too much noise—Mace had hidden the motorcycle several hundred yards south of the gate and begun what had turned out to be an arduous five-hour trek through the Appalachian forest—roughly paralleling the dirt road the truck had traversed—which had gotten him to this tree stump.

Mace took in a deep breath of the cold, clear air. Beneath his clothes he was perspiring heavily, even in the twenty-degree temperatures. Slowly he stood up again, moved forward to the edge of the tree line again, and peered down at the complex below through the branches of the pines on the crest of the ridge. He had come this far. There was no reason to make this long trek through the forest and not find what you had come to find—whatever *that* ultimately turned out to be. He laughed to himself. A New York investment banker prowling the dense woods of West Virginia in the middle of the night. Maybe he really was as intense as people said.

He took one more deep breath of air, pushed through the last line of trees out into the open, and began negotiating his way down the steep slope. He needed Slade here. Hell, this was probably what Slade did for a living, though of course he had never made that clear.

The snow gave way beneath his boots. For several moments Mace managed to remain upright, fighting the pull of gravity, but finally he lost his balance. He grabbed at several small trees growing out of the hillside as he tumbled downward but missed them or came away with nothing but a few twigs that snapped off in his large hand. Over and over he tumbled, unable to stop his fall because of the steep slope and the snow, until he felt the ground give way completely beneath him and he fell ten feet through midair into the soft powder at the base of the ridge.

For several minutes he lay still, covered with snow, listening for any sound that would indicate his fall had been detected, testing his body for any broken parts. But there were no sounds to indicate that he had been detected and no broken bones. Just a few bruises on his legs that would turn into nice strawberries in a few hours.

He had put up with much more than that on the University of
Iowa football field.

Finally he picked himself up, brushed the snow off his face and
jacket, and quickly moved toward the side of the large building.
When he reached it, he moved slowly against its edge, feeling his
way along the rough cinder blocks until he found what appeared to
be a door. He turned the handle and pushed gently. It gave way,
and he moved inside quietly. As he did, a smell of mildew and rust
rushed to his nostrils. Mace waited for a few moments for his eyes
to adjust to the pitch darkness inside the building, but nothing
came into focus. There was no light inside the building at all.

"Damn," Mace whispered to himself. He wanted to be back
into the safety of the pine woods well before the sun's rays began to
make their way down into this remote valley. But he also wanted to
find out what the hell was going on. Mace felt for the small flashlight in his coat pocket. He had no idea what he had just entered or
who might see him if he turned the flashlight on, but it was a
chance he had to take. He couldn't just stand here.

He held his breath and flicked the button. Instantly the room
was bathed in a soft glow. He glanced about, slowly gaining confidence that there was no one else in the small room. Then suddenly
the beam of light began to shake as his gaze focused on the letters
on the sides of the boxes piled to the ceiling: ammunition. He
stared at the letters for a few seconds, then moved slowly to the
boxes and pressed his gloved fingers against the letters inscribed on
the wooden crates.

"My God," he murmured. He flashed the light slowly around
the room. Lying open on the floor was a longer crate. He moved to
it, bent down and inspected the contents. Assault rifles. AK-47s,
the stencil on the side of the crate indicated. Mace had heard a
great deal about the weapon but had never actually seen one before. He was mesmerized by the sight of the sleek killing machine.

Mace rose from his kneeling position and glanced about the
cinder-block walls. What did this mean? It confirmed to him that

the fund was involved in something it should not be. How could this be anything aboveboard? Guns hidden away in a remote piece of the West Virginia backwoods. He had no other answers, but the stench of Broadway Ventures was beginning to overpower him. He needed answers to the questions that were rattling through his brain.

Almost four-thirty. There was little time left. He moved cautiously to a door on the far wall. Like the knob on the door from the outside, this knob turned easily. He pushed forward gently and peered through the space. Suddenly the crack of the door was filled with the bared, gnashing teeth and massive head of a huge German shepherd. The powerful rush of the screaming canine slammed the door shut in Mace's face, and he tumbled backward onto the cement floor of the ammunition room. "Jesus Christ!" He could hear the dog howling and snapping on the other side of the metal door in a frenzy, its front claws scraping against the metal like nails scraping down a blackboard. Then Mace heard a voice screaming at the dog.

Instantly Mace picked himself and the flashlight up off the floor and raced for the outside door. He paused only long enough at the entrance to make certain that it was closed tightly after him. He could hear the dog howling from inside as he moved quickly along the wall, back in the direction from which he had come. How foolish could he have been? How utterly foolish? He should have left at the first sight of the ammunition. He should not have attempted to find anything else. He should have simply picked up one of the machine guns as evidence for the state police and made his way back through the woods.

He ran alongside the huge building as best he could through the snow. Any normal person would never have come here. Any normal person would have stayed as far away from Broadway Ventures as possible.

The end of the building was coming up soon. He had to make a break for the woods. There was no choice. The longer he stayed near the complex, the greater the chance he would be caught. It was still very dark, but he was able to pick out a place where the incline of the ridge seemed less steep.

He pushed off from the building and broke for the woods. Fifty yards away from the building, just as the incline was beginning to become noticeable, Mace heard the outside door of the complex open.

"Go, Sasha! Find, Sasha!"

Mace glanced at the tree line. It was still a hundred yards away up the snow-covered slope. The thought of his successfully making it up the slope was preposterous. He would never reach the woods before the German shepherd overtook him. Mace sucked in a breath. Even if he made it to the cover of the woods, the dog would track him down quickly by scent anyway. Hell, the man would be able to follow the footprints in the snow even without the dog. And he was probably armed with one of those AK-47s.

The dog broke as the man released it from the leash and began to follow the scent along the wall, sniffing excitedly in pursuit of Mace. Tabiq smiled as he pushed through the snow behind the dog. It would be over in a matter of minutes. Vargus would be appreciative.

Mace moved sluggishly through the snow toward a large shack farther up the base of the ridge. It was his only chance. Adrenaline coursed through his body, pushing him beyond what he himself thought his capabilities were. He had been chased on the football field, but never by someone wielding a deadly weapon and following a bloodthirsty dog. It was amazing what the body could do when it had to, what the mind could make the body do.

Mace reached the front door of the shack, thrust it open, burst inside, and closed the door behind him. Quickly he snapped on the flashlight he was still carrying to see whether there might be any kind of hardware in the shed that could be of help to him. Immediately the light came to rest on the bodies of the man and woman Vargus had killed weeks before. Well preserved by the intense cold, the hikers hung side by side from the wooden wall by ropes, one end tightly secured about their chests, the other attached to hooks on the wall, their booted feet barely touching the floor of the shack. Mace took a step back, dropped the flashlight, and fell to his knees as the image of the almost headless corpse hanging next to the woman imprinted vividly on his brain, making him forget for an instant about the canine in hot pursuit. He had not eaten in several hours, but what was left of the meal—a hamburger and french fries—spewed immediately onto the floor of the shack. He could not control himself.

The German shepherd bounded through the snow, pointed directly at the small shack. It no longer needed to smell its quarry. The man smiled as he loped through the snow behind the dog. He had not bothered to put on a jacket, and he was glad that the chase would end quickly. The question now wasn't whether or not the intruder would be caught, but how Tabiq should deal with him when he caught him. Should he shoot him immediately or take him back to Vargus? Tabiq slowed as he neared the shed. The dog stood on its hind legs scraping at the wood as the man neared the door. He held the gun out, ready to fire if necessary.

"Down, Sasha," he whispered.

The dog obeyed, whimpering excitedly as it sat on its haunches outside the door, ears forward, foam building on its black jaw as it anticipated being allowed to enter the shack. Tabiq stared at the door. The intruder had to be in there. For a moment he considered retracing his steps to enlist help. There was only one intruder—he had determined this fact from the tracks in the snow—but the man might have a gun. Then the man shook his head. He had a dog *and* a gun, and he was a well-trained commando. Tabiq pulled the door open quickly, and the German shepherd burst into the shack.

In the next moment Mace moved quickly around the corner of the small building from the blind side, the side on which the door hung from its hinges. With a huge effort he slammed the door shut, trapping the animal inside, and then slammed the face of the shovel, which had been hanging next to the bodies, onto the other man's head. The man dropped into the snow unconscious.

The sun's first rays were just beginning to filter down into the valley, and Mace could barely make out the trickles of blood moving in rivulets down the man's face. Almost completely out of breath, Mace sucked in air as he stared at the fallen man, who had meant to kill him.

Quickly he bent over and picked up the AK-47. He might need it. He glanced back at the compound. Others would be coming soon. There would be more dogs and more guns. He had to go now if he stood any chance at all of making it out of there alive. He swallowed hard. Thank God the shack had had a back door.

Vargus pointed at Tabiq still lying unconscious in the snow. "Get him up," he growled at the other four men.

Quickly they picked up their fallen comrade and began to carry him back toward the facility. Vargus watched them go, his eyes narrow behind the dark sunglasses he wore against the brilliant sunshine. The compound had been broken into. The secrecy of the project had been violated. He could see the footsteps leading away up the slope from the shack toward the woods. On the very last day they were to be here. It defied all odds. It could not have happened this way. But it had.

He could not chase the intruder. They were on a strict timetable now. There was no way to stay another day to track down whoever had entered the base.

Vargus spit several sunflower seeds into the snow. The man in Washington would not be pleased. But there was nothing Vargus could do about it now.

His eyes fell to the doorway and the snow stirred up in front of it. This was where the critical battle had taken place, where Tabiq had failed. Vargus shook his head. Whoever the intruder was, he was resourceful. Tabiq was a practiced killer, one who did not miss.

Vargus pulled open the door of the shack. The German shepherd lay next to the headless body of the dead hiker, which the in-truder had removed from the wall and laid carefully across the floor of the shack. As Vargus watched, the dog sniffed at the thigh of the corpse without removing its eyes from him. Vargus shook his head again. He regretted not getting rid of the bodies now. Overlooking even a single detail could be devastating.

28

Janice Dolan moved out of the bathroom with only a towel wrapped about her. She shivered as the cooler air of the bedroom met her damp skin. The warm shower had refreshed her after a long day of teaching at the local public elementary school. She had been dreaming of the clear blue waters of the Caribbean as the streams of the shower had poured down upon her. But now the cold of the bedroom was a stark reminder that winter still clenched the town of Nyack.

Janice shivered again. She hated winter. She had been born and raised in Florida, and she had never been able to become accustomed to the constant cold here during the winter. But Jim's work was here, so here they would stay. At least the summers were nice.

If only Bobby would just come into the house when she first called him, she thought as she moved toward the large walk-in closet off the bedroom. Unfortunately Jim wouldn't be home until early tomorrow morning. Bobby knew that, and he was going to take full advantage of it, the way he did every time Jim worked the graveyard shift. It was going to be a struggle to get him to come in from the snow and finish his homework. It always was. She might as well resign herself to the fight.

At first the man's presence in the walk-in closet did not fully register. His hulking form was so foreign to what she expected as she slid the mirrored door across its tracks that she could only stare at his swarthy face and bushy silver-and-black mustache.

Janice turned to run, but Vargus was on her instantly, like a huge, agile tiger, throwing her face first into the floral-patterned comforter covering the bed. He overpowered her easily, pinning her tiny body to the mattress beneath his great weight. One huge hand grabbed a fistful of her long, freshly washed hair, pressing her mouth to the comforter so she could not scream, while the other removed a small piece of nine-ply rope from his belt. Deftly Vargus wrapped the twine firmly around her throat, crossed the ends at the nape of her neck, took hold of both ends with each hand, and began to choke her in a viselike grip. The woman's hands lay trapped beneath her body by Vargus's weight so she could not resist. Nor could she scream. The twine paralyzed her vocal cords.

Vargus smiled down at her as he watched the large veins of her neck begin to bulge. He leaned to one side so that he could see her face as it arched back against his pull. He jerked her neck twice as he pulled, and his lips curled into a tighter smile as he noticed a blood vessel below her left eye burst, filling the skin in the area with purple liquid.

She tried to speak, to utter only a word or two that would let the man know that he could have whatever he wanted if he would only relax the hold that was quickly suffocating her. There was cash in the house, and if it wasn't enough, she would drive him to a machine for more. There was jewelry he could take. He could even take her if that was what he wanted. She would not resist, and she would never say a word to anyone if he would only let her go. But she could not say these things because the rope was too tightly wrapped about her throat. Pleading silently with the man to have mercy, she stared into his cold dark eyes as he leaned to the side.

Just a few more seconds, and she would be gone. Just a few more hours, and the next step would be complete. Just a few more days, and the mission would be over and he would be worth twenty-five million dollars. Their faces were only inches apart, and for a moment, as he stared into the pretty eyes that begged for mercy, Vargus considered raping her. It had been a long time since he had sampled female flesh, and he was hungry for it. She was prettier than he had remembered, and she would put up no resistance at this point. But that would leave evidence that plastic surgery could not alter.

The boy was outside playing, as he was every night. That was whom he really wanted. But he had to finish her off first. If he took the boy without killing the woman, she would quickly realize that the boy was gone and alert her husband. That could imperil the entire mission. Before entering the house, he had considered showing mercy—taking both her *and* the boy—but had dismissed the thought quickly. The man in Washington was furious enough because of the West Virginia intruder. There would be no deviation from the plan. Vargus leaned over farther and pulled at the ends of the rope even harder. And then Janice's eyes rolled slowly back into her head.

"Get off her!" Eight-year-old Bobby Dolan screamed at the huge man as he tore across the bedroom and hurled his small body into Vargus. More than anything the impact surprised Vargus, and he tumbled off the woman, releasing his hold on her neck.

Her hands were suddenly released from beneath her body as Vargus fell from the bed. Janice grabbed the comforter and tried to crawl away. She tried to scream too, at whoever might be passing outside the house, but no words, only gasps, came from her throat.

At once Vargus was on his feet again. He glanced at the woman and realized that she would be incapacitated for several minutes. He turned to the boy, grabbed him by the back of the neck, and threw him into the closet. Within seconds he had immobilized Bobby with two of his father's ties hanging from the rack on a far wall of the closet and stuffed a third down his throat so he could not scream.

Seconds later Vargus emerged from the closet and was back on the woman as she crawled toward the bedroom door. He picked her up by the neck and slammed her against the wall. The towel fell to a heap at her feet, and for an instant he gazed down at her nude body.

With all her strength Janice shoved two long fingernails deep into the man's left eye. The eye filled quickly with blood. Vargus screamed in pain but did not release his hold on the woman even as the blood began to drip down his face. With a fury now driven by vengeance he wrapped both massive hands as tightly as he could around her neck and held on even as she beat him over and over about the face with the last strength left in her body.

Her death struggle did not last long. After a few moments her arms dropped to her side, her muscles began to twitch, and her eyes rolled far back in her head. Still, Vargus did not release his hold on her neck. He allowed her body to fall prone to the floor but maintained his grip on her delicate neck with both hands. The blood from his eye dripped onto her face, and still, he did not stop. The strain of the last two months rushed to the surface, and he vented his frustrations on her tiny body. Only when he became aware that she had lost control of her bodily functions did he pull back. She was quite dead now.

Vargus rose and moved purposefully toward the closet. The pain of his injured eye was excruciating, but he had endured pain far more brutal than this before, and the end of the mission still lay in front of him. The loss of one eye was a small price to pay for twenty-five million dollars.

He rolled the closet door open. Certain that there were just seconds remaining in his life, the young boy was terrified. But he was wrong. With a groan Vargus bent down and picked him up, carried him down the stairs to the first floor, turned out the porch light before leaving the house, and carried the boy quickly to the back of the Ford Taurus parked on the dark street in front of the house.

Vargus laid the small boy down on the snow behind the car for a moment, looked about quickly as he fumbled through his pants pocket for his keys, finally located them, and then attempted to insert the key into the trunk's keyhole. It took several moments to focus on what he was doing through the blood already beginning to cake over his eye, but at last the thin silver key slid into the lock, and the trunk clicked open.

Vargus bent down, picked up the struggling child, hurled him into the trunk space, and slammed the door shut over him. Calmly the dark man glanced up and down the quiet street again, then moved to the driver's side of the car, opened the door, and slid behind the steering wheel. He inhaled deeply several times, wondering if he should check the woman one more time to make certain she was dead. Far up the street he saw the faint glare of headlights and decided against the move. She was dead. There could be no doubt.

For a moment Vargus thought about the tracks he had seen in the West Virginia snow this morning. Tracks leading away into the woods. The only glitch in the plan. But there was nothing he could do about that now. He gunned the engine and guided the car smoothly away from the murder scene, which would not be discovered until it was much too late.

The Rotunda, the mammoth ivory-domed brick building that has served as the focal point of Thomas Jefferson's University of Virginia since the school's inception in 1819, rose into the night sky like a lighthouse over a calm sea, its pillared porticoes brightly illuminated by recessed high-voltage bulbs. The classic architecture of the building soared above the northern end of the Lawn, a tiered grassy area stretching away several hundred yards to the south. Lining the Lawn were the pavilions and hearth-heated rooms that had served as the classrooms and dormitory rooms of the university during its early days. Now the pavilions served almost exclusively as venues for social occasions, and only the best and the brightest students were granted the privilege of residing in the Lawn rooms.

Mace leaned against the smooth whitewashed wall of the

entranceway to the vaulted tunnel running beneath the entire length of the Rotunda. He stood in the shadows at the bottom step of the adit with his arms folded across his chest and looked out at the historic ground through glazed eyes. Typically Mace would have appreciated the rich tradition of this place, but he had not slept now in almost two days, and his attention at the moment was focused only on keeping his eyes open and remaining alert. They could be anywhere, whoever the hell "they" were. And if they found him . . . Well, that was something he simply could not consider.

It was long after two o'clock in the morning, and the catacombs under the huge building were deserted. He shivered. The February night air was cold. He would have given anything to put his head down on a soft pillow and pull the thick blankets of a comfortable bed up over him. But that was out of the question right now. There was one last thing that had to be done before he could climb back on the motorcycle and head for a hotel.

Suddenly a dull crash echoed toward Mace from the far end of the dimly lit, eerie tunnel, like a gentle wave rolling up on the shore. Mace turned in the direction of the sound. For a moment he swore he saw a shadow fade into a distant corner of the catacomb. He squinted to make certain the shadow had been just his imagination. But there was nothing there. Paranoia was already beginning to play tricks on his mind.

Mace turned back toward the Lawn and, as he did, came face-to-face with Slade Conner. "Jesus!" Mace stepped back instantly, then smiled. "I wish you hadn't done that." His words echoed away into the darkness of the tunnel.

"It's part of my job description to be able to do that whenever I want, a prerequisite for employment at CIA." Slade smiled back at Mace for an instant, then glanced over his shoulder. "Let's walk," he said firmly in a low voice. It was never a good idea to stay in one spot too long. It made you vulnerable. A moving target was always harder to hit.

Mace nodded.

They walked up the stairs together and began moving slowly toward the dark open area of the Lawn, away from the Rotunda.

When they reached the darkness beyond the arc emanating from the Rotunda's lights, Slade broke the silence. "So what's going on? You sounded upset on the phone."

Mace nodded. "I *was* upset." He hesitated. "First, I want to thank you for coming all the way down here from Washington to meet me."

Slade waved a hand. "It wasn't a problem. It's only two hours from Washington here to Charlottesville, and it's on open road. I've endured much worse, believe me." Slade stopped for a moment when he remembered the long dirt road to the remote airfield in Honduras. "But what in the hell are you doing down here away from New York?"

"Let me get to that in a minute."

"Okay, Brother." Slade held up his hands. He did not want to seem too interested.

They reached the edge of the first tier of the Lawn and shuffled down the steep five-foot slope to the next level.

"You said if I ever needed a hand, I could call." Mace's voice dropped to a whisper.

"Of course." Slade's expression became serious. He had a strange feeling about this, about what it entailed and who might be involved. He had hoped against hope that the subject of this meeting would involve something totally unrelated, that he wouldn't have to make the horrible choice if the reason Mace had called him here was what Slade thought. "What is it?"

Mace stopped walking and turned toward Slade. "I called you from a little town in West Virginia."

"West Virginia?" Slade stopped moving as well. "So that's why you wanted to meet here. It's on the way back to New York."

"Yes."

"What were you doing in West Virginia?"

Mace did not bother prefacing his explanation with a request for confidentiality. That was a given now. "Remember I told you when you were in New York awhile ago that I had taken on new responsibilities at Walker Pryce?"

"Yes," Slade said firmly, attempting to mask his trepidation.

"That we were raising a large fund to invest in Manhattan real estate and stocks on the New York Exchange."

"I think a billion was the figure you mentioned."

"Exactly." Mace smiled. "So you do listen."

"That's another part of my job."

"Well, don't ask me how, but I came upon some strange information with respect to how the money for the fund was raised and what some of it was being used for. I thought at first that I was just imagining things, but . . ."

"But you weren't." Slade finished the sentence.

Mace hesitated for a few moments before speaking again. "It doesn't appear so. There's something very wrong with the fund." He paused. "Some of the damn money was being used to fund some sort of . . . well, the only way I can describe it is covert activity."

Slade laughed, seemingly unimpressed. "Brother, are you sure you weren't secretly CIA-trained? Covert activity? That sounds awfully official and awfully suspicious. Even coming from the mouth of an investment banker."

It was unusual for Slade to be so casual, Mace thought. There was something amiss. "I'm not kidding."

Slade knew his friend was serious, dead serious. But for the first time in his life he did not want to face the responsibilities of a friendship. "I know you aren't." His voice became eerily calm. "Tell me more."

"I tracked a wire transfer out of the fund's account to this tiny town in West Virginia. To make a long story short, more specifically I tracked the cash to what was supposed to be an abandoned coal mine about ten miles outside the town. Except that the mine wasn't abandoned anymore. As near as I can guess, it was being used as some sort of training facility."

Slade's eyes shot to Mace's. He said nothing, but Mace understood the question anyway.

"I hiked through the woods last night, went into one of the buildings on the grounds of this place, and found a huge cache of weapons and ammunition. Unfortunately I went a little too far. Somebody heard me, and he and his hound from hell chased me across the snow. Obviously I escaped."

"So who transferred the money out of the account? I thought you were in charge of the fund."

Mace shook his head. "My job with respect to the fund was to raise the bank money and identify real estate investors. I didn't have anything to do with raising the equity, and I had no authority to transfer money out of the fund's accounts. I didn't even have authority to look into the account." He pursed his lips. "Only my direct superior could do that."

"Who was that?" Slade asked.

"Do you remember the woman I was with in Washington that day not too long ago? Leeny Hunt."

Slade nodded slowly. He hoped that Mace had not seen his physical reaction to her name.

"*She* transferred the money to West Virginia."

"But surely she isn't the only one with access to the account."

"There's just one other person with the authority to go into that account. Lewis Webster, the senior partner of Walker Pryce." Mace looked over Slade's shoulder at the huge oak trees, which were beginning to sway back and forth in an icy breeze. Again he thought he saw shadows, but it simply had to be his imagination.

"You're afraid that Leeny or Webster, or both, are involved in whatever was going on in West Virginia." Slade's expression became grim.

Mace nodded. "And I can't go back to Walker Pryce because if one or both of them are involved and the activity down there is actually something illicit . . ."

"You're a dead man." Slade finished the thought. "Because you haven't been to work and they will have been informed that there was an intruder. They might assume it was you."

"I wasn't going to call myself a dead man yet, but yes, something like that. It certainly wasn't a Boy Scout jamboree going on at the abandoned facility. Not the way the guy and his dog came after me." Mace paused. "A billion dollars is a lot of money. It could make people do funny things, especially if they are already involved in something they shouldn't be."

"Such as?" Slade's tone was terse.

"I have information that indicates that there was some sort of coverup at the job Leeny Hunt held before coming to Walker Pryce."

"How did you get that information?"

Mace did not want to drag Rachel into this by name if he could avoid it. "A little knowledge about your co-workers never hurts. You know that. I have friends in the business. A little digging, and I uncovered some troubling questions. But I don't have any answers yet."

"Uh-huh." Slade wasn't satisfied, but he didn't press. "Was there anything else strange going on in the fund's account?"

Mace nodded. "Yes. Almost all the equity money came through Capital Bank in Washington. It came to the fund in a roundabout way, but a friend traced all the money back as far as he could, and most of it went through Capital Bank. Nine hundred million of it anyway. And he couldn't get farther back than Capital. Except in one case."

"What do you mean?"

"He was able to get one of the account names at Capital Bank, an account where the money originated. But he couldn't get past the account. In other words, he couldn't find out how the money got into the account at Capital Bank."

"What was the name of the account?"

Mace smiled. Slade was on board now. He was asking all the right questions. "Pergament Associates." Mace hesitated. "Look, I need your help because I'm kind of cut off from my information sources. And well, honestly I don't know how to deal with the kind of firepower I saw in that building in West Virginia. I didn't know who else to go to. The local authorities probably would have thought I was nuts without some kind of tangible evidence. Obviously I couldn't go to Leeny or Webster."

"It's all right. I'll help. I'm your best friend. That's what I'm here for."

"I appreciate it, Slade." Mace looked around. "So let me get a little sleep, and we'll head back down to West Virginia together in the morning. I figure you ought to be able to go to the state boys down there. You'll have credibility."

Slade shook his head. "No," he said firmly. "I want you to drive to Washington tonight. Go to the Four Seasons Hotel in Georgetown, and check in. Wait for my call."

"What?" Mace stared at Slade.

"Do it." Slade's tone bordered at the edge of anger. "You came to me for help, didn't you?"

Mace nodded. He had never heard this tone before, not directed at him anyway.

"Then do as I ask. And don't call anyone."

Mace nodded again.

Slade stared at Mace. The choice was appalling. It was the awful choice. He inhaled slowly, showing nothing to his close friend through his facial expression. "So how did you pick this place for us to meet?"

Mace smiled. "We played the University of Virginia in football down here our senior year. Coach had us come to the Lawn the day before the game so he could feel as if he were actually educating us. Don't you remember?"

So many years. How was he supposed to remember some silly history lesson from so long ago? "Sure. Sure I do," Slade said quietly.

29

Liam's eyes fluttered open as he heard the door of the guard tower burst open. Instantly there were four of them, dressed from head to toe in black, standing before him, wielding impressive-looking hardware. Why in the hell did they need newer, probably more expensive guns just to shoot paint canisters?

The old man shook his head. So the guards at the gate had been caught unaware again, and as a result, he had been caught sleeping again. It would mean a written warning this time, and a possible suspension. Liam groaned as he leaned forward in the wooden desk chair. "Please don't use the ether again. It made me sick to my stomach for days last time," he mumbled. "Just tie me up and leave me here. I won't scream or yell or anything." He held his hands together in front of his face. "Well, go on. Do it."

Suddenly one of the intruders lifted the AK-47 to Liam's forehead and fired. The old guard's body crashed backward with the chair into a corner of the tower room. The men nodded at one another, then turned and moved quickly back down the way they had come.

Vargus was waiting for them at the bottom of the long stairway, grasping the little boy roughly by the back of his neck. "Done?"

"Yes," the first man back down the stairs grunted.

"Good." Vargus thrust the boy at him. "Take him and follow me."

Three minutes later Vargus stood before the huge chrome door guarding the control room. Behind him were thirty of the two-hundred-man invasion force—and the boy. Vargus turned toward the man clutching Bobby by the neck. "Bring him here."

The man pushed Bobby to Vargus.

Vargus smiled widely as he patted the boy gently on the shoulder.

"Please don't hurt me," Bobby whimpered, knowing he could take no comfort in the dark man's smile. "Please."

Vargus patted the boy on the shoulder again, then abruptly forced Bobby Dolan's mouth up against the metal speaker just to the side of the control room door. At the same time he pushed the young boy's left wrist almost up to the back of his neck.

"Dad, help me! Please!" the boy screamed.

There was no reaction from within, no sounds from the speaker next to the door, nothing to indicate that anyone inside the control room of the Nyack Nuclear Generating Facility had heard the boy's cries.

Vargus' expression turned suddenly sour, and he jerked the boy's wrist up above his head. There was a loud pop as Bobby's shoulder separated.

The boy began to scream again, reacting to the intense pain.

"What do you want? Don't hurt him. Please, for God's sake, don't hurt my boy!" a voice suddenly crackled through the speaker.

Vargus pushed the boy's face roughly across the polished wire mesh of the speaker, which also served as the microphone for those outside the control room. Bobby's upper lip snagged momentarily on a loose piece of the mesh, causing a deep cut on the inside of his mouth.

"Keep screaming," Vargus snarled.

Bobby cried pathetically, directly into the microphone.

"What do you want? Please!"

"You know damn well what I want," Vargus growled into the speaker. "Open the damn door!"

"We can't. God, the bars already slid into place! They aren't retractable for twenty-four hours at this point." Jim Dolan glanced back over his shoulder at the other engineers huddled around him. They did not want him to open the door. They did not care that Dolan's son was being tortured a few feet away. They cared about themselves, and they knew what opening the door meant.

"Bullshit. I haven't touched the lock. You can open this thing if you want to." Vargus paused. "If it's your close friends in there that are getting in the way, tell them I have a message for them as well. Every one of them has a loved one out here, and if you don't open this door immediately, I'll start chopping them up slowly so that everyone in there can hear them dying." It was a lie. Vargus held no other family members, but there would be no way for them to know that. "If you open the door now, I promise things will go a great deal easier." Bobby Dolan collapsed on the floor beside the door as Vargus let him go.

For several minutes there was no sound over the intercom. Then the huge chrome doors began to hum. The terrorists brought their guns down before them as the crack between the huge doors widened. But there was no reason to wield the weapons in such a way. The engineers inside were defenseless. The Nyack Nuclear Generating Facility was now securely in the hands of two hundred terrorists.

They poured into the control room as the doors stopped rumbling, Vargus leading the way. "Round them up," he yelled, pointing at the engineers. "Take them all down to the core and tie them up. We may need them later."

While seven of the terrorists laid their weapons down on desks and began to man the most critical positions in the control room—these men had had extensive training in the operations of a nuclear power plant—the remainder of the force jostled the engineers out of the control room and into the hallway outside toward the bowels of the plant. Vargus watched the group of prisoners shuffle away. It had gone so well. The man in Washington would be happy again.

"Sir!"

Vargus glanced at Tabiq. His forehead bore a long bloody scar, evidence of yesterday's early-morning battle with the intruder in West Virginia. "Well?" He spoke to Tabiq curtly. He was still furious at the man for allowing the intruder to escape.

Tabiq motioned toward the door. "He will not leave." Jim Dolan sat on the floor of the control room near the open doorway, cradling his unconscious son in his arms. "What should we do with them?"

The leader's eyes narrowed as he stared into Tabiq's face. "You need to toughen up, my friend." Vargus grabbed the man's gun, pointed it at the father and son, and unleashed a burst of fire. Instantly the man collapsed onto the boy. Both were dead. "Take them and throw them in the spent fuel pool."

Vargus pushed the gun back into Tabiq's hands and turned away.

It was just after the opening nine-thirty bell, and the New York Stock Exchange was a beehive of activity. Two separate hostile tender offers had been announced during the night, and the floor was frenetic in its pace. The arbitrageurs wanted in on the takeover action, and they had to execute orders immediately if they were going to make any money. Share prices of the two target stocks were rising rapidly. Both had already surged well past the initial offer prices laid out in press releases to the news services early this morning by the hostile bidders.

Men and women in brightly colored jackets crisscrossed the floor, searching for their traders to convey a multitude of buy *and* sell orders; investors who had owned the shares for some time were selling out immediately. They weren't going to be greedy. They were going to take their gains now and run, letting the professional arbitrageurs risk their precious capital to lay claim to the last few dollars of profit.

Traders formed chaotic semicircles in front of the specialists—
the men and women who made the market in a specific security on
the New York Stock Exchange—some frantically screaming buy
and sell orders at the specialists. Most of the older, more experienced traders simply gestured wildly at the specialists without
speaking, using hand motions to convey information.

Then an odd silence slowly overtook the great room. Even
trading at the posts where the specialists making the market in the
two takeover stocks resided ground to a halt. Everyone in the room
watched the ticker—actually a moving liquid crystal display—and
held their breaths, reading what they hoped was simply somebody's idea of a sick joke. The brief announcement rolled across
the screen.

Flash—the Nyack Nuclear Generating Facility, located approximately fifteen miles north of New York City on the Hudson River,
has been taken over by terrorists. The attack occurred at approximately four-thirty this morning.

The assembled throng on the floor of the Exchange continued
to gaze at the ticker for a few moments even after the last words
had disappeared. Slowly people began to move around the floor
again. Some began trading again. Some laughed, not choosing to
believe what they had just read. Others quietly left the building.

And while the share prices of the two takeover targets continued to be bid up in trading throughout the morning, the overall in-
dices did not fare as well. At noon the Dow Jones 30 Industrials
had tumbled more than three hundred points. Lewis Webster's
prediction was coming true, as he had known it would.

Kyle Mcyntire, commander of the one thousand Wolverines to
be deployed at Nyack, leapt from the passenger side of the helicopter onto the frozen ground of the field, then ran, bent at the
waist, out from under the rotating blades toward the uniformed

man standing before a grove of trees at the edge of the field. Leaves and twigs whipped chaotically about his body for several moments as the chopper rose, turned down at the nose, then sped away just thirty feet above the ground. Then suddenly it was quiet, noises effectively absorbed by the foreboding winter cloud cover.

"Sir!" The Wolverine had moved out from the grove of trees to a spot directly before Mcyntire. "Captain Thomas Ellet." The young man saluted sharply.

"At ease, soldier."

"Yes, sir." Ellet nodded smartly toward the farmhouse behind him. "We've evacuated the residents and are using the house as a command post. It's close, but not too close." Ellet glanced toward the far end of the field.

Mcyntire followed the captain's gaze and caught sight of the nuclear facility's huge cooling towers looming up from behind the tops of the leafless trees. "How far?"

"Just over three miles."

Mcyntire looked away from the plant and back at the younger man. "Give me a status report, Captain."

"Yes, sir." Ellet's posture stiffened. "There are approximately eight hundred Wolverines deployed, with another two hundred on the way from Fort Dix. They are expected here within the hour. We have the facility surrounded to the north, west, and south. On the east side there isn't enough room between the facility and the edge of the cliffs to position men without making them vulnerable to fire from the terrorists. But we do have boats out on the river."

"How about the intake and exhaust pipes?"

"Sir?"

"Upstream pipes bringing water from the river to cool the core water and pipes downstream sending warm water back out. I suggest we put cameras down there if we haven't already, just in case anybody tries to go in or out of the facility that way."

"Yes, Commander." The younger man was disappointed he hadn't already thought of that.

"How many of them are there, Captain?"

"We estimate several hundred."

"On what do you base that estimate?"

"Two security guards managed to escape through the woods during the initial attack. We've got them waiting for you in there." The captain nodded back at the farmhouse again.

Mcyntire sighed heavily and shook his head. "They'll be useless. They were running for their lives. I doubt they could have seen much, and whatever they did see, they won't remember accurately." The commander paused. "How many hostages?"

"At least a hundred."

"Anything else?"

"Just this." Ellet reached into his pocket, withdrew an envelope, then thrust it at Mcyntire.

"What is it?" The commander took the envelope without opening it.

"Correspondence from the terrorists."

"How did you get it?"

"They let one of the hostages go about an hour ago. Had her deliver it."

"What does it say?"

"It says they want a billion dollars. It says they want the release of certain imprisoned terrorists around the world, a list of whom they will provide later. And it says they want to be guaranteed safe passage to North Yemen, at which point they will free the hostages."

Mcyntire shoved the envelope into his pants pocket, then removed a pack of cigarettes and lighted one. "And?" His experience told him there would be one more piece of information.

"It says they have surrounded each core with five two-thousand-pound bombs and will detonate them if these demands aren't met."

"What's the deadline?" the commander asked calmly.

"There isn't one yet."

Mcyntire took several puffs from the cigarette.

"Sir?"

"Yes, Ellet?"

"If they were to detonate the bombs . . ."

"New York City would be uninhabitable within about two hours. Of course we wouldn't care. We'd already be dead."

30

Leeny watched carefully as Webster moved back and forth in front of his office window, pausing every so often to stare down at Wall Street. When he stopped to gaze down at the Street, still teeming with activity despite this morning's takeover of the Nyack plant, he would rest his chin in one hand and shake his head, mumbling something unintelligible into his crusty palm. He seemed distracted, showed a nervousness Leeny would not have thought him capable of. To be nervous, one had to possess feelings, and this man was the coldest human being she had ever met.

Perhaps Webster's agitation arose from the knowledge that together with the man in Washington, he had engineered the takeover of the Nyack nuclear plant and was therefore responsible for the havoc the terrorists had already wreaked upon New York City. Wire services were reporting above-average numbers of fatalities caused by heart attacks and strokes, particularly among the elderly, which medical professionals were attributing to the terrible stress brought on by the events unfolding at Nyack. Looting had begun to occur in areas where people had decided to desert the city.

But the thought that Webster really cared about any of those things was ludicrous. He was a callous man who didn't care about another's ills, no matter who he was, unless those problems directly affected him. The cause of his agitation had to be of a personal nature.

Leeny reclined on the comfortable leather couch of Webster's office. The plan was working. Exactly as they had anticipated. Manhattan real estate owners she and Mace had talked to were calling of their own accord, "just to touch base," they claimed. Just to see if the recently initiated Broadway Ventures was still in business or if it was in a holding pattern until the trouble at the power plant had been resolved—one way or the other. They tried to seem calm about what was going on just north of Manhattan—just north of their precious real estate—but she heard in their voices the panic lurking just under the surface. Though each investor was in no physical danger—they lived and worked in cities well away from New York—they still feared for their lives. Because their buildings—their net worths—sat directly in harm's way. Vulnerable and immovable. At the mercy of the terrorists who might detonate bombs at any second and rain deadly radiation down onto Manhattan.

They tried to project calm and confidence to her through the telephone, but they could not. At the end of the conversation they kept her on the line with idle chitchat, something they typically had no time for, as if they hoped that at the last minute she might make an offer on their buildings. They could not make the first offer because it was not in their nature. Savvy real estate investors never opened the bidding but waited for the other party to open up first, so they were certain not to leave anything on the table.

She did not accommodate them. She merely said a pleasant good-bye. Knowing they would call back. Knowing that when they did, it would indicate that they were beaten, that the pressure had become too much for them to bear.

She was already beginning to receive the second calls. And she was playing with their minds, making them grovel and still not giving them concrete bids, giving them no indication of what, if anything, she might offer for their properties. She was playing God again—and loving it this time.

"What's the matter, Lewis?"

The old man turned toward her, chin still resting in one hand. "Nothing."

The fire in the dark eyes seemed to be burning low, she thought. Something was definitely wrong.

The telephone buzzed loudly, interrupting the silence of the office.

"Hello," Webster whispered.

Leeny watched his face as she listened. Clearly the information he was receiving was not good.

"Yes." Webster nodded several times as he listened, then put the phone down. He stared at her intensely for several moments but said nothing.

"Lewis, what is it?" She swallowed hard. "Tell me!" The slow leak had become a torrent.

"It's Mace McLain," he hissed.

"What?" Leeny recoiled at the mention of Mace's name.

"We think he broke into the training facility in West Virginia just before the task force left for Nyack." Webster tilted his head forward ominously.

Leeny shook her head from side to side. "That's not possible. Mace McLain is dead. You told me he was to be killed last Friday night."

"He wasn't at his apartment when the assassin broke in. He was gone. And he hasn't returned," Webster whispered almost inaudibly. The accusatory glare became more pronounced.

"What?" Dazed, Leeny sat back slowly on the couch.

Webster's eyes narrowed. He watched her closely, searching for any clue that in fact she had tipped Mace off about the assassin. There was nothing in her face except shock. And he knew that while she was aware that the task force was training somewhere in West Virginia, she did not know the exact location. *She* would not

have been able to guide him to Sugar Grove. Therefore it was il-
logical to assume that she had tipped him off. Because that was
clearly why he had left New York: to go to Sugar Grove. "He isn't
dead," Webster said.

"But how? How did he find out about West Virginia?" she
asked, a feeling of desperation suddenly surging through her body.

"I don't know."

"But the people at the West Virginia facility must have caught
him." She was reaching for anything that would prop her up again.

"No. He escaped."

"Did someone see him? Is that how you know it was Mace?"

"Only one man. And that man did not get a good look at him.
Not a good enough look to identify him."

"Then how do you know it was Mace?" Leeny asked, her hands
covering her mouth.

"People in Sugar Grove recognized his photograph."

"So he knows what is going on." Her voice shook.

"I'd say there is a very good chance he has pieced this thing together. All he would have to do is read the paper and think a little.
We waited too long to kill him."

Leeny's breathing became short. "We have to find him."

"Of course we do," Webster whispered angrily. "And we are
looking everywhere. But he was smart. He withdrew almost twenty
thousand dollars in cash from his Chemical savings account before he left New York. He hasn't used a credit card, so we can't
locate him."

"Get the girl." Leeny's voice was an eerie monotone. Somehow
she knew that the answer lay with Rachel.

Webster's eyes flashed to Leeny's. "You mean Rachel
Sommers?"

Leeny nodded. "She'll know where he is. She'll probably know
a whole lot more as well."

Webster shook his head. "We've *been* looking for her. She's
nowhere. Columbia canceled classes, and she's vanished."

"Where is she from?"

"She lists no home address with Columbia except the apartment, and we've checked out every other Sommers in New York. No luck."

"God." Leeny swallowed hard and clasped her hands before her tightly so they would not shake.

Webster picked up the telephone and began to punch out a number. "Go back to your office, Ms. Hunt." His voice was still calm. "Continue to take the investor calls. Keep me informed of each person with whom you speak and any offers you receive."

Leeny rose unsteadily from the sofa and became dizzy. She steadied herself against the end table. Mace was out there somewhere, like a virus in a computer, waiting, biding his time. When the moment was right, he would strike, destroying all of them. She could feel it. They had to find him.

She stumbled toward the door. She needed to get back to her office quickly. She needed the pills.

"Commander?"

Mcyntire glanced up from the papers spread out across the top of the desk. "Yes, Captain Ellet?"

"They let another hostage go."

"And?" Mcyntire was curt. The pressure was already weighing heavily on him.

Ellet moved to the desk and laid the envelope down in front of the commander.

"What does this one say?" But Mcyntire already knew. It was simply a question of how much time he was being given.

"It says we have seventy-two hours to comply with their demands."

The commander groaned heavily and turned to look out of the farmhouse's den window at the cooling towers. "Okay. Call Ferris and let him know. Becker needs to be made aware of this as quickly as possible."

Roger Hamilton, senior vice-president of Maryland Mutual Life and chief investment officer of its thirty-two-billion-dollar mortgage portfolio, stared blankly at the television positioned in one corner of his ornate office. From his chair he had a beautiful view of the Capitol, one he generally admired several times a day. But this morning he had no interest. His focus was on the television and the situation at Nyack.

He watched the screen as if in a trance. The CNN correspondent was interviewing another physics expert, this time the retired chief of the Nuclear Regulatory Commission. The man confirmed that in fact the radiation fallout could easily render Manhattan uninhabitable. Worthless, in Hamilton's terms.

Hamilton glanced away from the screen toward the telephone on his massive desk. He had not tried to call Mace McLain yet. He had somehow convinced himself that all this was simply a bad dream or some horrible mistake. That either the government or the terrorists would quickly back down, that a settlement would be reached. And life would return to normal in New York City, in the country's most significant real estate market.

Suddenly the CNN anchor interrupted the interview. "We have, yes . . ." He paused, pressing the piece farther into his ear. "Yes, confirmed now. The terrorists have imposed a deadline. Seventy-two hours. If their demands are not met at that point, they will detonate the bombs they have positioned around the two nuclear cores at Nyack."

Hamilton shook involuntarily at this new piece of information. His career would be over. As soon as those bombs were detonated. If the unthinkable actually happened, billions of dollars of his mortgages would become worthless in a split second. The buildings would still stand, but they would be devoid of tenants and therefore devoid of cash flow—into eternity. At least his eternity.

He did not want to make the call, but there seemed to be no choice now. "Mace McLain, please." Hamilton fiddled with a matchbook as he listened to the secretary answer his call.

"He's not in today. I'm sorry," she said.

"Oh." Perhaps Mace had already opted to get out of the city. Perhaps Broadway Ventures wasn't as big and bad a vulture as he had hoped.

"Ms. Hunt is taking all his calls," the woman continued.

There was good and bad news to that revelation. At least the fund was still in business. But that someone taking calls was Ms. Hunt, and he hadn't been particularly friendly to her when she had visited with Mace. He hoped she had forgotten.

"I could transfer you if you like." The secretary's voice was strained.

"Yes, fine." Hamilton could hear the consternation in her voice. He could only imagine what it must be like to be living within range of the radiation's tentacles. If the bombs went off, he wouldn't have a career, but he'd have his life and his home.

The line clicked several times as the secretary performed the transfer. Hamilton rifled through his Rolodex while he waited. Walker Pryce, Walker Pryce. There it was. Kathleen Hunt.

The phone began to ring. An incredible choice the people of New York faced. Leave and possibly have your home looted for perhaps no reason if the terrorists didn't detonate the bombs. Or wait it out, take the chance, and face death. Because if the bombs exploded without warning, experts were predicting that it would take less than three hours for the radiation to reach the city. And there was no way that many millions of people were going to get out of New York in three hours. Manhattan was an island, for God's sake. Christ, they'd be swimming across the Hudson. Even if they got out, they wouldn't be able to return for years.

The meltdown of a nuclear power plant core had occurred several times in eastern Europe and in the old Soviet Union, and Hamilton had heard how devastating the results were on population and property. Those accidents, except for Chernobyl, had been kept quiet, but he had friends in those countries who had relayed what had happened. The fallout from those facilities had been small and quickly controlled, but the situation in New York City would be magnified many times if the terrorists lost their cool. "Answer, please," he yelled into the phone's mouthpiece, suddenly panicked. His prayers were answered immediately.

"Hello, this is Kathleen Hunt."

A wave of relief washed over him. "Ms. Hunt, this is Roger Hamilton at Maryland Mutual Life." He summoned his friendliest voice, which still conveyed a hint of arrogance. Even he could hear it. "I trust you remember me."

"I remember." Leeny's voice was cold. Despite the strain she felt over the news that Mace wasn't dead, she managed a smile. She was truly going to enjoy *this* call.

Hamilton heard the harsh edge to her tone. So she hadn't forgotten. Well, the hell with her. She still needed to respect him and the powerful position he held, the massive amount of money he controlled. "I just wanted to say that I enjoyed meeting you, Kathleen, and—"

"You are calling to see if we are still open for business, aren't you?" Leeny cut him off.

"Well—"

"Am I right?" she snapped.

"Yes." Hamilton's voice dropped almost to a whisper. His career was imploding, and she didn't care. He swallowed. It was time to grovel. These were uncharted waters, and he needed to do whatever it took to unload the bonds.

"You'll be relieved to know that we are still open. As a result, as I'm sure you can imagine, I'm receiving lots of calls. So my time is limited." She paused. She heard his heavy breathing on the other end of the line. He was sweating this out in a big way. It was wonderful. She could not help smiling again. Her next words were going to make him disintegrate. "I'll be generous and give you twenty cents on the dollar for your bonds, Roger. I'll give you two hundred million dollars for a billion dollars' face value of your bonds. There isn't any reason for me even to bother doing specific credit analysis on each property. I'm just going to give you one blanket offer."

"*What?* But that's ridiculous. It's insane," he stammered.

"Maybe, but that's the way life is in New York City at this point."

"I can't agree to twenty cents on the dollar. I was thinking more along the lines of ninety-six to ninety-seven cents on the dollar." Hamilton's eyes flashed around his office. Twenty cents on the dollar. That translated into an eight-hundred-million-dollar loss. He felt the perspiration bubbling from his palms onto the receiver.

"Clearly we are too far apart on price even to *begin* a discussion of the purchase of your bonds by Broadway Ventures. If you don't like my bid, I suggest you call other real estate buyers. If you can find any at this point. Or you can call me back when you are prepared to discuss your position more rationally. Thank you, Roger." She laid the phone back in its cradle gently and smiled. A thrill surged through her. The power she held was awesome—and intoxicating.

"Damn it!" Hamilton roared as he heard the line click in his ear. He slammed the phone down. "Damn it!" He screamed the word the second time. He knew there were no other buyers out there. Kathleen Hunt was the only game in town.

Leeny smiled at the phone, satisfied with her performance. She might as well have impaled him with a hunting knife. He was ruing the day he had been rude to her, ruing the day he had met her. Suddenly the phone rang again. Hamilton again already? "Hello."

There was nothing but silence at the other end of the phone.

"Hello," she said, loudly this time.

"Leeny?" A timid voice seeped through the line.

"Yes."

"It's John Schuler."

Leeny's eyes narrowed. "John, how are you? It's been so long since we've talked." She made her voice soft and approachable.

Schuler coughed nervously. "I'm fine." He had not expected so friendly a greeting. "In light of the circumstances." The experts were saying that the fallout from Nyack could reach Greenwich if the bombs exploded, that it was possible. But it would take much longer to reach Greenwich than it would to reach New York. And the effects would be much weaker. So he had left the bank immediately upon hearing the news of the attack, letting the more junior Turks risk their fool lives to keep the bank open. From Greenwich he could jump in the BMW and have enough of a head start to outrace *any* of the explosion's effects. In New York he was a dead man.

"I know." Leeny made her voice sound pathetic and scared. "I'm so frightened."

"But why don't you get out of there, for God's sake?" he asked.

"I'm going to. I just need to finish a few things, and then I'm leaving."

Schuler was relieved. It sounded as if Broadway Ventures was shutting down, at least temporarily. "So you and Mace and Webster aren't planning to speculate on what's happening, are you? You aren't going to buy anything, right?" He asked the question tentatively.

"Of course not," she lied.

"And you haven't already bought anything, have you?"

"No."

"Good." His voice was suddenly full strength. His billion dollars were safe.

"John?" Leeny made her voice extremely meek.

"Yes?"

"I really am scared. It's funny. I couldn't help thinking of you when I heard about the attack on the plant. I wanted to know you were all right." She hesitated. "John, I want to see you. Even if it's only for a few minutes. Even if it's only to have you hold me. I need to see you."

Schuler smiled. Mace certainly had his signals crossed about Leeny. Clearly she had loved what he had given her that night at the Inter-Continental. His self-satisfied smile became broader. So he hadn't lost his ability to overpower a woman with his love-making skills. He remembered how he had pulled her onto the floor, onto her knees, by the fistful of long golden hair. Immediately he felt the familiar throb in his pants. Sometimes you just had to be physical with a woman. "When were you thinking about?"

"Tonight."

"I'm not coming back into the city," he warned her.

"I wouldn't ask you to," she responded softly. "Why don't we meet at the Stamford Marriott? That's only about twenty minutes from Greenwich, isn't it?"

"Yes." This certainly was turning out to be a fortunate phone call. "What time?"

"Around ten. I'll have a room. Just call me when you get there."

"Fine. I'll see you then." Schuler smiled as he put down the phone.

Leeny hung up the phone, and the sweet smile that had played over her face during their conversation disappeared. But she had no time to think about Schuler. The phone rang again.

"Hello," she said softly, thinking it might be the little banker again.

"Ms. Hunt?"

She rolled her eyes. It was Hamilton calling back again already.

"It's Roger Hamilton."

The stodginess was completely gone from his tone. "Yes?"

"How about ninety cents on the dollar?"

"No." Her voice was suddenly steel tough. "Thirty cents. That's my final offer." She slammed the phone down.

Hamilton dropped the receiver and slowly allowed his head to fall to the blotter covering the desktop. His life was balanced on the razor's edge, in the hands of terrorists two hundred miles away. How had it ever come to this?

31

H ello," the familiar soft voice answered.
Relief surged through Mace's body. "Rachel!"
"Mace?"
"Yes."

"Mace, my God, I'm so glad to hear your voice." It was Rachel's turn to feel relieved.

From behind the curtain of his fourth-floor room Mace looked out over the brick courtyard of the Washington, D.C., Four Seasons Hotel, the room Slade had directed him to check into. It had been more than twenty-four hours, and still no word from Slade. "I would have called earlier, but I couldn't remember your stepfather's last name until now."

"Oh." She hesitated. "I've been so worried about you." Her voice was hoarse, showing her concern. "I called your office, but the secretary kept saying you weren't in. I called your apartment, but there was no answer there either."

"I've been away," he said quickly.

"I'm so glad you called. My stepfather was going to stick it out here no matter what happens. He doesn't think terrorists ought to be able to scare you out of your home. But Mom convinced him to go. And I'm going with them. I think it's the right thing to do. Especially given the deadline."

For a moment Mace did not answer.

"Mace?"

"Yes."

"Is everything all right? Where are you?"

"In Washington," he answered.

"What are you doing there?"

"Rachel, you remember that material you gave me?"

"About Leeny Hunt?" Her voice was suddenly unsteady.

"Yes."

"Of course."

"Well, you definitely uncovered something."

"What are you talking about?" She was frightened now.

"I'll spare you the details, but I don't think you need to worry about bombs going off at Nyack."

"What?" she screamed.

Mace hesitated. "Broadway Ventures has been funding a training center in West Virginia, a terrorist training center."

Rachel caught her breath.

"I traced some money out of the Chase Broadway Ventures account down to a little town named Sugar Grove and then found the actual site. And I almost didn't live to tell you about it. I haven't been back to the office since. For obvious reasons."

"This is incredible." Her voice was hushed.

"It gets better. I think the West Virginia people are involved with the Nyack situation. I think they were the ones that took the plant over. That's why I don't really think the bombs will go off. If there really are any bombs at all."

"What do you mean?"

"Think about it. Broadway Ventures was funding these people in West Virginia, a vulture fund financing a terrorist group. And Broadway Ventures was to invest in Manhattan real estate and Big Board equities, the exact securities that would be most affected by the Nyack takeover. Real estate for obvious reasons. Stocks because so many Fortune Five Hundred companies are headquartered and have significant operations in or near the New York metropolitan area."

"I can't believe it." But she saw the motive and the connection immediately. "It's perfect."

"Yes, it is. It has Lewis Webster written all over it. It was his way to save the partnership."

"But if what you say is accurate and he is involved, he has run a terrible risk. He could easily be exposed if something went wrong. Why would he do that? He's wealthy, isn't he?" Rachel asked.

"Yes. The rumor is that he's worth almost three hundred million dollars." Mace suddenly thought about Webster's meeting in Washington, the one Sarah Clements had told him about that day on the executive floor.

"So why would he do it?"

"To save the partnership, I suppose," Mace answered. "It sounds outrageous, I know. I can't see why he would take those risks either. But it's the only explanation I can come up with." It was a hole in his theory, and of course she had homed right in on it. "Please don't misunderstand me, Rachel. I want you out of that city now." Mace's voice was firm.

She did not answer immediately. "What about Leeny Hunt?"

"What about her?"

"Do you think she is involved?"

Mace inhaled slowly. "I have to think so. She raised the money for the fund way too fast. And—" He stopped. And it all came from Washington.

"What, Mace? What is it?"

"Nothing." He did not want to tell her what he was thinking. The implications were too severe.

"But have you gone to the authorities with this?" Her voice was high-pitched, nervous. If what he was saying was true, there would be people after him.

"I can't. I don't have any proof."

"But you can't do nothing."

He nodded. "I know. I'm just waiting here for some information from a friend. Then I'm coming to New York. There's one more thing I need before I can go to the authorities."

Rachel hesitated. "You're going after Leeny." Her voice was hollow. "She could tell you everything, I bet."

She was smart, thinking exactly as he was. "No, something else." There *was* something else he had to do, but Leeny was his primary target. He couldn't tell her what the other something was. He didn't want to scare her.

"Please go to the authorities, Mace. Right now. Please."

"All right." He couldn't go to the authorities because he didn't have enough to prove that his suspicions were correct, but he had to calm her down. "Look, I've got to go. So do you. Get out of the city. In case I'm wrong about all this."

A strained silence followed. They both realized that there was a chance they might never see each other again if Mace was wrong and the bombs were real.

"Rachel?" Finally Mace broke the silence.

"Yes," she responded quickly.

"Do you remember asking, 'What about us?' at dinner that night?"

"Yes."

Mace hesitated. This was difficult. He wasn't used to laying out his feelings. "I really do care about you. When all this is over . . . " He didn't finish the sentence.

"I know." She understood. "You know I—I care about you too."

He passed a hand through his hair. He had never missed someone this way. But there was nothing more to say now. "Okay, well, good-bye."

"Good-bye, Mace." Rachel hung up the phone slowly.

Mace put down the phone. It rang almost immediately. The caller could be only one person. "Hello."

"Mace, it's Slade."

"Where have you been?" A wave of relief rushed through his body.

"Sorry, Brother. I've been trying to get you this information."

"I assume you know what's going on in New York?"

"Yes." Slade's voice dropped.

"Do you know what I think?"

Slade answered without hesitation. "That the people who were at the facility in West Virginia are responsible."

"Exactly. Did you check out the Sugar Grove facility?"

"Yes."

"And there was no one there, right?"

"No, there wasn't anyone there." Slade removed a cigarette from the pack he held in his left hand and lighted it while holding the pay phone receiver in his right. He glanced at the Lincoln Memorial. He hadn't smoked in years, not since the Plymouth Home for Wayward Boys. The match shook in his hand. "But it was obvious to me that there had been people there. There were spent shell casings all over the place."

"Lewis Webster and Leeny Hunt are responsible for the crisis in New York, Slade. There aren't any bombs at Nyack. The whole thing is a conspiracy to speculate on Manhattan real estate and shares on the New York Stock Exchange."

Slade shook his head. Mace was too smart for his own good. "That sounds pretty ridiculous, Mace."

"Maybe, but I'm convinced it's the truth," he said.

"The bombs are real, Mace. My boss is in charge of the situation up there, for Christ's sake. The bombs are real."

"No, they aren't. You have to tell him that. Otherwise, if there is a raid by government forces in some last-ditch attempt to diffuse the situation, Wolverines will die needlessly."

"The bombs are real," Slade said persistently.

"Fine, they're real." Mace was irritated. Why was Slade being so stubborn? Suddenly a warning bell went off. It was faint, but it was there. "Have you been able to track down anything on Leeny or Pergament Associates?"

"No. I'm still working on it." He did not convey to Mace what he had learned about either one. He couldn't. Not yet. "Listen, give me another day." He took a puff from the cigarette. It calmed his nerves immediately. He had to keep Mace in that hotel.

"I can't. I'm going to New York."

"No!"

"I can't wait any longer in this hotel room, Slade. It's driving me crazy."

Slade glanced around the Reflecting Pool quickly. Of course New York was where Mace would go. He was convinced that he was indestructible. "All right. Look, I'm very close to the information you want. Pick a time and place to meet in Manhattan."

Mace thought for a second. Considering the situation in New York City, it might take time to get there. "Tomorrow night. Eleven o'clock. The skating rink at Rockefeller Center."

"Done."

Mace put the phone down. Slade was hiding something. He had known the man long enough to be able to tell when he wasn't being totally forthcoming. But what was he hiding? And why? Mace glanced back down at the courtyard. Even though Slade had disagreed with Mace about the fact that there weren't really any bombs at Nyack, he had suggested that they meet in New York City. Slade didn't believe there were any bombs either. Otherwise he would never have suggested New York as a meeting place. So why was he acting as if he were convinced the bombs were real?

Slade took one more long drag from the cigarette. Mace was right. Innocent men might die. Men of the Wolverines, men he knew. And some of the blood would be on his hands.

* * *

Schuler sat on the edge of the king-size bed in nothing but his boxer shorts. He stared at Leeny, who stood before him naked. She was gorgeous, a goddess. Just as he had remembered her.

He checked the television one more time. Nothing had changed. The terrorists were dug in, and the authorities were at a loss for an action plan. He reached for the remote to turn down the volume. Leeny had turned the sound up very loud, and it would distract him once they began to couple.

Leeny intercepted the remote, sliding it from Schuler's hand seductively and dropping it to the floor. She sank quickly to her knees in front of him, pulling his boxers off, kissing him even though there was no need. He was already as full as he could be.

After a few moments she rose from the floor, then pushed him gently onto his back so she could mount him. Seconds later she was on top of him and he was inside her.

Schuler watched her delicate frame as she moved up and down on him. God, it felt so good. He closed his eyes and forgot about Broadway Ventures, Chase Manhattan, and the threat of radiation. He moaned slightly as she leaned suddenly to one side. She was so good.

"John!" Leeny suddenly said his name loudly, over the sound of the television. She wanted him to see this.

His eyes fluttered open, and for a moment he could not comprehend what was happening. Then he understood. The thought of trying to move raced through his brain, but he was never able to act on the thought. The bullet tore through the nasal cartilage directly between his eyes and out the back of his head. He twitched spastically beneath her for several moments and then lay completely still.

32

F ollowing a brown Mercedes, the van moved slowly east on the lower deck of the George Washington Bridge, the double-deck suspension bridge connecting New York and New Jersey over the Hudson River. It was one in the morning, but the bridge was still crowded with people leaving the city. There was surprisingly little panic; people were generally calm. Despite the traffic, cars moved at a steady thirty miles an hour.

Suddenly, in the middle of the span, the van stopped. Instantly the cars behind began to sound their horns loudly. But the driver paid no attention. Calmly he pulled the keys from the ignition, jumped out of the vehicle, and ran forward to the Mercedes, which had stopped fifty feet ahead. People in passing cars screamed at him as he ran, but again he paid no attention. Seconds later he was safe in the backseat of the German car. The driver stepped on the accelerator and the car jumped forward, quickly lost in the flow of traffic.

Exactly two minutes and thirty seconds later the van disintegrated in a massive fireball. The blast blew out both decks of the east-bound lanes of the bridge. Cars and people on the bridge, those not incinerated by the blast, dropped sickeningly to the black waters below. Moments later the two ends of the east-bound lanes hung down toward the water by a few thin cables like the tongues of exhausted dogs.

Standing in the lookout tower of the Nyack Nuclear Generating Facility, Vargus had been able to see the fiery blast very clearly in the night sky. He smiled, imagining what was going on down there: the chaos and the panic on both sides of the bridge and the effect this would have on the city's inhabitants.

Bobby Maxwell, the New Orleans real estate investor, owner of twelve buildings on the island of Manhattan, slowly sat up in bed. His head hurt terribly. He had imbibed much too much wine last night. He laughed loudly as he rubbed his bloodshot eyes. At least it had helped him forget the situation in New York City. He groaned as he reached for the television remote and switched the set on. At once he forgot about his splitting headache.

The female reporter stood on the New Jersey side of the Hudson River with the sagging ends of the George Washington Bridge in the distance behind her left shoulder. Wind whipped her hair into a frenzy as she pressed a tiny speaker into her ear with one hand and held a large microphone in front of her mouth with the other. Finally she nodded and began to speak.

"Repeating, at approximately one o'clock this morning both decks of the east-bound lanes of the George Washington Bridge were destroyed by a huge bomb apparently carried onto the bridge by a truck or other large vehicle. Witnesses gave police the license number of a Mercedes seen speeding from the scene. Authorities located the abandoned car around four o'clock this morning in Westchester County, New York. No arrests have been made, and authorities are not willing to discuss fatalities at this time. The group now in control of the Nyack nuclear plant has claimed responsibility."

Maxwell swallowed, then rose quickly from the bed and rummaged through the nightstand, looking for the phone number. He didn't need to hear any more of the human-interest story. He didn't care about people. He cared about buildings. And his were in immediate danger of becoming worthless.

He needed to speak to Mace. Now.

*   *   *

At nine-thirty, despite what had happened on the GW Bridge, the Stock Exchange opened for business. The brokers and specialists who had come to the floor this morning, about half the usual number, were unusually quiet as they moved about the floor. They kept one eye on the tape at all times and traded only halfheartedly. By noon the Dow Jones industrial average had dropped one thousand points and the exchange governors closed the Big Board for trading; it was useless to continue. But the early closing bell did not sound before Broadway Ventures had made many extremely attractive purchases through sanitized numbered accounts.

Mace stared at what was left of his apartment. It shocked him. It had been gutted like a cow at the slaughterhouse. The leather couches and their cushions had been torn apart so that their innards spilled all over the floor. Pictures had been removed from the walls and smashed so that glass lay in and around the innards of the couches. There were large holes in the walls. Looters? It couldn't be, he thought. Most of the stereo components were shattered but still here.

Glass cracked sharply beneath his hard-soled shoes as he moved into the apartment and toward the bathroom, where he had hidden the package Rachel had given him, the package detailing Leeny's involvement in the LeClair and Foster insider trading scandal, a package the person who had broken into his apartment might have been interested to find.

Mace removed a tile from the bathroom ceiling as he stood balanced on the edge of the tub. A tremendous wave of relief surged through his body. It was still where he had left it. He removed the envelope carefully. Now Rachel was safe. Now they couldn't connect her to him. At least as far as getting in the way of their plans. If they had seen this package and the name of the addressee, they would have realized that she was involved, and she would have been in mortal danger.

He stepped down from the tub. It was time to find Leeny. Then he would go to the authorities with what he had.

Leeny sat in a booth at Joey's Place—a twenty-four hour diner directly across the street from Mace's apartment building—sipping slowly on a cup of coffee. Her eyes were sunk deep into her face because of the lack of sleep and the stress she had endured. She gazed through the diner's window at the apartment building's front door. Mace knew what was going on with Broadway Ventures. There could be no doubt. And he was going to destroy everything. Because of him, she would go to jail. Unless she could stop him first.

The image of John Schuler's dead body lying on the bed raced through her mind. She laughed out loud, then looked around to see if anyone had heard her outburst. But no one had.

From her purse she removed the Polaroid she had taken in the room of the Stamford Marriott. There was no need to have to look at his corpse in her mind. She could see the real thing. She put the photograph, a close-up of Schuler's bloody face, in her lap and glanced down at it. She ran a hand through her hair as she gazed at the horrible expression on the little man's face. A smile crossed her face as she admired her handiwork.

"Do you want anything else, lady?" The waitress stood next to Leeny, trying to see what was in her lap.

Leeny covered the picture quickly with her hands, glanced at the door of Mace's apartment building again and then up at the woman. "No," she whispered.

The waitress shook her head. This blonde was a strange one. She had been in here several times over the past two days to sit in that same seat for hours, watching the building across the way. The waitress on the graveyard shift had reported the same thing. She was a weird one, all right, and they had considered having the police haul her away. But she hadn't really caused any problems, and she tipped with twenty-dollar bills even though she only purchased coffee. "You sure you don't want anything else?" The waitress eyed the twenty-dollar bills spread out on the table.

"Yes." Her voice was almost inaudible.

"Okay. Well, listen, miss. We're closing down in a couple of hours and getting out of here. I suggest you get out of town too. Because personally I think those people are serious."

Leeny nodded at her but said nothing. She turned again toward the front door of the apartment building. She had to kill him. Otherwise he would tell. She felt helpless just sitting here, but it was the only thing she could think of to do, the only way she might possibly find him.

The assassin sat at the back of Joey's Place, watching Leeny from behind the side of a newspaper. Webster had finally given him the order to kill her. He smiled to himself. She was a goner at this point. The pressure had clearly overwhelmed her. Some people couldn't handle a situation as stressful as this one, and Kathleen Hunt was one of those people.

The assassin sipped from the glass of Pepsi. Webster wouldn't be happy if he knew what was going on. Webster had wanted the woman dead immediately. He had wanted the assassin to go down to her office this morning and take care of her right there, which seemed out of character for so rational a man. Then again, Webster was obviously rattled. Something the assassin had never witnessed. But the assassin had convinced Webster that killing Kathleen Hunt in her office was not a good idea, that he needed to wait and kill her in a quieter manner.

On the corner, just down the street from the entrance to Joey's Place, a lone figure waited, eyes glued to the diner's door. The person had been fortunate to find Leeny Hunt this morning, fortunate that Leeny had gone to work at Walker Pryce for a few hours as if everything were normal. She pulled the heavy winter coat up around her face.

Suddenly Leeny bolted from her seat and headed for the door. Nearly knocking over what remained of his soda, the assassin rose quickly from his seat, grabbing his wallet and keys from the table. What the hell was her problem? Had she somehow realized that he was following her and was she making a break for it? He raced toward the diner's door.

The waitress watched both of them run from the eatery. First the blonde and then the man obviously stalking her. She shook her head. It was a crazy city, full of strange situations. It was best not to get involved.

Slowly the waitress moved toward the table at which the blonde had been seated for the last two hours. She was curious about what had fluttered from the blonde's lap as she bolted for the door. Still holding a pot of hot coffee, the woman bent down to pick up the object and suddenly saw John Schuler's bloody face.

The waitress dropped the glass coffeepot at the horrible sight of Schuler's corpse. The glass shattered into thousands of tiny pieces when it smashed against the tiled floor, and hot coffee splashed onto her ankles. For several seconds she did not notice the pain, and then she began to scream.

Mace moved quickly out of the front door of the apartment building toward the subway. He hadn't bothered to leave by the back door, where he had surreptitiously entered the building to avoid being seen by anyone who was watching. Whoever had rifled through his belongings had long since left—the food in the open refrigerator had spoiled—and wouldn't expect him to return.

Mace began to run. He needed to get going. A fat man stepped suddenly to the left and into Mace's path at the last second. Mace crashed into the obese man and knocked him to the pavement. "Sorry." He stopped for a moment and held out a hand to help the man back to his feet. He glanced around as he pulled the man up. There were still a surprising number of people in the city. But then the deadline at Nyack wasn't supposed to expire until tomorrow at noon. Mace looked around again. This street would look very different then.

He ran toward the subway station. He had to find Leeny, and he would try first at Walker Pryce. She could tell him what he needed to know. She wouldn't do it willingly, but he would face that problem when he got to it.

The subway rumbled into the station, hurtling past the crowded platform filled with people carrying suitcases and bags, until finally it screeched to a halt. The doors slid wide open, and people waiting on the platform poured inside.

Mace moved toward the doors, following the crowd in front of him, but stopped as people started to scream. They began to part in front of him, pushing one another down in their frantic attempt to get out of the way.

At first he did not understand. Then he saw her. She moved down the platform toward him slowly, as if in a trance, eyes focused in a death stare, the gun, the same gun she had used to kill John Schuler, drawn before her, clasped tightly in her outstretched hands.

The conductor, leaning out of the fifth car in the nine-car train, suddenly saw the cause of the commotion. He closed the train's doors quickly and screamed into the intercom for the engineer to get out of the station. The train leaped forward instantly.

Leeny seemed a different person now from the woman he had met in the limousine on the way to Columbia Business School. The lines around her mouth had become distinctly visible. Her hair was a dull yellow, not the shiny gold he remembered. The eyes were dull too, almost unseeing. Her skin was a ghastly white.

She was twenty feet away, still moving toward him, walking only inches from the side of the train hurtling out of the station next to her, taking no notice of it at all, staring only at him, fixated on him. Suddenly she stopped, raised the gun in front of her face, and placed her right forefinger on the trigger. Then she squeezed.

Instinctively Mace brought his hands to his face. He had not thought her capable of violence. But now he remembered Rachel telling him that Leeny had spent time in a sanitarium. He had mis-judged Leeny Hunt.

Rachel sprinted the last ten feet. She did not hear the people screaming or the train rushing out of the station. She did not see the people tumbling over one another to get out of harm's way or the blur of the train behind Leeny's body. She saw nothing but Leeny's thin form pointing the gun at Mace.

Rachel crashed into Leeny at the last moment, just as Leeny pulled the trigger, just as the bullet exploded toward Mace. The violent, unanticipated impact knocked Leeny over and against the side of the speeding train's last car. Leeny slammed into the rush-ing metal and then pitched forward with the momentum of the train, toward Mace. She screamed as she fell forward, unable to control her fall. Her head slammed into a steel support column at the edge of the platform, and she dropped to the ground uncon-scious. The handgun flew from her grip and crashed to the cement, firing another shot at impact.

Mace gazed for a moment at Leeny, prone on the dirty cement, at Rachel, and then down at himself, checking for wounds. But he was unhurt.

Then he saw a man running toward him, dodging the people still cowering in kneeling positions on the platform. The man was coming for him. There was no doubt at all. He could see the gun and the way the man's eyes were fixed on him, just as Leeny's had been.

The assassin held the gun at his side as he churned toward Mace. He didn't care if people saw the firearm, but it would be bet-ter not to make it obvious just in case there was a hero in the crowd somewhere.

The man was coming fast down the platform, only a hundred feet away now. Mace glanced quickly at Rachel. Her eyes were filled with terror. She had also seen the man and realized that he was coming for Mace.

An extraordinary piece of luck, the assassin thought as he

dodged the people on the ground. Leeny Hunt's hunch had been right. Mace McLain had returned to his apartment for some reason; he recognized the young investment banker from the pictures the man in Washington had given him. Now he was going to finish the job Leeny Hunt had tried to complete. He had missed Mace at the apartment on Friday night, but he wouldn't miss now. Then he would make certain Leeny was dead as well and take off through the subway tunnel to the next station. It was incredible. Two for the price of one.

The assassin brought the gun up as he neared Mace. The man in Washington was going to be grateful.

Mace lunged for Leeny's gun, which lay on the platform five feet away, picked it up, and fired. The motion was graceful, not panicked but smooth and athletic. Mace remained ice calm as he went for the gun, realizing that he had to make the first shot count. He had hunted upland birds as a boy and learned that the trick to shooting was to take your time, even under pressure, and make certain you aimed carefully. If you rushed, you would miss. And he could not miss.

The assassin grabbed his left thigh instantly and fell heavily to the pavement.

Mace jumped to his feet quickly, raced to where Rachel lay, and pulled her to her feet. "Come on!" He moved to the edge of the platform and jumped down onto the tracks, then turned and pulled her down too. Through the darkness he could see the headlight of the next train heading toward the station. He grabbed Rachel's wrist and pulled her toward the darkness at the other end of the station. He had to get her out of here.

Mace kissed Rachel deeply as they stood together on the platform of track twelve at New York's Penn Station. Finally he pulled away. "You saved my life."

She smiled, and the dimple appeared in her cheek. "So I did. Guess that makes you my slave."

Mace nodded and smiled back. "Guess it does. But you won't hear me complaining."

"*Board!*" The conductor screamed the announcement up and down the platform.

Mace guided Rachel toward the door of the car. "Do you remember what I told you?"

Rachel rolled her eyes. "Yes. The Mountaintop Inn. Harpers Ferry. I take the train to Baltimore, rent a car there, drive to Harpers Ferry, and wait for you to call."

"Right. If anyone else calls you, get out. I don't care how friendly they sound. If you see anything remotely suspicious, get out. Do you understand?"

She nodded, hesitantly, suddenly scared again. But she saw the genuine concern in his face, and she liked it.

"Do you have money?"

"About two hundred dollars, I think." She had withdrawn every cent in her account before searching out Leeny.

"Do you have credit cards?"

She nodded. "One."

"Good, use it to rent the car in Baltimore. But *don't* use it at the Mountaintop Inn. Use your cash." He paused. "Do you understand?"

"Yes."

The door of the train car began to close. Mace held it, leaned into the car, and kissed Rachel one more time. He winked at her. "Everything will be all right. Promise."

"I hope so."

"*Come on, buddy!*" The conductor yelled down the platform at Mace. He wanted Mace to let the door go. He wanted to get out of there.

Mace glanced at the man, then back at Rachel. "Why were you there at the station? How could you have been there? How could you have known?"

"I picked up Leeny's trail at Walker Pryce this morning. I figured if I did, sooner or later I'd find you."

Mace shook his head. She was incredible. He kissed her one more time and then allowed the door to close. She waved at him through the window.

The train crept slowly out of Penn Station over the spider web of tracks. Rachel was safe. Mace glanced at his watch and began to move toward the stairs leading back up to the main terminal of the station. One o'clock. Ten hours until his meeting with Slade.

Vargus leaned back in the chair and rubbed his swollen eye gently. It had become infected, and the pain was almost unbearable. A gentle knock at the door distracted him momentarily. "Who is it?"

"Tabiq."

"Come."

The door swung open, and Tabiq moved into the office.

"What do you want?" Vargus squinted at the other man with his good eye.

"The men want to know if you've heard anything yet from the authorities." Tabiq nodded at the telephone on the desk.

"About what?" Vargus had destroyed the television sets at the facility. There should have been no way for them to know about his communication with the outside world.

"There isn't any reason to bluff." Tabiq was becoming annoyed at the lack of information from the leader. "You have made demands. Why else would you have released the two hostages?"

Vargus rubbed his eye again. "Tell the men to relax. The authorities are giving in to the demands. But it is taking them some time to meet what we have asked for. A billion dollars is a lot of money." Vargus smiled to reassure his second.

Tabiq was not reassured, but at least Vargus had admitted to making demands. At least he knew now that negotiations were in process. "I will tell the men. It will help." And he was gone.

Vargus shook his head and let out a long breath. Just a few more hours, and they would all be dead—except for him. As long as there were no screwups. As long as the Wolverine commander obeyed orders and didn't try to be a hero on his own. That was the only way it could unravel.

33

"Mr. Webster, this is Roger Hamilton of Maryland Mutual Life."

"Yes." A thin smile crossed the old man's face as he listened to the voice at the other end of the line.

"Up until now I've been dealing with a woman named Kathleen Hunt regarding some bonds my firm owns."

"Yes." He hoped the assassin had completed his task by now.

"But the secretary said you were handling all calls now."

"That's right," Webster said coldly. He wanted this man to sweat right up until he made the offer.

"What I have to discuss is rather urgent."

"What is it?" Webster snapped. He wanted to tighten the screws on this man quickly.

"Ms. Hunt and I had been talking about the purchase of a billion dollars of bonds my firm owns." Hamilton's voice was suddenly hoarse.

"And?" Webster was being curt to make certain that there would be no seller's remorse at the last minute.

The blood pulsed through Hamilton's veins. "I'll sell them to Broadway Ventures for seventy cents on the dollar." His voice was nothing more than a weak whisper.

Webster said nothing. Nothing at all. It was a negotiating ploy, one he had learned long ago. Most people detested silence on the phone and would keep talking just to avoid it.

"Mr. Webster?" Hamilton searched for a handle.

"Yes?"

"Did you hear me?"

"Yes." Again Webster paused and allowed the uncomfortable silence to continue.

Hamilton knew what was going on. He knew what Webster was doing. He was no babe in the woods himself. But he had no choice. He had to negotiate against himself. The CEO wanted *something* for the bonds. "Sixty cents on the dollar."

"No." Webster answered immediately.

"Please, for God's sake."

"No." The voice was stone cold.

Hamilton swallowed, then inhaled heavily. His hands shook. "Fifty."

Webster smiled. "Done. Send a fax to me immediately confirming the transaction. The money will be wired to Maryland Mutual this afternoon." The evil smile crossed Webster's face. He had just made half a billion dollars.

Mace slipped into Leeny Hunt's hospital room, unseen by the staff. Once inside the room, he moved quickly to her bed. He had to get her out of there—fast.

She turned her head slowly. As she recognized him, tears filled her eyes.

Mace glanced at the bandage wrapped around her head. "Come on, we're getting out of here."

She did not resist. She did not say a word. She simply rose from the bed with his help and slipped on her shoes, which the nurse had left by the door.

He took her by the wrist and guided her to the door, where he paused long enough to see if there were doctors or nurses in the hall. There were, but they were distracted by a constant influx of new patients. Mace moved quickly into the hallway, Leeny in tow, and hurried through the stairway door opposite what had been her room.

As they vanished through the door, a doctor moved out of the elevator toward room 425. He moved casually down the corridor, clipboard in hand, face down so that others would take no notice of him. When he reached the doorway, he felt for the gun beneath the white coat. The silencer was already attached. Despite the silencer, the shot would still make noise, but he was confident that the staff was so distracted that he would be able to make it out of the hospital with no problems after he had killed her. He smiled to himself. The first assassin had botched the job terribly and now lay in a hospital bed across town. Now *he* was their man. They should have sent him first anyway.

The wolf dressed in sheep's clothing glanced up and down the hallway one last time and entered the room. He stopped short almost immediately. Leeny Hunt was gone.

A half hour later Mace and Leeny entered the room of the New York Hilton. This would be the last night the hotel would be open. Management was shutting it down tomorrow at seven o'clock in the morning, the lone man at the front desk had warned Mace. No exceptions. You would be escorted out by armed guards at that time if you hadn't left by then. The man had been so insistent on this point he hadn't even noticed the bandage around Leeny's head. Mace had tried to hide it with a baseball cap, but it was still visible.

"Sit down," Mace said gently.

Leeny sat down slowly on the edge of the large bed. Her eyes were vacant, and she held her arms tightly across her chest.

Mace knelt in front of her and took her hands in his. He stared into her eyes. "You are going to tell me everything, do you understand?"

There was no reason to resist. She nodded obediently.

Mace stood and removed a small Dictaphone from his pocket,

then shoved a tiny audiotape into the machine. He sat down next to her. "First you are going to put it on tape; then you are going to write it down. Do you understand me?"

She nodded again, and suddenly the tears flowed from her eyes. Sobs racked her body, and she buried her face in her hands. "I'm so sorry, Mace. So sorry." They were the first words she had said since leaving the hospital.

Her shoulders shook uncontrollably as he watched her disintegrate. She was hardly a human being anymore. There was that little left. He shook his head. She had tried to kill him several hours ago, to kill him, for Christ's sake. But he couldn't let her sob this way without any solace. It wasn't in him to be that cold. He reached out a large hand and gently touched her shoulder.

It was all she needed. Leeny threw her arms around his shoulders, pressed her head against his chest, and held on for dear life.

Rachel moved down the lighted front steps of the Mountaintop Inn and through the darkness of the February night toward the car she had rented late this afternoon in Baltimore. The drive out Interstate 70 had taken less time than she had anticipated.

She shivered as she trotted over the gravel parking lot toward the car. It was cold out here, and she wanted to get back inside the hotel quickly. She had arrived at the Mountaintop Inn more than two hours ago and taken a long, refreshing hot bath right after checking in. But she had forgotten to bring the clothes she had purchased in Baltimore inside with her when she first arrived. Now she needed them.

When she neared the rental car, she removed the keys from her pants pocket and moved alongside the car to the trunk. The key slid easily into the lock, and the trunk popped open. She reached for the large paper bag that held her clothes.

As she straightened up and began to close the trunk after retrieving the bag, a gloved hand wrapped itself firmly over her nose and mouth from behind. Strange fumes filled her nose and lungs, and within seconds she was unconscious, dead weight in the man's arms.

The first man glanced at the second through the darkness. "That was easy enough," he whispered. "Put her in the truck. I'll go for McLain."

Ferris closed the door of Malcolm Becker's office, then turned toward the director of the CIA, who sat smoking one of his beloved Monte Cristo cigars.

"Well?" Becker asked.

The Rat Man could control himself no longer. He broke into a wide smile, exposing his long, curved front teeth. "They got Rachel Sommers outside a bed-and-breakfast in Harpers Ferry, West Virginia." His voice was triumphant.

Becker puffed on the cigar for a moment. "And McLain?"

The Rat Man's smile faded. "He wasn't with her."

Becker slammed his fist onto the desk. "Damn it!" He roared. He gazed out his window at the Virginia night. It was as black as his mood.

"It's going to be all right, Chief." The Rat Man made his voice soothing. "We have the girl. We can use her to lure McLain out. Conner will find McLain, and then we will smoke him out of whatever hole he's crawled into. It will work out."

Becker steadied himself against the desk. "Yes, we do have the girl. And McLain won't disclose what he knows until he's sure she's safe."

"Exactly." Ferris smiled. Becker needed him in moments like this. The general was an excellent planner, but sometimes he did not think lucidly under pressure. That was why they made such a formidable team. The Rat Man became the Ice Man under pressure. "We will smoke McLain out and kill him. Then we will be fine."

"Yes." Becker glanced up at Ferris. "I count on you, Willard. You know that, don't you?"

Ferris nodded. His eyes narrowed. "Have you talked to Webster?"

"Yes."

"And?"

Becker smiled. "It's unbelievable. Broadway Ventures has invested almost two billion dollars since Vargus had his men blow up the GW Bridge." The general shook his head. "Webster estimates that the market value of the securities the fund has purchased in the last three days is close to three and a half billion dollars. When the Wolverines retake Nyack and no bombs go off, the value of the portfolio will skyrocket back to its original value, back to three and a half billion. Webster will send the CIA's nine hundred million dollars back to us immediately through the dummy corporations. Then he will sell the securities Broadway Ventures has purchased. He'll sell them slowly and send us the proceeds over time, so as not to arouse any suspicion. Of course we still have to pay Chase back its one billion, with interest, as well as make the third-party investors whole, but it looks as if the CIA and Walker Pryce will net over a billion dollars. That will more than cover the overspending on the Wolverines and what I need for the campaign."

Ferris nodded. Becker was godlike in his ability to put together something like this, to assign each person his or her task, but not convey the scope of the entire operation to any of the individuals so that he was the only one who knew everything. The Rat Man's job had been to make certain the West Virginia operation went smoothly.

"It will be incredible when the Wolverines raid Nyack, Chief. The country will hold its breath, and the force, your force, will be victorious. Think about the press coverage after it's over. Think about all those people screaming at you, wanting a piece of you, wanting to *vote* for you. You'll say we had the raid planned the entire time. That we were just waiting until most of the people had gotten out of New York before we executed it." Ferris was ecstatic.

Becker sat on the edge of the desk. "Yes," he whispered

dramatically. He turned toward the Rat Man. "Willard, you are certain that Vargus was able to get the bombs into the plant."

Ferris nodded. "Oh, yes. When the Wolverines retake the reactor, they will find five bombs at each reactor. But they can't go off. Vargus neutralized the detonators. He's the only one who is supposed to have the authority within the group to set the things off, but if one of the other jokers tries to be heroic, they won't work. It's beautiful."

Becker laughed out loud. "I can't wait to see Andrews' face when he sees that the Wolverines have retaken the plant. He'll know the campaign is over."

"Right." Ferris was still excited. "It's amazing how well this thing has worked out."

Suddenly the two men glanced down at the floor. There were just two problems: Leeny Hunt and Mace McLain. Both of them had to be killed, and quickly, or the entire conspiracy could be compromised. And they knew it.

Becker inhaled heavily. "If it weren't for that goddamned Mace McLain, everything would be fine. That Hunt woman would be dead, and we'd have no worries."

"It will be all right, Chief. Remember we have Rachel Sommers. He won't screw with us while we have her."

Becker glanced at the Rat Man. "You'd better be right." He puffed on the cigar again. "How in the hell did the agents track Rachel Sommers down? I mean, they got her in Harpers Ferry, for crying out loud. That place isn't as remote as Sugar Grove, but it isn't Forty-second Street either. Did she use her credit card to pay for the room? Was she that stupid? I thought this woman was supposed to be so smart."

Ferris shook his head. "No, she used cash to pay for her room." The Rat Man hesitated. "The car the woman rented in Baltimore was equipped with a battery-powered cellular phone. You can track a cellular phone to precise locations at any time. And Bell Atlantic is very accommodating for the CIA."

34

Mcyntire leaned against a post supporting the farmhouse's front-porch roof and lighted a cigarette. The night sky was overcast—there were no stars—and he interpreted this as a gift from God.

The commander watched as a pair of headlights bounced up the long gravel driveway. The Jeep screeched to a halt before the small house. Captain Ellet jumped from the passenger-side seat and moved quickly to where Mcyntire stood.

"You sent for me, sir?" Ellet saluted.

"Yes." Mcyntire's voice was subdued. He looked at the driver of the Jeep who had gotten out and was standing next to the vehicle. But he couldn't hear; he was much too far away. "We attack in seven hours, at three o'clock this morning."

"A decision from Washington." Ellet had uttered the words as a statement, but Mcyntire heard the question. Ellet wanted to make certain that this order had come from the top, that the commander hadn't made a unilateral decision.

"Prepare the men, Captain Ellet," the commander said evenly.

The captain glanced down at his boots. "Yes, sir." He regretted the question now. It had bordered on insubordination. It was just that the potential consequences of a preemptive attack were so grave.

*   *   *

"There is movement in the Wolverine lines!" Tabiq burst into the office without knocking.

Vargus groaned as he came to. His body ached all over, a reaction to the infection bloating the area around his eye to the size of an apple. "What?"

"Yes. We can see them through the night scopes. They appear to be moving back."

Vargus checked his watch. Almost nine o'clock. It was too early. And why would they be moving back?

"The Mountaintop Inn, how may I help you?" The woman's soft voice drifted through the line.

"Betty Saif, please." It was the alias Mace had told Rachel to use.

"Just a moment and I'll connect you."

"Thanks," he mumbled. He had been shocked by what Leeny had conveyed to him at the end of her taped admission. The story was outrageous, but the last thing she had said was incomprehensible. He glanced at his watch. Eleven-ten. Slade should be waiting.

Several moments passed, and then the phone began to ring. After the tenth ring the inn's operator cut back into the call. "She's not answering. Could I leave her a message?"

"Can you tell me if she's checked in yet?" Mace asked.

"Just a minute," the woman said, in the same voice she was to use many times tonight. "Yes. She checked in around three hours ago."

Mace hesitated. That was strange. He had told her to stay in her room unless she saw something suspicious.

"Is there anything else I can do for you, sir?" the operator asked.

An uneasy feeling hit the pit of his stomach. "No, I'll call back later." He hung up, hesitated for a moment, then headed toward Rockefeller Center.

Malcolm Becker had assigned Slade the task of making contact with Mace months ago presumably as part of the conspiracy: to watch him; to make certain Mace didn't do anything suspicious; to offer help innocently if Mace ever needed anything. That was what Leeny had conveyed at the end of her taped monologue. It had so unnerved Mace he had been forced to stop the recorder. The contact with Slade had been anything but coincidental over the past few months, Mace now realized. Slade had been gathering intelligence, keeping an eye on Mace for Becker. Mace felt the anger rising again.

The Rockefeller Center complex was brightly lit but was empty of people. As a result, Slade was not hard to find. He was leaning back against a cement restraining wall next to the line of flagpoles on the south side of the famous rink, smoking a cigarette, something Mace had not seen him do since they had been at the orphanage together.

Mace watched his old friend for a moment. How could it have come to this? They had grown up together, been there for each other when times were difficult. Now he had come to find that Slade was part of a terrible conspiracy.

Cautiously Mace made his way to where Slade stood, moving in the shadows so that Slade wouldn't spot him. Mace was checking for others who might be waiting, others whom Slade might have brought with him to assist with Mace's capture—or worse.

"Hello, Slade," Mace said quietly.

"Hello, Brother." Slade dropped the cigarette he had been smoking to the pavement and stepped on it. "You didn't have to be so sneaky in your approach. There isn't anyone else here with me."

So Slade had been aware of his presence the entire time. "Smoking, huh?"

Slade nodded. "Yeah. I need it."

His voice seemed melancholy, but Mace did not ask why. And he did not wait to make known the revelations Leeny Hunt had conveyed to him in the hotel room. "I know everything, Slade. I know that Becker is responsible for the terrorist attack on Nyack. I know that he coerced Lewis Webster and Leeny Hunt into setting up Broadway Ventures for him. I know that he held the prospect of prison over their heads so they would acquiesce. I know that he's using the money he's making off Broadway Ventures to cover overspending and fraud at the CIA. I know it all. I have Leeny in a room at the Hilt—" Mace caught himself in mid-word.

Their eyes met instantly.

"At the Hilltop Hotel in Brooklyn," Mace finished. He hoped Slade could not see that he was so obviously making up the name of the hotel.

"I see," Slade said.

An uncomfortable silence followed.

Mace finally broke it. "How long have you known, Slade? How long have you been setting me up?"

"I've never set you up, Mace. I would never do that to you," he said quietly. "You know that. We go back too far." A gust of wind whipped up suddenly. Slade exhaled a cloud of smoke into it. "I've known about what's going on for a week. That's all."

"That's crap!" Mace was suddenly angry. "Leeny told me that Becker had you checking on me right from the start."

"That's right." Slade's voice was still quiet. "But I didn't know why he wanted me to check on you. Remember, he is my boss, and he is the director of the CIA." Slade hesitated, and his voice dropped lower. "Once he did tell me what was going on, because I pressed him after going to West Virginia from our meeting in Charlottesville, I agreed to help him, to be a part of the conspiracy, because that was the best way to help you. And because if he had seen the slightest trace in my face that I was going to try to blow the whistle, he would have had me killed. They would have just sent someone else after you. My God, they already have."

Mace could not believe him. "How do I know you are telling me the truth?" It could so easily be a lie. He could not trust anyone now, not even Slade, particularly after what Leeny had said.

"You don't." Slade turned so that he was facing Mace. Now *he* was becoming angry. "Look, I can't make you believe something you don't want to believe at this point. We've been friends since we were four years old. I shouldn't have to make you believe me. I'm telling you the truth. That's all you need to hear." Slade paused. "I had you at the Four Seasons. If I had wanted to, I could have given you to Becker then."

Mace disregarded Slade's last comment and stared directly into his eyes, looking for something, looking for a shred of truth or a shred of deceit. But the eyes were devoid of information.

Slade glanced around furtively. "I have information for you that will help you nail Malcolm Becker, the son of a bitch."

Mace heard the hatred in Slade's voice, but it could easily have been an act. "What?"

Slade produced a package from his coat pocket. "Take it." He handed the package to Mace.

"What's in here?"

"The names and numbers of the dummy accounts Becker used to send money to Broadway Ventures, advices signed by Willard Ferris okaying the transfer of money out of CIA accounts. It's the link you need."

Mace stuffed the information into his coat, still wary of being surprised by Slade's associates.

"Leeny Hunt was on the payroll too." Slade continued. "I investigated her for Becker some time ago. He knew that she had an insider trading problem and would be only too willing to agree to do what she did in exchange for not being prosecuted. Becker fixed that little prosecution problem, and she was his. Although I didn't know why he wanted her at the time."

"I know about her insider trading problem," Mace said firmly.

"Oh, that's right, you have her at the—" Slade paused—"at the Hilltop Hotel in Brooklyn."

"Yes," Mace said, relieved. Slade had heard the false address.

Slade took a last puff from the cigarette, then flicked the filter away. "Mace, there's something you need to know." His voice was deadly serious.

"What?"

"Becker has Rachel Sommers. He got her in Harpers Ferry."

For several moments Mace's expression did not change; then his head dropped. There was no reason to doubt what Slade had said. "Oh, my God," he said quietly.

" 'Oh, my God' is right, Brother." Slade pointed at the package he had just given Mace. "You can't give that information to the authorities if you ever expect to see her alive. I just talked to Willard Ferris, his assistant, a couple of minutes ago."

"So why the hell did you give it to me?" Mace's voice rose angrily.

"As a bargaining chip," Slade said calmly.

"What do you mean?"

"He knows you were in Sugar Grove." Slade lighted another cigarette.

"You told him that too? I can't believe it." Mace's voice rose.

Slade's eyes became nothing but slits. "They figured it was you who had broken into the old mining facility when you didn't show up for work. So they showed people in Sugar Grove your photograph, and a couple of them recognized it. IRS agent, huh?" Slade shook his head. "I know you've been through a tremendous amount. That's why I can't blame you for suspecting me."

Mace looked away. It was so hard to trust Slade at this point. He had answers for everything, and his answers seemed plausible. But Mace's gut was saying that Slade had been working with Becker the entire time. And if he had just gone with his gut in the first place, when Webster first approached him about Broadway Ventures, he wouldn't be in this situation now.

"Becker knows you figured out something, somehow. How else could you have found the site in West Virginia?" Slade hesitated for a moment. "I want that man. I want him to go down. But you have to take him down. I can't." He nodded at the package under

Mace's arm. "I'm going to tell him that I've talked to you over the telephone and that you have that information, that you quoted the names and account numbers of the dummy corporations to me over the phone. I'll convince him to make an even exchange. Rachel Sommers for that information. Without that package you can't prove anything. If he knows you have it, though, he'll know you could take him down, and then he'll deal." Slade puffed on the cigarette.

Mace smelled the cigarette smoke as Slade exhaled. It was all too neat. A baited trap waiting to be sprung. He was still suspicious of Slade. He couldn't help himself. But it didn't matter. If he didn't agree to what Slade was saying, Rachel was dead. He had no doubt of that.

Slade flicked away the second cigarette. He would have to call Becker as soon as he and Mace left each other to tell the general that Leeny Hunt was at the Hilton Hotel.

35

The assault helicopters bore down from the night sky on the Nyack Nuclear Generating Facility, diving swiftly, at forty-five-degree angles. At three hundred feet above sea level they delivered their lethal payloads onto the terrorist lines dug in on the perimeter of the plant's grounds. Missiles exploded in the midst of the militants, incinerating bodies instantly.

Wolverine ground troops began to pour into the compound, meeting little or no resistance. Actually entering and taking control of the buildings was not so easy, but within a half hour of the initial attack everything but the core room had been retaken. Twenty-seven Wolverines were dead, but so were almost a hundred terrorists, some of the most highly skilled men the terrorist world had called members.

Vargus gazed about the huge room that housed the nuclear re-actor. He was the only one left now. He sensed it. He sensed that they were close. He sensed his liberation approaching rapidly. Then the knock came, just as he knew it would. Two quick raps and then three short ones. Exactly as he and Becker had planned. His shoulders slumped. The Nyack nuclear plant was in control of the Wolverines, meaning that the mission was a success. Broadway Ventures had made billions, and he was just a few short days away from twenty-five million dollars for himself.

He moved slowly down the metal steps toward the door. Each

step was painful. The eye would never see again, but loss of sight in one eye was a small price to pay for so much money, he reasoned, as he reached to unlock the heavy door. It creaked as it swung open slowly.

The lone Wolverine, smartly dressed in his dark blue uniform, moved quickly through the opening. He hesitated for a split second, then raised his automatic weapon and fired. The burst of gunfire nearly ripped the man in two. He wobbled crazily for a moment, then fell to the floor dead, bleeding profusely onto the cement.

Captain Ellet stared down at Vargus for a second to make certain that he was dead, but there was no doubt. He smiled. The Nyack nuclear plant was back in friendly hands. And all the terrorists were dead, per his direct orders from Malcolm Becker, orders to which even Commander Mcyntire was not privy.

Preston Andrews and Robin Carruthers watched the television as Malcolm Becker climbed the podium for the press conference. Becker was to read a prepared statement that the Nyack plant had been retaken and that it was safe for the citizens of New York to return to the city. Once again the CIA Wolverines had proved themselves invaluable against terrorist guerrilla warfare.

Andrews rose from his chair, picked up the remote from the hotel room coffee table, and turned off the set. After replacing the remote on the coffee table, he moved slowly to the window overlooking the Los Angeles downtown area. He was in the city for a campaign fund-raiser, but now it didn't look as if there were any real reason to be here. Becker was going to win the election hands down. He was going to be all over every newspaper, magazine, and television screen in the country for the next six months. He was a hero again. This time he was larger than life. This time he had saved New York City from devastation.

"He's untouchable now," Andrews said quietly. "He's going to win this election in a landslide." His voice was almost inaudible.

Robin did not answer. She knew Preston was right.

Andrews laughed sarcastically. "He's the luckiest bastard alive." He snorted. "To have this happen now, to have it turn out the way it has. I suppose my contacts in the Middle East aren't as good as I thought they were." He said the last words offhandedly, almost to himself.

Robin glanced up. "What do you mean?"

The vice president turned away from the window. "The man in my room that night at the Doha Marriott, the one you've asked me about."

"Yes?" She stood, sensing she was about to hear something of great importance.

"He was an informer for the DEA. He told me that night at the Doha Marriott that this was in the works. Not the Nyack attack specifically, but an attack on an installation in the United States of these proportions. He must have meant this. But he could never uncover more than rumors and innuendo." Andrews hesitated, as if wondering whether there was anything he could have done. "If only I could have found out, I could have preempted the attack, preempted Becker's opportunity." He shook his head. "I had every intelligence unit in the government working for me to find out what was going on. Except the CIA, of course." Andrews laughed sarcastically again. "Those guys wouldn't help me. They are loyal to Becker."

Robin ran a hand through her hair. The dream was dead. It was over, she knew. As Preston had said, Becker was untouchable now. Becker was going to move into the White House, and Preston Andrews was finished in politics. So was she.

The two agents moved quickly down the hallway of the New York Hilton. They were to locate, detain, and bring her back to Washington, D.C., per Willard Ferris. They were not told why Ferris needed her or what he planned to do with her once they brought her back. But that was not unusual. They were agency veterans and had come to learn to expect the unusual at the CIA.

They had been told only that Leeny Hunt was here, no more than that. But it had not taken them long to find her room number. After flashing their badges at the night manager of the Hilton, he had quickly relented on his vow of confidentiality for all guests and let the agents see the hotel's computer register. One agent had remained behind to make certain that the manager didn't call the room to let the guest know that they were coming.

The men moved quickly down the hallway to room 1741, inserted the extra key they had forced the night manager to give them into the slot, and burst through the door. She was not in the bed. Instinctively the first agent into the room moved quickly to the bathroom door and thrust it open. But it too was unoccupied.

The second agent moved into the bathroom behind the first, glanced around, then shook his head. "I guess we got the wrong room," he said dejectedly.

"I don't think so," the other man said quietly.

"What do you mean?"

The first agent thrust at the second agent the pocketbook he had picked up off the double sink in front of the mirror. The men gazed down at the purse. It was stuffed full of pictures of what was obviously a dead man, shot point-blank several times through the face. There was nothing else in the purse but the Polaroids.

Wind whipped Leeny's hair across her face as she stared down from the roof of the Hilton onto Avenue of the Americas far below. Forty stories down. How would it feel as her body hurtled toward the concrete? How would it feel in that instant her flesh made contact with the pavement? What would she learn in that last second of consciousness before death? She had always wanted to know.

36

The sun shone down brightly on the Nations bank building, a seven-story edifice constructed near the southeast corner of the intersection of the Baltimore–Washington Parkway and Interstate 495, the Washington Beltway. Mace stood on the building's roof, at the northwest corner, as Slade had instructed him, watching the door that led down to the seventh floor below. Twenty minutes ago Mace had climbed up those stairs, half expecting to be shot as soon as he opened the door leading outside. But there had been no one on the roof.

The bag lay at Mace's feet. It contained the information Slade had given him, the bargaining chip, as well as the tape he had made of Leeny recounting all she knew about Broadway Ventures, Lewis Webster, and Malcolm Becker. Becker would need to see these things before he would release Rachel Sommers. That was what Slade had told Mace over the phone last night.

Cars on the Beltway roared continually past the building, but Mace did not hear them. He did not hear anything, so focused was his attention on the roof's doorway. It could open at any moment. Then he would be faced with the most difficult situation of his life. The other side wanted him dead, and he was trusting his old friend with his life. But this trust could be completely misguided. Slade could be selling him down the river.

Mace swallowed. Preparation: another key to success. Being

fully prepared for a meeting, having anticipated every question, every outcome, everything that could go wrong: that was standard operating procedure for him. But there was no way to be prepared now. It was all going to unfold at the speed of light, and he would just have to react on instinct. Otherwise, as Slade said, he was a dead man.

The door swung open, and Slade's hulking frame appeared. Malcolm Becker followed at a distance of ten feet. Then a thin man and Rachel followed close behind Becker. Mace felt a wave of relief as he saw her. He remembered the vulnerability he had seen in her eyes that day at the restaurant. How he had wanted to take care of her. Now that desire was going to be put to the ultimate test.

As the four of them approached, Mace noticed that the thin man was holding a gun to Rachel's ribs. Mace's eyes moved to hers. She was scared, but despite the gun, she managed a smile.

Slade moved forward, to a position directly in front of Mace while the others stayed back. His face was grim. Then his eyes moved slowly down to the bag at Mace's feet.

Mace's eyes followed.

"Turn around!" Slade screamed.

Mace's eyes flashed up to Slade's. "What?"

"Turn around!"

Slowly Mace did so. This wasn't part of the act. This hadn't been choreographed on the phone last night.

"Hands on the wall."

Mace put his hands down on the waist-high cement restraining wall. He gazed down at the ground seven stories below. Slade could throw him over so easily, and then Rachel would be killed. They would bury the bodies, and no one would ever know. He felt Slade's hands combing his body for a weapon.

"Turn back around."

Slowly Mace rotated back to face the others.

Slade nodded over his shoulder at Becker. "He's clean." He turned back to Mace. "Do you have it?"

Mace nodded slowly.

Slade bent down, keeping his eyes on Mace.

This was it, Mace thought. Slade could end it all now. Trying to push Mace over the restraining wall might have been risky. They had never tested each other physically. They did not know what the other was capable of. At the very least Mace might have been able to pull Slade with him. But Mace had no defense against Slade now.

Slade unzipped the bag slowly, fumbled through it for a second, and then removed the contents. He rose slowly, his back to Becker, so Becker and the others could not see his hands or what he held.

Mace eyed Leeny's gun, which Slade now leveled at his abdomen. This was it, the moment of truth. Slowly Mace brought his eyes back up to Slade's. There was no emotion on his friend's face, none at all.

"Slade!" the waiting general screamed at his soldier.

Instantly Slade wheeled around, aimed at Ferris, and fired. The Rat Man fell to the ground. Like a big cat, Slade darted behind Becker, and wrapped him in a choke hold with one powerful arm, leveling the handgun at Becker's head. Becker struggled for a moment, but he was no match for the younger man.

"Major Conner, release me! Right now!" The general's eyes were wide open with fear. The expression on his face gave away the terror he felt at the shiny barrel pushed against his temple. "This is treason!"

Conner paid no attention to Becker but locked him still more tightly in the hold, choking him, venting the hatred that had been building inside him. The man was a criminal, the perpetrator of a heinous crime against the country. And he had respected this man. The veins of Becker's forehead began to bulge grotesquely as Slade's grip became even tighter.

Still holding the bag filled with the information that would damn Becker, Mace sprinted to Rachel and wrapped his arms around her. She held on to him tightly, afraid to let him go. It felt so good to be in those arms again. She had been certain that she would never see him again.

Seconds later the helicopter dropped down onto the roof of the building, piloted by an old marine friend of Slade's from the Gulf War.

As soon as the craft touched down, the passenger door burst open. Slade began to push Becker roughly toward the craft toward the man beckoning from inside. "Come on!" Slade screamed over his shoulder at Mace while he pushed Becker to the side of the craft, bending at the waist when he moved beneath the rotating blades.

Mace grasped Rachel by the wrist and pulled her toward the craft urgently. He rushed by Slade, who had stopped to handcuff Becker, pushed Rachel into the chopper, and then followed her inside. Slade, having cuffed Becker, pushed the older man toward the passenger door. Together he and Mace forced Becker into the chopper.

Suddenly the door to the roof burst open, and CIA agents began to pour out of the darkness like aroused hornets from a ground nest. They did not know why their director was being loaded onto the craft like some animal, but they were going to stop the kidnappers if at all possible. Several knelt to fire immediately after making it through the door.

The pilot of the chopper saw the agents streaming onto the roof immediately and wanted no part of them. He revved the craft's engines suddenly and directed it upward.

Just as Slade began crawling into the cabin, the craft pitched forward at the touch of the pilot's hand on the controls, and his feet slipped out from under him. With both hands he grabbed the landing rod. He hung on to it in desperation, staring up into Mace's eyes wildly as the craft quickly moved up and away from the roof.

Mace leaned as far as he could out of the craft, reaching madly for Slade's wrist. He grabbed for Slade's fingers—but reached only air.

The agents' bullets smacked angrily into the side of the helicopter as it rose, tearing holes in the fuselage as the craft roared quickly away. Only a few more seconds, and they would be out of range of the gunfire, Mace thought. Only a few more seconds, and Slade will be safe. Mace stretched farther out of the door, until he thought that he must fall from the craft. But he almost had a grasp on his friend's wrist, and then he would be able to pull Slade to safety.

The bullet tore through Slade's right shoulder, paralyzing the arm instantly. For a moment Slade was able to hold on to the landing rod with one hand. But the chopper pitched crazily to the side, and his grip was broken. To Mace it seemed that for a moment, even though Slade's grip had come clear of the landing rod, his friend had remained in the air, suspended in space by some divine force. Then his own huge hand wrapped firmly around the short blond hair of Slade's left wrist. With one Herculean effort, Mace dragged Slade into the bay of the chopper.

Mace tumbled backward onto the floor of the helicopter with Slade on top of him. Instantly they sat up, and despite Slade's shoulder wound, they embraced, laughing and crying at the same time. Then Mace saw Slade's expression sour, and he glanced quickly over his shoulder toward the front of the helicopter.

Rachel lay on the floor, grasping her stomach, hands covered with blood. Another bullet had found its target.

Vice President Preston Andrews and his chief of staff, Robin Carruthers, stood on the lawn of the White House as the small helicopter made its descent. At first it was nothing but a speck, but it soon became recognizable.

Slade Conner had called Robin two hours ago to tell her what had happened, to tell her of Malcolm Becker's treachery, of Broadway Ventures, of who was responsible for the attack at the Nyack

Nuclear Generating Facility. She had listened, in disbelief, but here was the helicopter, just as Slade had told her it would be, coming down at them from the sky. Right on time. And there was the general.

Mace jumped from the chopper as it was still hovering five feet off the ground. He screamed at the armed guards to help Rachel even as they wrestled him to the ground and handcuffed him, unsure of whether he was friend or foe. But they saw right away that the young woman was in desperate need of assistance, that she had lost a tremendous amount of blood.

Several other guards wrestled Malcolm Becker from the helicopter, stood him up on the lush grass of the White House lawn, and jostled him to where Preston Andrews stood. For a few moments Andrews simply stared at Becker, saying nothing, his hands clasped behind his back. Then he broke into his candidate smile. "Welcome to the White House, Malcolm, although I'm certain this wasn't how you intended to get here."

Lewis Webster slammed the phone down. Where the hell was Becker? He glanced at his watch. Almost five in the afternoon. He had been trying all day to reach the man, but was still coming up empty.

Something was wrong. Becker hadn't sounded like himself yesterday when they had spoken briefly. Now he couldn't raise the man. And Ferris wasn't around either. He took a deep breath. Perhaps it was time to head to Switzerland—where most of his net worth had been sent over the past few years—and hole up there until he could figure out what was going on.

The office door creaked opened slowly. As Webster glanced up from his desk, he felt an intense pain shoot through his chest. Mace McLain stood in the doorway. Behind him were several unfamiliar men, guns drawn.

"Good evening, Lewis," Mace said calmly as he moved into the office followed by four federal marshals.

Webster stood. "What's the meaning of this?"

Mace stopped in front of the huge desk. "You mean those guys?" He pointed back at the marshals.

"Of course I mean them," Webster snarled.

Mace broke into a huge smile. "Funny thing. I just met these guys down on the street. They wanted to see the office of a major Wall Street executive who was about to spend the rest of his life in jail. I said I knew where they could find one. So I invited them up. I hope you don't mind."

The older man's eyes narrowed. "You're a cocky bastard. You always were. But you won't get me. There isn't anything you can pin on me. One call to my lawyers, and I'll be out in twenty-four hours. And I'll never have to go back."

"Wrong, Lewis." Mace's expression became serious. "These men know everything they need to know, including your part in the conspiracy. And how Becker got you to take part in it."

Webster stared into the younger man's eyes. The conspiracy was dead. He had been able only to delay his date with prison after all, not to avoid it.

37

Mace sat stoically in the chair at the end of the huge table, directly opposite Bentley Cox, the new senior partner of Walker Pryce & Company. Cox was not particularly charismatic, but Walker Pryce did not need charisma at the helm right now. It needed someone who could project a strong, stable image to the world outside, a man above reproach. Bentley Cox was that man: a Vietnam veteran, a devoted family man, and a civic leader. He would never be accused of being the brightest man in the world, but that didn't matter. There were plenty of other rocket scientists at Walker Pryce who could take care of that end.

Mace took in the surroundings for several moments as the other men sat down. This was a room he had never before been allowed to enter, the Partners' Room.

Walker Pryce was smarting from the terrible publicity it had suffered in the press. The executive committee—Webster, Marston, and Polk—was behind bars, awaiting trial, and the government had levied a half-billion-dollar fine against Walker Pryce. But Walker Pryce would survive—and prosper.

Mace watched Cox shuffle papers. The franchise was too strong. The firm had too many relationships and too many strong people to suffer permanent damage. And the half-billion-dollar fine was nothing more than a short-term problem for Walker Pryce. It was still going to earn a billion dollars this year.

Cox coughed several times, and the room became deathly still. "Mr. McLain, would you please rise?"

Mace pushed the chair back and rose slowly. His eyes flashed around the room at the assembled partnership. He did not know why he had been called here tonight. Perhaps they wanted to grill him on why he had not been smarter, on why he had not seen that there was something amiss with Broadway Ventures. It was the first time in six weeks he had been to the firm.

Bentley Cox began, speaking in a strong, nasal voice. "Be it known to all partners that Mace McLain has been awarded full partnership status at the firm of Walker Pryce & Company." Cox looked up from the leather-bound book and smiled at Mace. "Congratulations, Mace. You are the youngest partner in the history of the firm. And the only one who ever went straight from being a vice-president to a partner."

A huge cheer arose from the partners, and they stood and crowded around him to pump his hand over and over.

Rachel stood at the window of Mace's seventh-floor office, arms folded across her chest as she looked down on Wall Street. The wound from the bullet that had passed through her abdomen was healing nicely. It had been touch and go for a few days, but after convalescing for six weeks, she was feeling almost back to normal.

Mace moved through the door of the office, and she turned from the window. "So? What did they want?" She moved to him, and he took her in his arms.

"I could tell you, but then I'd have to make love to you again."

A look of mock irritation crossed her face. "Don't hold back on me. Tell me. Now."

"He's just been made the youngest partner in Walker Pryce history." Bentley Cox leaned into the office and winked at Rachel. "And now he's got to live up to that status. You two can take one week off, and then I want you both back here ready to go. Go to the Caribbean, have some fun, and then get yourself back here ready to work."

Mace smiled and then looked from Cox down to Rachel, who was still in his arms. "The Caribbean's for losers. We're going to Detroit."

"Detroit?" Rachel and Cox said the word in unison.

Mace raised one eyebrow. "Yup. That's where Andrews Industries is headquartered. Preston Andrews agreed to hire Walker Pryce yesterday. The assignment starts tomorrow. And there's a lot of work to do out there. That company's bleeding a million dollars a day of cash."

Cox shook his head. Mace was as driven as he had heard. Cox laughed and said good-bye.

Rachel turned back to Mace, a disappointed look on her face. "I was hoping we'd have some time together before you dived back into it."

Mace gently pulled Rachel close to him and laughed. "There's one thing I didn't tell Bentley."

"What's that?" She broke into a smile, not knowing exactly why.

Mace took her face gently in both his large hands. "I'm taking a deal team of five people with us out to Detroit. I'm going to spend one day at the company telling those people what to do. Then you and I are flying to Rome to get married." He paused and gazed into her sparkling azure eyes.

"But what about the policy?"

"What policy?"

"The one that says employees can't get married and remain at Walker Pryce."

Mace tilted his head to one side. "You aren't seriously thinking about working here. I mean, I'll be earning enough for . . ."

"Well, Mr. McLain," Rachel interrupted with mock anger. "I'm surprised at you. I worked my tail off at Columbia. I want a chance to be a partner here too."

"Oh." Mace pushed out his lower lip.

"So I guess we have a little problem." She smiled up at him coyly.

Mace shook his head. "No, we don't. We're getting married," he said forcefully. "I don't pay attention to policies anymore. Especially Lewis Webster's."

Rachel smiled and kissed him deeply. "I guess we're getting married then." She pulled back slightly. "Don't ever let me go."

"I won't. I promise."

ACKNOWLEDGMENTS

Special thanks to:

Peter Borland, my editor at Dutton. I am constantly impressed with his outstanding abilities.

Peter Schneider, Marketing Director at Dutton. He deserves a great deal of credit for this project.

Cynthia Manson, my agent. Every writer should be so fortunate.

Richard Green and Howard Sanders, film agents. Thanks for the tremendous energy and enthusiasm you put into this.

Mace Neufeld, Rob Rehme, Dan Rissner and Innes Weir. I'm grateful to you all.

Gordon Eadon, who was always willing to help.

Stephen Watson, a business partner and true friend.

Jim and Anmarie Galowski, pre-submission editors and great friends.

The Money Desk at WestLB: Chris Tesoriero, Jim McPartlan, Betty Saif-Bambara, Tom McCaffery, Mark Randles, Damian Harte, Bill McCormick, Chris Doyle, and Rob Ely—you all are the best.

Brooke McDonald, a big help at Bloomberg and a wonderful cousin.

At Dutton, I'd also like to thank:

Peter Mayer, Elaine Koster, Arnold Dolin, Michaela Hamilton, Leigh Butler, Denise Cronin, Aline Akelis, Lisa Johnson, Mary Ann Palumbo, John Paine, and Kari Paschall.

Others to whom I'm truly grateful:

Robert Wieczorek, Jr., Jeff Hilsgen, John Paul Garber, Roland and Susan Chalons-Browne, Rick Stoddard, Dileep Bhattacharya and Nita Mathur, Mark and Sharon Walch, Pat and Terry Lynch, Barbara Fertig, Walter Frey, Horst Fuellenkemper, Stewart Whitman, Kevin Erdman, Gerry Barton, Franz Vohn, Rick Slocum, Kheil McIntyre, Karen Hoplock, David Lawrence, Keith Min, June Drewes, Mark Rothleitner, and Glenn Stylides.